Jester in the Court of the Suicide King

by

Jack Voller

{ Graveyard Revels Press }

for

the queen of hearts
without whom this book would never have come to be

All sorrows can be borne if you put them into a story.
- Isak Dinesen

The jester is an affirmation of all that is uncertain in the universe, the random and unknown factors of existence. . . .
- Beatrice K. Otto, *Fools are Everywhere*

O noble fool! A worthy fool! Motley's the only wear.
- Shakespeare, *As You Like It*

contents

prologue

I seek in this book, this my recounting of a life spent in the luminous radiance of noble households and in the wan twilight of love's travails, to provide not a simple account of the plodding sequence of my days but of the unfolded truth of my heart. As I look back upon my time in the Created World, I find I apprehended this truth in fits and starts and out of all common order. But that is as it should be, for understand this: I am Jester, one for whom the common order never obtained. As Jester, I had license to turn the world upside down, to trick it topsy-turvy, subverting the powerful and exposing what others sought to hide while revealing truth through obscurities. Inversion and evasion were the everyday tools of my trade.

As such a man I lived a life that was, you might say, its own contradiction, for my purpose and indeed my very existence were refutations of the customary ways of the world. Yet – a grand irony – mine was a life lived in the service of those very men for whom the everyday world was the source of their wealth and power, the full scope and ground of their being. But what jester does not love irony, does not trade on it as a merchant does his common stock of goods?

As Jester I subverted all and defied the normal order. Born the son of a kennel-master I ended as counsellor to a King. I rode Fate's Great Wheel to an unprecedented height, finding there the culmination of an overweening ambition which in the very moment of its achievement began a descent into manifold sorrows. My apotheosis became its own undoing. In this life I have lived, a life of providential chance and harrowing loss, a life spent in the unmapped interstices of an otherwise-ordered Creation, I both found and lost myself.

What I found of myself was not merely a jester's competence in wit and common japes but a rare Gift, a curious skill in the reading of men's faces and the silent language of their bodies, even a trace, at times, of their thoughts and their futures. This Gift brought me both welcome renown and bitter enmity.

What I lost of myself, and in the losing thereof gained, well, that you shall see.

Know in the interim every word written here is true. 'He is after all a mere jester,' you may think; 'this impossible talk of knowing a man's mind, his future, is mere sport, an old jester's last and grandest trick to be played upon us all.' But in that you would be mistaken. If my life has been a jester's trick it is one played only upon myself, a self-undoing ironically unforeseen yet in the end a liberation, as my tale will show. What I present here is offered not as jest nor even strictly for my own sake but for the sake of a wise King I served and loved, one whose reputation and honor can be redeemed only by the truth. How I became Jester, and the nature of my self and my service, must be honestly told for it was as Jester my life unfolded, as Jester I succumbed to an unsanctioned impossible love of a Queen, as Jester I lost the daughter I loved and the wife I cherished, and as Jester I unwittingly helped bring my beloved monarch to a malign and untimely fate.

For all those many transgressions this tale shall be my recompense and atonement as much as it shall be my life's story. For King, for Queen, for family and for myself I would and must tell only a veridical tale or tell no tale at all.

And so my tale begins.

baronet

"Puppies!"

The cry startled me. I had been so enthralled by the se'en-week's running-hound puppy in my lap I had not heard his approach, had not noticed him standing but a few feet away.

"My puppies, you know." He dropped to his knees in the loose scattered straw beside me as I looked at him in startlement, as much for his claim of ownership as his unexpected presence in the kennel. He was about my age, I could see – I had recently turned four – but his garments were quite fine, beautiful in fact, the rich reds and purples of soft watersheen fabrics a world removed from my own garb of coarse brown woolen. I studied his face, its features soft and regular, almost beatific in the placidity settling over him as he turned his quiet attention to the wriggling whelps before us. He was familiar to me but only as a distant landmark is familiar to a regular traveler upon a road never approaching near to the object of his interest. And why had he said they were his puppies?

"They're not yours," I replied with quiet assurance. I pointed at the dam lying in the straw nearby, her mild eyes fixed on us as several of the pups clambered carelessly over her in their squirming play. "They're hers."

He glanced at me. "I know that. But she belongs to my father, so her puppies do too. And he says everything that is his shall one day be mine." His tone was measured and matter-of-fact, not boastful, his words for him a simple explanation of a irrefutable yet unremarkable reality. I was awed by his composure. "So the puppies *are* mine, you see." He smiled at me. "But you may play with them as you wish. I'll share."

So this stranger at my side was the Baronet's son, the boy my father unfailingly and reverentially referred to as Master Rupert. The Baronet's only son and indeed the inheritor of his father's vast estates. Though I had many times glimpsed him at a distance we had never before met, though it had never occurred to me to wonder why. Nor did it occur to me to ask what he was doing here now in the kennel, a place I had long thought of as mine by right of child-possession for it was not only my favorite haunt of all the estate's outbuildings but my home as well. For my father was kennel-master here, and we lived upstairs, our small chambers directly above the spot where Rupert and I sat with the puppies. Rupert's father might own the dogs, I thought, but no one knew them better or loved them more than my father and I.

"I live here," I said, perhaps wishing to establish my own right of presence. "Up there." I pointed helpfully to the low wooden ceiling.

Rupert looked at me. "I live there," he said, his voice still matter-of-fact and his arm pointing through the open doorway toward the Great House several furlongs off, its limestone walls now a warm yellow in the late afternoon sun. As he lowered his arm one of the puppies, one I had long recognized as the most exuberant, jumped for his hand in play and tooth met flesh. Rupert cried out as he pulled his hand sharply away. I expected him to strike the offending pup as I had seen others do but he simply put his finger to his mouth, though there was no blood, and looked at me calmly. "That hurts," he said, no trace of anger in his voice. "Their teeth are sharp." I was further awed, wondered if this was what it meant to be more than a commoner, to feel pain but accept it with grace and equanimity instead of curses and violence.

"I like you," I said with all the simplicity of childhood's feelings, thoroughly unmindful of how inappropriate the adults of our lives would find such a statement, how it would be for them a subtle but unacceptable breach of those rules of class and station giving all structure and much meaning to human life.

"I like you too," Rupert said. "Are there more puppies besides these?"

There were not, but we found sufficient delight and engagement in the litter before us and ere a ten-minutes' span had passed we had become the fastest of friends. It was with dismay, then, that I saw my father walk into the kennel and freeze with such astonishment upon his face he looked almost a caricature of himself, a minstrel-show embodiment of alarmed surprise.

"Master Rupert!" For an instant I thought my father had somehow lost the ability to move his limbs, so complete was his surprise. "Master Rupert! Y' should n' be here alone, lad!" he cried, his north-country accent thickened by sudden emotion. "Come 'way!" With those words my father regained the power of movement for he rushed to Rupert, scooping him up in his arms and carrying him from the kennel so quickly I had no chance to speak. I heard my father calling out as he carried my new friend toward the Great House, more anxious concern in his voice than I had ever heard before.

"Why did he do that?" I asked one of the puppies as I held the wriggling creature before my face, the warmth of its soft flesh almost a vital current flowing through my hands into my heart and I took its milk-sweet breath into my own lungs, sharing its life as it dangled helplessly in my hands, its tongue reaching vainly for my face. "He's my new friend. We were having fun." I wiggled the puppy so its head moved back and forth as though in negation. "I don't know either. He didn't need to," I said. "It's not fair."

My father returned a few moments later, sweat beaded upon his brow though relief now written upon his features, a broad rough-hewn face on which emotion rarely left more than a passing shadow. To most who knew him my father was stolid almost to impenetrability, yet to me, who always found great fascination in studying his face closely, a face which in fact formed my earliest memory, he was no more a cypher than the most histrionic stage-harlequin. To see deeply one need only look closely with heart as well as eye, I had learned very early in my life.

Rupert had escaped from his nurse in a moment of her inattention, my father explained, going on to declare it was great good fortune the boy had come first to the kennel so he could be rescued before any harm befall him. I nodded in dutiful agreement though I could not understand my father's concern, for Rupert was my age and I was given leave to wander freely among the outbuildings and pastures of the Baronet's estate, yet no harm had ever threatened me. Indeed, I never knew my father to express any overt concern for my safety in this regard though he was not a careless parent and I knew his love for me to be genuine and deep.

"Closer watch wi' b' kept now," he said portentously, "but if it be y' find 'im 'ere y' report t' me on th' instant now."

"Yes, father," I said, but even as I spoke my heart faltered within me for I knew I would not. I had no playmates my own age on the estate – nor did Rupert, who had only sisters and they all older than he – and having found one now I would not surrender him easily.

And I did not. My father's prediction was quite in error, for do what they might Rupert's nurses and attendants could not always contain an agile and quick-witted child who was a great lover of dogs and horses and adventures and no lover at all of the restraints and restrictions nurses and doting parents would impose upon a four-year-old child of the gentry. Rupert returned to the kennel as often as he might, and before he was caught and haled back to the Great House and I was punished for abetting his disobedience we would escape, with a dog or two for companionship, into the meadows or woods for as long as we could manage.

Though these adventures, as we called and considered them, occurred less frequently than either wished we nonetheless became devoted friends and within a six-month Rupert's visits were condoned by
his father, the Baronet being a man of kind and generous heart and a
great lover of dogs himself. Rupert and I would often elude the hapless
servants tasked with his supervision, and it was those moments, with
their frisson of disobedience and their greater freedom, that were the
richest we knew and which to this day live most vividly in memory.

This unlikely friendship was for me the first turning of the Great
Wheel, the initial stroke of the good fortune setting my life upon the
path it took, the first molding that began the determination of its final
shape. To be born the son of a kennel-master to a wealthy Baronet, one
who deeply loved his family, his books, and his hounds, who doted upon
his only son yet allowed that son to play freely with and befriend a commoner – this series of happy accidents, if such they were, made possible
all which subsequently befell me for the full number of my days.

Rupert and I reveled in our freedom and our friendship for two years,
having no concern but for adventures which seemed to know little restraint but our own physical limits. The cares and burdens of worldly
life and its grim travails were, as they should be but too often are not,
absent from the bucolic idyll in which we seemed to find ourselves. Life
on the Baronet's great estate felt to us a life charmed. Rupert's father
was a man of considerable wealth, important in the kingdom beyond the
usual status of his rank for his extensive lands were a prolific and reliable
source of timber and silver. His family was in those years complete and
a source of much joy and pride for him.

My father, it is true, knew the sadness of a widower, for my mother
and unchristened sister died during that childbirth, when I was not yet
two. But my father's work gave him great satisfaction. The Baronet's
running-hounds had been famed since his great-grandfather's time for
their excellence and endurance in the chase, and the Baronet had come
to rely entirely upon my father's wisdom and counsel for the management and breeding of his dogs, a responsibility in which my father took
great pride and which brought him considerable respect. He had great
perspicacity in all matters concerning dogs, a very knowing eye for the
qualities of a hound and how to breed those qualities true. While at this
time of my earliest youth I did not well understand the loss he had suffered and the lingering pain that was the trace it left upon his life, even

I could see my father often found a joy in his work, a gratifying absorption of his energies which must have been some recompense, for I never knew him to be lost to melancholy.

Those two years, it seems now to me, were as a blissful dream of childhood.

It is in the inexorable working of all worldly matters that simple joys must yield to the exigencies of life, and the beginning of Rupert's education marked such a yielding, the first of the many I was to know. Appropriate masters had been retained and a room of study prepared, but the fateful day began with poor auspices when the pupil could not be found. Yet as Rupert's proclivities were by now well-known, in short order the language master in the company of the Baronet himself arrived at the kennel where Rupert, with my assistance, had taken refuge behind a pile of straw in a remote corner of the building. He was soon discovered. The Baronet remonstrated with him briefly though with some asperity, ending with a firm command accompanied by a grand sweep of his arm as he pointed toward the Great House: "And now, child, to your studies and your future."

To my astonishment – for I expected some act of drama, an outburst of recalcitrance and resistance – Rupert quietly nodded. "Of course, father, yes," he said softly. And then I found my astonishment transcend astonishment and become incredulity for Rupert walked deliberately to where I stood in the shadows, my father's firm hand on my shoulder the only thing preventing me from bolting into the woods as I had been wishing to do as soon as I had seen the Baronet approaching the kennel. Rupert stopped directly before me, his eyes calm and the lineaments of his rose-pale face remarkably composed. Without a word he took my hand in his and turned to face his father. My eyes widened even before Rupert spoke for I suddenly knew with utter certainty – this, I would some years later realize, was the first manifestation of what I would come to call my Gift – the import of the words he was about to utter.

"I shall begin my studies as you wish," he said, "but I shall not begin them alone." He turned his head to look at me for a moment, his eyes steady, before returning his gaze to his father. I was astounded yet enthralled by this act of placid rebellion and self-determination from a child my own age.

My father's rough hand tightened on my shoulder for a brief instant, the release of pressure coming at the same moment as a short soft laugh from the Baronet.

"A companion for your studies as for your wanderings and your kennel-haunting, eh?" He laughed again as he glanced at me, not unkindly but I quickly looked down, unable to hold the master's gaze. "Well." He paused for a moment, considering. "Why not? Two may be taught as easily as one." I dared not stir nor lift my eyes from the ground at my feet lest that ground open suddenly and swallow me. "If you can spare your son, kennel-master, for some few hours a day, it seems we shall have two young scholars in residence." He laughed again, louder and with more pleasure, and I glanced up to see him shaking his head at the strange delight of the thing. I looked at my father in time to see such surprise on his features as I had seen only once before, when he first discovered Rupert in the kennel, and to see him nod his astonished acquiescence.

I had been in the Great House several times as a young child though my visits were confined to the kitchen offices or servant's hall. At least, those were the intended limits. My curiosity, however, could not always remain content with such small scope. So when one day I was left in the charge of a servant more interested in her gossip than in my supervision, I took advantage of her distraction to slip away, thinking to find Rupert though I had no idea where in the vast house his quarters might be. Hesitant and awed yet compelled by an irresistible urge to explore the extent of the house's mystery and grandeur while searching for my friend, I crept cautiously down a long hallway, the constant fear of discovery making my adventure all the more thrilling. A sudden noise behind me seemed to portend my capture so without thinking I slipped through a half-opened door to find myself in a room, fortunately unoccupied, of magnificent size and splendor as it seemed to me then, a room grander than any I thought could possibly exist outside of Heaven.

Rich furnishings of elegant somber walnut and ornate needlework, silver lamps, imposing portraits – oh, the portraits. It was they that most captivated me, held me with a paralyzing fascination. Stern confident men in armor or glistening raiment and women of impossible grace and delicate beauty peered down from glowing wood walls, their dark images in gilded frames seeming to me like moments of liquid time frozen and encaged forever. I had never seen such paintings before nor such people as were depicted therein, and as I looked up at them I felt in a manner new to me a sense of my own insignificance, my commonness. The world in which such people lived, which gave them such authority and presence, was a world I did not know, could not know, yet as I stood in that silent room, absorbed by one portrait after the other, I felt some vague stirring in my heart, the beginning of some inchoate but determined wish that I might someday know some share of their grace and potency. It was years before I understood this was the planting of the seed of my ambition.

So complete was my fascination with those portraits I had forgotten my design of seeking Rupert and exploring the reaches of the Great House, and only when I heard the repeated call of my name did I come back to myself. Those portraits suddenly seemed to me admonitory, aware of my presence as intruder and interloper, so with a shudder I flew back to the comfort of the servants' world.

The day our studies began I was given just enough time to clean my face and dress myself in clothes free of the mud and bits of straw that were the customary decoration of my garments before I was escorted to the Great House by my father who was, I could sense despite his usual reticence, as nervous as I. Moving with determined single-mindedness he led me through several rooms of uncertain purpose and along a dim hallway, halting abruptly before a closed door that to my eyes appeared much as the other doors in this hall. I wondered at his ability to know one from the other.

"This be th' room, boy. Mind th' master. An' y'r manners." Though this was but his habitual taciturnity I somehow felt he should have said more on what was, to me, a momentous if rather anxious and only dimly understood occasion.

Before I could respond or even bid a simple farewell he was striding quickly back the way we had come. I suddenly felt alone and anxious, my father's own nervousness and uncertainty, evident in his face and movements though I could not then have explained how I knew, having spread to me. I hesitated at the door, my stomach suddenly unsettled, unable to will my hand to reach for the handle.

At that very instant the door flew open and before me stood Rupert, hand on the door, eyes upon me. I read only quiet excitement and delight in his eyes and in the lineaments of his face and set of his shoulders. I was immediately reassured. He smiled.

"In, in, time to begin" he said gesturing, then laughed. "Ha! I've become a poet already, see?"

My heart's pounding slowed at Rupert's calmness and humor, and as there was nought to do now but as he bid I stepped across the threshold into a world that was quickly to enrapture me, change me utterly and make possible for me a life I could otherwise never have known.

The room was an instant astonishment to me, the grandest I had ever yet seen. To my six-year-old eyes it was a veritable hall of wonders and riches. For a moment I was near to overwhelmed and stood transfixed, my eyes sweeping the room repeatedly as I tried to comprehend all I was seeing.

"Such a grand room," I said at last, wonder in my voice. "We're to study in such a grand room?" Would I even be able to think in a place of such distraction?

"Not so grand as all that," Rupert answered carelessly. "Father's private sitting room." He pointed to a door. "The library's there but we're not to enter it without the reading master. Father says his books are too fine for boys who cannot yet read but someday we shall and then we may read them as we choose." His tone was so matter-of-fact I was as though in a dream. I had never held a book in my hands, their value too great and their contents inaccessible, yet here was the promise of a roomful of books awaiting only some learning and the passage of brief time before the wonders contained therein would reveal themselves. I felt a sudden vague excitement stir my heart. A new world was opening to me.

The dark paneled walls of this room bore half a score paintings of regal men and grand women, each reminding me acutely of those I had seen previously on my brief and ill-advised excursion in the Great House. But their intimidating character dissipated like the morning fog in sunlight as Rupert unfolded, portrait by portrait, their relationship to himself. Although I did not understand his solemn delight in his forebears it moved me to see him in his quiet pride even as it brought to my child's mind a first intimation of the great unbridgeable distance between our stations in this world. Rupert, I could see, lived and moved easily in a world which bestowed upon some a power and worldly presence I had already begun to find compelling but which I even then knew could never be mine.

But it was the marble heads of men – "busts" was proper term, Rupert explained, and I giggled at the word as children will when the sound of a new word catches their attention – which captivated me most that day. They were magnificent and frightening, somehow eldritch yet also moving, even inspiring in a way I only dimly comprehended. What sort of men must they have been that centuries later other men, wealthy powerful men such as Rupert's father, would keep stone facsimiles of their heads in their homes? I longed to touch the marble, to feel the cool soft-grained stone against my fingers but I dared not while Rupert was with me though on later occasions when alone in that room I would touch them, gingerly at first, later running my fingers lightly over their curves and hollows, the carven details of pale smooth stone which made these figures of old, these ancient masters, come almost alive for me even before I learned to read the words they had so long ago written. Their names, engraved on the base of each bust, were very poetry to me: Socrates, Plato, Ovid, Vergil, Cicero.

Everything in the room spoke to the Baronet's wealth. The original house, much expanded over the years, itself was quite old and though we were in that oldest portion of the structure nothing about this room spoke of age. Furnishings, rugs, lamps, even some of the portraits were not long from their makers' hands, and all was to me the epitome and manifestation of grandeur. The brass screens of the fireplace threw back the light of the lamps with a burnished intensity which made me avert my eyes; the lightly padded chairs in which we sat knew, it appeared from their condition, the press of no human bodies before our own. The windows in this part of the house were small and the ancient trees growing nearby kept the room in a perpetual half-light unless the fire were lit and the lamps aflame. Which, it seemed, they always were and the room glowed yellow-gold in the steady flames of wood and oil. To me the mesmerizing beauty of the room was near to magic, one which has never dimmed with time.

Like the physical beauty of that room what was given to me there lives redolent with glory in my mind down to the very moment I write these words. The act of learning was itself a delight to me, an opening of doors which I never imagined I would approach let alone through which it might be given me to pass. But pass I did to a world of knowledge that was ever an unknown realm to almost all of those born into my station, a world I imagined would be filled with strange tongues and ponderous mysteries presided over by imperious robed mages jealously guarding access to the mind's secret places and the treasure-rooms of ancient arcane wisdoms.

Yet this was not what knowledge was at all, I discovered to my surprise. As Rupert and I learned Latin and Greek (his gifts in foreign tongues much superior to my own, though my Latin eventually became

quite good) we began, haltingly at first then proficiently, to read the ancients, to engage the words and ideas of those men whose marble selves
kept watch, as it seemed to me, over our efforts to approach their august
thought. In this course of study I discovered that the knowledge contained in books, the vast trove of accumulated wisdom and lore available
to noble and gentry, was not of incomprehensible mysteries at all but of
the human mind and heart shared by all who live. After long study I
could read of Plato's shadow-filled cave and the slaying of Agamemnon,
of bold Aeneas and the civic conscience of Cicero, and I was transformed, re-shaped, by what I learned. I saw in these words and works
not the arcana of the upper stations, knowledge transcendent of common mortal concerns, but moving depictions of and meditations upon
those energies of the human spirit, fair and foul, for good and evil, that
contest ever for the hearts and bodies and minds of each of us, from
archbishops and kings to cottagers and criminals. I wished – oh, how
heartily I wished – those words and the wisdom they conveyed might be
available to all.

But the learning of ancient tongues is great laborious work. Even to
write and read the language of one's native land is a task of more labor
than I had supposed. Yet I loved it all, loved the effort and reveled in
the knowledge such effort unceasingly brought. Learning is struggle but
oh with what reward is such struggle repaid!

In my youthful enthusiasm I tried to teach my father, who could not
read and could mark only simple numbers, to write his name and to
acquire the rudiments of reading, but he would make no effort. He duly
recognized the great honor the Baronet had done us by allowing me to
be educated with his son but my father, I understand now, feared to
separate himself from the world he knew well and had mastered, a world
in which no man of his particular station had need of reading or writing.
For him to acquire those skills would threaten the serenity he had created for himself in the world of God and men, threaten the nature of all
the relationships with men and beasts and place which in their sum created the shape and meaning of his life. I soon contented myself with
regaling him with the adventures and tragedies and glories contained in
the volumes Rupert and I explored, and this was sufficient for my father
for all the years of my education.

beginning

My studies with Rupert gave me more than knowledge of Latin and Greek, history and mathematics and philosophy. They gave me myself.

All study I believe will do the same for those who commit themselves to the universe of knowledge with passion and diligence, but I mean here more than the discovery of the reach of one's thought, the development of wisdom built upon a foundation of accumulated fact and intellectual experience, the maturation of mind and judgement which are the natural consequence and result of sustained engagement with the bodies of knowledge come down to us from the time of the ancients. Such did happen to me, but along with it came the knowing of something more, something far out of the common run of life and beyond the customary order of things as I knew them from books and my own limited experience. What came to me in the course of those years of study and of growth from childhood to early manhood was my Gift.

Since that day, some years before, when Rupert had stood beside me in the kennel and I knew before he spoke he would tell his father I was to be his companion in study, I experienced similar premonitory moments with gradually increasing frequency. At first I found them merely puzzling, the source of some small if vaguely troubling uncertainty. I was a child, after all, and little understood the ways of mind or world. But as childhood ripened and knowledge and experience accumulated I came to understand such premonstrance was, if not extraordinary, far from a common experience. It was not written of in the books we studied though such books recorded many wonders still beyond my comprehension, nor did I ever hear any of my acquaintance speak of such matters. I well knew even at a young age that the faces and comportment of our friends and loved ones tell tales, and while I gradually came to suspect my experience was an unusual, perhaps preternatural, extension of that experience I also came to understand such extension was quite rare.

The very first day of my studies with Rupert acquainted me with the full reach of this aspect of my Gift.

We were to begin with languages, first learning to read and write our native tongue before progressing to the more rigorous study of grammar, rhetoric and logic, and thence to the ancient languages of the learned. In this Rupert had the advantage of me for already he knew the letters of our alphabet and could con some dozen or so simple words.

With his first questions to us the language master identified Rupert's advantage and though I did not yet precisely understand what I was witnessing I could readily see the change come over the language master's features when he turned his notice to me, a tension in his brow and the slightest narrowing of his eyes, a hinted pursing of the lips and though I did not then know the terms for what I was feeling I clearly sensed his condescension and misgiving.

After acknowledging I yet knew no letters I fell into awkward silence as the language master's eyes, cold and hard, lingered long on my face.

"My good lord the Baronet exercises unusual generosity," he said haughtily as he looked down at me, moving closer so as to tower over me in my chair. I could not quite take his meaning but his displeasure was evident in all the language of his face and form. Despite my confusion and growing discomfort I willed myself to stillness and the outward appearance of composure, for the desire to learn was already a fire in my heart, a fire from whose warmth I was determined to let no man drive me.

"I take no surprise a common child knows nothing," he continued, still looking steadily at me and I could see from the fractional widening of his eyes he was surprised I could hold his gaze. "Though I will make what effort I may," he said, stepping away from me, "I warn you now you will needs work twice as hard to learn half as much as Master Rupert." This was to prove far from the case, but at the time all I could think was to give the language master no cause for complaint against me. I remained still and held his look without defiance or fear.

He looked at me a moment longer before sniffing and walking away, taking a few steps toward the front of the room before turning around then looking deliberately from Rupert to me and back to Rupert. "One may regard it," he said with a slow shake of his head, "as axiomatic that distinctions of station serve the inscrutable purposes of Divine Will. It is a truth, one may rightly say – " here he paused in the pedantic manner of one flaunting his learning before completing his thought " – incontrovertible."

In a jumbled instant I realized I had somehow heard in my mind that unfamiliar word while the language master still held a finger to his closed lips and it was only an instant later I saw and with my ears heard him say "incontrovertible." I was aware also of a strange sensation I could not then name nor describe except to call it a sensation of thought, if one might use such a phrase. I glanced at Rupert to see if he had remarked anything unusual but he sat quietly, eyes upon the slate tablet which lay on his desk and signs of impatience in his features and manner.

"Nonetheless," the language master concluded, "we shall proceed as best we may despite the evident inequalities and most unorthodox arrangement. Let us begin."

Thus my introduction to the world of letters commenced, though my concentration that day was much strained on account of my lingering confusion. Yet I struggled to remain attentive for I was more determined now than ever to acquire all the learning I may and to acquit myself to this tutor whose disdain for me I could neither fully comprehend nor ignore. But after our lesson concluded that day it was not the alphabet which dominated my thought but the inescapable and inexplicable fact of my having somehow heard a word that had not yet been spoken. To all appearance the same had not happened to Rupert and for my uncertainty and doubt I could say nothing to him of this matter though I longed to understand it. I knew I could not in some mysterious fashion have anticipated the word for it was a word unknown to me before this day. And what of the strange sensation in my mind, some curious dreamlike feeling of a barely hinted-at presence of . . . something? I lay awake long hours that night considering the matter though when I at length fell asleep I was no closer to understanding than I had been the moment it happened.

And it happened again, a dozen times or more on random occasions over the course of the next several years. Each time was much the same as the first: our language master pausing, in his pompous scholarly manner, before uttering some grand word meant to impress his pupils and I somehow hearing the word in my mind the instant before it was spoken, a silent hearing (if I may use such a phrase) always accompanied by a vague sensation, almost as if thought were somehow made tangible and lightly, very lightly, brushed my mind in passing. I can come to no better description of a phenomenon which to the best of my knowledge has been experienced by none other, though in my heart I suspect I am not the only to have ever known it. What it meant, and what its purpose might be, I could at that young age form no meaningful supposition. I was similarly baffled as to its provenance, and fortunately it did not yet occur to me its origin may have been something much less than providential.

I said nothing of this, not even to Rupert or my father, but applied myself to my studies with all the diligence and application I could summon. I soon was Rupert's equal in the mastery of letters and words and we remained peers for the entire course of our study in the reading and understanding of works written in our native tongue. The language master's haughty disdain of my common origin never disappeared entirely but did soften to such degree that he was able to praise my work, even quite warmly at times, and to report approvingly to the Baronet on my progress. When eventually we began the study of Latin and my command of the language proved equal to Rupert's his manner toward me eased further to such extent he seemed, at times, to have forgotten my low station and begun to see me as a true lover of learning rather than an interloper in a world beyond my station. I felt no small measure of vindication.

I also felt, increasingly, the operation of the other and earliest aspect of my curious Gift, my strange sensitivity to the subtle text of the human face and form.

Rupert and I were ten the year natural history was added to our curriculum of study. A new tutor for the subject had been hired, and on the day of his arrival we waited eagerly in a front parlor so as to catch a glimpse of him as he rode to the house.

The anticipated hour had passed and Rupert, having lost interest in our vigil, took up a volume and retreated to a chair in a corner of the room. So it was I who saw him first, a slender figure on horseback, shoulders hunched and cloak wrapped tightly about him for protection from the cold. Light snow had fallen during the night and as I watched the horse's slow approach, wet white clumps dropping from his hooves at every step, the steady rhythm of his motion almost hypnotic in its effect, a vague but irrefutable sense of forlornness came over me. The rider adjusted his cloak about his shoulders and seeing that motion I spoke without intent. "He's terribly sad," I said, the words startling me as I realized I had uttered them aloud. Behind me I heard Rupert put down his book and rise. Before he reached the window our approaching tutor glanced toward the Great House. It was clear to me from the motion of his head, a slight movement upward and immediately sideways, subtle but unmistakable, that he did not see me in the window, though what struck me more was the impression of melancholy upon his features, readily evident in the vertical lines of tension in his cheeks and horizontal tautness below his eyes, a rigidity about the mouth, all suggestive of a hollow ache, some deep discontent. He was too distant for his eyes to be visible in sufficient detail but I had no doubt of the sorrow gripping him.

Rupert stepped to the window and waved cheerily at our tutor.

"He can't see us," I said.

Rupert waved again, more broadly, but there was no response. "I guess he can't. Angle of reflection, you know."

"He's quite sad. Something's wrong."

I could feel Rupert glance at me though my eyes remained fixed on the forlorn horseman in the drive before us.

"How do you know he's sad? Why do you say so?"

I shrugged, unsure I could explain. "I can just tell. The way he sits upon his horse, how he looks about him, the discomposure of his face . . ." I let my voice trail off, feeling I couldn't risk saying more without sounding the fool.

Rupert sighed. "He's probably just cold, and who is made happy by heavy clouds and wet snow?"

I shook my head as the tutor passed out of sight behind the far edge of the house. "More than that," was all I said.

"We shall see," Rupert said brightly. "Come. We'll wait for him in our study and see if it is cold or melancholy. Loser translates winner's Greek for tomorrow."

More than an hour passed as we waited with growing impatience to meet our tutor and have our plan of study laid out before us. When the door to the room finally opened, however, it was the butler who entered. He glanced briefly at me before addressing Rupert.

"The new tutor begs leave to delay his introduction and first lesson until the morrow, Master Rupert. He received word but yesterday of his betrothed's death and asks a delay to compose his spirits after travel." The butler turned to leave, paused, looked back at Rupert though with his eyes now narrowed in thought. "The young gentleman seems quite undone," he said, pursing his lips tightly. "It is a wonder he made the journey, for he seems only to half-know himself or what he does." With a sad shake of his head he left us.

The translation from Ovid I submitted to our language master the next day, blithely pretending it was my own, was, he exclaimed, the best work from Greek I had ever done. The natural history master we never met, for in his overwhelming grief over his lost love he surrendered his position and left the Baronet's the very next day, even more defeated and forlorn, it seemed to me as I watch him ride away, than he was upon his arrival.

I came to understand, as such incidents occurred with growing frequency, that I was in a manner of speaking somehow unusually well able to "read" the faces and bodies of men (and, with much less perspicacity, women, for reasons which eluded me). The subtle signs, often unseen by others, that were manifested in face and form were to me as are the signs of an animal's passage through the woods to a skilled hunter or forester. As they may glean from an indentation in a bed of moss or the dangling of a broken twig the pace and direction of a deer's movement or the state of a fox's mind, I could read in the body's visible language of skin and muscle the state of a man's mind and even the bent of his character. The set of a man's shoulders, the tautness of the skin about the eyes, the tilt of the head, the shifting contours of cheek and chin and neck, the movements of the lips, the rhythms and nuances of speech, the conformation of his features – all these, taken together, I learned to read as though they were words upon a page, mutable and ephemeral but there nonetheless to be perceived and understood by one sufficiently acute of eye and mind and trusting of instinct.

It soon became my great passion to test and perhaps begin to comprehend this strange skill, to determine if I could its nature and provenance as well as the extent of its utility. I began to study with great care the faces and movements of all who came within my ken, at first in a manner clumsy enough to earn me rebukes for unmannerly staring but I cultivated subtlety and discretion as best I might and soon found I could scrutinize those about me without drawing overmuch attention to myself. I endeavored also to learn how the signs I observed in feature and form manifested in the words and actions of those I watched, to thus put to the proof the insights I gleaned. I was particularly interested to "read" those who were unknown to me for this, I felt, would provide the surest validation of my efforts.

I began to spend what time I could in those spaces of the Great House most frequented by servants and staff. The kitchen offices were my favorite haunt for there I could plead hunger to gain some morsel of food and retire to a corner to eat as slowly as I might. Amidst the regular bustle of the place I would become all but unnoticed while closely observing not only the household staff, who too soon became so familiar to me they were little challenge to read, but the merchants and tradesmen who came upon business. They were the favorite subjects of my study. I heard the poulterer ostentatiously declaim the quality of his geese while the signs of insincerity were thick upon his face and in his voice, in his ever-shifting eyes and heavy repetitive gestures, then later hear the under-cook who had agreed to the purchase berated for her ignorance in buying such overaged gamey birds as were unfit for the Baronet's table. I saw the mercer's boy explain to the housekeeper, with all evidence of honesty, that the foreign linens purchased by her Lady-ship had been lost when the ship transporting them foundered in a storm, only then to receive a great tongue-lashing for being a liar and the servant of an even greater liar. I slipped away into the nearby village the next day to learn the truth or falsity of his report, and there I heard it confirmed by several merchants.

I even found occasion to test my curious Gift during the greatest servant scandal of all my time in the Baronet's household.

Rupert and I were fourteen. He had recently begun receiving instruction in some of the arts and refinements of which all young men of the gentry and nobility are expected to have command, and that included dancing, an activity he whole-heartedly loathed. His parents insisted, however, so Rupert's pleas to be excused from such instruction fell on decidedly deaf ears and he was forced to suffer the compounded indignity of learning to dance while his sisters served as partners. I secretly envied him. As a commoner I was of course excluded from all lessons intended to develop those social graces expected of gentlemen, and being forever barred from that world I longed all the more ardently for the very instruction Rupert seemed to find almost excruciating. I resented also that the time Rupert was required to devote to these lessons was time I spent laboring in kennel and stable for my father rather than in those pursuits of the mind which I so loved.

The near-by village could support no dancing-master so the man hired as Rupert's teacher was resident in the Great House. Soon after his arrival rumor quickly spread he had fallen in love with one of the parlor-maids and she with him, and as the Baronet was quite tolerant in all such matters provided the proprieties were observed the issue seemed to follow its natural course. Prior to this I had given scant attention to the romance-gossip which seemed always on the tongues of servants. But this matter caught my interest, in large part because my own attention I found was increasingly drawn to the younger women who crossed my path in the course of daily business, my own nascent manhood beginning to manifest in the avidity with which I followed the movements of their limbs and bodies and studied the soft contours of their faces. (Such distraction, I came to believe, was the principal reason my skill in the reading of women fell far short of my skill applied to men.) I also found myself quite envious of the dancing-master, a comely man not yet thirty whose elegant fashionable clothes and easy masterful command of the social graces seemed to me the very manifestation in human form of that worldly milieu to which I found my heart and imagination ever more powerfully drawn though it was a world forever denied me. In my heart I longed to be him.

Walking through the Great House to mathematics instruction one afternoon I passed a parlor the door of which was ajar. I heard within the voice of the dancing-master, quiet but intriguingly earnest. The behavior which followed on my part was inappropriate, I confess, but so fascinated by the man, by his worldly air and sophisticated manner, was I that I stopped in the empty hallway and, seeing no one about, inched closer to the half-open door so I might eavesdrop upon him.

The dancing-master was in close converse with the parlor-maid of whom he was said to be enamored, speaking in dulcet tones to her such fulsome declarations of ardent affection I nearly blushed to hear him even as I sought to commit his phrases to memory for my own future use.

The maid shifted her position, moving closer to him upon the sofa, and as she did so some extraneous motion on the wall beyond the lovers caught my eye. A large mirror above the fireplace had reflected her movement and I suddenly realized their faces were thus presented indirectly to my view. I crouched low, mesmerized, willing myself to be invisible so I might avoid detection as I watched and listened with rapt if guilty fascination.

As I watched and listened my heart slowly began to grow cold within me, for in the dancing-master's animated face and graceful sinuous movements I read clear signs of insincerity and falsehood. The gleam of eye and eager tension about the mouth and jaw and cheek, the subtle theatrical edge to his importuning voice, the practiced gestures, the self-awareness of an actor at work – in these combined tokens I saw nought but deception. This was seduction, not love. No, I suddenly realized, not seduction but its aftermath, for the closeness of their bodies and frequency of intimate touch indicated to me, even in my virginal naiveté, that whatever emotions flowed between them had already been physically consummated. I blushed again at the thought.

A sudden noise in the hallway behind – merely one of her Ladyship's lapdogs chasing some insect or vermin – caused the dancing-master to glance toward the door and though I felt certain he did not see me I hurried away to my lesson, unsure of the full import of what I had seen but determined to bring Rupert into my confidence.

"I think this is your fevered imagination at work," Rupert said with a sly smile when I had finished my tale. "Neither you nor I have as yet any direct experience of the treacherous pathways and murky complexities of romantic love, so what can either of us know with any certainty of the heart-matters of another?"

"I have not yet been in love," I agreed, surprised to feel myself blushing yet again, for to my mind came unbidden the image of the young scullery maid whose blue eyes distracted me near to confusion whenever I saw her. "But the dancing-master's falsehood is plain upon him. There can be no doubt."

"Nor is there any evidence. False in what way and how is this known?"

I glanced at the floor. "I do not in what manner he is false, only that he is."

Rupert sighed. "My father would intervene if what you say is true, but I know his first questions would be 'What evidence do you have of this man's misbehavior?' and 'How do you know of this?' There is no credible answer to either. Besides, if decorum has been kept between them – "

"It has not."

"Again, what proof of any of this? To the eye it is but a fashionable young man wooing a young woman, nothing more."

"Not to my eye," I said firmly. "I know what I saw and what I saw was deception. He is false to her in some way, I am certain of it. I know not why nor even in what manner but he is. Your father is a proper upright man and I would not repay his generosities to me with a silence that allows the moral tone of his household to be sullied."

Rupert smiled. "You will out-Cato Cato yet, my friend. The reputation of no ancient Roman moralist is safe from such austere scruples as yours." He laughed aloud. "Yet," he said, "as I would well like to see this dancing-master and all his ilk banished from my presence forever, and as you were correct – though I think by chance – about our natural history teacher, I will do this much. I shall insinuate to my father that the old villain Rumor has infiltrated his household and sown vague reports of this fellow's romantic duplicities. Then the matter becomes his concern, not ours. Agreed?"

"Agreed."

Rupert did speak to his father who, as predicted, dismissed the matter for its lack of credibility and proof. Yet before banishing the matter from his mind he must have mentioned something of it to his wife who, much less sanguine than her husband and indeed somewhat shrewish in manner, descended upon the dancing-master like a Harpy enraged. As besuited her natural temper she confronted him with no consideration for privacy or decorum, it apparently being a firm conviction with her that berating a servant within earshot of others would have an improving effect upon the entire household staff. How the Baronet, ever the kindest and mildest of men, could come to love such a woman as she was always a mystery beyond my power to resolve.

Subsequent gossip reported the dancing-master held his ground in the face of her Ladyship's onslaught, deflecting her accusations with such deft grace and charm that by the end of their confrontation her initial vitriol had been subdued to mildly admonitory bromides. Indeed, the dancing-master's defense of his interest in the parlor-maid was so ardently eloquent – and gossip's inevitable enhancement of it so robust – her Ladyship's harangue came only to further his cause, seeming as it did to convince all in the household, including the object of his declared affection, that his love for the parlor-maid equaled that of Orpheus for Eurydice.

But it did not.

Some dozen weeks later, having been briefly absent from the estate helping my father convey a half-dozen weanling running-hounds to a gentleman residing at some distance, I returned to find upon entering the Great House a scene of great confusion in the servant's hall. The parlor-maid so passionately beloved of the dancing-master a few weeks ago was sitting upon the floor, her back against the wall and her head in her hands, her body convulsing with sobs of such intensity as I had never witnessed before. Two servants knelt beside her, caressing her and offering words of consolation to which she could pay no heed even had she wished. Her hands were wet with her own tears and the great gasping intakes of breath between her wracking sobs sounded to me like misery made audible. I stood transfixed, horrified, disrupted in all thought and feeling, my scheduled lessons forgotten. Being but fourteen it was not much for me to say I had never seen one in so much pain of heart before, and certainly I had no personal experience of such terrible emotion – though I would in due time become acquainted enough with sword-sharp grief – but I nonetheless felt in my heart a great welling sorrow as I helplessly watched the parlor-maid's hysterics. Tears came to my own eyes out of some dimly sensed sympathetic instinct but there was no action I could take, no words I could utter, which I felt would prove of any consequence or consolation. Yet I knew in some instinctual way I must do something, that it would be inhuman simply to walk away from such terrible suffering. I found myself approaching her without conscious volition and even as one of the servants kneeling by the parlor-maid glanced up at me in irritation I reached out and gently placed my hand on the maid's head and spoke words that came unsummoned to my mind.

"Heart's ease, mistress" I said, having almost to force the words from my quivering lips as my own tears began to roll. She paused in her sobbing without looking up and after a moment I turned away, as confounded by my actions as those about me. Even more so, for in the instant I touched her I knew the full cause of her terrible anguish: she was with child. I felt a hand upon my shoulder but did not even turn to see who was guiding me away.

"Come away, lad." The under-butler's voice, firm but without anger. "There's nought to be done by any. She needs the purge her cry will give her so let it be. She'll have more an' enough before her yet."

"What – "

"She's dismissed. With child by the dancin'-master an' her Ladyship will have her gone immediately, sent back to kith to fare as she may."

"The dancing-master," I said almost to myself. I turned a look upon the under-butler. "And what of him?"

He snorted his contempt. "Gone i' the night three days ago leavin' neither word nor trace. A sad an' bitter business is such a fall."

Was this, I wondered, the deception I had seen in the dancing-master's face and manner all those weeks ago? Was his falsity a simple insincerity, a pretense of abiding love for the sake of fleshly gratification? I supposed it must have been this which I had seen.

Yet it proved to be more than that, we were all soon to learn, for in less than a month's span good-dame Gossip brought from the village the news that the mercer's elder daughter was with child by the dancing-master. What vindication I felt for the accuracy of my observations was left hollow by the memory of the parlor-maid on the floor, overwhelmed by pain and grief and the prospect of lone bitter hardship before her. I had never met the dancing-master but I cursed him in my mind and my heart as though he had been my life's greatest nemesis, and I pray the judgement upon him is severe and the flames which await him bring to him a thousand times over all the pain he caused to others in the name of false love.

Two more years passed while I continued to enjoy the Baronet's indulgence and the intellectual companionship of Rupert, though as those days went by the growing demands and expectations of his station and its great distance from my own began inexorably to draw us apart. We were I thought as two vessels which for a time sail in close company, their proximity permitting the exchange of warm greeting and companionable talk but as tides and winds and purpose will always draw such vessels apart, slowly at first but with greater speed as time passes, so it was, inevitably, with us. As we crossed the threshold of manhood Rupert received ever-more instruction in the accomplishments expected of titled gentry and the knowledge necessary to oversee a large and thriving estate, and as I had nought to do with such matters our time together in that magnificent study, that warm refuge of learning where we both felt the great pleasure of the mind's delight in putting itself upon stretch, began to grow ever less, waning like the light in the far last days of autumn. I found myself spending more time helping my father in kennel and stable, as he had now been given oversight of the Baronet's horses as well, and although my love for all creatures was undiminished I found the work increasingly uncongenial to my yearning spirit.

My greatest satisfaction in those days of increasing stable-work came from the opportunity to improve my horsemanship. Though not permitted to ride the Baronet's proud hunters or the coach horses, I would at every opportunity saddle the palfreys, the quiet-tempered riding horses used by Rupert's sisters, and slipping away into the surrounding meadows or woods imagined I was upon my own pacing steed, lordly master of my own fate. At times I would imagine myself some local squire surveying his holdings with proud possessive eye. Sometimes I was a knight-errant from an old *romaunt* of chivalry and adventure such as those Rupert and I had studied, riding forth to prove himself through valiant deeds and heroic rescues. Always I returned to the stable with an air of dejection and disappointment as the empirical reality of my life yet again closed in upon me and drained my dreams and fantasies of their consolatory power.

This my father noticed.

"Y' lose y'r way, lad," he said to me one day as I unsaddled the old mare I had been riding. I had not been lost at all so it took me a moment to realize he was speaking figuratively, a practice quite rare with him. "I c'n see y' ride t' avoid work an' t' dream th' dreams I see in y'r eyes when y' return. Bu' that's never goin' t' be y'r horse, nor will any oth'r. Th' books ha' gi'en y' grand ideas an' they'll bring y' nought bu' trouble. Y've been educated out o' y'r own proper station but int' none other, an' that's unnatural."

"It feels quite natural to me," I said, tamping down my indignation as best I might. "It cannot be wrong to learn."

"Not f'r them tha' needs it." My father shook his head, turned away. "I should ha' kept y' out o' th' schoolroom. Y' learn what will do y' no good an' I see it bring y' nought but ambition an' unrest."

I opened my mouth to protest but found I could not. My father was right: my learning had unsettled me. I could find in myself no wish to follow my father as kennel-master nor even to be estate steward, a position my ability to read and write would put within my reach and which the Baronet had already hinted might indeed come to pass should I so wish it, for the reports he received from our various tutors always were encomiums to my surprising aptitude and abilities. But I did not wish that fate either. In my heart I longed to be a tutor, to instruct others and open to them the same delights I found in the acquisition of knowledge, instill in them the same love of learning that burned in my heart. But this was impossible. No family of rank would engage as tutor to their heirs a commoner who had never *seen* a university let alone never attended one, and no commoner's family had much need of what I could offer even if they could afford – as very few could – to pay for a frivolous education. In consequence, I had no sense at this time of what path my life might take that could bring to me some measure of happiness and fulfillment.

The next day I spoke with Rupert upon this. We had been unlikely schoolmates for ten years now and my respect and admiration for him had only increased with those years. He was in the main the better scholar and student yet never once, even in our earliest school days, boasted or exalted himself above me. From the very first his placid temperament – placid through the personal calmness and the innate dignity of his nature, not through lassitude nor languor – had awed me, and had long led me to regard him as both capable advisor and trusted confidante and, as much as our differing stations would allow, friend. It was as such I approached him after our studies this day.

"I know not what to do," I lamented after recounting the previous day's brief exchange with my father. "I fear he may be correct, that I have become dissatisfied with the common station, the only station which is my lot. For all my love of beasts and of my father I do not wish to spend my life in a kennel, yet I know no other work."

"What of my father's suggestion you be apprenticed to the estate steward so – "

"I cannot find it within myself," I said with the urgency of a young man's despair, "to regard that as anything but an offer I would only resignedly accept, not one that would delight me. I am truly grateful for your father's continuing generosity but with such work I know my heart would remain restless. Yet neither do I know what my heart would seek. It seems I have found, here at the end of all my learning, only unseemly ambition and great irresolution." I paused, shaking my head with eyes downcast. "Perhaps my father was right. Perhaps I have become unnatural."

"And perhaps you have become too melancholic at too young an age." Rupert's bright tone brought my eyes to his face, upon which played an almost impish smile. "You resign yourself to failure in life before you have rightly begun. We have not yet reached the end of our learning, as you say. Indeed, no truly wise man ever reaches that end. We have more than a twelve-month yet before I go to university and who can say what knowledge or opportunity may or may not come to one in a year? Or in the year which follows?"

I forced a wan smile for Rupert's sake. "I wish I possessed even half your phlegmatic nature," I sighed. "Though I misdoubt if any nature could withstand such displacement as I feel and fear has befallen me." Was my father indeed correct? Was it my fate to be disjunct, forever discontent with those prospects open to me while forever barred from those which drew me as the song of the Sirens drew those ancient sailors to their doom? To what mast could I be bound so I might achieve the enrapturing fulfillment of hearing their song while yet holding fast to my own life and self?

"Come," Rupert said. "My eldest sister insists upon playing for us upon her new harpsichord. Let us find some wine and give her an appreciative audience while we leave these fears for the future."

I smiled to myself at the accidental congruence between my thought of the Sirens and Rupert's musical suggestion. There are no Sirens here, I thought wryly, only three maidens all set upon the determined pursuit of husbands. Well, I can applaud with as much feigned enthusiasm as any young beau and will help make up an audience for the sake of my friend and his sister – and for the excuse it gives me to avoid both kennel-work and more of my father's doleful reminders of my dislocation from the world of my birth.

The year of which Rupert had spoken passed all too quickly though progressively less of my time was spent in study as more of Rupert's was given over to preparation for university and for the life of a wealthy man of rank. And in due course of time Rupert did depart as expected, and on that day my heart knew a heaviness it had never felt before, a grim weight bearing my spirit down almost to darkness. My time of study had come to its formal conclusion, though the Baronet had kindly granted me free use of his small library. Most burdensome to me was the loss of my childhood's friend and scholarly companion, the buoyant spirit of one whose character and temperament and intellect were always an enduring inspiration to me and a bulwark on which my own more turbulent character could find support and sanctuary. Upon the occasion of his departure I knew also for my life's first time the sorrow which attends the closing of one stage of life. We were both seventeen now and the last vestiges, the final lingering traces, of childhood vanished from our lives forever on the day of Rupert's departure. He was leaving home and childhood behind for a world of great promise and possibility, a life that would include not only the further broadening of his mind's horizons but of the world's as well, for the plan of his life now included extensive travel in foreign lands.

But there was no corresponding promise for me, no grand vista of life, no anticipated experience promising to provide the bracing challenges to mind and spirit I so craved. My future, I thought on that day, held the promise of only kennel-work or perhaps the overseeing of household business and estate ledger-books. My heart sank at either prospect. I felt thoroughly lost, for the first but far from the last time in my life, unmoored and drifting in the interstitial spaces of the Great Chain of Being, those shadowy silent gaps between the fixed stations of human order now seemingly destined to become my spirit's permanent abode.

I certainly could not know — and just as well that it was so, for the knowing then would have been too painful to confront if even possible to apprehend — that this would indeed prove the condition of my entire life. For such is of necessity the jester's lot, after all: of the low but among the high, more than common yet neither gentry nor noble, neither servant nor master. A jester is a rare sort of man but that rarity is predicated upon his having no established or certain station, no solid place upon which to stand and claim as the foundation of self, so his feet must forever move in a mad unceasing dance on a path that led, for me, to a place which brought me both renown and opprobrium, accomplishment and loss, great comfort and greater anguish of heart.

jester

The second stroke of what I cannot now identify as simply my good fortune — say, rather, the accident that ensured my perpetual residence in those in-between spaces of the fallen world — was the arrival at the Baronet's Great House, a year after Rupert's departure for university, of a throng of guests come to celebrate the marriage of the Baronet's middle daughter to the second son of an Earl in the north of the kingdom, an Earl who later came to play a signal part in shaping the course of my own life.

To my great delight Rupert returned from university for the occasion, though I could as a commoner share little of the company's amusement. Yet to his credit and my heart's pleasure Rupert always treated me as a respected friend and sought to include me in those simpler amusements whenever my presence could be justified. It was one such simple outing, a visit by a group of the younger guests to stable and kennel, that set my life upon the path it would take.

And again puppies played a role.

A just-whelped litter of the Baronet's famed running-hounds drew the excited attention of the ladies of the party. Their affected laughter and animated chatter worried the dam, and as one of the ladies reached to caress the nursing and still-blind pups the dam growled and snapped once at the air to warn her off. It was but a harmless warning in the common way of dogs but the young lady started and squealed as though fang had torn her flesh as she half-tumbled backwards into the straw which covered the ground. She was instantly rescued by one of the young men of the company — it had been obvious from the moment they entered the kennel he was her favored beau — who helped her to her feet with many polished turns of phrase and an air of solicitous gallantry. He followed this with a simple jest, as is the way of such lovers, accompanying a glance at the wary dog with a remark about her being "a very bitch indeed."

I took some offense. The dog in question was a favorite of mine and my father's, a prime breeding bitch of excellent qualities, and had been carelessly provoked by a thoughtless woman. My only recourse was to jest in return and with due regard for station.

"Indeed, honorable master," I said lightly — the honorific was excessive but I could see it flattered his vanity, as I expected — "and what bitch in a box will not guard her charges against incursion?"

My lingering emphasis on the second syllable of "incursion" was of no avail, for their mild looks showed the pun had escaped them all —

except for Rupert, whose arched eyebrow suggested he understood I had just compared a baron's niece to a cur. While I could explain away the pun had it been necessary I took from Rupert's reaction that it would be best to further distract the party with diverting words. And words suddenly came to me, fully formed as though delivered upon the instant by the Muses themselves and I half-chanted them with dramatic exaggeration of voice and look and gesture:

A bitch in a box will guard her pups,
Let all young ladies beware;
For a bitch will do as a bitch must do
Whether she be dark or fair.

I bowed an exaggerated bow, confident none would understand the last two lines as redounding to the discredit of the fair-haired young woman who had provoked the nursing dog.

Several of the party laughed and one clapped his hands and declaimed "Rupert! Most men keep their jesters in the house, not confine them to kennel with the hounds. Or do you hide your jester from your guests so none may steal him?" More laughter and the first young gallant spoke again. "I say a rhyming jester will be a great relief. If I hear yet more tedious talk from our grey fathers of their vanished youths and long-ago glories I shall go mad. Let us have this fellow in the hall tonight!" General assent followed and Rupert, struggling to hide his astonishment, looked to me, his eyes wide in question. I nodded and Rupert, somewhere between amazement and disbelief, said simply "So be it."

Much of that evening's laughter was not at my puns and rhymes but at my expense. I was the kennel jester, fool of the fox-hunters, wonder of the stable, Pretender to the Whelping Box Throne. But I did not much mind, for though my jests and rhymes met with less approbation than I would have wished – and they were in truth paltry things in the main, for this was no skill I had been cultivating, yet – I found to my pleasant surprise and great comfort that words came easily, snatches of song again appeared almost fully formed in my mind and puns were ever ready at my lips. From the earliest days of my instruction alongside Rupert I knew I had more than fair measure of facility with our native tongue, but this gift of wry amusement and sharp humor took even me by some surprise. Yet by the end of that first evening I knew I had found that which I could do well and felt the dawning hope it might be the path leading away from the kennel and a cottager's common life. I knew my wit would improve and, wedded to what I had already begun to suspect was a deft and subtle skill in the reading of men beyond the common measure, it could make me – and here I do confess a failure of the humility so prized in Heaven – a jester of some skill. Perhaps even renown. Thus it was I hoped, and as you shall see it was a hope which came to be realized.

The Baronet was sufficiently pleased by the evening's diversion and amusement I provided that I was called upon to reprise the role nightly for the duration of that festive week. So bracing and rewarding did I find the first night's experience I began immediate study to improve, and by the end of the week had accumulated a small store of jests and tales, some of my own invention, and had begun to teach myself juggling and a few simple gambols and gestures which I found lent much comic force to my puns and poems.

I was saddened when the party of pleasure disbanded and Rupert left to resume his studies, the return of the household's customary routine bringing a quiet and tranquility which magnified my sense of loss. I had in those few days fallen in love with the idea and experience of jesting, for in the performance I drew from within myself what I valued highly and in its jest-expression felt it become something uniquely mine. In creating tales and puns and witticisms I was putting to use the knowledge I had so painstakingly yet delightedly gained, turning my learning, my wit and my love of language into both a source of amusement for others and a celebration, as it were, of my own self. A new self, for when I donned the scarlet costume Rupert's youngest sister had quickly fashioned for me and painted my face and gave my wit and tongue free rein I performed without conscious effort some manner of personal alchemy. I and all that I drew from within myself were conjoined and transmuted in the crucible of my longing and ambition into one who through the act of performance became more than he had ever been before. As a jester I, a commoner, a kennel-master's child, acquired power over gentry and noble, directing their minds and hearts this way and that, as I chose, with my tricks and tales. I became, for a brief span, master, and in the brief inversion of the common order of things I found a gratification and exhilaration of spirit which surprised and delighted me. And I wanted more. I became hungry for a steady diet of such experience. If I must live in the in-between spaces of the Created World then let such experience be my sustenance there, I thought. I became even more ambitious and determined.

I became Jester.

Though the Baronet was hardly a reclusive man his parties of pleasure and gatherings of friends were neither frequent nor large, and I found myself oft distracted with longing for the opportunity to be jester again. When guests gathered I was, to my great relief, regularly invited to entertain, and these performances quickly became the greatest source of pleasure in my life and each occasion I awaited with almost frantic eagerness. I worked continually to improve. I avidly composed and memorized tales and comic verses, I practiced gambols and tricks before uncomprehending dogs and horses, I visited the nearby village on market days to bribe with what small coin I earned itinerant musicians and entertainers to teach me the rudiments of their arts. I was in a sort of heaven, for I knew I was now discovering my true self, discovering a path leading I knew not where but which drew me as a shrine draws the pilgrim.

My father was dismayed, more disturbed by this new passion in my life than he had been by all my years of eager learning.

"A gran' foolishness tha' suits y' for nought an' gives y' more dreams t' lead y' nowhere." He shook his head in grim determined frustration. "Th' books lead y' t' a cliff an' now y' step off like a damn fool."

"I am paid for my efforts, father," I said, awkwardly aware of the petulance in my voice. "Our master and his guests sometimes together give me more in coin in one night than your wages of a fortnight." That should count for a great deal, I thought. "It gives me pleasure to entertain others and my mind and wit and learning are put to use. I cannot see this as folly."

"B'cause y've lost sight o' yourself an' y'r station, boy! Y'r learnin' gave y' foolish gran' dreams and now y' mistake 'em for the world. There's nought f'r y' that way bu' trouble."

For three years we disagreed, though we seldom spoke on this matter for it was clear neither of us saw hope the other would change his thought. We disagreed until the very day my skill as entertainer, my identity as Jester, took me to greater heights.

For those three years I served my master the Baronet, first merely as occasional jester but as the months passed I gradually became more to him. With Rupert away, his three daughters all finally married, and his wife having died within a twelvemonth of my first night of experience as jester, I became in some manner a companion to him. It was not unusual for me to be his only company at table, and I was one of few on the estate with whom he could discuss topics of timely consequence, works of literature and questions of philosophy as well as the daily business of the estate. Too, I could understand his reminiscences and listen with patient sympathy when his mind turned to memories of his family, whose absence was a constant source of sadness to him.

"We have educated you better than we knew."

The Baronet and I had been lingering over wine at table and his sudden words caught me by surprise for neither of us had spoken for several moments. His tone was kindly, and I knew he felt, as deservedly he should, in great part responsible for my perspicacity and wit as though it were a reward for his generosity, and this I would not dispute. "Here we set you to read books," he continued, "and you go beyond us leaps and bounds, learning as well how to read men." His smile slowly faded and he leaned toward me and with a father's gentle firmness placed a hand upon my shoulder, holding my eyes with a clear and steady gaze beneath thin grey brows. "I've known you all your life, known your father and your mother God rest her soul, and watched you grow in mind and body alongside my only son, to whom you have been a great friend and boon and who bears great affection for you." He lifted his hand and rose from his chair, moving toward the low fire in the hearth. When he spoke next, his back to me now, his voice was soft and weighted with thought.

"The ways of God are beyond mortal knowing, and so it must and shall always be." He slowly turned from the fire to look back at me, still in my chair and holding a glass of wine which I had completely forgotten. "How you knew, when we met with the overseer of my mines, that he had begun to steal from me, I still do not fathom, but you knew. Somehow you knew." He shook his head as if still lost in amaze, then walked back to me. Again his warm hand on my shoulder for a moment. "You do me many good turns, and have my love and thanks for your pains. God works His ways through you to our betterment!" He then bid me goodnight.

His silver mines were the single greatest source of the Baronet's income, greater than his rents and timber combined, yielding an ore of unusual purity and consistent quantity. Rumor held the Baronet had as much wealth as any duke, and for his support of and service to the crown would someday soon be elevated to Baron, though that never came to pass for him.

In the capacity of a sort of minor scribe I had begun to accompany the Baronet on his visits to oversee his domains and their condition, for he was an active and interested master concerned for his estate and for those who lived and worked upon it, though in truth he first invited me more for my company than for my abilities to read and write. The Baronet's usual companion on such visits was his estate steward, an estimable and honest man but dull and Lenten company at table, taciturn and little given to humor or witful conversation.

But even in my initial capacity as little more than table company I had occasion to attend the Baronet when he met, as he regularly did, with the various petitioners, tenants, and under-stewards who on some days were an almost constant audience before him for hours together. These experiences I loved, for in watching and listening and studying the men who appeared before him I found rich opportunity for the application of my Gift. I would with increasing ease read the language of the human forms which appeared in a steady parade before me, the signs of sincerity and deception, deep-rooted honesty and practiced dissimulation. It was the richest field for the cultivation of my Gift I had yet known, and I applied myself assiduously to its improvement. I continued also, as I long had now, to catch as it were a word or sometimes two from a man's mind the instant before it was spoken. After some several months I realized this was occurring with greater frequency, though was still from a regular or common occurrence, and this gave me some hope that the power of my Gift might yet increase further. Of this aspect of my Gift, however, I could as yet determine no practical benefit.

When I first began aiding the Baronet in matters of estate business I would offer only the briefest of remarks, knowing well even those were somewhat of a boldness on my part. But the ambition and desire burning within me would permit no silence. I would prove my skill and my worth to those whom I would help and who could in turn help me along that path whose destination I still could not discern but which seemed to offer only more possibility the further along it I proceeded. Initially my remarks were tentative and offered almost in the spirit of jest, but as the weeks and months passed and the accuracy of my observations was regularly confirmed, I grew more confident and experienced and within a twelve-month had become a trusted confidante to my master. The matter of the mine overseer confirmed absolutely to the Baronet the value of my insights, while to me it confirmed the vague intimation I had long sensed in the shadowed corners of my mind that the full reach of my Gift was still to be discovered.

On the Baronet's last visit to his mines he met as was his custom with the mine overseer to review the records of production. The estate steward and I joined our master in the overseer's house, located hard by the workings of the most productive of the Baronet's mines. The overseer, a tall, ascetically thin man with quick movements and long greying hair which appeared never to have known any management, ushered us into a small room arranged so the account books might be examined in relative comfort, though the house was in the main rather small and dark, with ceilings so low I feared the overseer was in constant danger of striking his head. He was, I could see immediately from his manner and the set of his features, making great effort to appear at ease. Yet effort and ease are each exclusive of the other, so instinctively I began to watch him closely. He seated us at a worn oaken table, dark and scarred with decades of use, which nearly filled the room. Setting large pewter goblets before us he filled each with wine almost to the brim, and though the Baronet remarked on this as a kindness it was clear from my master's words and manner such hospitality was unaccustomed. Yet the overseer had been in the Baronet's service for many years, I knew. What had brought about this change?

When the overseer left the room to fetch the account books I slipped quietly from my seat, gliding silently to the doorway to observe him. The Baronet looked at me curiously but I only held up a cautioning hand. The overseer had gone to a bookshelf in the next room – the house as I said was quite small, a cottage really – and as I watched he began to remove a large leather-bound volume. As he slid the book toward him a small roll of parchment, tied in black ribbon, came out from the shelf as well, one end of the ribbon being caught underneath the heavy book. The overseer stopped suddenly when he saw the parchment, reaching out to push it back into the recess of the shelf. But in his nervousness the heavy account book began to slip from his other hand and nearly fell before he mastered its weight. These sudden movements allowed the rolled parchment to fall to the floor. The overseer snatched it up quickly and with furtive clumsiness thrust it back into the gap in the shelf where the account book had been.

I slipped back into my seat just as the overseer returned, my eyes intent upon him to see what I might read in his face. There were now beads of perspiration on his brow despite the relative coolness of the day and his movements were more abrupt than they had been, a sign of the mind's discomfort. He was making an effort to compose himself, not without some success, suggesting a brief moment of fear now being replaced by relief. Yet it was merely a parchment that had not quite fallen to the floor. A parchment not kept with the others in the pigeon-holes of the desk on the other side of the room. A parchment kept out of sight, hidden behind a shelf of account books. Something quite amiss, I thought.

The overseer placed the account book on the table before us and began some explanation about a sickness among the miners as the cause of decreased production and those reduced revenues upon which the Baronet had remarked during our earlier survey of the mine's workings. But I still could see the signs, in the overseer's darting eyes and still-sharp movements and the lines of tension in his face, of a mind not at ease. I rose and stood behind the Baronet, feigning interest in the notations and figures upon the page – in truth I have no great head for numbers – to which the overseer was pointing with an earnestness and energy almost unmeet for the pragmatic matter at hand. He struck me now as a man *playing* the role of overseer rather than *being* one. As he spoke I stepped silently away and slipped into the next room to retrieve the parchment roll from its dark niche in the shelf. Not a man much accustomed to deception is our overseer, I thought, for a clever thief would more carefully conceal the evidence of his theft. For theft, or some similar malfeasance, I fully suspected it was.

With quiet stealth I returned the room, my absence unremarked, and resumed my place behind the Baronet's chair until the overseer's review of his figures was complete. I well knew my next gambit entailed some risk but I was not overly concerned. The eager cultivation of my Gift had given me much confidence in my instincts, and I knew as well no jester worth the name could live in fear of risk.

"That is how matters stand now," the overseer declared as he closed the account book with a firm clap of its cover, relief contending with finality in the tone of his voice. The Baronet sat back slightly in his chair and the estate steward, who had asked several questions and seemed satisfied with what he'd heard, sat silently. "The sickness has much abated among the miners," the overseer said, "so we shall see more silver and more pleasing numbers next quarter-day. Revenue will be as it was, quite soon. I am confident."

I laughed sharply, startling all.

"Perhaps revenue still is as revenue was, and what revenue will be is what revenue is," I said in bright jester-fashion, "and it is the overseer who will not be as the overseer was." And with that I tossed the roll of parchment to the table before the Baronet, who like the others was gaping at me in wonderment. I continued before any other found voice.

"My experience with speaking parchments is quite limited, good masters, but I believe this may be just such a thing before us, for I avow it has the ability to explain much."

His brow furrowed, the Baronet removed the ribbon and unrolled the parchment, looked for a moment at the dates and numbers written thereon before handing it to the estate steward. Consulting it closely, then again opening the account book and comparing some of its entries to those on the parchment, the estate steward's face grew grim, darkening as its lineaments grew stiff.

"Theft," was all he said, his eyes remaining on the figures before him. "Certain theft." He rattled the parchment. "These numbers show what has been held back."

"O, overseer!" I cried dramatically, "had you been a proper magician you might have made your master's money disappear entirely." I shook my head in mock sadness. "Alas that you are instead but an alchemist who merely sought to *conceal* his money by transmuting it into a sheep." Here I took the parchment from the estate manager, turning it over and pretending to exam it. "Yet even then you could manage only to turn it into a dried piece of a sheep's skin. As poor an alchemist as an overseer." I shook my head in mock sympathy as I returned the parchment to the steward. "And now I believe I shall summon the coachman," I added, for the Baronet had risen to his feet and turned a glowering eye on the overseer.

"Indeed you shall," the Baronet said, his face taut with unaccustomed severity. "Indeed you shall, and then to the constable."

That was the chief incident to which the Baronet had referred when thanking me for the good turns I had done him. Or at least that was the incident as he knew it. I did not tell him, then or ever, of its strangest aspect, the feature which startled me and, in the following hours and days, confused and vexed me as I reflected upon it. That moment occurred while the overseer was pouring wine and I was watching him closely, reading in his face the subtle signs of turmoil within: the lines and contours of his cheeks somewhat taut, a tension about the mouth, his hard bright eyes and the slightly puckered skin around them all gave indication of unease. I also detected the flux of these features that is common among men struggling to balance how they wish to appear with what they would conceal, for their passions ebb and flow as one impulse struggles with the other, and as expected I did see such alterations as the overseer worked to assert some pretense of composure.

What I did not expect was to hear, suddenly, two words ringing clearly in the room as though spoken with deliberate emphasis and clarity: "better hidden." For an instant I thought I indeed truly heard them in the common manner of hearing, and so glanced quickly at the Baronet and the estate steward. Yet neither showed any sign of anything unusual and at that moment I realized I had also registered the same peculiar sensation I felt whenever I caught from another's mind a word about to be spoken. It was that mere and fleeting intimation of touch as if thought had been made palpable and brushed against my mind so quickly and so lightly the sensation was all but undetected yet was irrefutable, existing in the gap between what is hinted and what is unknowable.

What was strange here, a puzzle to me, was that the overseer was not speaking nor was he about to. What this meant I could not quite say. Was my Gift still revealing itself? Was I still in the process of discovering its full range and power, its nuanced possibilities? In the days that ensued I came to expect other incidents of hearing thoughts never intended to be spoken would soon follow (and they did, though they were relatively few in number), and I wondered as well what if anything might come after. Might I yet perhaps gain more mastery of this Gift, discover new aspects, command it at will? So far those moments of catching words from the mind of another had occurred with no volition on my part, no effort of will, though I certainly had tried to force the experience many times, never with success.

Yet with this awareness of a heretofore unsuspected aspect of my Gift came uncertainty, a new and discomfiting misgiving regarding its nature and provenance. What, I wondered increasingly, was the purpose of such a Gift, this strange sensitivity to the thoughts and feelings of others and the outward signals thereof? Was there a purpose? And why had such a thing been bestowed upon me? The Baronet had understood the consequences of my Gift to be the mysterious working of Divine Will, and I had eagerly taken that understanding to heart for I did long to comprehend this Gift, to ascertain as best I might its role and place in the moral framework of the Created World and thereby its purpose in my life. Or perhaps it were better to say the role of my life in its purpose.

Yet was the Baronet's belief nothing but the consequence of the good my Gift had brought to *him*? He was a kind and generous master, as good an exemplar of virtue as I had yet known, but my service to him had been solely in matters of commerce and the management of his estate's business. I had remarked on the character of men coming before him upon that business and I had uncovered the perfidy of his mine overseer, but was not all this in the service rather of Mammon than of God? I had, years ago now, seen at a glance and from a distance the heavy grief of the natural history tutor and I had readily escried the deception of the dancing-master and felt the bitter misery of his victim, but to what end? What had changed as a result of my perceptions? What suffering had I averted? None. I have seen truths and falsehoods and dissimulations aplenty in the faces of servants and tradesmen, but how is this in the service of Divine Will? Why should such a Gift come to me, I a commoner with an education which has unfitted me for my divinely appointed station yet ushered me into none other? If I am, as my misgiving heart whispers ever to me, a lost man, a displaced man, is not my Gift fully implicated in that displacement, in the growing unquiet of my spirit? Along with my education is not this Gift my only companion here in the in-between space I have come to inhabit?

I had come to find I was a placeless man. Not in the sense of position, of course, for I held a place in the Baronet's household though it was one of my own making, one which did not exist prior to me and which will cease to exist after I have gone. I was placeless in a sense more troubling and profound, placeless in the sense that on no mind's map of the Created World was there a location marked for me. In the Great Chain of Being there is no link graven with my name, no direction for my role in the vast pageant that is the slow mysterious unfolding of Divine Intention.

My placelessness, the growing sense of the in-betweenness of my life, was already for me the disquieting theme of my days and nights, and as I began to ponder anew this elusive Gift I felt doubt return to my mind. If my Gift were indeed an instrument of God's will would I not be given greater scope for its use? Why should such a Gift be bestowed upon a kennel-master's son, now a simple scribe and jester, a minor advisor to a baronet? Would not such a Gift better serve God's purpose if it were bestowed upon a monarch or some minister of state, some noble man of worldly power whose words and decrees might alter the destinies of kingdoms? Why to a fool in a country Great House whose study-texts are the faces of farmers and tradesmen and servants? If I were to be an instrument of God, my Gift given by Him so I might in some wise further His Will, would I not know this? Surely there would be some sign, some holy vision, a consuming sense of grace in my heart to suggest the hand of God in this matter and in my life. I had read much of saints and martyrs, prophets and visionaries, and while I understood doubt was not unknown even to the holiest among them I also well knew I was no saint, no man in whose heart burned the holy fire of God's higher purpose.

In this uncertainty and questioning my restless mind found its way to the antipodal thought: perhaps this was not a Gift from God after all but a snare laid by Satan, some trick of the Devil's to draw my soul to him. Could this in some manner be a test of my will and my faith, my ability to resist temptation? If I embraced this Gift, followed the path it led me down, would I perchance become lost to grace, doomed to eternal torment? I could for no effort of thought understand how this might be so, lest it be that somehow my abilities led me to sacrifice moral virtue to Mammon, but as I felt thoroughly disinclined toward any fashion of trade or commerce I could not see there was danger in my Gift. Yet for all these considerations I was unable to free my mind entirely from doubt.

Life in the Baronet's household grew quiet when the last of his daughters married, and while the tranquility of my master's life was pleasing to him in the main, it was becoming for me an ever-greater goad to my ambition and my restlessness. I loved him as well as any man loved a good master but I could find no contentment in the prospect of a life spent as secretary or steward upon a quiet country estate. The fear that such might prove my fate brought still greater restlessness to my mind and spirit, an unquiet at times accompanied by a touch of despair, but still I could form no clear plan for a different future.

Little it mattered in the end, for at the age of twenty-two I suddenly found my future thrust upon me, ready or no.

The Baronet had always been a hale man if not robust, and the bodily troubles he knew were of the same order as come to all who tread the soil of the Created World. It was with great surprise, then, that I was greeted at servant's breakfast one day with the news the Baronet had suddenly taken quite ill, suffering constricting pains in the chest and laboring to breath. A physician had already been sent for, and arrived just in time to usher our master to the presence and mercy of God.

The household, which had been in well-ordered state for such length of time we all seemed to have forgotten the possibility it would not be thus eternally, was now both stunned and in silent turmoil. All of us felt

some measure of true grief for the Baronet, as kind a master as any servant might wish for. My grief felt – as I suppose most griefs do – particularly acute, for though my father still lived, albeit in the waning health
which is the customary lot of the aged, the Baronet had become to me
somewhat of a second father. We shared conversations which could
occur only between men who had read and valued the same books; we
discussed various matters of business and estate management, and some
questions of political consideration, that none without interest in the
larger world would comprehend. The more I learned of that larger
world the more fully I understood how generous and tolerant the Baronet had been in educating me alongside his own son, and how rare such
beneficence was. No wonder, then, the two of us had grown companionable during the three years I was formally in his service, for after returning from his travels Rupert chose to live in a far-off university town
so he might pursue further study, a choice which pained his father but
which he accepted with silent resignation. I became, in some small manner and for a few brief years, a surrogate son to the Baronet. I treasure
even now in my own advanced age the memory of our shared delights,
and most of all the memory of his great kindness to me. I hope and
trust he has found his fair meed in God's presence.

Word of his father's illness had of course been sent to Rupert, but so
sudden had been the Baronet's decline that seven days passed before
Rupert could reach his father's home.

No. Not his father's. Rupert's home now, a home nevermore to be
what it had been.

The Baronet's funeral was the darkest moment of my young life, a
wave of grief washing over me and leaving a deep lingering melancholy
though I took some comfort from the breadth and depth of feeling manifested by household staff in eye, face, and heart. The weight of our
sorrow in the face of this sudden loss was also, I knew, the weight of
love, intangible proof of the genuine human sympathy and compassion
ever in the Baronet's heart and which always drew from those who knew
him and who labored in his service, regardless of station, a commensurate elevation of heart and spirit and a bond of mutual affection, gratitude, and love. He was not a demonstrable man yet with his quiet care
and deep human feeling embodied a nobility of heart, mind, and spirit I
have seen far too seldom in my days upon this earth.

It was near a fortnight after the funeral when Rupert asked me to
meet him in the private study which once had served as our schoolroom,
where under the tutelage of various masters and the watchful eyes, as I
had then imagined, of those marble busts we had been introduced to a

dazzling expansive world of knowledge and possibility. It was a room I frequented often after I was granted quarters in the servant's wing of the Great House. While I had been given the freedom of much of the house I most preferred the erstwhile schoolroom where I might read in peace while enfolded in memories made warmer and more comforting by the passage of time. But as I entered the study that day and though greeted with an almost fraternal affection by Rupert, the room seemed altered, somehow rendered alien to me. None of its physical aspects had changed but it was clear upon the instant of my crossing the threshold that all the room once held for me and all it represented had inexplicably receded. Our *quondam* classroom had become but an assemblage of surfaces and objects towards which I might stretch my hand but which never, it seemed, would again yield familiar sensation, yearn as I might. It was suddenly a stranger's room, impassive and remote. I needed no glance at Rupert's face to know the words he would speak to me that day would alter the course of my life.

In truth this was not entirely unexpected. The Baronet often remarked how Rupert's travels abroad had changed him, how a mild melancholy had been settled upon his brow ever since his return. His father first thought this merely a temporary unbalancing of the humours, a consequence of long travel in foreign lands which would correct itself upon Rupert's return to his native country and his home.

But Rupert never returned home, entirely. To his native country he returned, yes, but he established for himself residence in a university town in the east of the kingdom and made clear his intention to remain there for some years pursuing further studies. He had visited his father's house only once since returning, and that for little more than a week. His son's intentions pained the Baronet though he loved Rupert too much ever to command his son against his own expressed desire.

I knew my master had feared Rupert's plans portended unwelcome alteration in the course of his family's history for we spoke of this matter once, the Baronet's mien clouded with its own melancholy and his voice weighted with sorrow. He loved his only son but he loved also the life of the landed gentry, living it much as his forebears before him had done for generations. They he felt had bequeathed to him a manner and mode of life almost as a responsibility and obligation upon the past, an entail of the heart.

"It is a tradition rooted in this very land," he had explained to me once, "rooted in and belonging to this place, bound to it in gratitude and duty and love." Thus it was his heart misgave him for he now believed

Rupert would not be bound to that place, the grand house and all its estates and the family's rootedness in the land and its traditions as he himself was. I had nodded my concern and spoke some words of encouragement neither of us believed, all the while feeling acutely my own ever-growing sense of dislocation and rootlessness. Everything, it seemed, was changing in ways beyond the reach of any of our efforts to resist or deny.

So it was Rupert's words to me that day in our former schoolroom fell on ears not entirely unprepared to hear them.

"I know my studies," he said quietly, his manner and tone intimating the scholar he was becoming, "will occupy my mind for some long span of years, and they cannot be pursued here. There is a sense among some of us in residence at university that a new spirit of inquiry is being born, a slow-dawning realization that our veneration of the ancients, while enriching in many ways, has served somewhat as a brake upon our learning." He shook his head, lips pursed in thought. "The world changes, my friend, and I would be among those ushering in that change. There is nought I love so much in life as the pursuit of knowledge, nought which satisfies my heart to such fullness. I cannot leave off what I so love, what makes me in heart and mind and spirit who and what I am. So I cannot remain here. Nor in truth do I find in my heart a wish to follow the manner of life so beloved by my father and his fathers before him." He paused, his hand almost of its own accord reaching to the book I had left on a table, his fingers for a moment resting upon its cover almost as though to begin a caress. "The estate and its tenants," he said, "I do cherish for reasons beyond the lucre they provide, and while I thank my father for the love of learning he passed to me I share in no degree his love of the chase and field and country affairs. The estate will continue much as it long has, but this house will not be as is the house of active country gentry, for my residence, my life, will be elsewhere and my visits here infrequent and brief. Those who manage the affairs and business of the estate shall of course be retained, but house staff need be but few." Here he paused again, his gaze directed out the window into the green shadows cast by the large tree which had shaded that window even when as mere children we studied here. Did he see in his mind some innocence of childhood he would preserve with those continuing studies which promised to disengage him from the world? I wondered this as I waited in silence.

"I propose," he said at length, "your father remain as kennel-master, for though I have no taste for the hunt I would not forsake entirely the long labors of my forefathers, my own father, in breeding running-hounds of such quality their fame reaches the corners of the kingdom. Your father has had no small part in the cultivation of that quality so I hope and trust he will remain to oversee what breeding shall yet take place. It will suit his –" and here in the instant of Rupert's pause the word "honored" formed instantly in my mind as if spoken aloud, my strange Gift again – "honored age that such oversight shall be less burdensome than formerly, for most of the hounds shall be sold. No need now to keep a full hunting-pack; breeding stock shall be sufficient. Your father himself shall choose which are retained. As for my father's boarhounds, in their far-distant kennel, well – " and here he turned to me, a smile playing upon his lips " – that brings me to you and your fate, my friend."

"To me?" I said in genuine surprise. "What have the boarhounds to do with me? I love them best of all hounds, yes, but –"

"The boarhounds themselves will soon be gone," Rupert continued, "for they are sold already to the very Earl whose son's betrothal to my sister, you will recall, was the occasion of your ascending The Whelping Box throne." He smiled broadly at the memory, as did I. "And which began," he continued, "your career as my father's jester, though I know you soon became much more to him." He studied me again, his eyes narrowing slightly in his thought. He turned to a small table standing against the wall and briefly lifted a sheaf of papers stacked thereon. "He praised you in his letters to me – I retain them as memento, you see – and indeed wrote of you and your value to him in rather striking terms." He looked to me expectantly.

"I am sure he did me courtesy out of all proportion to my value," I said, bowing my head in reverence to the Baronet's memory, "but then your late father was ever the kindest of men."

"Your words are accepted with gratitude and affection, my friend, yet I think you are unjust to yourself and to your insights, as my father called them. 'Curious and striking perceptions, at times almost wondrous' he wrote, if I may quote with a scholar's dry pedantry." He smiled.

"And the boarhounds?" I asked.

"Yes," he said, redirecting his thought. "My sister tells me her father-in-law the good Earl is in need not only of more boarhounds – though I suspect that need exists more in the fullness of his love of the hunt than in the emptiness of his kennels – but he also now finds himself in want of a jester." Rupert's wry grin and arched eyebrow indicated well enough his assessment of that particular need. "It seems several of the

Earl's noble acquaintances have retained the services of such fellows recently and the Earl is not a man who will be outdone." Rupert approached me, laying a hand briefly on my shoulder in the manner of his father. "My heart is a scholar's heart, and my house will be a scholar's house, dry and solemn and no fit habitation for a jester of any sort, let alone one of your wit and capacity." He looked away for a moment, then slowly faced me again, hints of sorrow, and the effort to control it, now evident in his face.

"You have been a valued friend to both me and my father, and I would reward such friendship as best I may. You have I know been a valuable adjunct in the management of this estate and if you wish you may remain here to assist the estate manager in whatever capacity most suits the need, and likely succeed him in the post. But this will be a quiet house," he continued with a slow shaking of his head, "and I cannot think you will find much satisfaction here, with so little that will be congenial to your spirit and wit. I know little of the Earl beyond my sister's occasional remarks of his love for all sports of the field during the day and love of company at table in the evening, but such a life surely must offer rich scope and opportunity suited to your gifts and which cannot be found here." He paused, hand on chin and oh, the scholar in him was as evident as a lamp in the darkness. Even in my present state I almost smiled. "Your mind and your fate are yours to decide, of course, but as one who has known you long and known you as friend, I cannot but encourage the latter choice."

I had known when I crossed the threshold into the study that when I went back out that door it would be to a world different from what it had been when I entered. Such are some moments of our lives, whether we will have them so or not, for the Wheel is as implacable as it is eternal and no creature on this earth holds over it any sway.

I rubbed my eyes, suddenly weary though the sun was yet high. Before I could speak Rupert continued.

"You need not answer now. Take what time you will to consider your choice."

I shook my head. "I need no time. Your offer of some employ here is a true kindness and I am humbly grateful, but with a scholar's perspicacity you see that my spirit and, yes, my ambition are too restive to be long content with such calm as will descend upon this house when you return to your studies." My gaze drifted to the deep-shadowed window, lingered there. "I sought, when we were young, to pass some measure of the learning we acquired to my father. He wanted nought to do with the world of books and the knowledge they offered. He had found his place and had become in it as an oak in the forest, strong-rooted and flourishing because of that rootedness in congenial soil. To move such a tree is to kill it. This he knew, so he would risk no disruption nor embrace any change which would threaten the comfort of such belonging and rootedness." I paused. "He was in his way of much the same mind as your father in their valuing of place." I faced Rupert. "From my deepest heart I thank you for allowing my father to remain here for what span of earthly days remains to him. But I am not like him in that way, this you know. So into the Earl's service I will go, and will take with me a heart heavy with my father's absence yet full of gratitude to you. This my spirit tells me I must do." Tears began to well in my eyes, I who was not yet much accustomed to them, and for the upwelling sorrow in my heart I could speak no further. Rupert extended his hand to me and I clasped it in both of mine before bowing my leave.

Back in my chambers I sat on the edge of my narrow bed, my face buried in my hands and my mind in a growing turmoil, racing thoughts contending with one another in a flux of confusion. I had long wished for more in my life, wished to engage a larger world, and now with the opportunity before me I suddenly felt only doubt and fear. If I should fail? If this unknown Earl is not the indulgent master the Baronet was? And my father. I strained against the thought of living his life yet as I faced a parting from him I did not know if my heart could stand such loss. Two of the great forces within me, my ambition and my love for my father, were now determined antagonists.

I was at war with myself and no armistice was possible. Yet I knew I must go.

Rupert returned to the scholar's life he loved scarcely a month after his father's funeral. What I believed would be our final parting in this world brought a settled gloom to my spirits, no suitable thing for one seeking to be jester in a new grand household. Yet I was overborne by sorrows. I was leaving the only home I had known, losing my benefactor and friend, leaving my aged father. Only at this time, with a poignancy and a belatedness of regret I found almost unbearable, did I fully come to the realization that the price of my restlessness and ambition would be the loss of the only world I had known and all in it whom I loved.

Though pained by Rupert's departure I knew a still greater pain awaited, for the day of my own leaving followed closely upon his. My new master the Earl had sent a retainer as guide and escort, and after two days' rest both man and horses were intent and eager to return.

I found my father in his quarters above the stables, those self-same small dark rooms, rough-walled and low-ceilinged, in which I lived for the first nineteen years of my life. It suddenly occurred to me I had not visited my father here since I moved into servant's quarters in the Great House; since that time all our converse had been in kennel or stable or at table in the servants' hall. Surely for this reason the thick smell of horse and hay in his rooms struck me almost viscerally even though I had just passed through the stables and kennel below. Had I ever noticed the smell as a child? I paused for an instant searching my memory, finding nothing. Unremarked for near twenty years and today filling my nostrils to distraction. How could I not have noticed? The answer followed the question as swift as thought: it was of course that I had been living in the Great House, away from these rooms, the stables, the kennels – away, I realized with an unwelcome sting, from the common world into which I had been born and which, in my secret heart, I wished fervently if vainly to leave. Had I now become an interloper here, already displaced so far from the milieu of my inescapable origin that its native condition strikes me almost with dismay? I would not have it be so, would erase such feeling from my heart, yet had not the prospect of life as kennel-master been for me almost anathema? Even the promise of stewardship in the Baronet's household was insufficient meat for my ambition's appetite. I had wished to leave this world and for days had thought I was about to, but in that long moment at my father's threshold I discovered I already had.

I realized also my father must have known this, felt it in some way he could not or would not articulate. The Baronet in his kindness had once offered my father lodgings in the servants' quarters when I entered service, but my father refused, insisting he needed to remain close to the creatures in his care and that he would find sleep impossible without the sounds of animals stirring beneath him. What, I wondered, had it meant to him I could sleep so soundly elsewhere?

My father's age had taken much of the acuteness from his hearing and he had not yet noted my entrance. He was absorbed in some leatherwork he held in his lap as he sat near the room's sole window, the ancient stool beneath him worn, I noticed for the first time, to glossy smoothness with long use. I rapped loudly on the open door and from his stool my father glanced up at me for the briefest instant before returning to his work. His face was impassive, as it customarily was, and I waited for him to speak.

"So y' go t' grander house now, ah? Now t' serve an earl," he said at length. He had always retained the accent of the north country, land of his birth and childhood, and in the depth of his feelings his accent always thickened. "Come t' take y'r leave." It was statement, not question.

"I have. The Earl has sent man and horse for me and they await me even now."

He was silent for a moment, his attention seemingly given over to the bridle he was repairing but I knew his hands, rough but grown expertly skilled with years of such labor, could do the work on their own.

"I do have fear for y'," he said at length, head bowed and eyes intent on his work. "T' leave place an' station. . . . " He paused, leaving the thought unfinished. "But much o' th fault be mine, I know. I should ha' tol' the ol' Master 'no' when he asked f'r y' t' be schooled alongside Master Rupert." His hands paused in their work. Without lifting his eyes he shook his head slowly. "'Tweren't natural an' I knew so, b't surprise an' foolish pride bettered me. Said it many times an' it's true as e'er: y' been schooled out o' y'r station but int' none other." He slowly raised his head and our eyes met. "An' now y' leave. Master Rupert says y' could stay t' aid th' steward but y'd rather lay y'r head in grander house still. Y've had tha' dream years now." With a pursing of his lips he looked away. "I hope y'r head lies easy, lad, I do f'r y'r my son an' I love y' proper as I can. An' so m' heart fears."

My father had always been among the most taciturn of men. To hear him speak even this much at a stretch was rare and it both surprised and moved me now. These words, all of them, were in my father's fashion the fullest possible token of his love and care and with that realization there came tears to my eyes.

"Y' were always a great hand w' th' dogs, boy, so look upon th' boar-houn's there t' see they be well-kept. Th' Earl gets m' son an' under-master as well, but I be glad o' the latter f'r at least he knows th' hounds well an' is a good man t' care f'r them. O'er fond o' his ale, though, so keep some watch."

I nodded my reassurance. The under-kennel-master had, like my father, been many years in the Baronet's service, moving north with the boarhounds when they were sent to the Baronet's hunting lodge. "I leave this place, father, but never the love of creatures I learned here. Learned from you. You have my word the boarhounds will be well-kept."

My father glanced at me briefly. "'Tis sad news master Rupert will sell much o' th' pack. 'We shall keep but half a dozen,' he says t' me.

'Not enough,' I tell 'im. 'Not enough f'r proper breedin'.' He agreed t' ten but n' more. Still not enough but 'is mind's made up. A great hand wi' books 'e may be but dogs 'e does n' properly ken. And with no hunts, no chase, how can we know which t' breed? True measure of a runnin'-hound can only b' taken in th' field, I tell 'im. He says perhaps th' vicar will run th'm from time t' time. Vicar's from gentry so it be proper but 'e has n' real heart f'r th' hunt. Won't be 'nough. This family's pride 'as long been in th'm dogs but in six gen'rations they'll ha' lost much o' what makes 'm rare. Great sad shame 'tis." He had stopped working on the bridle, merely turning it slowly now in his hands as he spoke, his fingers absently caressing the supple leather and glistening fittings. I don't know that I had ever heard my father speak so many words at once, and truth to Heaven I was unsettled by the strangeness of it.

"But th' great folk always will do as they do. Th' old Master, though, he wouldn' like th' thought 'f it, no. . . ." His voice trailed off and his hands, for the first time since I entered the room, fell still.

"Rupert's heart draws him elsewhere, and should not a man be true to his heart?" I asked, finally finding words.

"Don' speak t' me o' hearts, boy, till y've come to know y'r own." Although he spoke with an unwonted gentleness, his voice almost a whisper half-swallowed by the acute stillness of the room, his words took me aback. Yet before I could reply he continued, his hands again caressing the bridle as he lifted his head, his gaze directed to the room's single small window but his eyes, I could see, focused far beyond, into the distance of memory.

"Hearts. Yes." His jaw worked and I knew he was struggling with some tumult of his own heart.

"N' man knows 'is own heart till 'e knows love," he said finally, an abstractedness about him now but his voice quietly firm. "An' then he mus' lose 'is heart. When y'r mother came t' me my heart took her shape, as damp clay takes a hoofprint. As though God himself had shaped it so. An' my heart was full. But after tha' it could take n' other shape. An' when y'r mother died, well, n' other could fit th' shape o' my heart. None other would fit there." He turned to me, his own eyes now moist. "An' in that emptiness I've missed her f'r nigh twenty years. Hearts, aye. We know th'm only in the losin' o' th'm."

My father rose from his chair. Unable to trust my voice I embraced him in silence. All these words from my father, more than he customarily spoke in a se'en-night, revealed more of his own heart than he had ever given expression to before. I blinked back tears and wanted to speak but no words would come for a long moment. "I love you father," I finally managed to whisper. "I may not yet know my heart but do know you shall always be in it." He nodded, tears in his eyes and his lower lip quivering. He had never looked so old to me before, vulnerable and insubstantial the way an aged man becomes when he knows his days may be counted with no great effort. I had the sense even a light tap upon his chest could have knocked him over. I suddenly felt a touch almost of panic, like a man suddenly realizing he has forgotten some urgent business. I understood with a great press of guilt I had allowed time to pass and age to happen to him while I was a foolish youth, heedless of all that should have been said and done. Now it was too late. We have no means by which we might fill those voids of the past, bridge the gulfs our carelessness kept us from seeing until belatedly we recognize what can bring us only regret and sorrow, the lingering guilt of unnecessary but now irredeemable absence. I gave my father a final embrace and though tears blurred my vision rushed downstairs to the horse waiting outside and instantly set him to a gallop, surprising the servant of the Earl who had been sent to guide me north, to conduct me to my new life.

My guide, a fleshy man of pale complexion and flaxen hair, was as loquacious a fellow as I had ever met, able, I was soon sure, to match word for the word the most chattering kitchen gossip that had ever been. It did not matter whether I hearkened or no; his volubility was a constant torrent flowing unimpeded regardless of reception or obstacle. He spoke as though his material existence depended upon speech, that were he to fall silent for even a moment he would vanish on the instant, cease utterly to be. There was nothing upon which he would not expound: the shape of a cloud, the condition of a village, the profusion of roadside vegetation, the quality of the inns at which we stayed, the trattle of sheep in the roadway, the dust in the air, people I did not know — all was grist for the implacable mill of his relentless verbosity.

This was precisely what I did not wish for. My world in flux, my heart as upon the rack for its recent losses — my thoughts and spirit needed tranquility, not the relentless buzzing of this rhetorical gadfly. I could hardly bear the distraction of his endless travelogue, the tedious jejune narrative of a mundane and uneventful journey.

Uneventful, that is, until we stopped for the night at a miserable inn still several days' journey from the Earl's seat. Not a proper inn at all, really, but the merest pretense of a cottage to which had been appended – to all appearances, appended in great haste by grievously unskilled carpenters – several small rooms for the lodging of travelers.

This inn was closer to achieving a state of genuine wretchedness than any at which we had yet stopped. Low-ceilinged and dark, its hearth too small to produce sufficient heat and drafting poorly, the small public room was redolent of raw smoke and grim despair. My guide and I took the only two chairs at the lone table in the room, furniture which merited not the dignity of the word for like the walls it was dark and greasy to the touch, worn and chipped with hard use and long neglect. The chairs creaked ominously as we sat, the noise startling several rats scavenging beneath the table. I doubt the food is fit even for them, I thought glumly.

We spoke briefly with the host, a small dark man of curiously quick movements and evidently the only person beside ourselves within sight or sound. I felt an instant instinctive dislike for him though I took great care to show no reaction. There was an ominous distant light in his eyes, something remote yet with a strange intensity. Almost ferocity, I thought. His mouth seemed set in a permanent half-snarl and the tight, lined leathery skin about his eyes gave him a peering and almost furtive air.

As we waited for what I was sure would be a poor and meagre meal I grew increasingly uneasy. Not merely on account of the repellant dinginess of an inn built as much out of reified wanhope as of lumber, nor on account of a host who seemed as likely to murder us as bring us food and drink. No. My spirit's unrest was consequent upon the growing recognition of this squalid inn as a dramatic, irrefutable marker of my own displacement. As I contrasted the lost comforts of the Baronet's home and the anticipated greater grandeur of the Earl's with my sordid surroundings I felt more than ever before, and with an immediacy and acuteness which startled me, the in-betweenness of my life, my station that was no station, the drifting indeterminate island of which I would, I feared, be sole inhabitant for all the years remaining to me.

Had I known at the moment this feeling would never fully leave me as the years accumulated, that it would often manifest in mind and heart as a bitter loneliness and a dark shapeless dread at times casting itself over my spirit like a funeral pall, I may well have despaired, abandoned my escort and returned to Rupert's estate to suffer the stifling boredom of a steward's life.

But I did not know, so there I sat, disdainful to the point of contemptuous of that inn and its host and all the travelers who found it sufficient. The travelers especially, for those who could find such a place adequate must necessarily and without awareness leave behind some trace of their own lives' unrecognized futility and despair which would necessarily accumulate over the years like an invisible crust upon the walls until the very weight of those failures brought the building in upon itself to collapse in a damp mass of rotting lumber and leaden sorrows. It was this more than the thin smoke from the faulty hearth that darkened the walls and gave to that shabby room its great down-bearing weight upon my heart and spirit.

Yet why should I feel thus? This was a commoner's inn and was I not a commoner? A most uncommon one, I smiled grimly to myself, but irrevocably by all the laws of God and man and nature a commoner. Inns such as this would have been my ordinary lot, the quotidian and unremarked experience of my world and condition were it not for fortuitous chance. Indeed, but for that chance an inn such as this would be to me as recognizable as my own dwelling, perhaps even a comfort for which I could not afford to pay. The Wheel was at that very moment carrying me upward with a rush of exhilaration and promise from a Baronet's service to an Earl's, yet as I sat in that inn eating a wretched meal of boiled mutton and stale brown bread washed down with thin, bitter ale I felt ill at ease. Not only with my surroundings, but with myself. Pride is a cardinal sin. Was I succumbing to it already? Good fortune and serendipitous chance may befall any man and I knew I should not let mine turn my head from a due humility, not allow my stroke of fortune to lead to the imperilment of my soul. Of my skill and my learning I was justly proud and of my ambition I sought to be wary though I could in no manner refute or deny its taint upon my nature. Yet ambition is not evil in and of itself if it lead not to hubris or sin. If I guard myself against overweening pride I am subjected to no moral danger, no risk of my immortal soul. Thus I reasoned with myself.

These thoughts troubled my mind as I sat in that sordid unpleasant inn made more unpleasant by those thoughts, my ambition and pride pitted against my belief in the need for humility, the squalor of the room in which I sat in stark contrast to the comforts and beauties of those noble dwellings, real and imagined, which I was already coming to feel were my due, having been duly earned.

I struggled also to pay no heed to my companion, his volubility slowed but not halted by the loud and careless chewing of his meal. So weary was I of him I felt a surge of relief when our host approached us.

52

"Nought more f' ya sirs." He could it seemed speak only in a thick and gravelly mumble; I'd understood scarce half of all he'd said since our arrival. As he stood stolidly by our table I could not determine if his words had been question or declaration.

"We needs retire," I said as I rose, seizing the opportunity to separate from my companion, "for we start early." The Earl's steward had instructed my guide to pay only for a single lodging room each night, but unable to bear the thought of yet more inane chatter – I half-feared even sleep would be no impediment to my companion's prolixity – I had myself been paying the cost of a second room at the inns where we had stayed, and gave thanks that each night a second room had been available.

"Reach home t'morra then, do y'?" our host asked with a sidelong glance that caught my attention.

"No," my guide answered briskly as he too arose. "Three days' travel yet. We reach the Earl my master's seat on Thursday, God willing." He wore no livery so we might attract no unwelcome attention but, loquacious fool that he was, missed no opportunity to tell any with whom he spoke he was in an Earl's service, even after I had twice remonstrated with him to be more circumspect. Any man with a meet sense of caution and sufficient store of wit would have kept such information to himself, for while service in such a household indeed confers much status it also may tempt those who believe, often rightly, that noblemen's servants are more likely than most to carry coin or other objects of value; often even their raiment has value enough to make it worth the taking. To blithely announce such service to all and sundry upon the road with no regard for caution was to court trouble.

The innkeeper regarded us in silence, his eyes taking our measure. His gaze lingered on our garments and our saddlebags, none of them of any particular worth but no doubt superior to what was normally seen in his grim hovel of an inn. His eyes narrowed slightly as he looked again at our faces, studying us each briefly in turn, the slight pursing of his lips and lift of cheeks suggesting a turn of some sort in his thoughts.

"Main road north b' plagued wi' highwaymen o' late. Some's been robbed only b't there been murder too." He shook his dark head in a theatrical gesture of pity. My distrust of him was now earnest and active. His manner seemed to have grown guarded and more furtive even though to all appearance he was aiding us.

"None's been taken yet f' the crimes," he continued. "Dangerous clever men they be I s'pose."

"Robbers and murderers," my guide said, evident anxiety in his voice. A fearful man for a guide, I thought wearily. Why could the Earl's steward not have sent some resolute and taciturn yeoman instead of this chattering mouse? He gave me a worried look.

"You passed safely as you traveled south," I said reassuringly. "Why should the journey north not be the same?" I glanced at the innkeeper, who was watching me closely, his eyes bright and hard. "Perhaps the matter is not so grim as our host reports," I said, smiling to soften the import of my words. "Tales grow in the telling, perhaps travellers' tales most of all."

My guide shook his head. "I came not this way," he said. "The steward had given me other matter as well that sent me east before I fetched you, so my road south was not this one."

The innkeeper turned to my companion. "Aye, other roads for now be safer if not s' straight. Stick t' those an' you'll be well." His tone was as solicitous as his graveled growl of a voice would allow but his manner was at utter odds with his words. My suspicions darkened further.

"Y' be honest men an' good, I can tell," our host continued, "an' I would see n' harm come t' any such that's sheltered under m' roof. I be rough in m' ways," and here he glanced pointedly at me, "but not in heart. Take another road, a safer. Three leagues on y' come t' a village, just beyond it a narro' road branches east. Not s' trafficked as formerly but sound an' safe, an' adds but half a day's ride. Take that an' y' be t' th' Earl's grand house without trouble."

My companion looked at me, his eyes beginning to widen with his growing concern. "What say you, Jester? Let us take the safer road." His tone was imploring. "Half a day's a small price to pay for surety." He turned abruptly to the innkeeper without waiting for my response. "Yes, I believe we shall take that way, skirt the highwaymen, confound them all. What's half a day? Less perhaps. Our mounts are fine sturdy creatures, they can keep a good pace if so commanded. Among the Earl's best."

A foolish and foolhardy exaggeration, I sighed inwardly. I know horses better than most commoners and I certainly know a dull-spirited walking horse when I ride one.

"Two horses."

The words were the innkeeper's but they were not spoken. As before, I heard the word in my mind with all the force and ringing clarity of a word spoken aloud and again accompanied by the same indeterminate sense of palpable thought brushing lightly, momently, against my mind. My Gift now in my service, I thought, for in catching the word my suspicions and observations cohered into the realization we were being deceived, decoyed into the purlieus so we might be robbed of coin and horse. The main road was not beset by highwaymen. It was the route suggested by the innkeeper which harbored the danger, leading us to confederates who would be prepared and lying in wait.

Catching my companion's eye and giving him a knowing look which he seemed not to comprehend I repeated our desire for rest and an early start. The innkeeper took his leave but as my guide and I turned to our rooms I suddenly stopped him and with feigned surprise exclaimed "Oh! The horses. Let us look in upon our mounts before retiring." My guide began to demur on account of the cold but my voice and my hold on his arm grew firmer as I insisted and with no further complaint he accompanied me outside. Although but of middling stature and lean of build I pulled him along almost as one would a child's rag puppet. He was a man possessed of little strength of character, anxious and timid and as empty of will as he was full of words. I felt for him something between pity and contempt.

A lean-to so dilapidated it seemed in imminent danger of collapse served as what our host had referred to as "the stable" and my heart sank further at yet more evidence of squalor. I grew angered at both the innkeeper and myself when I saw the horses not been unsaddled though they had at least been given hay, as poor as it was. As we tended to the horses I explained, in little more than a whisper, my suspicions of our host and his report of highwaymen, saying nothing of course of the words I had caught from his mind.

My guide was unmoved by both reason and entreaty, his fear countermanding all other considerations.

"He may be a rough man and his inn uncouth," he said, "but I believe him to be honest enough in this regard. If he were such as you say surely he would have been discovered by now. I will take no risk with my life or the Earl's horse. Half a day's further ride is nothing." His mind was fixed and I retired to my miserable room with a sense of mingled despair and resignation not unmixed with contempt for the man's gaping foolishness.

My guide held to his intention the next morning. I had neither the wish nor the strength to argue with him further, having spent a restless night on a thin foul mat of decaying straw, half-fearing we would be set upon by robbers in our sleep. So my guide and I parted company. The innkeeper explained the path he recommended rejoined the main road north just below a village some two days' ride by the path my guide would take, a day and a half by the main road on which I would remain, so I agreed to wait for my companion there. With that we went our separate ways, he as full of misgivings for me as I was for him.

I wondered, as I rode north, what the Earl would think of his guide allowing me to ride alone. I considered also whether my erstwhile companion would plead with me to say nothing, perhaps offer me a bribe for my silence. Would I accept it? The thought of accepting some compensation for having to endure his foolishness and loquacity was tempting, and I confess I could bring my deliberations to no firm conclusion on that question.

My ride proved as uneventful as I anticipated. Every traveler I met on the road I greeted with the same inquiry – "Is the way safe?" – and all answered in the affirmative.

I reached the village that was to be our meeting place where again I heard no word of highwaymen or other hazard. I waited impatiently for my guide, and when the time of his expected arrival that evening passed with no sign of him my concern began to grow.

As a second day passed from morn to afternoon I began to fear outright for my escort's life, though I also knew whatever harm befell him was a consequence of his own folly. Nor would I, out of concern for my own safety, go in search of him. I told myself should a third day pass without his appearance I will send report to the constable and make my way to the Earl's on my own.

But this did not prove necessary, for a few hours after sunrise on the third day my guide appeared in the doorway of the inn where I waited. He was disheveled and dirty, exhausted from two days of foot travel and famished. He was, however, uninjured. The robbers who had left him bereft of coin and goods and horse had offered no insult to his person. He all but fell upon me when we met, words of gratitude, apology, and explanation tumbling from him in equal incoherent measure.

We departed the next day, both of us on my horse as I had not coin enough remaining to hire another. My companion's loquacity had quite abandoned him, for which I gave silent thanks, though he was repeatedly effusive in both his gratitude (though in truth I had done nothing for him) and in his praise of my perspicacity regarding the duplicitous innkeeper, which he seemed to regard as little less than miraculous.

The only other matter prompting him to speak at any length was our catching sight of the great cathedral in the town only several leagues from the Earl's principal estate. Even from a distance the cathedral struck me with a sense of the wondrous. I had never before seen such a construct except in the pages of books, and the sight of its spires, still incomplete yet thrusting triumphantly above the low stolid roofs of the town, touched my spirit and my mind in some way I could not name, nor forget. I vowed to visit it as soon as I might.

My first sight of the Earl's great country house, his most magnificent home yet one he used but sporadically, also put me into a state of quiet awe, one which my companion's low spirits and consequent silence allowed me to savor. As it came into view I stopped the horse and for a long moment sat without speaking. Considerably larger than the Baronet's great house or any other I had seen except from great distance, its brilliant white stone caught so much of the early afternoon light the eye was almost pained to look long upon it. The expansive façade of the house was almost as a second sun, so dazzling was its reflective, radiant presence in the dark landscape which was its setting, surrounded as it was at some remove by dense forest while from the foot of its walls and porticos spread a vast green-velvet lawn. The eye was drawn by line as well as light, for the house sat at the end of a long avenue of towering lime trees. It seemed to me almost as a planet at the center of its own cosmos, the ordering entity around which all other material elements gather and from which their significance derives. Seated there upon my horse, desirous of comprehending the size and grandeur of the building before me, I realized its true significance and power upon the mind and spirit inhered not in its breadth or height, not in the immense value of its materials and furnishings, but in its transformation of the world about it. Its sunlit brilliance seemed almost a distillation of light, a refulgent declaration of being outshining all the colors of the surrounding earth while its imposing elegant linearity overbore and interrupted the contours of rolling hills and huddled forest. The house arrested attention with quiet majestic grace, commanding awe with unforced irrefutable dignity. Insisting upon nothing it was freely given all. Even the cathedral had not struck me in such manner. I had never known an experience of mind such as this.

That realization struck me as fitting, for there before me was not simply a building of such size and grace and symmetry it could reorder the very landscape it occupied. There before me was my new life, its shape and nature waiting to be determined. The thought broke my reverie and I urged the horse forward.

Our approach upon a single horse was enough to set the household into such a state of excitement we were surrounded by servants before we could dismount. My escort, whom it quickly appeared was something of a favorite among the female staff for no reason I was ever able to ascertain, seemed on the instant to recover his wonted loquacity and his tale began to pour out of him in a breathless rush. We were led into the kitchen and only when meat and ale were set before us did he pause in his narrative, and then only briefly. He related his misadventure with an almost histrionic drama while his audience of clustered servants listened with rapt attention and commensurate wonder, further fueling his self-importance which led to even greater theatricality of voice and gesture. I was half-forgotten – until my guide, concluding his account of the robbery, stopped abruptly to point dramatically at me, his eyes widening for greater effect. Oh, this foppish fellow is in his element, I thought. Being robbed was a great good fortune for him, for he will trade off of the tale for years to come.

"He was right," my companion declaimed. "He saw true when I was blind." I was no longer forgotten. "You knew, Jester. You read the innkeeper's dark soul aright, read him as a monk reads Scripture while I was the true fool, not you. Oh, my reason swooned in the face of fear, I do confess it. What a folly, what a folly." He lowered his head and swung it slowly from side to side as though he were a tragical actor upon a stage lamenting some pitiful unwarranted tragedy. I wanted to laugh. "I shall harken to all your words now, Jester, by God's wounds I shall. We had heard here, all of us, some small report of the Baronet's man, said to have uncanny insight or some such, but we knew not whether to credit the gossip or no. Oh, more true than the report is the fact." He nodded and looked about him at the rapt faces of the servants, one or two of whom now glanced nervously at me. "I saw it myself," he continued, "there with my own eyes I saw this Jester peer into the innkeeper's black soul and see there the mark of the devil's damning hand but I was too much the frightened fool to heed him. I confess it. I paid for that folly, friends, and only by the grace of Providence do I still possess my life." He raised his mug of ale to pledge me. "And again I say never henceforth shall I have misdoubt of this Jester, this man of wonders."

I knew not whether to thank the man or mock him. I merely smiled and nodded, half-raising my own mug to acknowledge his words as some few of the gathered servants now stared openly at me though their faces betokened not wonder but suspicion, even here and there a hint of budding fear. I had no sooner set my mug down when it was refilled by a young kitchen maid, her hand trembling and her eyes staring fixedly at my mug as she strove to mask her nervousness. "Bless y' sar," she said quietly before retreating.

This I saw was an important moment, one which could shape all of my time in the Earl's service. I could have minimized my importance in the guide's recounting of his misadventure, gainsaid his exaggerated recital of my prowess, insisted it was all chance or luck or mere nothing. I could have shifted their perception of me away from wonder and superstitious fear and brought it back to sensible earth and the ordinary ways of the mind's knowing. Back to the safe quotidian. But I did not. In part because my guide's account was, despite his many exaggerations and flourishes, accurate in the main. In larger part, though, because in my pride and my ambition I would miss no chance to accrue what power and cultivate what reputation I could, and if the servants of the household I was joining should from the start think me a special sort of being, a figure of some mystery whom they believed able perhaps to glimpse the secrets of their hearts, well, this would suit my desires well. So I said nothing, allowing the servants gathered round to think what they would, knowing their reports of my guide's story and of me would grow in the telling and the re-telling, knowing that by the time their gossip reached the neighboring estates and town it would tell that my escort single-handedly dispatched a band of robbers instead of the two highwaymen who waylaid him while I will have become some sort of minor prophet or wizard. Let them talk in such wise, I thought, for the effect of such gossip will but redound to my reputation.

My guide, glorying in the continued attention of his auditors, resumed his discourse, beginning his story anew with yet further embellishment. I had had my fill of him, for this day and forever, so I asked for direction to my new chambers. My new home.

Thus did my time in the Earl's service begin auspiciously.

cathedral

In the days following my arrival at the Earl's grand estate I found myself much unsettled. All about me was less familiar than I had anticipated: people, environs, dialect, customs, routines, manners – all were further from what I had known my entire life and had assumed to be more or less the given state of things across the kingdom if not beyond. The Earl's household, much larger than the Baronet's, was ordered with a regularity and formality alien and uncongenial to me, for though the Earl himself was, I soon learned, not given to formality himself he took little interest in the management of household or estate affairs, leaving them in the hands of his butler and several stewards who managed with a firmness to which I was unaccustomed. Right glad was I jesters were held to few of the expectations placed upon all others in service.

The Earl was away from his principal estate when I arrived, and more than a month was to pass before I met my new master. Having little to do then in my first weeks in the Earl's service other than acquaint myself with the Great House and its ways, I found myself with overmuch time to dwell upon the strangeness of my surroundings and the consequent sense of my own further displacement. I felt, too, with a great acuteness and sense of emptiness the absence of my father, of Rupert, of the Baronet and all that had grown familiar to me in my former service. I had expected much upon my entrance into the household of an Earl. What I did not expect was to find that by the end of my first week there I was already bored.

I sought distraction and as well felt the need, indeed a longing, to learn more of the new district in which I found myself. To this end I began to wander the streets of the grey cathedral town not far distant whenever I could, dressing in common raiment so as to be inconspicuous and unknown to all – or so I thought – and in this way I began to learn much of the Earl and his domain and of those who lived in this reach of the kingdom, knowledge which came to serve me well in my time there. This habit of wandering unknown among the people of my own station, watching them in the course of lives which were as my own might have been had I remained among them, has never left me since and has often proved of consolation to me as well as of value to those in whose service I labored.

My thoughts kept returning to the great cathedral I had glimpsed upon my arrival, and on one of my first forays into town I made it my goal. As I approached, my steps slowing as though of their own accord,

I could feel a strange stirring within me, vague but of an undeniable potency. I found myself enthralled by the cathedral's twin spires rising as it seemed higher with each step of my approach, their stone a pale grey against a darkly clouded sky. The wooden scaffolding which embraced various unfinished parts of the edifice detracted for me not at all from the impression of earthly substance and mass transformed by the labor of men into heaven-reaching grandeur. Never had I seen such a construct before, and while the ways of churchmen even then did not much inspire in me the reverence I knew I ought to feel, that yearning prayer in stone was a glorious magnificence to me, greater even than the glistening declaration of self-importance that was the Earl's Great House.

For minutes I stood silent and motionless in the damp, rutted lane before the great church under the clouded skies I had already begun to fear were a permanent fixture of this part of the kingdom. About me was nought but stillness: no tradesmen at their daily labors, no carters leading rumbling wagons through the street behind lumbering oxen, no ringing of steel on stone or hammer upon wood. Only the promise of more rain and the great edifice before me, impassive and monumental and seeming almost to swallow sound, to challenge and refute the very idea of motion. Here you will stand, it seemed almost to say. Before me you will be transfixed by a power you cannot comprehend and a longing you cannot name. And in your heart you will love that power and longing and will surrender yourself to them without thought of what you may lose by so doing.

I had already learned there had been for some years now insufficient money to continue work on the cathedral, and some small signs of neglect were evident where scaffold timbers sagged and birds built ragged nests in grey alcoves meant to house statues still to be carved. Yet my spirits remained moved almost to joy by this celebration of God's greatness and our human longing for a transcendent love promising redemption. I was at the same time chastened and subdued because what else may a man be before such a towering magnificence of stone demanding of him the acknowledgement and worship of a glorious and kingly Omnipotence to whose Heaven it leads both eye and mind? What else may a man do before such a construct but drop to his knees and avow to himself his own insignificance in the complexity of ordered Creation? In such wise the building spoke to me. Yet in that subjection also lay an exuberant joy, for this vast subtle orchestration of carven stone was also a soaring song of the human spirit, an exulting testament to those aspirations to the Godlike within us and a celebration as well of our richly varied gifts, of the skill of many hundreds of men who devote to God's purpose what God has given them so we may cause to rise from a plot of flat earth an enduring monument of unimaginable strength and sublime power to testify for ages to the highest and most ennobling yearnings of the human spirit. To be unmoved before such glory, I felt instinctively, is to be inert in heart.

I could smell him before I saw him. Enwrapped in my thoughts I did not hear his footsteps in the damp dirt of the road but the sudden unmistakable smell of ale brought me back to myself. I turned to find I had been joined by a friar, standing close enough that the sleeve of his ample garment touched my cloak. The bitter reek of ale was strong upon him but much of it was the sour smell of old ale, no doubt spilled days or weeks ago on the frayed woolen of the grey habit which was his sole article of attire, though I could also smell fresh ale upon his breath.

"Even now a magnificent monument to the Creator, and I pray daily I live to see it complete. What grandeur then! What glory!" His voice began to rise in pitch and grow in volume even as I turned to look at him. "An expression of man's love for God and in turn God fills it with his eternal Love for us. No room for the devil's purpose in the presence of such love, such power. Drive them away, drive them all away!" His arms flailed as though enacting the promise of his words. "The full and absolute power of God. You feel it now, feel it like a hundred fires no hiding the fires of God, eh? The Love flowing from Heaven is a love that sets the spirit aflame. And when it is complete! Complete! A thousand fires then, a hundred thousand, a beacon to souls for leagues and leagues and all the devils begone!"

He stopped abruptly to rub his face with a curious vigor and I took the moment to study this odd friar. Beneath an utterly bald pate his face was heavy and round, pocked considerably beneath the thin white beard which grew in uneven patches along jaw and cheek. Perched on a thin neck above narrow shoulders, his broad head seemed out of place, a seed-laden flower grown almost too heavy for its stalk. But his eyes struck me the most, animated by a wild bright glitter even on this sunless day and rarely still, darting about as though he were urgently drinking in the world around him, or dreading assault from unseen forces.

Unsure of the man I uttered some simple innocuous words regarding the cathedral only to be startled by the abrupt swivel of the friar's ponderous head and the quicksilver narrowing of his eyes as he studied me closely. Ah, I thought, my accent.

62

"A visitor here I hear, I hear, in your voice I hear . . . ." And in his pause the words "the west" sounded in my mind, words again accompanied by a sense of thought made palpable, and though I knew not why I suddenly felt with full surprising conviction it was now right and proper to surrender completely to this aspect of my Gift, for when this holy man, an absolute stranger to me, continued he said "the west of this kingdom." "The kingdom of God knows no region," he continued with rapid speech, "but here we are divided like birds and beasts, like creatures of forest and sea, like the squeaking bat and the burrowing mole, we fallen creatures we the inheritors of the crumbled remains of Babel's tower, no?" He stopped, looking at me expectantly, intently, his round face seeming to quiver with some strange excitement. He was clearly mad, not drunk, and I confess I began to grow somewhat nervous for to this point of my young life I had had no direct experience of madmen.

I nodded. "Yes," I said, "my home was in the west but I am now in the Earl's service." I spoke with deliberate calm, hoping not to excite him further and already beginning to think how I might escape him.

"The Earl's man!" he nearly shouted as he clapped both hands to the side of his head with a violence that startled me. "I would keep no man of the Earl's service here in the wind and rain" – the air was utterly still and though clouds lowered above us no rain fell – "to do ill service to the health of him in service. You understand me you see." It was a statement, not a question, and he nodded vigorously for no reason I could determine. "Come," he said, clapping me on the back with surprising strength, "the house of God awaits. Myrmidons and mongrels see not the empyrean but we do, though fallen sadly from God's grace if not his love. Inside you shall understand me, all shall be clear. Come." I would have torn myself away from any other such man but rudeness to a friar, even a mad one, no, that I could not manage. And I did long to see inside a work of such somber majesty and inspiring promise.

With his sinewy arm about me the friar hurried us to the cathedral door and into the most dramatic space I had ever encountered, a vast grey lithic enclosure which immediately and for a long moment overwhelmed me to stillness, almost to rapture as my spirit seemed to reach of its own accord for the vaulted roof so expansive and so far overhead its further corners were lost in shadow. Seen from the interior the cathedral's structure was more complete than I first imagined although the empty alcoves and niches and the simple wooden altar and pews testified to the long hiatus in construction and adornment. Yet that engulphing cavern of a cathedral was no less impressive, no less able to abduct the

spirit, as it seemed to me, to hold it ransom for the mind's acknowledgement of God's sublime and transcendent grandeur of which this monumental absorbing space, surely the greatest and most complex expression of which human mind and body are capable, was but pale attenuated metaphor of the divine magnificence for which it stood. Tears
welled in my eyes and I felt pierced, transfixed by a power which should
have been impossible – I was surrounded by mere stone, after all – yet
irrefutably and undeniably *was*. I trembled for I felt with certainty my
spirit had somehow gone from me and I knew not if it would return.
For a brief span it seemed as though I had lost cognizance of myself, my
being somehow absorbed into the space and power and grandeur of this
incomprehensible achievement, overwhelmed by a towering frozen
wave of stone which bore my spirit away in an irresistible surge. In the
gloomy half-light of the sunless day that vaulted multiform space should
have been given over more to ghosts than to God but I know it was an
indefinable yet insistent emanation of Divinity filling me then and my
spirit falters still at the mere memory.

This moment proved even more transformative in my life, for I believe it was the power of that unprecedented experience, sublime and
transcendent and enrapturing, and the accompanying disruptive shock
to my mind and spirit in the o'ermastering space of that cathedral which
opened to me the third and final aspect of my Gift: a vision of what was
yet to come.

In an instant the cathedral before me, raw and incomplete, was transfigured into a glorious house of God. Gone were the dirt and shadows,
the piles of lumber and veneer of dust and litter of crumbled stone, the
plain wooden benches and the mad friar next to me. In their place was
the light of a sun-rich day streaming through brilliant jeweled windows
to illuminate a space of gilded glory. The vaults overhead, painted in
warm hues, glowed in the reflected light of the sun; the choir and altar
screen gleamed with highlights thrown from their dark polished wood,
richly carved with impossible intricacy. Painted statues of saints and
martyrs in ordered magnificence filled the niches ringing nave and tran-
sept. An altar of gleaming marble was draped in a brilliant rich cloth
which rapt the eye and upon that cloth stood a bejeweled monstrance,
its lustrous gold a beacon to the yearning spirit in that holy place.

The vision left me in an instant but it had come with such a sense of
pressing, tangible reality I could only stumble to the nearest bench and
slump weakly upon it. I recognized immediately this strange inner sight
was in some fashion another manifestation of my Gift, for it too had

64

been accompanied by the sense of palpable thought touching the mind which I always experienced when catching words from another's mind. Yet in this visionary instance the sense of mental touch was much more potent, not a mere brushing against my mind but something more, a firm impress which in its swift registration and departure left me with a sensation akin to vertigo, but a vertigo of the mind rather than body, if such a thing may be.

I confess I cannot even today confirm the accuracy of this vision, cannot determine whether it was truth or merely inspired wish, for the cathedral remains incomplete, remains still as I saw it that long-ago day. Other such moments have occurred to me, however, as you will learn, and from their validation I do believe what I saw of the cathedral will yet come to pass. I am certain, as certain as I am of the lingering power of that vision and its numinous glory, pulsing and alive in memory yet. I have since that day had many an occasion to be angered with God, so angered I have cursed and denied Him, but I cannot forget the searing vision of that holy place in its completion.

The friar, I suddenly realized, was speaking to me but so lost was I in the aftermath of my vision I at first did not hear him, had in fact forgotten his presence until he paused to slap me on the back hard enough almost to jolt me off the rough bench of a pew upon which I sat. He nodded, smiling hugely.

"Full fruition, yes," he said nodding but I did not take his meaning.

"All in a muddle here," he continued, sweeping his arm at the space before us, "but clear to God, clear to Heaven and there's no telling what a man will see when he looks." He stopped suddenly, dropping to the pew beside me to peer intently at me, his eyes yellow and rheumy but still madness-bright and boring into my own with disconcerting intensity. I wished to be free of him, to consider alone and in quietude what had just occurred. I struggled to clear my thoughts so I might cast my mind about for a way to leave without insult.

He held up a shaky hand, a peremptory gesture of cessation. "No, no no no." I was suddenly struck by the possibility he had read my thoughts. Has his madness given him some Gift beyond my own? Or – and this thought came to me with such fear in its wake I suddenly felt a cold dampness on the back of my neck – is it the Gift that has driven him mad? Is this *my* fate? I felt a sudden urgent floodrush of panic and made as though to stand but the friar pulled me back to the pew.

He continued to look at me, nodding vigorously now and in my confusion I knew not what to think or say. "It is here," he said, his calm voice disconcertingly at odds with his glittering eyes and antic manner.

Again he rubbed his face with that same curious vigor so when he looked up at me his cheeks and brow were glowing even in the half-gloom of the nave where we sat. "It is here but we don't know it, what it is why it is we don't. We stumble about in blindness through our own error, our own sin." He jumped to his feet. "Sin! Sins of our fathers. Sins of our mothers. The worst sins those of ourselves," his voice now a shout, both arms raised above his head as he shook his fists at the ceiling far above us. I thought about running but he abruptly sat down again, so close to me a fold of his robe lay across my thigh and the smell of ale again filled my nostrils. "We inherit sin and make it our own, yes, we grow it like a weed and water it with blood and tears and vanity. We inherit frailty and feed it, make of it a vast world of troubles and disorders and only love – " He stopped suddenly, his last word seeming to hang in the damp cathedral air as he put a hand to his face.

"But some," he said slowly after a moment's pause, his eyes closed tightly as though in pain, "some are born out of order." He stopped, nodding vigorously with his face contorted by a grimace which would have been comical if not for his madness and its incongruity with the vast expectant space of the cathedral around us. Of a sudden his eyes flew wide open and his finger was suddenly pointed at my face and he spoke softly though his voice was almost accusatory, "You are such a one!" He leapt to his feet again, laughing and clapping his hands, almost dancing in some mad merriment I could not fathom. I began to rise, thinking to utter some word, any word, of hasty farewell before fleeing but suddenly he was still, frozen in mid-motion, his eyes locked on mine as I stood.

"You are such a one, yes," he repeated, this time his voice modulated to scholarly seriousness. His eyes held mine. "You, the Earl's new jester. You are the man out of place, out of the order of things, yes, you are such a one. The displaced man among us." He dropped to the rough pew again, his shoulders slumped, his massive head in his hands, all trace of manic energy instantly gone. Without fully knowing what I was doing I sat back down beside him.

"I am mad," he said before I could form the words to ask how he knew I had come to serve as jester. "I am mad, sad, would climb the mountain to bask in God's great Love above forever but the world holds me back, the things of the world surround me, swell around me to distraction." He shook his head. "This robe the birds the stones about us the very butter in the dairy and the hops in the field all put me into a confusion and my dreams – " he stopped abruptly, looking about him now; pursing his lips he held up a finger, wagged it at nothing – "my dreams stop not when the sun arises I know but I would clear this confusion oh I would clear it in the cleansing power of God's Love if I might." He sat fully alert now, eyes straight ahead but seeing I knew not what.

"How know you I am the Earl's jester?" I asked before his lunatic's rant could resume, for the matter so troubled me my desire to flee his presence was now utterly forgotten. "I've said nothing to you beyond the fact of my service, few here know me yet –" My voice trailed off as I sought the courage to ask the question I half-dreaded to ask. But in the pressing stillness of that grey holiness ask it I did: "Have you some Gift from God to know such things before other men?" I could not bring myself to utter the remainder of my thought: "and has it driven you mad?"

He turned his orb of a head slowly, blinking and narrowing his eyes as though seeing me for the first time, studying me as he would a curious insect or hothouse flower. There was a calmness in his face now, an uncanny repose of feature and lineament as though no fierce passions had ever touched his heart or mind. Was his an intermittent madness, a flow of fits and frenzies now suddenly in abeyance? I had read of such things but without direct experience of men disordered in their minds I could only guess. My uneasiness increased but I needed to hear him speak, to answer my question.

"Gift?" he said wonderingly. "The gift of God's grace and love as given to all men, yes. But my knowing you are the new jester? That comes not from God but from the greengrocer's wife." He laughed softly, with no trace of his former mania. "She is my niece and accompanies her husband to the Earl's great house though more to gather gossip than to deliver roots and vegetables. We are not so grand here that news of your coming and word of your wit hasn't been the talk of the servants for weeks." He laughed again. "A Gift from God." He smiled for an instant then abruptly rose, rubbed his face again but this time slowly and with evident weariness.

"I would rest, Jester. I would rest. Weariness takes me suddenly in my age. . . . " And with that he turned and walked slowly toward the door by which we had entered the cathedral, his massive head drooping. I watched him in silence, pitying him for his fits of madness yet glad for his departure. Halfway to the door he stopped and turned slowly to face me.

"Word of you preceded your arrival, Jester, and has grown since in the gossiping. Expect the tales only to continue here in your time upon

God's earth, if even only some small part of those stories be true. Already — you are a young man, young — servants' ever-wagging tongues tell of your acumen in the ways of men more than of your wit and rhymes. They whisper even of some strange power to know a man's heart purchased through compact with the Devil at the price of your soul." He paused, again rubbed his face as though thoroughly fatigued.

"You fear this, Jester, do you not?" He spoke slowly, taking several steps back toward me across the dusty stones of the cathedral floor. "You are troubled by this acumen, this uncanny knowing you are said to possess. Perhaps you wonder if it comes not from God but from the Great Deceiver, from Beelzebub. Ah, Beelzebub!" His look suddenly became almost ecstatic and I could see another fit of madness coming upon him. He stood for a long moment as still as the statues which would one day fill the niches ranged around us. The sudden silence following his shouted reference to the Devil, here in this holy place, descended on me like a palpable weight in the half light of the cathedral, every piled stone of which seemed now only to be waiting for the friar's terrific damnation of me, a curse to bring those stones showering down upon me, the agent of the Evil One daring to desecrate this holy place with his polluting presence. Perhaps such should be my fate, I thought as I began again to tremble. The Baronet had once saved me from doubt, I had believed, but doubt had slowly returned and now, here in this sacred stonework monument with a man of God whose flitting turbulent madness must surely be the oracular touch of that God to whose service he had given his life — now the reassurances and persuasions of the Baronet seemed hollow and as remote as the days of Solomon.

In that moment of my fear and my weakness I did what I never had done before and never done since. I acknowledged to that man, that holy lunatic of God, the nature of my Gift as I then knew it: not just reading of men but catching words from their minds and thus knowing something of their hearts. I said nothing of my vision only a few minutes ago but already growing distant, for I suspected he may already have had some sense of what had happened to me, and as well I did not wish to speak of what I myself did not yet understand. I sat down heavily upon the bench and across the distance between us confessed to the mad friar my fears and doubts about the Gift's origins, my hands beginning to shake as beads of sweat formed upon my brow even in the cool damp of the cathedral. I spoke of the Baronet and his kindness, the words tumbling forth in an ecstasy of relief, and how my small Gift was used in the service of a kind and honest man and how I expected the same in my service to the Earl, God willing. I shook with the effort as I spoke.

"I cannot fully lose my doubt though I see no hand of evil in this matter," I concluded, worn with the effort of speaking aloud what had so long been restrained within me. "I am no saint, father. All mortals are the fallen children of our first parents and I am mortal and therefore a sinner, but – "

The friar's laugh startled me. "Logician as well as jester! Oh, a wise jester for a fool!"

I thought again of his madness, said nothing. Tears had come to my eyes as I had spoken and I feared to say more lest I cry openly in front of him.

"You do not speak of all, Jester. You do not mention your vision of this cathedral's glory, or perhaps would forget it, would pretend it was the imagining of your mind for you are afraid of yourself still. But I could see you in your own way of a mad fit, Jester, I saw it in you so few moments ago." I was right. Somehow through his madness, or because of it, he had understood something of what I had seen in my mind. He walked slowly toward me. "As you do not mention it with your Gift you either fear it most of all or do not yet know such visioning as part of your blessing." He sat down on the pew in front of me so we faced each other, he upright with his pale pumpkin face and I with my head hanging almost to my knees. I could not hold his gaze.

"You were born," the friar continued, speaking slowly now with his voice seeming to come from a distance though he was close enough for me to touch, "into the house of a good man; this is the handiwork of God. You were given a nobleman's learning out of that good man's love for son and servant; that too is the handiwork of God. This learning you put to the service of this good man; is this not the proper harvesting of that which God himself has sown? All of this, sad Jester, marks the path of a life in service to a master who acknowledges in the actions of his life the righteousness and the glory of God and his teachings. As does our Earl, in his rough and careless way." The friar paused. I could still not lift my eyes to his face. "You see, Jester, I too am a logician. And no small fool!" He laughed and I looked up, watched him wave one hand before him in a gesture I did not understand. The mad fit returning? "Along this path you discover a Gift," he said, his voice rising now and his words coming more rapidly, "yet you fear the provenance of this Gift, doubt the Giver from whom you have received it. Ha! Perhaps you are a poor logician after all, Jester, for the Devil is evil as evil is but wastes no cunning and no Gifts on a man who misleads no Baronet and who comes to an Earl with no trickery in his heart. Not in his heart, not in his head – " The friar threw both hands above his head now, closing his eyes for a moment as in ecstasy. The madness come again, surely. "You who have had in God's own house a vision of that house in its coming glory! You have seen it, the triumphal celebration of God that is yet to be! Yet you doubt, you doubt, you doubt. . . ." He shook his great head as his features began to twitch and contort as if alternating between sorrow and ecstasy. "A fool of a jester and a jester for a fool, a tool yes but of God not Beelzebub." He was animated now, antic, a mad puppet gesticulating at random as he leapt to his feet and looked wildly about while his face lifted to the dusky vault of the cathedral ceiling far above us.

"You read men, Jester, the gossips say, aye and some gentry say it too. So they say so they pray but I pray too. The salvation of souls, Jester. I read too, the great Book, God's Book, the very word and being of my life's reading my heart's bleeding and there – the Prophets! The Prophets!" He stopped suddenly, eyes on me, arms spread wide. I too stood, helpless, uncertain, almost mesmerized.

He nodded vigorously. "The Prophets, yes. In the great Book the given word of God the Prophets. Oh, ours is a fallen world, Jester, sadly fallen in well-earned sorrows a sinful world abiding only by the grace and forgiveness in the endless Love of our Heavenly Father. No Prophets among us now, none such as Ezekiel or Isaiah, none such as they now to point the way across the desert of our woes past our foes but for all our trespasses the Father of Forgiveness has not forsaken us!" He was leaning toward me now, his entire body tense and though I now met his gaze he seemed not to see me. "No," he said, his voice suddenly soft, barely a whisper, at such incongruous odds with his contorted posture I nearly smiled. "No," he said again. His gaze suddenly sharpened and he saw me now, his eyes bright and he raised a finger to point at the bridge of my nose from only inches away.

"You. No prophet no but all gifts are not denied to all men here in the swampy fen of this sinful world God still gives us a taper to light our way a grace given in love from above given to guide those who would still listen who still would hear without fear. Small graces small traces but all we deserve, yes, but grace yes still grace given in love from above given oh Jester!" His voice rose so sharply in pitch and volume on that last word I took a step back in startlement. "Jester," the friar repeated but now his voice had returned to a whisper, soft yet intense, "oh still

70

to come is the fullness of the Gift, Jester, still to come is the fulfillment of your greater purpose, what you saw here today of tomorrow just the beginning." He stopped, nodded. "God in his mercy is great but all gifts have their price. No giving is truly given except by God and his Son, exchange, yes, invisible perhaps but the Gift will have its price, oh Jester you will see, you will see and you have my pity Jester. And my poor blessing." He made a rapid sign of the cross only inches from my face, looked at me a long moment in silence.

"A mad friar for a Jester!" he suddenly laughed. "I choose the friar for I know, Jester, this I know – " and again he stopped abruptly, his hands open rigidly before him and a look on his face which in its sudden severity and blazing obscure passion froze me where I stood. "This I know – " and now his breath was coming hard and he seemed almost to be forcing the words from his chest. "I know that coming events cast their shadows before them, so I would not be I would not see as you Jester not as you, no. I am mad enough mad enough indeed. Oh it weighs upon me!" He shook his weighty head as though to free himself from confusion. I suddenly felt empty, frightened by fears I could neither name nor understand. I waited desperately for him to continue, prayed he would stop.

"Coming events cast their shadows before them," he repeated, this time to the empty air, yet still I could take no meaning from this for the fear and confusion in my own mind. "You will see, Jester. Through your tears you will see."

With that he straightened abruptly, glanced furtively about him for a moment as though in frantic fear then hurried to the cathedral door. I felt the urge to call out to him but no words came to my lips, only a hand half-reached toward him in uncertain supplication.

At the door he stopped, whirled to face me, his face wracked with emotions at which I could not even guess.

"Coming events cast their shadows before them, Jester." His voice was nearly a shout. "And to you some small glimpse of those shadows is given. Ha! I would not be you. God have mercy on you Jester, in his Love."

In a moment he was through the great door and flying down the steps to the road like a man possessed though it was some emanation of the Divine possessing him, I believed then and still believe now, not some agent of the Devil. His last word seemed to linger in the air, a haunting hollow echo, for what seemed a preternatural length of time. I waited until the cathedral's pressing stillness silenced that echo, then waited longer, much longer, before I followed the friar's path to the lane outside. It was empty except for a butcher and his cart trundling slowly by, his large black dogs panting from the weight of the load they pulled as they eyed me suspiciously.

I never set foot in that cathedral again. The Earl was little interested in matters of the spirit, rarely attending religious service himself and giving little thought to the souls of those in his service beyond vaguely ordering them to attend those services he himself eschewed. Yet often in my time there I would stand before that monumental ascendancy of stone, haunted forever for me now, and I would wonder, relentlessly and without resolution.

I never saw the mad friar again. Within a month of our encounter I made inquiries but learned only he had disappeared from the house used by those of his order, none knew why or whither. He never returned.

I suffered misgivings about my cathedral vision for many months. That I had never before experienced a prophetic vision did not, to my initial surprise, much trouble me, for I believed it was the effect of the cathedral upon me which was as a shock to my mind and spirit, opening to me what the friar intimated was a third (and, as it happened, final) aspect of my Gift. I accepted now that my catching of words from men's minds was a true part of the Gift I had for whatever reason or purpose been given, and while my vision of the completed cathedral was a mystery to me I felt no need to explain it away as some trickery of the mind. I would let it be what it would be, for I felt now I had assurance of sufficient strength within myself to embrace whatever my Gift would prove to be.

What most clouded my thoughts in the days and months which followed was fear I might end like the mad rhyming friar. He had known of my vision even as it beset me so he must, I reasoned, be in some way sensitive to whatever agency or power bestows or informs such visions. And he was mad. I feared greatly to end in such a state, for what had I but my mind? My learning, my wit, my Gift – I dreaded the prospect of losing myself in my mind, for was I not already lost enough, as it were, to the ordered world?

earl

The mad friar's pronouncements on my Gift gave me to hope I would find it much called into service in an Earl's household, as indeed had already been my expectation. His station far exceeded that of Baronet, and as an Earl's duties, domains, responsibilities and wealth were all commensurately greater they surely must actively and comprehensively engage my new master in the affairs of business, the kingdom, the world. Life in his service would surely be a ready feast of opportunities.

Or so I had thought.

What I found in my Earl was instead a man devoted wholeheartedly to worldly pleasure, a man decent enough in the main but whose words, deeds, and deliberations betrayed scant evidence of the workings of any greater purposes or higher interests. He was a proper master when not vexed. His servants were treated reasonably well and paid fairly, he took no advantage of the female staff (I cannot say quite the same of myself, but then I am a commoner and my dalliances were shaped by nought but mutual desire), and though his pieties were oft enough invoked by himself they never had sufficient passion to send him to confession or to Mass. The Earl saved his passions for the hunt and the table, the true loves of his existence. There was in him no trace of concern with those issues of polity or statecraft which consume the hearts and minds of so many men of power, no concern with matters of business or trade except they continue profitable to him, not even much concern with the doings of his own family though he treated them kindly enough when he happened upon them.

As he had no concern for the quotidian workings of his own domain, the administration of all its aspects was left largely in the hands of a personal secretary and several stewards. I found myself fortunate in the character and humours of the estate steward, a robust sanguine man, serious but not solemn. He greeted me with fair warmth upon our introduction, delighted he said that the master had retained one who would bring learning as well as levity and wit to the household. That we could discuss the likes of Pliny and Vergil in Latin (though his rather halting, I must say) was a source of pleasure to both of us.

Just beneath him in rank was the house steward. He was said to be a fair and conscientious man and I found him to be so, though quite saturnine in character. I sought to cultivate his friendship but with no success, for he ever remained cool to me. He had suitable education as well (though no Latin), and that had given him airs. Though my education was quite superior to his he gave me to understand in ways subtle but undeniable my position as jester put me beneath his serious notice and certainly beneath his friendship. I regretted the loss for both personal and pragmatic reasons but let the matter pass with the best grace I could. It was my determined plan to befriend all who would have my friendship and do all I could to remain in the good graces of those who would not, for one never knows from which quarter allies and assistance may one day need be summoned. I was most fortunate that even in one of the most troublesome matters from my time in the Earl's service, my involvement in revealing an under-steward's thieving ways, no setback occurred in my assimilation into the household.

Still fairly new to the Earl's service I was in the kitchen offices one morning in my usual way of gaining the confidence of the servants as well as learning the ways and customs of my new home when a wagon-load of foodstuffs arrived. Several times a week the kitchens were put in delivery of such goods, paid as rents by tenant farmers with all supplies being duly noted on a bill of lading. As servants unloaded the wagon I, out of an idle curiosity fueled by boredom, picked up the bill of lading from where it had been left for the house steward's principal assistant. A tedious list it was, quantities of this and bushels of that in a crabbed hand difficult to decipher. Yet decipher it I did, my boredom being a powerful goad to even the most trivial of amusements. In further frivolity I found myself glancing from the bill to the various goods being stacked against the wall and strewn haphazardly upon a table. And I began to count those goods.

"Is that all, then?" I asked one of the under-cooks as she closed the door to the wagon-yard.

"Is't not enough?" she said shortly, her round face red from exertion. "'Tis a long day's work waggoner's brought an' past usual time again."

There must be some error, I thought, for there was evident discrepancy between some of the goods carried in and the quantities noted on the bill of lading. Four bushels of potatoes marked but only three in the kitchen, eight chickens noted but only six upon the table, on and on it went.

"The bill shows more than what is here," I said, holding out the document to her.

Her look was sour. "I canna read," she said in the tone one would use with a wayward child. "What's on paper is under-steward's concern, not mine. These chickens are my concern." Her annoyance was overt but I had one more question.

"These bills go to the under-steward then? Always?"

"Y' are fool, aren't y'?" she snapped without looking at me. "To under-steward then I suppose his master the estate steward, for them's rents. Now leave me t' m' work if y' please."

A simple error? I wondered as I left the kitchens. Or something else? It's but livestock and vegetables – would I trouble myself over trivialities? But thought of the Baronet's overseer came to me then, sowing a seed of suspicion that was watered by my boredom. I returned to the kitchens on the next delivery day and again found the unloaded goods to be scant of the bill of lading. I repeated my visits over the next several weeks, with each experience the same. There could be no explanation but systematic diversion and theft.

I first queried the kitchen staff but learned nothing, for none were able to read the bill of lading. I began regular converse with the waggoner – always the same man – but even my most innocent questions concerning route and tenants caused him to become guarded, the comport of his eyes and movements conveying suspicion. His answers were evasive though couched in the tones and language of common gossip, effort at pretense evident in his voice and face and manner. This was no innocent drayage, I could see.

I considered what action next to take. Surely it was unlikely multiple tenants could be party to ongoing deception yet still avoid detection. Occam's Razor, I thought: the simpler theory is the more likely to be valid and here the simpler theory was a waggoner complicit in some scheme to deceive illiterate servants. This meant an under-steward careless of his duties, though such would hardly be unprecedented. Indeed, I had never seen him in the kitchen offices during deliveries, evidently regarding such matters as beneath him. All to the advantage of a thieving waggoner, I thought.

To spy upon the waggoner, trail him in his rounds and discover his perfidy, was my first intention but the Earl's return to the Great House put sudden demands upon my time. He planned to remain some weeks before removing to the grand hunting lodge that was his preferred residence, and as my conscience had been pricked by this kitchen-door intrigue I desired prompt resolution to the matter. By good fortune I had to hand the means to effect my purpose.

One of the stable boys, a thin and eager lad named Jaim, had taken a liking to me, impressed by my knowledge of horses and the simple sleight-of-hand tricks with which I entertained him when visiting the stables. Him I could trust, I felt, so with many a firm admonition to keep the matter strictly secret I paid him to follow the waggoner on his rounds, giving the boy the pretext I suspected the man of mistreating his horses.

My plan succeeded. Jaim proved admirably stealthy and without detection followed the waggoner scrupulously. The horses were treated adequately and all was routine, he reported, until after the final stop. Instead of driving directly to the Great House the waggoner detoured to the old grange, unused since a newer and larger was built several years prior.

I spoke my thoughts aloud, nodding to myself. "And the waggoner took some few goods from the wagon to the grange."

To my surprise Jaim shook his head. "Not alone. He had quick help – the house under-steward himself."

I looked at him dubiously. "You are mistaken."

"No mistake," he said, stung by my remark. "My eyes are sharp an' well enough I know the under-steward from other men."

Astonishment overtook me but I said nothing. I gave the boy more coin than promised and repeated my injunction to share this matter with no one yet.

I had no good reason to doubt the boy but given the stakes of the matter felt I should verify his report myself. On the next collection day I secreted myself ahead of the waggoner's expected arrival in a copse near the old grange. Some while later a figure emerged from the woods nearby and proceeded directly to the building: the under-steward himself. Shortly thereafter the wagon arrived and, as Jaim had described, the two men unloaded some small part of the wagon's freight into the building. The waggoner then drove off in the direction of the Great House while the under-steward remained inside.

'You wait so I shall as well,' I thought, and in short order a small cart pulled by a single grey-muzzled pony appeared around the corner of the road that lead to town. The driver, hooded despite the warm sun, drove directly to the grange. The cart was quickly loaded with the selfsame goods the wagon had brought but a short while earlier, and after they were covered hastily with straw the cart set off toward town at the best pace the old pony could manage while the under-steward hurried away in the direction of the Great House.

I shook my head in mingled wonder and confusion. This was a great deal of risk and trouble for what small profit could come from the sale of roots and meats, it seemed to me. A foolishness surely unnecessary. The Earl paid fairly. Why the under-steward would risk place and prison for small coin I could not fathom.

As I studied what to do my heart sank somewhat within me. I felt no enthusiasm to expose the under-steward for such trivial theft, yet at the same time theft it was, and ongoing. Over time the gain to the under-steward must be sufficient that he endures the risk, so perhaps the cost to the Earl is not entirely negligible. True he is a wealthy man and would not much miss the sum, but that it no way excuses theft.

Thou shalt not steal. Oh, the moral aspect of the matter was as plain as life itself. To say nothing and thus condone theft is no better in the eyes of Heaven than to have taken those goods with my own hands. A good man, a man of probity and virtue, would act, I told myself. Was I not such a man? Certainly I believed myself to be.

But was I? I was vacillating, half-minded to ignore the under-steward's petty thievery, leave him to a greater justice. Yet would this not constitute moral laxity on my part? To my thought came suddenly the mad friar and his declamations in the cathedral regarding the divine source of my Gift. I bethought myself too of the Baronet's kind words of gratitude upon my exposing the perfidy of his overseer. Were these not proofs of the virtue I believed inhered in the purpose of my Gift? If I believed so then I must act in this instance as well, as small a matter as it was. Perhaps precisely because it *was* a small matter. Small stakes may seem to excuse inaction but at Judgement no excuse will be brooked, no stain upon the soul go unnoticed.

What action to take, then? Surely some measure of charity is to be considered, for should not sin be met with virtue rather than self-righteousness? To expose the under-steward directly to retribution might only harden his heart. To offer some amelioration, to demonstrate the working of charity and considerate kindness, might open his eyes to the influence and beneficence of moral rectitude.

Not being without my own endowment of shrewdness I knew that before taking action it would be necessary to secure further proofs. To this end I enlisted Jaim's aid again, hiring his surveillance of the grange as oft as he might in the next three weeks. With considerable misgiving, for I wished to involve as few as possible in this enterprise, I also bribed a kitchen maid to secretly tally the goods delivered by the waggoner. I hoped to deflect suspicion from both waggoner and under-steward by telling her there was some question of the tenants' accuracy in noting the goods provided, and she seemed to accept my explanation. She was of course illiterate but I made for her lists of the foodstuffs commonly delivered using my poor sketches in lieu of words and showing her how to make simple marks denoting quantities.

At the end of the determined period I collected the kitchen maid's lists and met secretly with Jaim, who confirmed the continued clandestine behavior of waggoner and under-steward at the grange. I thanked him with word and coin, failing not to enjoin him to continued silence until this matter had concluded, then began to take my leave.

"Jester," Jaim interrupted, "how shall this play out? What will you do?"

I hesitated a moment but could see no harm in giving the boy some sense of my intentions. "I would treat the under-steward with charity, Jaim, even if it be more kindness than he deserves. I will confront him directly, him alone, with my accusations and proofs. If he then on some suitable pretext depart the Earl's service the matter shall end there."

I was surprised to see Jaim shake his head. "I have no gift to see into men's hearts as you have, Jester, but the under-steward will have little care for your offer. I wager half a quarter's pay."

My brow furrowed in surprise. "Surely not, Jaim. The evidence is against him and should he refuse I shall take the matter to the house steward. Certainly the under-steward would not risk such exposure."

Jaim shook his head again. "Not all gossip has yet reached your ears, Jester." He paused, looked down at the ground and when he raised his head his cheeks were flushed. "'Tis a matter against God and nature, and I do not care to speak of it but for your kindness to me, and I would not see your plan come to nought." He swallowed hard, steeling himself for something I could not guess. "Steward will take no action for – " he looked away again for a moment, his jaw clenched "– for the steward, it is whispered, is mad for the under-steward, mad as a dog for any bitch in heat." He blinked hard several times, the summoning of effort evident in his face. "Buggery, Jester. The under-steward earned his position not with his wit but his arse. Many know of it but none will speak openly of it for fear of losing their place." The boy's cheeks were crimson now.

I was not surprised he knew. Little which happens in a noble household remains secret for long. Let the wiliest man stealthily conduct clandestine business in the quietest time of the darkest night in the most private corner, and within three days his actions and intrigues will be fodder for gossip from the nursery to the mews.

"Sodomites," I said musingly, half to myself.

"Aye, that's the word, as in Scripture."

"Yes, in Scripture. And in other ancient books, Jaim. It is called now the sin against nature but it was not always so. Greek love, it was once called, in pagan times when it was no sin at all."

The boy's eyes widened. "No sin? Buggery? God save me from being pagan then!"

I half-smiled at the boy's naïve alarm. "You are safe, Jaim. We are no pagans." I then grew serious. "What you say troubles me. Sodomy and sin I leave to God. But this theft, no, that may not stand unchallenged." I paused, considering matters for a moment. "Your part in this ends here I hope, Jaim, and I do trust you will come to no trouble on its account. But remember: strict silence yet. If matters stand as you say and troubles ensue I would not have them touch you if such may be. Keep silence." He nodded, a trace of worry in his eyes, and with a handshake we parted company.

In the next days I made what inquiries I could and heard enough to corroborate Jaim's story. So be it, I thought. Whether the house steward would indeed act as Jaim suggested, defending the under-steward against my accusation and evidence, I could not say. Nor could I determine if the under-steward's thievery was known to any beyond himself and his accomplice. I had no wish for this matter to extend to the house steward despite his disdain for me, in part because the matter was small but more because I would not have my earliest weeks in the Earl's household marked by challenge and conflict that could perchance trouble the remainder of my time in service. The house steward's tenure in the Earl's household was lengthy, mine of little more than a month, and I doubted not the house steward could make a formidable enemy. On the other hand, to act anonymously in this matter was impossible as my proofs were dependent upon witnesses I would protect as well as my own active involvement.

Well. I would to the under-steward, confront him and see how the matter played. Perhaps his confidence in the house steward's support was not so great as Jaim supposed. And should it prove so, then I would consider my recourses anew.

Like the house steward his master, the under-steward felt himself superior to servant staff and held himself aloof with his own not inconsiderable airs, so for me to find him alone at table was a matter of no effort. I approached him from behind as he ate, walking as silently as I might – a skill at which I had already become adept, for surprise and stealth are a jester's friends – then with a sudden jump landed upon the bench beside him, startling him tremendously. He leapt to his feet with a cry, mingled fear and anger upon his face as he turned toward me. Precisely the reaction I sought, for an unsettled man the more readily reveals what he otherwise might comceal.

As he struggled to steady himself the under-steward's features hardened into anger, the narrowing of his eyes and slight sneer upon his lips signaling the disdain I suspected he felt for me. As jester I believed I would soon enough have sufficient of the Earl's confidence and trust to rise higher in his estimation than any under-steward ever might, but I could not yet press such advantage, being too new in service. 'Let him have his sneer,' I thought. 'It will soon enough yield to dismay.'

"Sit again, master under-stupor," I said brightly, patting the bench beside me. "One of your exalted station should stand upon no formalities with such as I, though should you sit upon those formalities I would lament your absence most joyously."

He shook his head, his flaxen hair (much longer than was then the fashion) shimmering in the streaming sun. He was a comely youth indeed, tall and slight of build, and clearly one who took fastidious pains with his appearance and raiment.

"You make no sense, Fool, though I suppose such is your purpose." He slowly sat, eyeing me warily and keeping some distance between us. When he suddenly realized he could not reach his plate he sat confused for a moment until I slid the plate to him with a nod. His eyes flickered from my face to the plate then back to me. "Why do you trouble me with your child's nonsense?" He wished to sound authoritative but the uncertainty in his voice was unmistakable.

"Oh, master under-stupor, I speak not nonsense but a caution. As there are no formalities between us, for as Jester I answer to none but one and then not even to him, to sit upon formalities would be to sit upon nothing, and to sit upon nothing would cause a man to fall . . . into . . . the abyss." I wiggled my fingers as I extended my hand toward his face then slowly lowered my arm toward the floor as I spoke, peering comically at him from under lifted brows.

The under-steward's sneer deepened as he regained some measure of self-control. "Your words are empty," he scoffed derisively, "and I have nought to do with fools whether they be dressed as such or no." I had indeed worn jester-costume, this one an insistent brilliant scarlet impossible to ignore. "Leave me to my meal in peace."

"Yes!" I shouted with arms suddenly raised overhead. "A pox upon peace in pieces!" I abruptly leaned toward him and spoke in conspiratorial tones. "Should a man not enjoy what peace he may while such peace may last? For which of us knows, master under-stupor, when what peace we possess shall be shattered into pieces? Perhaps even by one," and here I glanced in the direction from which I had snuck upon the under-steward, "who creeps upon us unawares and startles us out of our peace. And who then shatters it into pieces irrecoverable."

His eyes narrowed as he studied me closely, struggling to make sense of my words, some instinct telling him of an under-meaning his mind had not quite the dexterity to discover.

"Take your folly to his Lordship's table for I value it not." His voice betrayed his growing nervousness. Now to put him upon stretch, I thought.

I stared at him for a long moment, slowly rising then abruptly turning about to lift myself so that I was seated upon the edge of the table, my torso turned to face him.

"You mistake me, good sir under-stupid. You mistake my very na-ture, which is not whimsical but kind and good and generous, as you shall see." I was smiling broadly, jester-fashion. "Indeed, so mistaken is your assessment of my nature it would seem almost to be – " here I paused dramatically " – against nature." As I spoke those last words I spread my arms in a slow sweeping gesture, palms facing the floor, will-ing the words to linger in the air. I looked at him intently, hoping he would begin to take my meaning. While his sodomitical practices were of no concern to me I would nonetheless have him realize they were known, for I needed him to be anxious and fearful of discovery. This was a deception and an unkindness on my part, I realized not without some regret, but it was in service to my lord and to virtue. That we may allow unvirtuous actions to serve a virtuous cause, well, it has been long since I have read Aristotle or Epictetus or Augustine, and my concern then was not with ethical nuance but with a thieving servant. And, per-haps most urgently, my own need to prove my own goodness.

The under-steward's eyes narrowed, the effort of thought and effects of confusion written plainly on his features. 'The boy was right,' I thought. 'It is not by wit this fellow earned his post.'

"I would not see you, nay, nor any man . . . against nature," I contin-ued, again drawing out the phrase. "I would have you understand me aright, not with a crooked understanding, one that is, say . . . bent over, struggling under the weight of error." With a quick and sinuous motion – for in my youth I could well move adroitly if not with much grace – I pushed myself off the table and, landing lightly on the floor, immediately turned my back to the under-steward and bent over, my buttocks almost in his face. "For in such position, master stupor, a man may well have thrust into him – oh pardon my error, kind sir, I did mean thrust *upon* him – yet more and more error. And that will not do." I abruptly stood erect and turned to face him. "The understanding between us must be as straight and true as a . . . pudding-prick." I paused a moment, then quickly straddled the bench next to him, putting my face only inches from his own. His eyes were wide still with uncertainty and confusion though comprehension was beginning to dawn upon him.

"You see, master under-stewpot," I continued in a low conspiratorial whisper, "I do regard the presence of error as a most lamentable and tragical thing. I would have all such presence become absence for even in the smallest of matters error is ever an enemy to my thought and comfort." I paused, nodding. "To be made distraught by error is my curse, master stupor, the bane of my waking hours but I am helpless before it do as I may and what I will." I shook my head in mock self-pity, enjoying myself now as a cat which plays with the hapless mouse it will soon devour. "I can do nought but labor to correct all error and banish it from my presence." I put a hand to my chin in scholarly manner as though deliberating some fine point of philosophy. "In the smallest of matters it troubles me," I continued, my tone scholar-solemn. "Yes, I seek out error in the most miniscule of matters so I may correct it. Even in a matter as small as . . . oh, let us say a few chickens, or few several bushels of turnip and potato. You understand me, master stupor? A few of this, several of that – such small errors as few would notice, few could perceive especially when those few cannot read even . . . oh, say . . . a bill of lading. Such a small error then for who can even detect it? Not those who pay their rents in goods for they commit no error and ergo may see no error. Not those who receive those goods for they are unable to detect discrepancy between what is on the wagon and what should be on the wagon." The under-steward's face was rigid now and growing pale, beads of sweat beginning to form on his brow. "Such small errors, so small they are known only to those few who commit them. Though in the end such errors accumulate." I paused, sitting back, my eyes locked on the steward's. He seemed almost paralyzed, rendered immobile and inarticulate by rising fear commingled with anger.

"Oh, but known to one other as well," I continued lightly. "One who can read. And count, yes, that too. And who has eyes to see. And feet to carry him hither, thither, yonder," as I made a running motion with two fingers. "Even as far as the old grange. I have been told it is long disused but who tells me so speaks a falsehood for I have myself seen it frequented of late." I smiled. "Another error, you see." I shrugged in mock resignation. "I suppose my work shall never be done."

The under-steward was visibly struggling for composure now, the lineaments of his face working this way and that in his anger and uncertainty. Finding some measure of control at last he spoke. "What is your meaning, Jester? What is your purpose?" His hands gripped the edge of the table fiercely, the joints almost white.

"I would have you fall no further into error, master stew-bum, no, for my love of you I would not. Nor would I have my words be misunderstood. So I shall speak plainly. And simply too I shall speak, for I see well enough you have but scant stock of wit. *Res ita est*, master stupor: you are known. I have watched, another has watched. Secret tally has been kept and it will not match the bills of lading you have given to the estate steward." I held his gaze and nodded once. "You are known."

He opened his mouth as if to speak but closed it again quickly, lips pursed in frustration and confusion.

"Surely you see your position," I said. "It is one disadvantaged in great degree, for your theft is documented and witnessed and I think you would not have that exposed. Are you not vulnerable enough, master bung-hole?"

He wiped his brow with the back of his hand, his clumsy motion and clenched jaw betraying the tumult within him: anger, fear, greed, self-protection all contending for mastery. But still I did not think he was ready to agree to the bargain I would soon offer him.

"I think your words are idle, Jester," he said, finally finding his voice but the taut unsteadiness in it gave the lie to his words. "You have no witness and no tally and would frighten me to do some bidding of yours, bend me to your will." The word gave him the thought. "Perhaps you would seek to blackmail me into some buggery of your own," his voice petulant and rising as the fear in him began to mount toward panic.

I waited a long moment, letting the silence weigh upon him. "I would give you my cap, sirrah," I said, taking it from where I had tucked it into my belt and holding it toward him. He looked at me in bewilderment. "Pray," I said, "take it good sir. It should rightfully be worn by you for of us twain you are much the greater fool. You have been the more careless, and foolish enough to found your petty scheme upon nothing more substantial than illiteracy." He sat motionless, helpless in his confusion and staring blankly at the cap I held toward him. "No?" I said. "Well, so be it." I placed the cap on my own head before rising.

"Believe what you will," I said, my voice level and firm. I decided at that instant to play a bluff. "Time crawls on whether we will or no and

I have exhausted what small store of it I had allotted to spend on dull thieving fellows today. The matter stands simply. You may leave the Earl's service and may even take with you your shopkeeper's gains, or you may remain to be exposed. Decide now. Either you leave this room to collect your goods and give what pretext you may for your departure, or I leave this room to call upon the estate steward. Which shall it be?" I held his eyes steadily, watching the shifting lines of his face, his mouth and jaw as his heart and mind struggled in confused combat with one another. He rose clumsily, fists clenched but trembling and when he spoke his voice was tight with anger even as it betrayed his fear.

"I leave this room but to collect nothing," he said with forced and unconvincing acerbity. "The house steward will protect me from your lies and your forged tallies and your bribed false witnesses and it is you who shall live – shall leave his place in shame and . . . and ignomy," he stammered, his voice rising as anger and confusion came near to over-mastering him. "And when you are miserable and alone and . . . and – "

As he stumbled in his heated speech I caught "forlorn" emerge from his thought, felt the light touch upon my mind. I spoke instantly.

"Forlorn? Oh, not I, Master Stupor." He started, astonishment in his eyes now. "A good word, fair mistress," I said with a nod, pressing my advantage and my bluff for I could feel his resolution faltering, "but I fear your prediction is but another error. Though let us cease this quibbling, for it wearies me now. I propose you a contest to settle this matter. We shall upon this moment each to our respective stewards go: you to the house steward so you may ask him to stake his place and livelihood on the agitated words of a foolish young fop for whom he has a passing fancy, and I to the estate steward with documents and witnesses and – did I fail to mention this? forgive me, an error of my own making – fresh wagon tracks about the unused grange and yesterday's delivery still stacked and untouched, by persuasion of my coin, in the kitchens where it may be counted and compared to the bill of lading." I removed my cap and bowed with great flourish, then spun on my heel and strode from the room.

I had taken but a few steps down the hallway leading to that part of the house where the estate steward kept his quarters when I heard rapid footsteps behind me. I paused but did not turn, waiting in stillness for the under-steward, relieved he had fallen for my threat to involve the estate steward. As he stepped in front of me I again felt the touch of his agitated mind and caught the word "betrayal" from his mind.

Instantly I held up my hand to silence him then spoke quickly. "Not betrayed, master-stupor, merely discovered. Your hubris is as egregious as your folly, for only one besotted with himself could think thus." I stared at him, my eyes cold and hard and I could see fear now thoroughly in mastery of him. The Gift has come to me as I sought to do good, I thought with a relief I kept from my face and manner. Oh mad friar you were right.

"I go, Jester," the under-steward said, almost spitting the words, "but your meddling shall be remembered and repaid and you returned to the Devil whence you came." With that he rushed back the way he had come.

The under-steward made good upon the first of his words, leaving that day upon the pretext of having received word of his father's sudden death and declaring he would return after the funeral. He was never heard from again.

Yet the under-steward had not fully departed from my life, for though I lack firm proof I believe he endeavored to make good on the threat contained in his final words to me. He, I am convinced, was responsible for what would be the first attempt on my life, this one motivated by a revenge he sought in the following manner.

I had fallen already, as I have said, into what became a lifelong habit of making frequent forays, always in some manner of disguise, into the towns and hamlets neighboring the estates and residences of my masters. These visits were a double delight to me, for as I learned news of the people and their concerns I also witnessed and in some small tangential way participated in their lives as I watched them go about their business, their entertainments, their joys and sorrows. These were the people with whom I shared station of birth, and while my education and my ambition held me aloof from any desire to live as one of them now I still felt drawn to those commoners living their common lives. I felt toward them an attachment tinged with melancholy and accompanied by a longing, idealized I am sure but undeniable, for the sense of belonging, the sense of rootedness-in-station, if I may name it thus, of which those people were unwittingly possessed and which I believed was forever beyond my grasp now. Their lives felt natural to them, and they lived those lives with an innate and intimate unquestioned acceptance of their place in the Great Chain of Being, grounded comfortingly in the Created World. True, in those lives they knew deprivations and sorrows but in compensation while they did not consciously know it they lived a participation in a communality that began with family and extended by due degrees to Heaven. Their lives were shaped and their hearts and spirits buoyed by a *belonging* as present in their lives as the very air they breathed. From this came my sense of melancholy, I knew, for though I could travel among these people and be taken for one of them, I was not. Oft in these visits to town and village my father's words would come back to me: "educated out of your station but into none other." I envied those whom I observed in their belonging, their natural assured place in God's grand order, and I believe this envy as much as any desire for news and knowledge kept me a regular visitor among them. Indeed, as the Earl showed only intermittent and cursory interest in news of his people, I came to regard my forays as largely for my own purposes.

My visits to town were known among the servants, for I was given fabrics for my disguises and had also the use of a horse, and such matters can have no secrecy about them. Indeed, the gossip concerning my visits soon grew to include the suspicion I was capable of transfiguration, able to assume the visage and form of another or to render myself invisible if I wished. As all such gossip well served my purpose I made no attempt to gainsay any of it.

I have no doubt the under-steward was aware of these visits of mine, nor do I doubt it was he who hired the ruffians that set upon me one evening, less than a fortnight following his departure, as I prepared to ride back to the Earl's Great House from the cathedral town.

In order to avoid attracting undue attention on these forays into town, for I typically dressed as one for whom use of a horse would have been unlikely and ownership impossible, I stabled my mount at a small hostelry on the very edge of town and from there begin my explorations, as I came to think of them, on foot after completing my disguise.

I had returned to the inn after half a day among the townspeople and was about to mount my horse when the stable dog's sudden alarmed barking spurred me to instant alertness. In my mind flashed the image of something I had half-glimpsed just a few moments earlier while crossing the inn's small stableyard: a furtive movement in the shadows, an uncertain glint of light. I had dismissed it as a trick of my eyes at the end of long day but now, upon the barking of the dog, I felt come upon me a sudden and overpowering sense of threat. I leapt upon my horse just as a man burst into the tiny stable, another man half-visible behind him in the fading sunlight. The first man, stocky and heavily bearded, dark of hair and scowling of mien, sought to push the stable's rough door closed behind him and I saw in his hand a long knife, the glint I had seen in the shadows earlier, but I had started just soon enough to ride the horse into him while he was still off-balance and I knocked him back from the door. He slashed at me, missing, called something to his companion who reached for me as I rode by, the horse almost already at gallop, and I felt his hand brush my leg and an instant of fear but his grip never closed. Urging the horse to its utmost capacity I raced into the road leading back to the Earl's park. There was no pursuit. When I arrived at the Earl's stable, the horse sweating beneath me and my hands and heart still trembling, I was met by a groom who before I had dismounted suddenly cried aloud as he pointed to the horse's hindquarters. There on the animal's rear flank was a still-bleeding wound, a clean-edged gash the length of a man's hand made, I realized, by the ruffian's slashing knife. For days I smuggled sweets and fruit from the kitchen to that horse, who recovered without incident, in gratitude for my life.

The attempt was never repeated though a search for the ruffians proved vain. Not until after I entered the King's service some years later was harm again threatened to my person.

Ingratitude is a dark stain upon a good man's character and a stain I have always sought to avoid, so I do wish it clearly understood that the Earl's kindnesses to me over the five years I served him were never met with anything but my honest appreciation and genuine thanks. He was, despite an occasional irascibility that was the consequence of a humour which tended toward the choleric, a good enough master in the main. Yet I was not saddened to leave his service when that time finally came. My departure from the Baronet's household had brought tears to my eyes and my heart into my throat, for my love for him and for Rupert was deep and true. But no such feelings, no deep stirrings of the lachrymose emotions, attended my departure from the Earl's service. He was, as I have remarked, a man little given to exercise of the mind or appreciation of wit, and though educated properly enough in his youth he now read nothing and pursued no learned conversation. The visits he made to the grand houses of his peers and the feasts he himself hosted never had as their prime objective the statecraft and political intrigue which I knew would interest me and provide a rich field for the exercise of my wit and my Gift. No, for the Earl a good day's hunt and a groaning board at evening were life's highest pleasures and the object of all his interest. The world beyond those experiences was to him a world of tedious shadows, too thin and tenuous to engage his passion and which must merely be endured until he could resume indulgence in the two true loves of his life.

Of me the Earl knew not quite what to make. He had come to believe he must be possessed of a jester, but did not really know why he believed that. To him a jester was an accoutrement, a living signifier of his worldly achievement and status akin to the gold and jewels with which he adorned his wife, the fine tapestries he hung upon his walls, the costly horses he was forever purchasing. Some few of his peers had jesters, therefore must he too. To him one jester would have done as well as another.

And so I was bored, for five long years. I would find many months together pass without any manifestation of my Gift, lacking as I did regular opportunity to put it to some proper meaningful use. In fear it would atrophy I began to haunt the mews and the kitchens, the kennels and the dairy, anywhere I might engage in conversation and again experience that soft brush of thought against mind as I caught a word or thought from another before it was spoken. I had but few such experiences in this time, leading me to conclude that the more trained and active a man's mind, or the more he was under some duress, the more likely I was to experience the Gift in his presence. That I only once caught a word from the Earl's mind only confirmed my conclusion.

The Earl and his companions were, in the main, more entertained with minstrelsy and comic dumbshows than they were by my jests and rhymes which, like my puns and witticisms, often were lost upon men whose minds were little shaped by learning or too lethargic for the effort of thought. So his house hosted, much as it had before my arrival, a regular stream of itinerant entertainers of all sorts, for word travels swiftly among those whose meager living derives from their ability to make others clap or dance, laugh or cry. Yet even though my jester's skills were little in demand my presence at all feasts and entertainments was always expected. In such a household I became bored, profoundly bored, and remained so for those five o'erlong years.

Yet as stultifying and unrewarding as was my service to the Earl, the lowest point of all my time in his household had nought to do with him or his myopic devotion to the hunt and table. The low point came, some four years after I began to serve him, in the form of a letter from Rupert carrying the heavy news my father had died.

I was but little surprised, for my father's health had been in decline well before I left the Baronet's house. But a sorrow settled upon my spirits nonetheless as I read Rupert's sympathetic words, a dark press upon my heart that left me as it were in a daze of melancholy. To this point in my life I had loved none so deeply as I loved my father. He was the font of my being, the only caregiver I had known owing to my mother's untimely death, the steady source of the deepest and most binding feelings I knew as both child and man. For what love is like that of child for parent? It is an amalgam of dependence and awe and devotion wrapped in a simplicity of affection that knows no equivalent the rest of our days. The course of no love runs with uninterrupted smoothness here in the fallen world but if this first of loves goes not awry it is not only the foundation of our formative days but the love which gives shape to all we will become and to all the love we shall seek and know thereafter. And now I had lost that love.

No.

Not lost. The object of our love may pass from our sight and grasp to Heavenly grace but such love is never lost, never dead. Such love is forever memorialized, not in the manner of a marble effigy upon a tomb, for such love lives in the heart, in the warm quiet pulse of our being day after day through the course of all our vital years. Child loves parent because in great measure the child *is* the parent, the living expression of another's love however much we achieve our own distinction, our own separate self. Forever endures a bond we cannot sever even should we wish to, for we are forever shaped by a parent's love. My father spoke of his heart taking the shape of the woman he loved but does that metaphor not obtain for filial love as well? And that shape may never be entirely forgotten or forsaken. Never may we fully escape our origins, never erase the line linking us to our source any more than the ocean may forego the river's tribute of waters from distant mountains. In my heart, to this very day as I write these words, my father lives in my heart, and my spirit is in joyance thereof.

Thus it was Rupert's letter brought me sorrow but not despair. No, the source of my despair was the ongoing agony of my boredom in the service of a man who had no real appreciation for my wit and my skills. And yet – oh, another grand irony impossible not to love – the very cause of my became boredom in the end the agency of my liberation, the stroke of great Providential fortune bringing me into the King's service and all the joys and sorrows I there found.

There was as I have said no greater source of joy for the Earl than the hunt, and of all the many creatures he pursued – and he was thoroughly indiscriminate in his tastes, riding to hounds or hawk for any creature, great or small, depending upon the season – his greatest passion was the hunting of boar. His boarhounds, bred from those he had for years purchased from the Baronet, maintained their quality and ferocity, which I knew would have reassured my father's heart though he would not have approved of the manner of their keeping. Much was done in the Earl's kennel to encourage the natural fierceness of their nature, including denying all access to these creatures by any except their keepers, for the Earl believed lack of human contact would keep their spirits fierce and their instincts true. It was a pain to my heart, for these giant hounds were my favorites among all their kind.

The Earl's ordinary boar hunts were held with little ceremony or splendor, for his interest and his love was given wholly to the hunt proper rather than its trappings, and his few companions on those hunts were men much as himself, nobles hale and bluff for whom the chase was perhaps the greatest pleasure they could know on earth. These men were also much like the Earl in their preference, for most of them loved no chase better than the boar hunt. Could the Earl hunt boar every day he would surely have done so, though of course neither man nor hound nor horse could long endure such regular exertion and danger. For there is no fiercer beast in the forest than the boar.

"Only through the chase does a man fully prove he is a man." The Earl had, for reasons known only to himself, decided one evening while sitting at table with none other but myself in the room to reveal the great significance of the hunt. That such activity was irrevocably and forever beyond one of my station seemed not to have occurred to him.

"The chase alone gives a man the chance to prove his true mettle, Jester, even more than warfare." He nodded sagely in agreement with himself, his always-florid face beginning to grow redder as he warmed to his subject. I stood by helplessly, my eyes upon him out of courtesy but I wholeheartedly wished I were elsewhere.

"In warfare, you see, a man now is never alone." I had no knowledge of the Earl's experiences in war. When I later queried staff regarding the matter, none reported ever having heard of him being in battle. "Not as in the old times, single combat, that was a fair test of a man. King-doms in the balance, decided by a single stroke." His look was almost wistful, as though recollecting some long-ago time when he himself had been tested on a field of honor and emerged victorious. I grant such would have been likely, for he was a large robust man of surprising agility for one so stout of limb. "No," he continued, "now it is all armies and strategies, leaders in tents and troops shoulder to shoulder with hun-dreds or thousands just like themselves. No glory there. But the hunt, the hunt. . . ." His eyes half-closed for a moment as he savored the thought. "In the heat of the chase," he said as he turned toward me and held up an explanatory finger, "the true full heat of the chase, mind you, a man comes upon himself alone, is tested alone." He paused, drawing a deep breath in preparation for plunging ahead. I thought of all the many hunt preparations I had already witnessed in my young life, the throng of grooms, beaters, pages, huntmasters, foresters, gamekeepers. Alone?

"Alone," he said, savoring the word. "Man alone. And in mastery of the world. A great hunter beneath you responding instantly to your slightest command, indeed the best of them needing no command. A good horse is an extension of yourself, you know, carries you through the woods as though on wings. You have some knowledge of horsemanship, eh, Jester? That's why I let you ride. Stableboy or something in your youth, no? So you have some sense of what I say."

"Indeed, my Lord, I –"

"It takes no thought. A man's mastery of horse complete, it surrenders its will to yours. And its spirit, fully given to the pursuit it knows in its very heart is its life's purpose. All in unison. It is a beauty, Jester. A beauty, to race as on wings." He stopped abruptly, his eyes narrowing. "The horse with the wings, what was his name?"

"Pegasus."

"Yes. It's like that, the smooth rapid gait of a good hunter, all management of the horse unnecessary, the creature's great pounding heart felt through your flesh as though his blood mingled with your own, the great muscles flowing, driving beneath you." He closed his eyes again, reliving the feeling, draining his glass of wine.

"Man and horse almost as one. A great glorious thing in itself. Glorious. The ancients knew, didn't they? That half-man half-horse, the . . . satyr was it?"

"Centaur, to the Rom –"

"But the great true joy is the chase itself." He shook his head in wonder at the thought. "Your kind cannot know that joy but it is the greatest joy, a glory here on earth unlike any other a man can experience." He gave me a sly sidelong look, the effect of his wine evident in his eyes. "To make the beast with two backs is a pleasure yes but to hunt to the death a true beast is a greater, I say." He chuckled at his own joke, as he always did, for he and his companions traded the same tired jest a half dozen times a month.

"And when the beast finally stands at bay, ah. . . ." He again closed his eyes in recollected delight. I wondered, idly, if he would notice were I to slip away.

"That is the culmination, the climax of all preparation and exertion and struggle. And there is no more noble antagonist than the boar for with his wild fighting spirit it is he who demands the most from a man who would take him in proper fashion, with spear or, best, with sword. Ha!" He scoffed and raised his glass to his lips only to realize it was empty. Before he could look at me I fetched a flagon from the sideboard and refilled his glass.

"Even a woman could take boar with a bow were she unnatural enough to learn the weapon. But a proper man engages the boar in a true mortal test, on foot, sword not spear in hand with dogs to distract but it is man against beast, raging slashing beast angered and frightened to madness in the full frenzy of a death-struggle. The man who loses mastery himself in that moment, loses himself to fear or uncertainty or even blood-lust, is a man who will be carried home either dead or forever marked with the scars of his failure." He shook his head, drank again. "For more than thirty years I have hunted the boar, always with spear or sword and have never been scarred. Few can say as much, Jester, this I warrant. Few can say as much." Another drink, a long pause. "Better to die in the field than be so shamed but best of all to vanquish, to face down all doubt and fear, face without flinching the rage of the beast, all the fierce wild energy of the forest gathered into that beast's terrible heart and those gleaming tusks I have a dozen times seen spill a dog's entrails upon the ground before the dog even knew he was struck. And when the boar charges, a man faces not mere beast but in that beast his own death and to defeat that death, to feel the sweet pleasure of the death-thrust, is to gain dominion over all fear, all doubt, all that would drag a man down from the pinnacle of himself." He paused, eyes half-closed yet again as if in transport. I had never heard my master so eloquent, for it was his custom to speak of the hunt at table with his companions when the drink flowed more freely and the conversation grew ever coarser.

"That is the hunt to a proper man," he said with finality. "A victory not over beast or nature only but over. . . ."

And in his pause I caught a word from his mind, the only such instance in my five years of service. "Negation."

". . . negation, over all that would o'ermaster a man, deny him to himself. For to be mastered is to be negated." He slowly shook his head firmly, lips pursed and eyes hooded. "No proper man can allow that to happen and still live with himself." He paused, then almost as though recollecting himself looked at me. "That is why like all proper men I love the chase more than aught else in the world. Without it a man loses

92

himself, and with it a man finds his truest self and claims it. And if a man own not himself what value has his life?"

After a moment's pause he dismissed me with a wave of his fingers, to my great relief.

So it was the hunting of boar was for my master not merely the greatest pleasure any sport of wood or field could provide but something approaching nearly to a necessity. This was why he had become a connoisseur of boar and why also he would regularly grieve the decline of their quality of late. The boar had grown small, he lamented, less robust in body and deficient in the ferocity of spirit they once possessed, too soon to stand at bay and too small to fend off the giant hounds, too easy to finish with thrust of sword or spear. This for the Earl was the unforgiveable fall from grace, the greatest sorrow of our age, and when he and his companions were well steeped in their drink it was the inevitable and tedious subject of all their impassioned argument. I was repeatedly and thoroughly bored.

One night five years into the Earl's service and more than half drunk myself out of boredom I again found my efforts at entertainment pushed aside by talk of boars. But this time I began to grow irritated as well, annoyed beyond sufferance that my talents were being wasted and my ambition stifled as I sat all but idle in a grand hunting lodge which was beginning to feel more and more a prison to me. These feelings mingled in my mind, strengthening each other in endless round and I began to grow anxious with frustration. Then suddenly from this mix of feelings transmuted by my mind's mysterious alchemy came a thought, an inspiration to give me hope that I might effect some change in the dull routine of the household.

I impulsively took advantage of a pause in the regular litany of complaint to jump up on a chair which had been pushed back from the table, instantly commanding all attention,

"Would you, my lord, care for more of this marvelous ale?" I asked, pointing somewhat unsteadily to the pitcher on the table before me. It had stood there untouched for some time, for the hour was tediously late and the servants had been dismissed. "It is an excellent brew, most worthy to be quaffed by one of your station and discriminating taste. One of the finest ales ever to cleanse a man's palate," I declaimed, though in truth it was but of the Earl's customary quality. I took the pitcher and held it aloft as though in celebration of its virtues.

He looked at me in deliberation. "Yes, Jester, another," he said, his speech slurring slightly with what he had already consumed. He held his tankard toward me to be filled.

Instead of complying I walked to the far end of the table and with a flourish set the pitcher down at its very edge, as far from the Earl as could be. With great nonchalance I walked back to where I had been sitting, humming.

The Earl watched me as steadily as his inebriation would permit until I resumed my seat, studiously ignoring him. The several other men seated at table looked at me with various measures of confusion or with half-smiles as they anticipated some jest.

"The ale, Jester," he said after a moment, his voice firming as he set his tankard on the table with clumsy force. His manner was never far from imperious and drink typically brought this aspect of his character to the fore. Yet despite the firm tone of voice which was his usual means of asserting his authority I continued steadfastly to ignore him though I knew I needed to proceed with care. He was not a patient man at any time and when in drink was even less so.

"You offer me ale, Jester," he continued, his voice louder now, "yet put it as far from reach as may be. Has tonight's drink drowned your wit? Has it truly made you – " and here he paused to look knowingly at the other men at table, drawing them into his joke " – a fool?"

Sycophantic laughter greeted his remark but still I remained silent and unmoving until the last echo faded. Then with all eyes on me I spoke quickly.

"Such a prized ale, my lord, surely is worth some little effort, some small journey," I said grandly as I rose, gesturing with a sweep of my hand at the distant pitcher. "Much as, say, a prized and worthy boar is worth the effort of the chase."

I hurried on before either his anger or confusion could grow. "You declare the boar of these forests have grown weak and of little spirit, have robbed the chase of its challenge and sport." I had his interest now, speaking as I did of his favorite subject. "So. If boar of quality no longer come to your forests – perhaps they have learned of your prowess and they fear you" – here I paused for more of his companions' laughter – "then you should go to them! Find boar of proper quality in the domains of another who will share the hunting with you, and teach *those* boar to fear you." I smiled broadly to coax the other men into laughter again and in their drunkenness they obliged.

The Earl looked at me steadily, the turning of his thought apparent in his eyes. "I see your game, Jester, though I will still have my ale. But I go you one better in the game: I shall bring those boar to me!" He dropped a heavy fist on the table, rattling tankards and plate. This was always for him the sign of a decision reached, however rash or foolhardy, for he was a man for whom all decisions were instantly and forever beyond reconsideration.

His proposal, though audacious to the point of folly and utterly impractical, did not much surprise me, for the Earl was rather averse to travel. It seemed always to cost him great mental effort even but to uproot himself from one of his estates and journey to another. With the death of his wife some scant two years earlier – a shrewish woman who never ceased to regard me with aught but a vague settled distrust though I never gave her cause – the Earl's inertia grew so that now he spent half the year or more together at his hunting lodge, and other than the Great House and one small estate in the southwest of the kingdom where the deer hunting was excellent his other homes had not been visited since his wife's passing.

"I shall have the boar brought to me," he said again, savoring the words and the genius of his idea, turning over in his mind the delightful thought and the joys of the fierce chases his scheme was already promising him.

"I shall import them to the park here," he continued, "the finest fiercest boar men can catch alive and then release them into my forest, yes" – another resounding thump on the table so firm it caused him to sway slightly – "and reinvigorate the fading stock that remains to me. Ha! what hunting shall we have then, my friends. To chase again boar possessed of fighting spirit, long of tusk and huge of girth" – one of the men at table began slowly to applaud – "to pursue them with the great hounds through league after league of forest – the chase as it once was and will be again I say!" And here the Earl stopped, both hands raised as though to ward off an excess of delight and red face aglow with a fierce drunken smile. His eyes closed and his companions fell silent. I wondered only what magnitude of expense such an undertaking would require, thought also of the unfinished cathedral only a few leagues from the Earl's Great House. But I said nothing. A jester may talk his master out of much folly – indeed, it is a duty and long-hallowed tradition among those of my kind – but I was determined to say nothing on this head. He is rich, let him have his folly. It was nought to me while being all to him, and any pains I took to dissuade him would surely be met only with impatient dismissal and annoyance.

"It will," the Earl said, his eyes still closed, "be glorious."

And in some regards it was. The expense was indeed tremendous but the Earl put the necessary machinery into rapid motion and was within less than a year importing foreign boar, a practice he continued well after I left his service, according to report. He sent to various noble families in several kingdoms, paid handsomely, and in due time the creatures began arriving at his lodge. Many perished en route and more died within weeks of their release into what to them was a foreign landscape fully claimed by the native boar, as the gamekeeper explained. But enough of the beasts survived to further inflame the Earl's passionate love of this particular and most special chase.

The new beasts were indeed impressive, larger and more fierce in visage and manner than the native boar of this kingdom and with thick tusks that gleamed in the forest shadows like the glint of a Saracen blade. How such beasts were captured, caged, and transported by ship and wagon such great distances was a wonder to me and remains so to this day.

The unloading and freeing of the boars quickly became a spectacle *sui generis*. On account of the danger few were allowed to participate or observe, but though a jester is not among the many he is certainly among the few, and as a retainer whose status was clearly understood by none beside myself I was able to insinuate myself into this most unusual enterprise. But only once did I do this, for while fascinated by what I saw during the almost otherworldly experience I witnessed, what I felt I did not wish to feel again.

Those boar which survived the ocean voyage were transported to the Earl's hunting lodge on heavy, creaking wains pulled by oxen visibly straining under the weight of the iron-and-oak cages, three to a wagon. The boar typically were sent from abroad in groups of six, though with the deaths en route it was rare that more than three or four lived to see the Earl's extensive forest. On the day I watched there were four to be released.

A clearing had been made in the forest a league or more from the lodge, the rutted track so narrow tree limbs brushed our shoulders and the sides of the wagons as they lurched and swayed over the rough ground. From the cages came groans and thumps and strange snortings I had never heard before, all these noises combining to create a cacophony of sounds denoting an uncertainty and fear I think no man nor woman can ever know. Even those captured and taken as slaves must understand in some manner what has happened to them, but no boar nor other creature in the Created World knows as we do, can comprehend an experience for which God and Nature never prepared them. They are only animals, most would say, the object of sport or service to a greater being created in God's image and given dominion over them. True indeed, but just as the God-given power of noble over peasant must have its moral limits, should this not be true for our dominion over the animals? To put them to our service or on our table or to the chase for sport is the Heaven-ordained order of the Created World and therefore good. True also it is they have no souls but I who grew up among beasts almost as though they were my familiar playmates believe the higher animals do have hearts. They cannot feel as we do, but they feel. I believe this in my own heart, believe the fear and terror I heard and felt from those encaged boar in those bouncing wagons was an expression not of mere instinct alone but of genuine and terrible feeling, a grim and confused distress. I have spent too much time in the company of animals not to believe they have some experience of the rudimentary passions. And for that my own heart misgave me as I rode on the swaying wagon with its load of bellowing fear and frustrated, confused anger just behind me and I regretted my part in the moment that lead the Earl to his scheme.

I turned to the waggoner beside me as we rumbled slowly through the forest. He was a short thick-set man, dark of hair but with skin surprising pale for one whose work kept him much out of doors. What little he had said when we met at the lodge stables marked him as a man not much inclined to conversation.

"Are they always so distraught?" I asked, struggling to raise my voice above the noise of the boars.

"S' what?" He looked at me in puzzlement and I realized he did not know the word.

"Unhappy. Do they always paw and grunt and squeal so?"

"D' know. First time drivin' 'em."

I glanced back at the cages. "They seem in much agony of mind and heart."

He gave me a curious look, the sort one gives an unfamiliar object of doubtful purpose.

"Mind and heart? They be boars. Wild pigs, sport for gentry an' such. They'll be dead soon enough."

I sighed inwardly and returned to my thoughts. I was grateful when we reached our destination a short while later.

In the clearing stood a winch-tower which the Earl had caused to be built for this sole purpose. While one wagon drew up at the far edge of the clearing the other was slowly eased between the legs of the tower, stopping when the crates were below the mechanism. An iron hook secured to the end of a thick rope was lowered to within reach of the hindmost cage and secured to its top where an iron loop, placed in the center, would allow the crate to be lifted. Four men on the tower strained at the winch-wheels, lifting the cage off the bed of the wagon so it could be driven to safety at the clearing's edge. The cage was then winched to the ground, all the while the boar within snorting in rage, pawing the oak floor of the cage until splinters flew and lurching about with an abrupt violence that caused the cage to rock and sway until finally it was on the ground. The hook was then moved to a loop upon the top of the cage's sliding gate, the securing pins of which were then removed. A half dozen men, experienced beaters all, stood in front of the wagons at the clearing's edge, each armed with bow or spear lest the newly freed boar in its frenzy should charge wagons or oxen. Several of the great boarhounds were before them, their long massy chains secured to oak pegs as thick as a man's wrist which though pounded deep into the ground yet appeared to me in constant danger of being pulled from the earth or snapped by the wildly straining dogs, whose frenzied barking at the mere smell of boar seemed blood-lust made audible. Never had I seen, despite all my experience, dogs so taken by the wild fierce forces that were the legacy of their wolfish forebears. They put me in mind of the hell-hound Cerberus.

On prearranged signal the door of the cage was raised and after a moment the boar rushed out, ferocity and fear contending with confusion as it halted, snuffing and grunting and pawing the ground, making small frantic runs in all directions, pausing often in strained confusion. During one brief pause it looked about wildly before dashing suddenly to the refuge of the sheltering woods before it. It was all in all an exhibition of such animal intensity that had I not witnessed the scene I would never have credited the tale.

And it was a tale that spread. Word of the Earl's improbable project caught first the ear then the imagination of many of the kingdom's hunt-loving nobility, and life at the hunting lodge began to grow, at long last, interesting on account of the greater traffic of guests. Nobles of even the most remote relation or most transient acquaintance came to see and hunt the marvel of these foreign creatures, and the Earl's vainglory was equally well pleased with both the notoriety his folly and great expenditure had brought him as well as with the grand company now surrounding him at table.

Then the crowning glory (and as Jester I must be allowed the pun): the King himself was coming to hunt the foreign boar.

The news instantly turned life at the hunting lodge into a frenzied whirl that could not have delighted me more. From five years, five long years of boredom suddenly to more frantic activity than could be readily comprehended. Such was the turmoil of preparation it were as though a mad jester had founded his kingdom of misrule in the surrounding forest.

As no more captive boar were en route at the time the Earl had no choice but to cease his own hunts so the King's sport would be assured. But there was much to distract even him. He managed to shake off his habitual disinterest in the affairs and management of his properties and began to oversee preparations in a meddlesome manner, the prime consequence of which was to create yet more work. Again coin flowed freely from his coffers but he took no care. Artisans of every sort were hired to repair and replace and refresh. Farmers and mercers joined the steady flow of servants and entertainers who arrived at the lodge almost daily, a flow that grew heavier as the day of the King's arrival drew near. Merchants brought food, linens, tapestry, carpet, furnishings by the wagonload. Entertainers auditioned before the Earl himself, though he had sense enough to know his acumen in this area was limited so it fell largely to me and the lodge steward to decide among the mummers and musicians, acrobats and jugglers, who would be hired to amuse the King and his retinue each evening.

For two months this circus of activity was our daily life. When news of the royal visit first reached the household we felt the day of the King's arrival would never come, but when that day was finally upon us it seemed to have arrived unexpectedly, far sooner than any could have anticipated and well before we were prepared. Such is the effect of a King and his movements among men, epochal in anticipation and memory because so transformative in the present, the center of an irresistible vortex drawing all to itself and altering forever the world through which it passes.

The King's visit was to be a brief one, ten days only, yet somehow brevity had become monumental, a titanic disruption of every custom and routine of the Earl's household. Every moment of that disruption was joy to my heart and spirit though to household staff it brought only consternation and near-ceaseless labor. And that was but a foretaste, for labors would be redoubled upon the King's arrival, for as always he travelled with a retinue, no inconsiderable number of nobles and gentry and of course their servants, a company which, taken in the main, would place considerable demand upon the staff of a Great House let alone that of a hunting lodge, however supplemented for the occasion it might be. My sympathy was given to those servants for they were my fellows, commoners all of us, yet I was right glad I was not as they were in household status and station. I was, I thought yet again, of them in origin but not among them in practice. Or in life.

The King's entourage did not on this occasion include his Queen. I have many times considered whether my life would have been different had she accompanied her husband. Would I have felt some stirring for her even then? Would she have proven a distraction to me which might have kept me from succeeding as I did? Or would her presence and my reaction to her have somehow alarmed me, deterred me from ever agreeing to enter the King's service? Would that have been blessing or curse? I have often wondered thus yet for all my wondering have arrived at no convincing answer. Well enough. The Wheel turns as it does, and turns only forward, and as it turns we forever and inescapably find ourselves where we are.

The first evening of the King's visit was to be occasion for the grandest feast ever held within those lodge walls, an event which to this day looms large in memory for me. This was to be the first grand lavish feast I witnessed as well as the occasion for my coming to the attention of the King. It was, in short, the night which forever altered the course and tenor of my life.

I had been in rigorous preparation for that night since word of the royal visit first reached the lodge. I considered carefully what I might do, and prepared and stored in memory all manner of jests, puns, tricks, tales, and gambols. I spent much of the coin with which the Earl had rewarded me acquiring such appurtenances as my tricks required and purchasing new jester-garb, for all depended upon my ability to catch and hold the notice of the King's company, perhaps of the King himself. To ensure the freshness of my learning I re-read some of the Latin texts I had found in the Earl's disused library, to which I had been given free access. The Earl himself had forgotten what little Latin he had ever learned, and I hoped for the chance to come to the notice of those guests who knew the language. It was imperative I prove myself to be a jester capable of much more than common tricks and ribald jokes.

All this preparation I undertook assiduously because the stakes could be no higher for me and my ambition. It was my express goal and aspiration to leave a signal impress in the wild hope the King or some member of his retinue might sufficiently delight in and appreciate my talents so I would be rescued from the enervating boredom of the Earl's service. Fawning adulation and hollow flattery would, I believed, elicit only indifference, for the King was known to be a man of learning and said to have little tolerance for the sycophancy that is the common blight upon every royal court of which I have ever heard or read. My effect upon the King or any of his company must come from a much richer lode, suggest much greater depths. True, I was a jester but I knew I was much more than that, knew the strange Gift which had for unknown reason been given me surely could not be fated to languish in a household devoted only to hunting and feasting. I could not then nor cannot now in my late age say precisely what I was beyond a mere jester, but the knowledge I was filled me with a sense of determination I could not ignore. To be in the service of a peer engaged in statecraft and intrigue, or – apex of my ambition! – to be in royal service, would be as a dream realized, for such service would provide the richest and most fertile ground for the flourishing of my Gift. I readily confess such ambition was most unseemly for one of my station, a hubris for which I must some day answer. But then, I reminded myself, as Jester I had no precisely demarcated station after all. If I were fated – and by this point in my life I believed my Gift surely must be the work of some Fate or Providence – to inhabit the gaps of the Created World, why not live that interstitial life in royal service where my Gift would have greatest opportunity to stretch itself, to stretch me, and to serve the highest purposes of God and man? Yes, that was my ambition, my goal. My dream.

So it was I watched the arrival of the royal retinue not, as did many of the household, from courtyard or roadside but from a high window, unobserved but giving careful scrutiny to all, to their manner, their raiment, the fashion and sequence in which they were announced, the very manner of their movements. I had already learned from the royal envoys (and their servants) who had arrived several days earlier the identity of many of the prominent personages accompanying the King, and had learned as well that some believed the King's true purpose was not to hunt but persuade the Earl to consent to an arranged marriage for his youngest daughter.

Most interesting to me was the rumor an intrigue of some dark political consequence was afoot. Though specifics were few I learned a certain Baron had fallen under some grave suspicion and it was believed he had been invited to accompany the King so he might be kept under some scrutiny or some insidious action of his be forestalled. All of my instincts came alert the instant I heard the gossip. Here is an opportunity indeed. This Baron, I thought, was the man I should study as a cat does the bird upon which he is set to pounce.

As the night's feast commenced and the guests began their orchestrated entrance into the lodge's Great Hall I stationed myself in a servant's hallway so I might observe the nobility as they entered the room and assumed their places. At the time I knew little of matters of precedence but a remark by the butler had suggested something out of the ordinary in the seating, and when I pressed him further learned that the Baron in whom I was interested was seated much closer to the King than would have been customary. The butler was puzzled, thinking perhaps the Baron's proximity to the King was a sign of some impending favor, but I took the matter quite differently. 'This is a clever King of ours,' I thought. 'He wishes this Baron to know he is under scrutiny and thus unsettle him. A man at ease hides what a man under duress may reveal.'

When the Baron was escorted to his seat a flash of surprise crossed his face, as evident to me from across the Hall as if he had been at arm's length. He glanced at the King's chair, back at his own, said something to the page escorting him who shook his head and spoke briefly before departing. The Baron sat slowly, looking about him at the other members of the King's party. 'Are you wondering if your secret is safe, my Lord?' I thought. 'Your doubt grows, does it not?' I nodded. Yes, he is my prey and now the cat creeps closer. I hurried off to prepare for my entrance.

That first evening's feast was to be the grandest, and I knew also it would be my critical moment, the prime opportunity for the execution of my intentions and the greatest chance for the fulfillment of my ambition. All my forethought, my planning, my wit and knowledge would be put to the test that night. Indeed I myself would be put to the test, and at stake was nothing less than the very shape of the remainder of my earthly days. The impression I made that night was the impression which would be remembered and which would determine my future.

The feast was well begun when I made surreptitious entrance into the Great Hall. I had contrived a new costume for the occasion, disdaining the customary jester's motley the Earl – a man of little imagination and less originality – preferred for me to wear. Tonight, on my own cognizance and at some risk of incurring the Earl's displeasure, I was garbed entirely in black, a glossy silken black, my only concession to color being a crimson belt and crimson sashes tied about my upper arms and thighs. My face I had painted a glistening white with a large black diamond surrounding each eye. I slipped into the hall just behind a press of servants entering from a side passage and into a shadowed nook, standing still and silent, willing myself to blend into the shadows. I waited until there came a lull in the music, and in an instant I was in the center of the Great Hall. Having spotted a momentarily empty chair near where my master sat next to the King I leapt onto it.

I bowed with dramatic flourish and as I stood erect boomed in my most theatrical voice, "Here is one, grander than all the rest, whom I most humbly, warmly, and felicitously welcome to a noble domicile which now stands graced and exalted in consequence of his most beneficent, gracious, and transformative royal presence." And then, in Latin, "Hail to our glorious regnant monarch, forger of a more peaceful and magnificent kingdom through the greatness of his will, his wisdom, and his love." I paused, quickly scanning the faces of those seated near the King to see who understand. Most, except my squinting master, seemed to have followed but it was with the King I was truly concerned for it was he I most wanted to appreciate the quality of my learning. I would at no time be mistaken for a common japing fool, but on this night of all nights it was imperative to my hopes I be understood as much more than the common run of jester.

"I fain would entertain," I continued, speaking slowly enough for the rhyme to be noticed even by those distracted with talk or wine, "but can only dream I would seem a sufficiently comical thing to entertain an honored king." Another deep bow with a flourish which left me gesturing directly at the King who was smiling slightly, his head cocked at that subtle angle which always denotes the mingling of surprise and interest. Boldly enough for a dozen men I made direct eye contact with him and held his gaze for a long moment. Jester's license.

My heart bounded when the King arose and spoke, for his words were in Latin. "A gracious welcome, Jester, and I thank you. Excuse my showing no astonishment at a greeting worthy of a schoolman but your reputation precedes you. I see now I was well informed when told my host had in his service a jester raised in a kennel yet who could speak a priest's Latin and who besides was possessed of . . . curious wisdom." We held each others' gaze and my heart leapt again. This was more than I could have hoped for, that some rumor of my Gift had reached the King's ears. I allowed myself a slow smile, visible to all but for the King alone, and the light in his eye told me he understood.

I nodded then continued in Latin. "Your Majesty's notice of my foolish self does me much honor. I humbly express the wish my wit and my small entertainments during your sojourn here in these remote woods shall prove adequate recompense for your courtesy." I bowed again as I shifted my position in preparation for jumping down from the chair.

But the King held up a peremptory hand. He said something in Greek but as I have said my command of that language had even at its height been weak, and lacking both texts and the opportunity of practice I could now understand but little. Attempting even a rudimentary exchange would be embarrassing. So I smiled and bowed again. "I do confess to his Highness," I said in the vernacular, "your speaking the language of Homer and Herodotus is now Greek to me."

The King smiled as he resumed his seat and I took this chance to jump down and, to cover my embarrassment, quickly pulled three brightly colored balls from a pouch under my tunic and began juggling them as I moved to the center of the hall.

"One may juggle for a King," I proclaimed loudly, managing the balls expertly for indeed I had fair skill in the art though it bored me prodigiously, before suddenly spreading my arms wide and letting the balls fall to the floor beneath my outspread arms. "But name me a monarch who has seen too little juggling and you will name me" – I paused here, arms still outspread – " a blind king." Some laughter and light applause.

"One may rhyme for a King," I declared as I struck an exaggerated theatrical pose.

Oh great King you are as the sun
That upon the meadow shines.
Yea, you are as the stealthy snake
Which around the mouse entwines!

I stopped abruptly, a look of mock horror on my face. "No, no, no, that will not do, sirrah, that will not serve at all," I said dramatically, slapping myself on the head and staggering comically sideways. Just a light touch of simple comedy, I reminded myself as some in the company chuckled or smiled. I would at whiles engage those who require simple humor but it is to the King I most direct my efforts.

"Flattery, fool, flattery," I said as though expostulating with myself. "It is a delicate thing. To the ear it must be as euphonious as harmonious, while to the mind's eye it must present images of greatness and . . . and . . ." I looked about me as if in confusion. "Oh, whatever rhymes with greatness, yes, that!"

I turned as though facing someone standing where I had been a moment earlier.

"Inchoateness. That fits the rhyme."

I slapped myself upon the head again and reversed my position so as to continue the mimicry of argument between two persons.

"That is thrice a rhetorical bauble, sirrah, for, one, you mis-speak the word. Two, none knows what it means, and three, what it means is in no wise flattering."

I turned again. "How is it you know the meaning if as you say none knows? Answer me that."

Another change of position and I drew myself up to my full height, arms crossed imperiously. "Do I look like 'none' to you?"

Change again. "No, indeed," I said, shaking my head. "Nor like priest neither, in such foolish garb."

Some amused groans and tittering laughter met the pun and I bowed with exaggerated flourish.

"One may cut a caper for a King," I continued as I danced a few comically awkward steps, in truth the only sort of which I am capable, "but why weary royal eyes with such flopping about when one may perform" – and here I reached into a voluminous sleeve and pulled out a crimson silk scarf which appeared to lay flat in my open palm. I extended my arm, my other hand poised dramatically above it, then abruptly whisked the scarf away – "Magic!" There in my hand was a small brightly colored paroquet. I had purchased it, at great cost, several weeks before from one of the many itinerant merchants seeking to profit from the King's visit. I had kept it secret from all, hiding it in my quarters, but I knew nothing of such creatures and by this point the poor bird was close to death despite my best care. But no matter on this night: applause greeted my simple trick and I bowed, noting as I did the King's particular pleasure and approbation.

So, sleight of hand it is, then. I waved the scarf over the stuporous bird in my palm and the paroquet seemed to disappear on the instant. More applause. I secreted the scarf and bird and procured a small coin from an inner pouch of my garment, keeping it hidden. I approached a page standing behind the chair of a nearby nobleman and with dramatic flourish appeared to produce the coin magically from his ear. I bid him hold out his palm, into which I dropped the coin. I closed his fingers upon it, stepped back, bid him to show us the coin – and his palm when opened was empty. Simple tricks, really, learned from a travelling conjuror, but when several such are strung together and performed briskly they prove entertaining enough.

But now the time had come for the cat to pounce.

With a twirling flourish and flow of crimson scarves I spun away from where I had stood only to stop abruptly in front of that Baron who was the object of my special interest.

"Legerdemain, tregetry, or prestidigitation?" I asked in a voice all could hear. "Which would you prefer, my lord?" I smiled broadly – those terms are nearly synonymous, and under ordinary circumstance I would have hoped my word-play jest was understood and perhaps lead to some countering remark upon which I might play. Though play was not now my deep purpose.

I held my pose before the Baron so I might scrutinize him closely. In his face and manner were tokens of a man not at ease, unsettled in heart and mind. The King's plan had worked, I thought. And I would take his plan one step further, push this nobleman one step closer to his edge to see what I might learn.

"Have I posed you a puzzle, my lord?" I asked after a moment had passed with the Baron offering no reply to my question. "I do beg your mercy, kind sir, for I would not lose my lord's good graces. No, by my faith I would not." I took a step closer, removing as I did so one of the long scarves tied about my upper arm. "Why, I would rather lose my way, lose my heart . . ." As I spoke I twirled the scarf so it formed a narrow circular band and when I paused in my speech wrapped it quickly around my throat, a brilliant crimson slash at the point where an executioner's axe would fall. "Or even my head, rather than my lord's good graces." My voice was hard and my eyes locked on his as I spoked so I readily saw the edge of fear touch him as he made great effort to maintain visible composure. Despite that effort his face darkened slightly and the shadows in his eyes and the shifting of the small muscles of cheeks and mouth hinted at growing unease. I smiled, studying him still, seeing in his eyes the scrambling effort of his mind. He was frightened, he was wondering what I knew, whether I was an agent of the King.

The source of such fear and confusion could only be guilt. I had succeeded. The cat had pounced upon the prey and the prey was his.

Still smiling at the Baron I took several steps away from him so I could be the more readily seen by the assembled company. I stopped and with a flourish brought my hands together, wringing them briskly, then opened my palms to reveal a small white egg in my left hand, nothing in my right. I then closed my palms, placed my closed fists against my chest, crossing my arms as I did so, then slowly extended my arms toward the Baron, fists still balled tightly.

"In which, my Lord, is the egg?" To all appearances it should have remained in my left hand. To that hand the Baron nodded once brusquely, annoyance competing with all other signs of emotion on his face.

I turned from the Baron to address the assembly. "The left hand, he declares," and here I raised it with a dramatic gesture, "is where the egg is to be found, and I – " Here I deliberately crushed the egg, a look of sudden and exaggerated shock upon my face, and slowly opened my raised left hand, allowing the shell to drop to the floor and the thick yolk to drip slowly from palm and fingers. I looked comically about me as though in dismay and embarrassment while the guests roared. I shook my head in apparent dejection as I waited for the laughter to subside.

"What now shall I give this worthy Baron?" I asked with theatrical pathos, drawing attention back to my person. "I meant to give him my egg, my last beautiful snow-white egg from my beautiful snow-white dove. . . . I see now I have no choice" – and here I held my still-closed right hand toward the Baron – "but to give him this!" And there in my open palm was a gilded egg, glittering in the torchlight.

"I testify to nothing about its contents, sir, I do warn you. I fear that in this our fallen world a noble exterior all too often hides foulest corruption. But I do wish you well of it."

With a bow I tossed the egg to him. He caught it clumsily and handed it instantly to the page behind him. (Though the gilding was thinnest foil the egg still cost me a fair sum, but the trick was well worth the price.) With my eyes again upon the Baron I made a slow bow to scattered applause.

I turned and saw the King had risen, applauding, and was now motioning me to him.

"This Jester of yours is a most capable entertaining fellow," he said to my master, "and amuses us well. We give him great thanks and this token – " here he paused to remove a ring from a finger of his right hand and hold it out to me – "of our appreciation and gratitude, for we are pleased to discover such a one as he here in this forest fastness."

I approached, dropping to one knee as I accepted the proffered ring with lowered head. "Your Majesty does great honor to a simple trick-ster, one who wishes only that his diversions had entertained all in your retinue as well as they had entertained Your Majesty himself." I then switched to Latin. "I know grave matters may well distract the uneasy mind even as one seeks to present to the world a mask of composure." Here came my decisive moment, a bold gamble upon which I knew the success or failure of my hopes might hinge. Raising my head I looked directly into the King's eyes then deliberately shifted my gaze to the Baron seated next to my master, then back to the King, who was now looking at me with a focused intensity and traces of surprise and curios-ity evident about eyes and brow and mouth.

At that instant I believed my gamble had succeeded, though proof would have to wait.

I bowed myself from the King's presence as a troupe of mummers was introduced. I passed among the guests for the remainder of the evening, offering jokes and japes as opportunities arose and though I lingered much near my master I was not again addressed directly by the King.

The feast concluded early by the customary standard of the Earl, a man whose ability to carouse late yet arise early for the hunt was a won-der to me, especially for one of his age, but the King had travelled that day and wished to be well-rested for the morrow's hunt. I bowed him a good-night as he passed and he caught my eye with a strangely knowing look. A moment later a royal page pulled me aside.

"His Majesty the King would speak with you, Jester," he said softly as though wishing no other to hear. "In his private chamber, anon," he added, his voice giving an emphasis to "private" which made clear the importance of discretion. I nodded, then made my way indirectly and as unobtrusively as I might to those rooms given over to the King's use. A guard at the door admitted me without greeting or acknowledgement.

I was suddenly struck – no, "astonished" better serves – at finding myself alone with the ruler of my native land, a man who had been but an abstraction to me, a name and concept only, until earlier this selfsame day. Now he was before me, stepping up to me, greeting me before I could summon the presence of mind even to bow let alone kneel, an egregious breach of protocol of which he took no notice.

108

"Your entertainments were pleasing to us, Jester," he said, "and I thank you again. Your master," and here he turned slightly away from me, his gaze shifting to the low flames dancing in the great stone fireplace, "is a devoted loyal friend to us, and is valued accordingly. But we know him to be a man of . . . narrow interests, and in confidence I say to you I did have some concern how heavily our time not spent in the chase here might pass. But you have helped put my concern to rest, and for that my gratitude."

He turned to face me.

"But that is not why I speak to you now," he said, abruptly switching to Latin. "A serious matter concerns us now, and as no tongue is as well suited to such matters as Latin and as you are an educated Fool, I would fain speak with you in the language of Cicero and Vergil, Catullus and Tacitus."

"An excellent conceit, Majesty," I replied in the same language, "and I trust my wise foolishness will culminate in no foolish wisdom, in Latin or in any other tongue. For 'tis better for one's lasting fame to be a witty fool than a foolish wit."

He smiled briefly. "I had thought, upon first hearing gossip concerning the Earl's Jester, that I would discover it to be as insubstantial as the common superstitions of peasants, but such is not the discovery I have made." As he spoke his look grew serious, the change coming over his features, evident even in the shadowed half-light of the fire, making clear we were broaching some weightier matter. Even the tenor of his voice had altered slightly.

"You remarked upon some dissatisfaction in the company this evening, and as you did so gave particular notice to one at table, one to whom you had already paid some special attention." He paused, holding my gaze, and I felt a sudden feverish rush of uneasiness. Had I made an error, committed some inadvertent but egregious offense, somehow miscalculated or perhaps been misinformed? My mind misgave me as it began searching wildly among possible explanations but before I could do aught but struggle to contain my confusion the King continued.

"You were reported as a man of uncommon insights, even said by some to have purchased those powers through compact with the Prince of Darkness." He smiled briefly to signal his disdain for such gossip. "I would hear those insights, Jester, and why you did single out one among all our grand company. I would have your further thoughts upon this man of whom I speak – thoughts that may be offered with fullest freedom and impunity, with full jester's license upon my word and honor as man and monarch." He stopped, his face calm and his eyes expectantly upon me.

I had rolled the dice already; now it was time to see how the pips came up. My slow single nod acknowledged his reassurances and I began, choosing my words with great circumspection.

"The noble guest to whom my Majesty refers" – I of course knew the man's name and title but followed the King's lead in leaving those unspoken – "did seem from the outset to display much unease. I had heard some rumor of him as having fallen into disfavor, and though I heard not why that should be so it is widely known he is a man with strong interest in matters of state as well as one with an extensive circle, extending even to foreign lands, of active men who share his interest. Tonight I saw him surprised to discover he would be seated so near your Majesty, a signal honor to most but in him at that moment I saw but consternation and concern." The King's mouth shaped a subtle half-smile, gone in an instant but I knew then he indeed had the Baron placed near him to bring unease to the man. "There was through the evening a disquiet evident in his eyes, ever shifting; his face, taut despite his efforts at dissimulation; his bearing, oddly tense during an evening of feast and entertainment; his movements, abrupt and irregular as though made by a man whose mind and body do not well coincide. His thought and heart were elsewhere. But I think this not an instance of unbalanced humours or any illness of the body." I paused to read the King's face though it was half in shadows. His eyes had narrowed slightly and his brows drawn closer together as I talked, signs of his increasing interest in my words. A short sigh escaped him.

"You would now read me," he said softly, "as you read the man of whom we speak. As you read most, I suppose. A clever Fool indeed. But I now deprive you of that advantage" – here he turned his back full upon me – "and bid you speak on. In particular I would hear of the jest involving the scarf."

I smiled to myself at the King's acumen and my respect for him grew.

"I have found men unwittingly reveal much when they are distraught or their feelings in some manner are put upon stretch, and such was my purpose at that moment. What I saw in that lord's eyes were signs of fear and growing uncertainty. My little jest struck him to the heart as would happen only to a man of troubled mind and conscience. There is with him something most certainly amiss. Yet there is also somewhat of the cunning fox about him, I believe, and like the fox may prove wary and a source of much trouble." I smiled grimly though the King could not see me. "I would, if I may expand my bestiary, recommend to my sovereign he trust this man as he would an adder fanged." I paused. "Had I greater acquaintance with this lord and his habits I might say more and speak with fuller certainty, but even now I trust the truth of these few words I have spoken."

Then came another stroke of such great good fortune as I could never have imagined, never have thought even to pray for, so fortuitous was its occurrence. Can you see, my reader, why I felt for days after this occasion the great Wheel was indeed whirling me upward? That my life was destined by a beneficent Providence to some measure of great reward and fulfillment? Such was the spirit filling my heart.

A vision, a visitation of my Gift at a moment that could not have been more opportune or more of a blessing. It was as momentary and overwhelming as all my visitations have been, yet fully transformative in my mind of the world around me. I seemed not to be in that shadowed parlor in the Earl's grand hunting lodge, the King standing with his back to me, nearly in silhouette as shifting firelight played upon the walls. No. I saw as though in a living dream I were before the King in some grand room, a reception hall perhaps, opulent in its furnishings. But though I seemed to be in that room it was not I who stood before the King but the Baron of whom we had been speaking. The same Baron but an utterly different man now. I saw him as though I stood but a short distance behind him, his face invisible to me but the set of his shoulders and the feckless but impassioned gestures of hands and arms marking him with defeat and despair as surely as if he had just been unhorsed on the field of battle. The King's face was stern, hard as I would rarely ever see it in all the years I would spend in his service and his every motion carried gravitas and iron judgement. The Baron abruptly dropped to his knees and though I heard no words his gestures now were those of desperate supplication. Upon the instant the vision faded and I came to myself to see the King facing me, his look one of puzzlement mingled with great interest.

After a pause he spoke. "This is no fit or ague, Jester," he said softly. "I am no physician but my heart tells me this is more. Speak."

A moment passed before I could collect thought and wit enough to speak with care.

"One may call it a brief experience of premonition, Majesty," I said quietly. "Some are said to believe that coming events cast their shadows before them" – here I thought of the mad friar as I borrowed his phrase – "and while such matters are the provenance of God not jesters, I accept it as metaphor at least and say that at moments, rare and beyond reach of my will, the outlines of such shadows do briefly seem to appear before me."

"A most curious jester indeed," he said softly. "And now? What . . . shadow did you seem to see?" The King stepped closer as he spoke, his eyes intent upon me.

As I told him my vision his eyes narrowed slightly as his lips spread almost to a smile.

"Oh," the King said as I fell silent, "the gossips did not do you full justice, for your uncanny knowing outstrips their tales. You are half-wizard half-jester, it seems." He turned from me, stepping toward the fire into which he gazed briefly before speaking.

"I too leave such matters to God, who gives to men a world seeming as full of mysteries as the sky is of stars." He was silent for a long moment before half-turning toward me. "Some days prior to my departure for this place I set in motion certain plans concerning the man of whom we have been speaking. I will tell you only that this man has fallen into irrecoverable disfavor with us for reasons of the greatest moment, reasons involving the peace and security of my kingdom. Those plans will have, soon after my return to court, precisely the consequence perceived in your . . . glimpse of shadows. I do confess some amazement at your words, wizard-jester, but the ways of the Creator may be trusted even when their working is beyond our ken. The wisdom of the holy Prophets assures us of this. I find in your observations and your shadows full justification and confirmation of my decision. There is, I would say, a convergence here which gives much ease to my mind and my spirit." He turned from the fire and approached me, studying me closely. I stood statue-still, waiting for I knew not what.

"Accept, Jester, another token of my esteem," he said in the vernacular, dropping a small hard object into my open palm. Without a glance I secreted in my tunic what I later saw to be a sapphire. "And know we shall soon speak further. But for now, even a king must rest himself against the rigors of the morrow's hunt."

I bowed my way out of his chamber in silence and gratitude.

The days that followed brought hunts and feasts and entertainments enough to weary all but the Earl and his most stalwart boon companions, and though in this time the King never summoned me again I watched him and his retinue closely, even contriving one day to accompany the boarhounds to the field. I saw little of interest, though, other than to note that the Baron seemed ever more disaffected, for several days excusing himself from the hunt on the pretext of ill health and spending much time in his chamber. I learned also – oh, the cultivation of servants' friendships has ever been a great boon to me! – the Baron had quietly dispatched several letters during these few days, a curious practice while upon a hunting trip. While I could learn nothing of those letters I suspected they concerned the royal disfavor into which he had fallen. Indeed, he seemed to my mind to be behaving ever more like a man grown suddenly aware a trap is closing in upon him.

I also learned, in this time, that his majesty had indeed not come principally to hunt the foreign boar, as most assumed, but to negotiate with the Earl an arranged marriage between the Earl's youngest daughter and the second son of a nobleman whose fealty the King was most determined to secure. Such practice, I came to learn in following years, was one to which my King devoted much calculating thought and energy of intrigue and from which he seemed to derive a genuine satisfaction. I well understand that the responsibilities of a kingdom and the management of its ways are forever beyond my reckoning, and there can be no question of a monarch's need to cultivate a trusted alliance of loyalists, without which no royal position would be long secure. Yet I confess this practice of arranging marriages gave me pause. For a King whose own marriage, I would soon learn, was a source of the deepest joy, to devote himself so assiduously to the arrangement of life-long bindings only for the sake of political expediency and with no regard for the feelings of those most directly involved – well, to this day it is a mystery beyond my ability to fathom. It is for me the only shadow upon the King's character, a small taint upon a character so admirable in so many ways I quickly came to love him both as monarch and man. But a taint nonetheless. Love must be allowed to be love, and for those entangled in these marriages it was not. I always strove to forgive my King his trespass against love for the sake of the love I bore him.

Ten days passed at rapid pace and the King and his retinue were to depart the Earl's lodge the following morn when, shortly after the final night's feast had ended and all had retired to their rest, I was again quietly summoned to the King's chamber. Again he greeted me in a room filled with shadows, a low fire the only illumination. Again we conversed in Latin, the King's language of gravity and secrecy.

"Would you see more of the world, Jester?" he began abruptly, though his tone was familiar, even gentle. "Or are you content here in the deep shade of this northern forest?"

"I have had full meed and measure of boar and pine and fir, your Kindness," I said, then added quickly in the vernacular for the sake of the puns: "For the boar do most certainly bore, and I pine not for the fir."

I just caught the King's half-smile in the shadowed room before he continued in Latin. "I hoped for such answer and am glad of it. This is no place for a man of wit, let alone one of your special gifts. You languish here, Jester. That may readily be seen even by me. Join my household and your reward shall be commensurate with your value to me, which I doubt not will prove considerable."

My heart leapt but I forced the smile from my face as I knelt at the King's feet, lowering my head in heart-true gratitude and a flood of relief. For I was indeed now to go from the stale prison of a remote hunting lodge to what I imagined as the world's grandest stage, bathed in brilliant light and across which flowed an endless stream of richly appareled figures, powerful men of great renown and women of regal beauty, all of them commanding and captivating as they conducted the world's great business.

A foolish thought, I knew, even at the very instant it formed in my mind – a young fool's naïve fantasy. But a true expression, I aver even now in my old age and hard-won wisdom, of the sense of possibility and promise that at the King's offer blossomed instantly before me like some fabled flower of a far-off land. I remember nothing of the words of thanks which flowed from me at that moment and recall only that the next fortnight passed with an excruciating and plodding slowness as I waited for the King's promised messenger to arrive. I watched with silent joy as the Earl's lodge was returned to its customary state. Before, such dismantling of the trappings of grandeur and delight would have filled me with melancholy, presaging as it did the return of customary routine and stale boredom to the Earl's rooms. But now I smiled to myself as rich elaborate decorations were removed, the low stage in the Great Hall disassembled, its timbers stacked to be burned in the great fireplace on the cold nights fast approaching. Servants hired for the occasion of the King's visit were dismissed, entertainers paid and sent on their way, tradesmen removed their goods and departed. The descent of silence and routine was as a funeral pall draped solemnly over a coffin and I cared not a whit. I burned with anticipation to be gone.

At last my emancipation, my new life, arrived in the form of a carriage bringing a royal messenger accompanied by two of the King's household guard. The messenger was presented immediately to the Earl and I was summoned. I know not the particulars of the arrangement reached by my former and new masters but the leather pouch delivered to the Earl was, I could see, quite weighty for its size. There was a letter, too, but the Earl gave it the merest glance. There was a letter for me as well, in elegant Latin, warmly welcoming me to royal service and bearing the King's own seal.

With that and a perfunctory farewell from the Earl my new life began. It was, I thought as we set off for the King's primary residence, a grand and ancient castle as I had heard in the south reaches of the kingdom, exactly what I had wanted, longed for, plotted for. It was a life's desire realized.

But with its price yet to be paid.

castle

Limestone, I think.

No stonemason I, so take my word for what it is, an aging Fool's supposition, but limestone, yes, I believe limestone. The king's grand castle, his beloved and primary residence, was made of limestone.

I do not know why it never occurred to me to ask. Perhaps because I thought I knew, perhaps because it never really mattered. It is, after all, the effect of the stone, not its actuality, its *species*, which drew me then and which still lives so vividly in memory for me now.

No work of man I have seen was ever constructed from more affectingly beautiful stone. There was gold enough in the color of it that even the midday sun in a cloudless sky couldn't burn it away, a gold that was you might say just below the primary yellow-brown of the stone, a dense subtle underlayment of gold that made the heart surge toward apprehension of some ineffable beauty of color. The Earl built in white, the cathedral near his Great House was a heavy dark grey, and the Baronet's ancient home was the light gray of the western fieldstone but this castle, older far than the Baronet's, was suffused with a color that seemed to my imagination to be the hue of the earth in a hopeful young man's ecstatic dream of life, the rich tone of a world filled with the promised consolation of satisfied longings.

Oh, and when the low sun was upon the stone, morn or eve but especially, it seems to me, in the evening, in the warm palpable air of the day's departure, that stone's textured surface, once crisp and sharply grained but long since softened by the effects of time and weather, was thrown into rich relief and bathed in such deep yellow-gold or dark near-crimson the color stopped my feet, my breath — almost, it seems, my very heart.

Color. Life in royal service was a feast of color such as I had not known before, for there I was always among those possessed of the wealth that allowed them to fill their lives with color. It was upon their walls, beneath their feet, borne on their bodies. The raiment of the wealthy is the greatest glory of their wealth, I think, for to them the cost of richly colored cloth is nothing, the rare dyes that create the reds and purples so favored at court being easily within their means. Their very nature seems to revel in the competitive display of wealth and taste. None of the muddy browns and dark rusty reds of coarse wool for them, the colors and textures of the common cloth in which the common people dress, in which I came of age. Nobility can array itself in the blinding white of ermine and the dense purples and crimsons of dyed silks no others can afford. And this, I confess, I loved. From my first day in that castle I found myself astonished by color, seduced by it as only one to whom it was not birthright could be seduced.

Such color as I was forever encountering there produced in me almost a sense of rapture, a fleeting transport out of self into a realm of abstracted beauty whenever I found myself in the presence of fabric and fur rich and intense in color. I was oft astonished to a momentary incapacity. The insistent beauty of such clothing as I saw in the court, and the mind's aching attenuated reaching for such beauty and the unnamable fulfillment it promised, overflowed my heart yet was a knife to my heart in the self-same instant. The sharp longing for those things we cannot have but which we fully in our minds comprehend – riches, possessions, the alluring man or woman – this longing is known to all and is cause for pain enough in this sublunary world, but to feel such longing for color? I half-wondered if my mind had been unsettled by my new life. How could color, which is both reality and abstraction, demand such possession? Color draws and defies equally with a strength beyond mortal reckoning, and in those early days in royal service my eyes at times would fill with tears if I thought too long upon this.

This was so, I understood, because the rich explosive hues in which the royal world is forever bedecked were not to me simply a beauty of the eye but a beauty which by the very strength of my heart's response to it reminded me I was not of that world. Raiment of the sort customary among royals and nobility was a declaration of insurmountable difference whether the difference be merited by the man or woman inhabiting the raiment or no. Even the costliest clothing does not make the man, I have well learned in my time among the wealthy, but that matters little for rich clothing reminds all who see it that rank and means carry with them privileges and powers independent of virtue or merit, and of the myriad ways in which the fallen world rewards the former more often than the latter. I, a commoner, had no business being in love with color and raiment such as that which filled the court, for in its dramatic irrefutable presence it marked a station which was not and never could be mine. In the royal world, that stage upon which I realized the fulfillment of my greatest ambition, I was constantly reminded I would inhabit the in-between more completely and insistently than I had ever yet done.

Perhaps for that very reason I chose for my new jester-garb to be devoid of rich color, deliberately muted. I put aside the brightly colored costumes I had worn in prior service and from my earliest days in the court my costume was of an deep inky black fading, through the careful work of the Queen's weavers and tailors, to dark grey from center to sides. Only occasionally did I adorn myself with colored scarves or other accoutrements. The effect of this costume was striking and it served me well in my duties.

It also brought some measure of peace to my mind as well, for in its way this distinct costume was a means by which I acknowledged and even embraced my own distinction, my own idiosyncratic place in the world of royalty and power. Were I to dress in some mimicry of the clothing I encountered around me I would feel false to myself, feel as if I were seeking actively to submerge my identity in the waters of a world which could never be my own. With this new and curious costume I resolutely marked my separateness from all, from royal, noble, gentry, servant, commoner. It even marked a separateness from myself, from the Jester I had been to the Jester I was now becoming, a new costume for a new service, a new self.

Though I kept none of the costumes I had worn for Baronet or Earl I did retain my common clothes, those garments of rough wool or cotton in dull hues which I wore when I walked town or field or when I sought some reassurance that though the Wheel had carried me to a great height, it had not carried me completely away from the world of my origin. Had not left me entirely dispossessed.

118

queen

"So you are my husband's new jester."

With that simplest of statements the track of my life was altered irrevocably and all I had thus far gathered to myself of myself was irrecoverably scattered.

It was but the third day of my royal service and I had yet to meet the Queen. Having seen her only once and then only from a distance and from behind I had no sense of her appearance or character beyond what I gathered from servant chatter, which told that she was generally well-loved, kindly and free from haughtiness. Preoccupied with my new life and station, I had so far given her little thought.

She had come upon me unawares while I was in close converse with some minor officer of the house. In startlement at her words I turned and in an instant my mind and body seemed suspended in motion and being, emptied of all capacity of will and self-knowing. This was the effect of surprise, yes, and of royal presence, but in the strange and sudden vacancy which a moment ago had been my present self it was also an undoing, an unraveling of the threads of minded being and a revelation of some heretofore unsuspected susceptibility to an agency of power whose nature and influence I did not fully recognize, though I later realized the experience seemed somewhat akin to my initial reaction to that unfinished cathedral five years before.

A short, sharp gesture made by one of the Queen's ladies-in-waiting brought me back to myself as I realized I had made no reverence to her Majesty. With the widened eyes and flushed cheeks of upwelling embarrassment I doffed my jester's cap and dropped to one knee with head bowed so deeply and for so long it were as though I offered my neck to the executioner.

"My husband has chosen curiously. Never before have I met or even heard tell of so formal a jester." I looked up in surprise to see her smiling gently, and though transfixed by the elegant bowed curve of her upper lip – a curious detail to notice at such a moment, I realized with some part of my mind – from the corner of my eye I could see one of her ladies rolling her eyes in amusement and I realized I had responded with a great excess of formality. Before I could bethink myself to rise the Queen extended a hand toward me, wrist bent and palm facing down. "I would meet your kind formality in consonant manner, O formal jester," she said, and I knew to kiss her ring.

As I think on the experience now, writing these words a quarter century later, a lifetime later, that memory is still limned with vivid fire in my heart and accompanied by a renewed pang of sorrow. For that occasion, our very first encounter in this world, the first of many thousands over the course of twenty-five years, was the only time my lips ever touched the woman I came to love more than any other in Creation.

"Rise, formal Jester, and accept my thanks for the kind honor you do me." As I stood I looked for the first time full upon her face and saw in her half-smile and the mild softness of her eyes her wish to ease my embarrassment and for that kindness my heart went out to her. This, I would soon learn, was her way always, to apprehend with intuition as well as understanding the actions and words of those about her and to respond with a natural grace of kindness requiring no conscious effort or thought but which was innate and inevitable as the song of birds or the opening of the bud.

Indeed, I eventually came to understand this as her Gift. Far different from mine, certainly, but perhaps more powerful in its constancy, and in the myriad days of my time in royal service I felt her Gift whenever in her presence, whenever we spoke, and I witnessed its action as well upon almost every other with whom she conversed. She understood it not as any Gift but simply her manner of being, but for me it was the touch of the Divine upon her.

Her Gift was a nature animated by a quiet yet potent spirit which moved outward toward and embraced all the vital life before her, a spirit so sensitive to the pulse of life, the full complex humanness of those in her immediate presence, that when she spoke to man or woman each felt, for that span, that all her being was directed to them, all of her life flowed toward and enfolded them in compassion and heart-felt understanding to such degree it seemed only they two alone existed on earth and none other. To me the effect was writ plainly on the face of each to whom she spoke. Upon me – ah, upon me in these first days of our acquaintance the effect was merely disconcerting. Alas that it did not remain so.

"Will you walk with me, Jester?"

"Majesty," I managed, bowing my head again as I struggled to compose myself. 'She is beautiful,' my first coherent thought concerning her, still floated in my mind though already it began to be crowded by others I could not, in my confusion, quite distinguish.

The steward with whom I had been speaking, who had throughout managed himself with the grace and perfect etiquette borne of long practice, excused himself and I walked with the Queen as her ladies fell some steps behind.

"My husband says already he is quite pleased you are in his service, for he reports you to be a man of uncommon wit and learning."

"His Majesty does me great honor, for in truth it is but the case that what tumbles into my head readily tumbles out again, there being little therein to detain it. My good fortune was to be raised in the household of a kind man who, finding himself aghast at the emptiness of my head, did seek to fill it, though with only partial success." And here a comical flourish. I was beginning, to my relief, to regain some small presence of mind and, with it, some jester-wit.

The Queen smiled briefly and in the momentary transformation of her face, the widening of her mouth and lifting of her cheeks and the subtle spark in her eyes I felt a strange elevation of spirits and a sense of sudden tightening within myself, not of body but of spirit – or heart, I cannot say which. But I did know I very much wanted to see her smile again for its effect upon me. That thought was instantly followed by a vague intimation of dissonance, some hint of an undiscerned agency causing to tremble that which should be as immovable as the very foundations of the world. I knew not what to make of this even as I sought to convince myself it was but the effect of royal presence upon one unaccustomed to it.

"Other tales swirl about you, Jester, like dried leaves in the eddying winds of a fading autumn."

I glanced at her in quick surprise at the simile only to see her giving me a sly look and the hint again of her captivating smile.

"Yes, I have had uncommon education too, and though I have no Latin I read the poets and playwrights of our tongue and take great delight in the beauties of their language. Melodies of the heart and spirit in need of no music." Her smile was full now and again I felt the disquieting tremble within, the disconcerting feeling of a pleasure haunted by a shadow of uncertainty. I knew not what to make of it so spoke quickly to cover my confusion.

"Well said, mistress." I was pleased to note I had no reluctance to address her in common terms, as jester's license would allow. "The poet's metaphor is as a pebble of gold upon the verdant hillside, unexpected perhaps but token of a rich load beneath."

"Oh," the Queen said lightly, "I fear my lode has little depth or quality, but my small treasure brings me joy nonetheless."

"As it should, madam, for learning which pleases not is learning not worth the having. We must acquire only what is of value." I felt myself warming to my role and was glad for the distraction it provided from the nebulous disquiet within. "The squirrel gathers only what sustains him in winter, the ant gathers only what will feed his children, and the crab gathers – faith, I know not what the crab gathers for he is a mysterious fellow. I would not be a crab for all the coin in Christendom."

"Why is this, Jester?" she asked, the hinted smile still upon her lips and my eyes drawn to her face like moth to candle. 'She is beautiful,' I repeated to myself.

"Why madam," I said, recovering, "the crab can move but sideways yet his eyes look only forward. The poor creature must spend all his days moving toward that which he cannot see while seeing that toward which he cannot move. No, if I could not be man I would be not crab but bird."

"And why a bird, sir?" Her tone was light and I was joyed that even while somewhat distracted I found wit enough to please her.

"Your bird sees with great acuteness, majesty, and may thus espy the creeping cat far off, if he have wit enough to look. At that he may soar and thus escape his danger. I would be such a creature, and grieve that all men have not the wit to escape that which they might see if they would but look."

"Yet does not trouble sometimes come upon us unaware and unexpected? Neither man nor woman nor beast may flee that which may not be seen until it is upon them."

"True, madam," I said nodding, "and for such reason I would be a dog, for he may see his enemies and, if he see them not, may nose them out. Yes, I would fain be a dog were a saint my master."

She smiled yet again and I felt almost as one who awakens from a dream and, opening his eyes, fails for a moment to recognize his surroundings though he be in his own bed. How came it no woman's smile ever struck me so before? Is this but the common effect of royalty? I had neither read nor heard of such, though entire volumes are given over to the grandiloquent praises of queens and countesses and other such deities in human form uniformly possessed of alabaster skin and rose-red lips and eyes which outshine the moon and stars. But within me was a feeling not born of any courtier's florid flattery, though I knew not, in truth, the true nature of what I felt.

"Dogs, Jester, are what I would speak of with you, so let us set aside the rest of our bestiary. It is said of you the dog is your special friend, that your skill in the discernment of a man's character extends also to the dog. Is this gossip true?"

"Gossip is the lifeblood of folly, 'tis said, so thus it is we have among us more fools than flowers upon the orchard trees in spring. But it would seem you have been informed by a very Diogenes, madam, for like him I am indeed a great admirer of the dog, though would fashion myself in the dog's manner only in that I would sink the teeth of my wit into those who would abuse me or my master's family." I paused for effect. "Though 'tis true I will also bite my friends to save them."

"More plainly if you please, Jester. I know not this man, this . . . Dodgy Knees you speak of."

"Oh mistress, the plain suits me not, though I confess beauty addles my wit at times, such as the present," I said, bowing slightly. She smiled and nodded at the compliment and in my surging heart I wished to say more. And was grateful a jester's freedom allowed me to say even that much.

"But dogs, Jester."

I nodded. "Indeed, madam. Dogs I hold to be the greatest friend to man other than woman. But only if they be loyal. And so I find a thousand of my friends are dogs but none are women."

She laughed sharply. "Oh, such harsh judgement upon those of my sex, sir. I do pray that will change for you now you have joined our household, for I would have it that you find many loyal friends among us. And I would have it, too, that as a good man you do someday know the felicity of faithful love."

"As would I, mistress," I managed to say despite another vague deep stirring of my heart. I hurried on so I might not consider it. "Dogs indeed I know well from my earliest days. My old father was kennel-master to a Baronet who cherished his hounds above all else but family and learning, as good a man as any kingdom may hope to boast. So one may almost say I was whelped in a kennel, raised by Cerberus, and instructed in the ways of life by Argos."

She shook her head slowly. "Your learning outpaces me again, good sir."

I gave her a flourishing bow. "I do beg your forgiveness, madam. There is wit enough in your eyes for a hundred scholars, which leads me to forget myself. Do forgive my foolish allusions, which are but poor errant things besides."

She lifted her head as she laughed brightly. "Oh, Jester, you have been among us so few days yet already you speak like a courtier long-accustomed to courtly life. I daresay in another month you will have learned all a man might know of us and, being thus sated with the knowledge, leave us for fresh adventure."

That thought struck me strangely as being out of keeping with our light banter, and it was a thought somehow unwelcome, as though its surface masked troubling intimations I could not discern. "Keep no such thought, your Majesty. I could search an age of ages and find no life richer than this." I gestured expansively at the castle around us but my heart held another meaning. At this instant the thought of leaving royal service was as a towering wall of black adamant in my mind, unapproachable, impenetrable, a negation obscured in darkness. I could not think it. I had, after all, just arrived, and found myself falling deliriously in love with the swirling entrancing life of the castle and its ways and inhabitants. I could imagine nothing which might compete with such a richness.

"Dogs, mistress, yes," I said, pulling myself back to the moment and the immediacy of the Queen's presence. Such beauty, such easy grace. . . . "To speak as plainly as fool may speak I do indeed hold in my heart a deep and enduring love of all dogs, than which there is no more honest creature in all Creation. In their usefulness they love us, though scanted food and affection they love us, in their extremity they love us, and they are incapable of deception. I would have all men be as honest as dogs for then I would love them as well."

She smiled briefly. "Attend me then, Jester, at the royal kennel in three days' time. I will send for you shortly after prime that day. I would have your sense of my particular favorites among the royal dogs, for though the kennel-men treat them well and speak of them fondly their true love is for the dogs of the chase, and I would have the thoughts of one well versed in dogs and more catholic in his love."

I bowed my leave, my mind aswirl with thoughts I could scarce contain and had no wish to identify.

I had much to occupy me in the ensuing three days but what held most sway in my mind was thought of the Queen, a thought unbidden but as insistent as the mid-day August sun in a cloudless sky. Despite many demands upon my attention and the myriad distractions great and small invariably attending the beginning of life in a new household, especially one so grand, I could go no more than two hours' time together without finding myself distracted by contemplation of her. Nor could I determine why this was so.

Her beauty? Yes, indeed, she had beauty enough: her skin touched with the palest rose freshness, her face elegant in its symmetry and form, lips richly curved and expressive, hair of a warm honey-gold – oh, I could prattle like a foppish courtier for half the day but it was not her physical form alone which drew my thought now, this much I knew. For I know of myself that beauty alone – and I have seen more than a man's fair share of it, seen the Queen's equal or superior in it many a time – has not the power to distract me to such degree.

But I had not met beauty in the form of a queen before, I told myself. Perhaps it was merely that, beauty conjoined with royal power, that left such lingering impress upon me. And to encounter this at such a time and in such a state as I was in, my mind and spirit newly aflame with the grandeur and complexity of a new home and the still-incomprehensively rich life with which it throbbed, the aesthetic glories around every corner and the beguiling possibilities of every room, every outbuilding, every face. . . . Perhaps she was simply the point of consolidation, as it were, of all in this new world with which I was already falling in love, this profusion of regal glory and human complexity that in its embrace of me seemed almost a consummation.

This, at least, is what I told myself for three days.

My visit with the Queen to the royal kennel gave me my first look into that building, a look which left me astonished. Never before had I seen such richness given over to the accommodation of simple creatures. The wood-and-stone kennels of the Earl had been much like those of the Baronet, if somewhat newer and larger, sound and functional but in their construction and appurtenances nothing more than utilitarian and serviceable. The royal kennel made those seem as some shepherd's byre made of wattles and daub.

The kennel had been rebuilt upon the King's order but some two years prior, and in its materials and disposition was now as fine as the house of any landed gentry. My first thought upon recovering from my surprise was the wish my father could have seen such quarters devoted to the housing of dogs, though upon reflection I suspect the still-pristine stonework and fine forged-iron fittings on varnished oak would have left him uneasy, have spoken to him of a world distressingly far from the necessary comfort he found in the ordinary and the common.

Motion at the kennel entrance caught my attention as four large black dogs burst in confused tumult from the shadowed interior of the kennel into the bright sunlight, their glossy coats streaked by shifting highlights as they bounded toward us, jostling each other in seeking to fawn upon the Queen. The kennel page who had accompanied them sought to call them off but they paid him no heed. In their delighted spasm of affection and liberty the dogs in turn sought all of us – Queen, ladies-in-waiting, pages, myself – but it was to the Queen they always and reflexively returned, leaping and spinning in their transport and I feared for a moment they might turn upon each other as dogs will sometimes do even in their frenzies of affection. But these were no fierce dogs of the chase, I could see. Their dominant spirit was that of the domesticated greyhound, energetic and passionate but without viciousness.

They were not quite like any dogs I had seen before. Larger than the common flushing dogs, much smaller than the great boarhounds, they also lacked the depth of chest and length of leg which give the greyhound the speed and durance of breath so suited for the running down of swift game. Yet their build was robust, dogs of the field unquestionably, their energy evident in the light quick movements of their restless gambols and their shining eyes. Their long heads were narrow and sleek, their coats a rich glossy black and of some slight length upon tail and leg. Beautiful they were to look upon but their purpose I could not quite discern. This was some indulgence of royalty, surely.

"Are they not fine, Jester?" The Queen's delight was evident in her voice, drawing me from my thought.

"Indeed, Majesty," I answered, rubbing underneath the muzzle of one which had ceased its cavorting play long enough to lean against me. "Dogs of great beauty and energetic grace, but of a sort unknown to me." Another approached and leapt upon me, paws high on my chest, its bright eyes inches from my own as it licked my chin once before leaping away.

The Queen laughed. "It seems you shall soon know them as well as you care to." She paused a moment and when she spoke again her voice was softer, richer. "These are my favorites of all the kennel, good Jester. Of all in the realm of dogs these beautiful creatures possess my heart like none other."

I glanced at the building behind me, surely large enough to hold two hundred dogs. They must indeed have some magic about them to be the graced favorites from among so many, I thought. To be in such grace. . . . I turned my mind abruptly from the thought and spoke to the kennel page, who having abandoned all attempts to control the dogs stood silently some yards off. "How many altogether does the kennel hold, lad?"

He ducked his head in a quick bow, his eyes widening slightly and tokens of nervous fear in his face now. So you have heard rumors of me, I thought. "Near eight score sir," he said quickly, "with room for more, perhaps a dozen."

"And in the other royal kennels elsewhere?"

"I've not yet seen the others, sir. Forgive me. Somewhat new to service, sir." He ducked his head again. "Some several dozen as is told." I nodded him my thanks and turned to the Queen.

"Your heart is a gift not lightly bestowed, Majesty. These must be princes among dogs indeed."

"Oh, we will indeed make a courtier of you yet," she said, smiling again. I would jest all the day to see such smiles, I thought, then shook the thought off, speaking quickly to distract myself.

"Oh no, madam. I would be no courtier, for their words always prove much lighter than they seem, the wave-borne foam which vanishes even as one watches. They are men who labor mightily upon witticisms having no more meaning than that. Much rather would I be what I am, for my words are weightier than they seem, the very waves beneath the frothing foam." I leaned toward her and whispered conspiratorially. "Yet pray tell none I say this," I said, "for then my disguise is lost and I shall indeed be taken for a fool, yet being so taken shall be mistakenly took."

She looked at me curiously for a moment, her eyes searching my face as her hands absently fondled the dog pressed against her. "Your words fold back upon themselves, Jester, even as they turn themselves inside out and in their acrobatic trickery say not what they seem but what you would have them mean. I cannot say I always follow these convoluted turnings but I do begin to see, I think, why my husband speaks fondly of you."

I bowed again. "You do me great honor, madam," and again I felt that vague inner trembling, as though my spirit were a lute whose strings had been touched by a hand unseen. I hurried on so I would not dwell upon such feeling. "I shall repay your kindness in the manner of a wise man, for I shall ask you a question concerning that which is close to your heart and which therefore you will speak upon with delight."

She looked at me silently, eyes widening in anticipation.

"'Tis this, madam. These creatures of your heart," I said, gesturing at the dogs who had now begun to turn more of their attention upon each other, "serve what role in the royal kennel? Do they put the game upon chase? They seem not as suited as the blooded hound for larger game, nor do they seem as made for the task as the running-hound or greyhound or lymer for swift game. Do they flush bird and small game, giants among pygmies?"

The Queen smiled impishly. "In truth, Jester, their chief purpose is to be the dogs of my heart. Oh, my husband will tell you they are a rare dog, newly bred by several worthy gentleman hereabouts for the fetching of birds the falcon has struck but let slip his grasp or the small game hunted for active sport which the archer has but wounded. Two were presented to my husband for use in the field but those dogs took my heart as no other has. For that love my husband procured for me two more of these dogs and though he still says he will take them into the field so they may earn their keep he speaks in jest, for he knows I would fear for their safety. Indeed, they have at my request had no proper training as I would not have their native spirit compromised. And my kind husband indulges my whim."

I studied the dogs frisking about us for a moment, then whistled sharply. Two looked at me instantly. I was already in the act of taking from my pouch a few scraps of dried meat I had brought for just such purpose and they dashed toward me, their movement catching the attention of the other two and soon I had all four dogs seated before me, upon which they were rewarded.

I turned to the Queen. "The dog may keep his spirit even while keeping decorum, Majesty. It is but a matter of exercising some subtlety and care in their management."

"I am pleased of this, Jester. The kennel-master and his men train well for the field and chase but with a firmness I would not have applied to such as these. Yet I would have them mannered." She studied her dogs, still seated with their eyes on me. "What I have heard is true, that you are skilled in the ways of dogs. I would, then, ask this favor of you, that you do instruct some kennel page, one of your choosing who possesses the proper manner, in those techniques of management which will not break their spirits. For this you will have suitable reward and my thanks and love."

I glanced at her involuntarily before lowering my eyes. "As you wish, Majesty. It is my honor and delight so to serve." My heart had caught at the word 'love' as though hooked by some invisible angler though I could not think why.

Or, rather, I would not allow myself to acknowledge the reason. But I believe, now, that I knew well enough even then, somewhere in a shadowed region of the mind where are born the thoughts we do not summon or even wish but which will intrude upon awareness nonetheless.

The several weeks which passed before I next spoke with the Queen I occupied with further learning my way about the castle and fulfilling her injunction regarding the training of her beloved black dogs. I found a kennel page who had a suitably gentle disposition, for I knew the

Queen would command her dogs with a light touch so they must be trained for such. The boy proved an adept learner and the dogs made excellent progress in learning the various calls and commands in which we instructed them.

Some of these commands, I confess, I did not teach the Queen, and not only because they were commands given by whistling, an action unseemly for any noble woman. That I taught such commands to the dogs was perhaps a shameful transgression of propriety and a foolishness, I grant, for I did so in order to keep for myself as best I could a special means of managing the Queen's dogs, one unique to me. I did not at first ask myself why I did this, but soon enough was compelled to recognize I acted so in the hope and expectation my superior and particular command of the dogs would bring me more often into the Queen's presence. In this I was, for better or worse, correct.

For all the dizzying amazements of those heady early days it remained that the greatest source of my mingled delight and confusion was the Queen. Despite my efforts and the many distractions she occupied my thought out of all proportion to our acquaintance. Unlike my former master the Earl, the King did not require my presence at nearly every evening's meal so I could often go a se'en-night or more without speaking to the Queen in any manner of substance. Yet I could not go half a day's span without thought of her, and I did not know why.

Or say rather I deceived myself. I told myself it was merely the distraction of her beauty, our shared love of the dog, her calm and regal manner, her graceful bearing, the Gift of her warm all-embracing sense of empathetic presence. I told myself everything but the truth.

I redoubled my efforts of self-distraction, of dispelling from my mind what I thought I could not understand. Ever more assiduously I explored the castle and its outbuildings and its grounds, even to the furthest reaches of the surrounding royal park. I took myself more and more into the bustling great city just beyond the park, always in some measure of disguise as was my accustomed habit. I spent much time myself in the training of the Queen's beloved dogs, though this proved not distraction from thought of her but rather goad to further contemplation. Yet I persisted, visiting those dogs almost daily, sometimes several times a day, to train them, yes, but even more to ingratiate myself to the Queen, to do all I might to bring myself into her company and to her approving notice. I did it, perversely, to think about one whom I should not have been thinking of at all.

My efforts at distraction faltered and likely would have failed altogether had I not discovered that drink proved a potent balm to soothe
my vague disquiet. After several pints of ale or cups of wine I found
pleasant distraction indeed, especially when drinking in company, so I
sought the taverns of the city with ever-greater frequency, for there I
was unknown, unfeared, the object of no whispered gossip or becloaked
doubt, and boon companions were always ready to hand. Even when
making my way unsteadily back to the castle alone and thought of the
Queen came upon me I would feel no vague troubled stirrings but instead a thick, sodden pleasantness seeming to hold me at a safe remove
from all conditions and concerns of my unquiet heart.

At such moments I could convince myself all was well.

princelings

Every common hovel is a stage upon which all the dramas of life, from birth to death and all the ragged victories and wrenching losses in between are daily enacted, but a royal castle is the grandest stage upon which the greatest spectacle of the human pageant is performed. That pageant is present in its highest estate – matters of great political consequence, treaties and declarations of war, high alliances altering the destinies of kingdoms and their subjects – as well as in its meanest and most ordinary – the scowl of the weary scullery maid, the dalliance in the mews, the emptying of chamber pots in those rooms far from the *garde-robes*. Life in a royal castle is life writ large, throbbing insistently with the comings and goings of noble visitors and their servants and all the sundry folk who have business there. It is a place frantic with preparations for grand occasions and as still as the tomb when King and Queen are not in residence. The fullest range of human experience, there in full display in all its intensity. The castle certainly became, for me, the place wherein I knew both the greatest sorrows and the greatest joys of my life.

Sorrows and joys. They attended my life in royal service from the start.

Human life knows no greater sorrow than the loss of those we love and it knows no joy greater than the joy of love. That these two antipodes of human feeling should be so intertwined, obverse and reverse of the same intransmutable coin, is a matter of necessity, a fundamental condition which can never yield, never be altered or evaded. Without one the other would be a blankness as day would be nothing without night.

Sorrow and joy came closely intertwined for me in that castle, yet first they did so for the King my master in the form of a tragedy that despite its gradual eclipse by a compensating joy eventually ensnared us all.

The King's tragedy was the loss of his beloved younger brother, his only sibling, who died suddenly of some uncertain ailment shortly after I entered royal service. The loss was bitter hard for my master, for he loved his brother as we should see all good brothers bound in fraternal love. I knew the Prince by reputation only, but could read in my master's face and bearing and feel in the darkening of his spirit the grievous pain and sorrow which touched him upon the occasion of his brother's death. The court was draped in mourning for months and the King conducted as little of the kingdom's business as he could in that time. I did not yet know him well but could feel the profundity of his heart's pain and though distracted by my own growing emotional confusion I felt his sorrow with an acuteness sometimes moving me to tears, though I suspected even then those tears were for myself as much as for him. I did what little I could to lighten his burden but this was no time for ribaldry and jest so in the main I felt helpless, a supernumerary of little account.

Abruptly one day the King summoned me into his presence and addressed me in Latin, to my momentary surprise. This was the language of our more delicate conversations but I had no thought as to why he might use it now.

"I fear I have brought you unwittingly from your forest fastness to a house of gloom, Jester, and I regret this sorrow should be one of your earliest experiences of us. But you are astute enough to know this to be an unprecedented occurrence, far from the normal course of our life."

"Your compliment is as kind as your apology is unnecessary, Majesty," I said with a slight inclination of my head. I could already read his face and manner well enough to knew he had much more to say on this occasion than these words of loss and regret. There was a firmness in his bearing and a tone of resolution in his voice that had been absent since word of his brother's death first reached his ears. Something, I knew, had changed for the King, some decision reached, and this struck a small spark of relief and hope in me as I waited for him to continue.

"You know, Jester, the two sons sired by my brother the late Prince?"

Ah, there it is, I thought with satisfaction. His way out of the darkness in which he has been lost these past several months.

"But slightly, sire. Fools and sorrows make poor companions." My first experience of them had been upon their arrival at the castle for their father's funeral, and I had spent so little time in their presence they were all but ciphers to me. The oldest, Arther, was an engaging child five years of age, and Edwin, overwhelmed and uncertain, was but two. They had no sisters.

"Here, Jester, is what I ask of you, and I ask it in this language of ancient Rome because this is a matter of special import and delicacy." He paused, the effort of collecting his thoughts visible in his countenance.

"I have," he said, "a concern I know you will share with no one." His eyes narrowed slightly as he spoke and he looked at me with dark intensity.

I spoke quickly. "Why Majesty! A command, a threat, and a declaration of trust have rarely been so compactly made and delivered, I am

sure." I smiled tightly and tipped my head slightly. "I salute your rhetorical economy," I said lightly. Jester's license. My directness had
caught him off-guard but in his eyes I could see surprise give way to
respect. A corner of his mouth twitched slightly in what under happier
circumstance would have been a smile. We are learning well to understand each other, I thought with no small pleasure.

"The Queen and I have been wedded but these three years," he resumed, his manner growing serious again, "and as yet have no issue.
This I am sure will change, as I trust the matter to the working of Providence, yet. . . ." His look drifted away, eyes focused on some far distance for a moment before returning to me. "Yet I will not fully surrender the matter of my kingdom's stability and future entirely to chance or
to any power I do not understand. I need thus consider what might be
should my queen prove barren. I would not disclaim her, Jester, I would
not though already I hear those whispers, for she is to me the warm
eternal light in the chill darkness of this endlessly mutable and ever-frac-
tious world. Yet I cannot disregard the demands of my station, of what
my kingdom requires of me. Succession, Jester, is a paramount duty of
all monarchs, a tremendous burden and so be it, and already I find my
nights clouded by this matter."

I looked up sharply at his last phrase, my ability to guard my thoughts
softened by the frankness of his speech. He caught my glance.

"Aye, Jester," he said with a wan smile, "Many a night finds me sleep-
less, staring at the stars and imploring them for a wisdom they never
deign to provide."

I had heard already some talk of the King's nocturnal visits to the
Astrologer's Tower, a bartizan that was the highest point of the castle,
long-disused, but had thus far given the gossip little heed, plumped as
gossip always is with the superstitious finery with which servants are so
enamored. Now, I knew, those whispers were not only true but hinted
at a matter of some substance.

"I have found little wisdom in the stars myself, Majesty, but then I
am of but middling stature and they are thus farther above me than they
are you."

Again the brief smile. 'Your burden of sorrow lightens,' I thought.
'Your plan begins to ease your heart.'

"The empyrean is the realm of angels not of men," he said, "so in its
mysteries and inscrutability men should expect to find no consolation.
Yet still we gaze and wonder and implore." His voice trailed off as his
look grew serious, and he turned it on me. "I ask this of you, Jester, as
one I already begin to love and trust, and as one whom I already know

has uncanny insights into the ways of men. I ask you to give great care and attention to the young princes, for I would know with all the certainty that might be the sorts of men they will become. All possible care will be taken with their education and their character, but I want not only the reports of tutors and guardians. I would have as well the insights I think only you among my household can provide. Watch them, Jester, watch them with your special scrutiny and keep me full informed of all you learn. Though I pray this matter resolve differently I have no reluctance should God ordain it so: Arther and Edwin will be my heirs and successors should the Queen produce me no children. They are of my blood as close as may be and I will not abandon my Queen" – here a flitting wry smile crossed his face and he stepped close enough to put a hand on my shoulder – "You know her, Jester, with all your skill in the reading of men you must know her though you have been with us but a short time. You will understand, I think, the love a man must feel for a woman such as she. That is the love I feel for her and I will not part with her."

I was concerned lest I betray the sudden confusion I felt as he spoke of the woman he loved, the woman whom I could not think of without vague unsettling stirrings, but I kept mastery of my features and my heart. "Indeed, Majesty, I do comprehend such love, I think," I said, "and I applaud your wisdom and your love for your Queen, whom I already know to be most excellent among women. Your plan is a wise one, and I give you my pledge to keep it as secret as it will be most forward in my thought and vigilance." I bowed slightly.

"You give my heart ease, Jester," he said warmly as he pressed something small and hard into my hand, a small ruby I saw when I glanced at it later. "For me there is quiet joy in knowing that regardless of the workings of a wayward fate I may secure succession and the peace of my kingdom. They are promising princes and will, I trust, turn out be the most admirable of men and leaders of men."

In all the years following I never forgot my King's injunction and did all I could to fulfill it. Arther exceeded the King's expectations. The young prince spent much of his life at the castle, taking to the life of a young royal with due dignity and exemplary virtue. He proved to be an excellent student and a kind and humane young man, unspoiled and uncorrupted by the great favor in which he was held. The more I watched him grow and the more I learned of him the happier I felt for my King and kingdom, for I had no doubt Arther would prove to be the monarch his uncle wished him to be.

Edwin was less enamored of life at the court and from the first much preferred to remain with his mother at one of her country estates. As he grew older he began spending considerable time travelling abroad, giving none in the royal household much opportunity to observe him directly. The reports which reached us were equivocal in the character they painted of him. Some indicated him to be a young man of self-possession and cultivated manners while a few whispers were less reassuring, suggesting as they did Edwin was restless and much enamored of intrigues. Rumor, or more than rumor, held that Edwin spent much time in curious low company: alchemists, mountebanks, medicasters, herbalists and the like. I suspected that, as is common with all the stories men tell of other men, the tales of him grew in the telling as they travelled from distant shores to our own. Yet concern remained to me, for I could find no satisfactory explanation for Edwin's reported behavior even should only some small part of it be true. The King, however, soon came to take little more than cursory interest in Edwin's doings, and I do confess that with the passing of time my own interest in the few and meager reports we received of him also waned.

This plan of succession was, for the King, the quiet ongoing joy that arose from the sorrow of his brother's loss.

But perhaps because it was a joy born so directly of sorrow and tragedy, it proved a joy eclipsed by tragedy in the end.

gift

I was not long in royal service before I realized to my quiet delight that my Gift was coming to its fullest fruition. The hope which had withered during my tenure in the Earl's service – the wish my Gift might well serve a man engaged in weighty matters of state and business – blossomed anew and soon flourished in the King's service. All that I had longed for in thinking of what would most test and develop my Providentially-bestowed skill was at last realized.

As the ways of courtly life unfolded themselves to me in the months following my entry into the King's household I found myself immersed in a near-constant stream of delights and confusions which intermingled and succeeded each other in a manner impossible to untangle. In matters grand and mundane, from the entertainment of visiting nobility to mastering the castle's webwork of rooms and passages, I found myself in a hectic exuberance as I thought upon – indeed, gloried in – the achievement of my ambition's grandest dream. For such a fate to have befallen me seemed at whiles a chimera, an exultant fever-dream from which I feared I might momently awaken. So potent and fulfilling did my accomplishment seem I felt at times almost as in a glory such as are depicted in illuminated books and the sun-glowing glass of cathedral windows surrounding saints as they ascend radiantly to Heaven. I attended the King and his chief ministers at parleys and audiences, my observations and insights quickly being acknowledged as uncommonly astute and thus soon granted, by the King himself, as much credence and weight of argument as those of even his most powerful counsellors. The fact some of these men, foremost among them the old Lord Chamberlain, came to resent me only fueled my sense of importance and achievement. Only the King's estimation of me was of any real consequence and it was evident to all he had come to value me highly for my advice and insights, not merely my japes and jests.

Word of my effectiveness in counsel and my value to the King spread quickly beyond the court, adding to the reputation I had long ago begun to acquire. But I was on a much grander stage now than the distant lodge of a hunt-loving Earl. This was the stage of a kingdom, a busy stage of the world, and the reports of visiting envoys and foreign delegations became the basis of a rapidly growing renown which pleased my ambition and my pride, against which I struggled to guard myself with only limited success.

Rumors and gossip fly from a royal court with arrow swiftness and the swiftest rumors grow largest. Soon it was bruited about that the King's new jester was some species of wizard leagued with the Devil, and it was not uncommon for those who met me in castle hallway or public road to cross themselves if I were recognized, though I took great care to avoid being recognized beyond the royal grounds. Some servants there were who actively avoided me, for the sudden turnings down hallways and abrupt reversals of direction never escaped my eye. To my great delight I began to hear in taverns and at market-fairs, on those occasions when I ventured incognito into town, ballads and poems which treated of me in terms preternatural, such as this, one of the first I e'er encountered.

Show me a man who knows the future,
One who knows the minds of men;
I will show you the monarch's jester,
All does fall within his ken.

He knows all that one may think on,
Sees in his mind what soon will be;
Coming events do cast their shadows –
He alone those shadows sees.

Dreams in the night are horn-books to him,
Secret thoughts are a child's toy;
Fate stands by to do his bidding,
He commands with a master's joy.

So all beware of the monarch's jester!
Avert your eyes and mask your thought.
Should he cast his spell upon you,
All your life will come to nought.

In court, envoys and courtiers began to request my exclusion from council or parley, though such requests were never granted for only the King himself determined my presence or absence. In my majesty's closest circle most believed my simple explanation of my talents, that my education in a Baronet's household had given me a great knowledge of words and my prior service much experience in the ways of men, and thus my insights were little more than an educated mind leagued with a sharp discerning eye and unerring instinct. The King himself believed neither the gossip or my public explanation. Nor did his priest, a mild-eyed man who, certain I was sent from God to assist the King in his mission to consolidate the kingdom under the rule of law and God, would bless me every time we passed. Though I have come to have little use for men of God I always smiled my thanks at him, for he was a good man and ever a friend to me, and his belief in the divine provenance of my Gift was a reassurance. But many of those whom I knew or encountered in the daily course of my life in royal service came to mistrust or even fear me, though this never troubled me much. Their fear and the deference they begrudgingly showed me I took as irrefutable evidence of my achievement. I had come into the renown and, one might add, the potency for which I had longed.

For my Gift, then, I was by those around me both cursed and blessed, at once an agent of God and of the Devil. This amused me considerably, for surely there could be no fitter mark of a jester's uncertain status in this sublunary world, caught between stations with no true place of rooted belonging, at home everywhere and nowhere, a common man with uncommon context. At the margin of the royal world while standing in its very center, I had become a man of paradoxes.

The growth of my reputation was most fueled not by my ability to read the character of men in their forms and faces, though that ability grew ever more acute given its frequent exercise in court, but by the second and more mysterious aspect of my Gift, the catching of words from the mind of another. This strange skill, manifesting only on rare occasion before, came during my time in royal service to grow into a potent power.

Appearing before a monarch puts most men in a heightened state of mind and spirit, and as I have said it is in the presence of men in such a state that my Gift becomes most active and acute. When such men as appear before a king in the customary course of their lives begin to speak, they often do so in a manner rhetorical or even theatrical, choosing their words with care and speaking at times almost in the manner of a player, with affected gravity or pomposity. Their deliberations and their pauses serve the purposes of my Gift to perfection.

The words I hear in my mind are always words of some consequence, words of significance in a speech or statement and which shape a man's message and give weight to his meaning or thought, and it is precisely on the very point of speaking such words that a man mannered in his discourse will often pause. It is because of such pauses, whether they be natural as a man considers the appropriateness of his word or merely an affectation of manner by one who is self-important, that this aspect of my Gift came to serve as well as it did.

I had for years questioned the practical import of this aspect of my Gift, for prior to this the words I had caught from the mind of a man who was speaking would be pronounced almost at the instant I became aware of them, to be heard by any. This part of my Gift seemed to have no meaningful purpose, unlike my more-rarely-active ability to catch words a man is only thinking.

But in royal service I learned I had been mistaken. When men speaking before the King affected their declamatory manner and their pauses became pronounced, I discovered that if I caught their word and spoke it instantly most men would become in some measure discomfited in thought and manner. I learned to stand as near a man speaking before the King as I might so if I caught a word from him I could speak it not in grand declamation but softly, almost as though it were intended to be heard by that man alone. With practice I became quite adept at this, quite quick, and the intended effect was almost always achieved. Sometimes the man speaking would, upon hearing me utter the very word foremost in his mind, start and turn abruptly to look at me, his eyes revealing a confounding startlement often quickly followed by the awakening suspicion I could know his thoughts. This was the reaction I most sought. Such men would instantly grow nervous and their speech perhaps falter and stumble. A few of the more superstitious even crossed themselves and once one, an emissary to my master from a foreign potentate, blurted out "What deviltry is this?" as he leapt away from me as though he had touched fire.

Not all such moments were thus, however. There are some few men of sufficient cunning and strength of both mind and will who could restrain their surprise enough to appear unperturbed. More than once such a man turned to me and offered some such remark as "A most rhetorical Fool! Just the word I was looking for."

A clever pretense, but of course these were educated and important men, never truly at a loss for words, so their remarks were but an attempt at dissimulation. Most understood they had already betrayed themselves by the sudden darting of their eyes and the subtlest twitch of their heads in my direction when I spoke, and they sought only to dissemble, to cover their inadvertent display of weakness.

"Shall I find you others?" I would ask, my face suddenly serious and tilted slightly toward them as I held their gaze steady with narrowed eyes, a posture of challenge always recognized. When even the boldest of those men resumed their speech it was always with some hint of doubt now apparent in their voices and bearing, the benefit of which always redounded to my King.

Being able so effectively to serve such a man as my master was a gladness to my spirit, for as the months passed my respect for him grew to admiration and my admiration in turn grew to love. He was a thoughtful man and fair, not given readily to anger or spite or fearful jealousy. Few of the monarchs or emperors of whom I had ever read could match him in kindness and nobility of spirit. He truly loved his kingdom, loved it not for the power it gave him as much as for its very idea, for the high nobleness of its purpose. The governing of subjects was less to him than the concept of the state and his manifest duty, as he understood it, to devote himself and his energies to that state. He was never harsh or unfeeling in policy or judgment, but it was the almost transcendent nobility of kingdom-as-ideal which held greatest sway over his heart and mind, and the passion of his life was to secure that ideal, to realize it as comprehensively as he might in the here and now and future of the Created World.

love

Several months passed before I again accompanied the Queen in review of her dogs, though on several occasions she brought one or two on a brief visit to me and had been quite complimentary on their improved comportment. I was pleased inordinately by her praise, pleased out of proportion to the pride I took in my management of dogs. Why was this? Was it her royalty, the simple fact of her station? As my acquaintance with her and with the nobility passing always through the royal court increased I found it ever harder to convince myself this was so. Nobility was fast becoming my routine acquaintance. What else could her praise mean to me then? I did not wish to allow myself to think much upon it.

When again she summoned me it was not for a kennel visit but so I might show her, in the freedom of the field, all that her dogs had been taught thus far. Companioned by a small entourage we took the dogs beyond the castle's outer ward to a broad meadow separating the castle from the forest fringe of the royal park.

"This is the proper world for dogs, Jester, is it not?" she said happily, watching her favorites cavort sportively in the initial exuberance of their freedom. "I would take them on such rambles as these daily if I could, just to watch them thus. Just to delight in their joy."

I smiled as we watched the dogs course through the summer-flowered meadow, imposing upon them no restraint of command so they might revel freely in pure physical delight of animal being. They were a beauty to behold in their swiftness. With sculpted heads craned forward on sturdy yet elegant necks, sleek of form and glistening black in the brilliant sun, they seemed joyous dark wraiths of the field. Upon full stretch their motion was effortless grace given tangible form before us, their turnings and gambols as they engaged each other, leaping and rolling about in mock combat, no less than visible proof of the vital joy inherent in animal Creation.

I glanced at the Queen. As she was intent upon the dogs I allowed my gaze to linger on her features. Our walk through the meadow had caused a few strands of hair to escape her cap, threads of honey-gold gossamer trembling in the light breeze. She was smiling slightly at the dogs' frolics and for a moment I looked in gathering delight at the elegant bow curve of her upper lip, the pale rose warmth of her skin, the arresting dark green of her eyes —

— and upon the instant I felt as though my spirit had been seized in implacable bands of iron, my breath arrested in my lungs and my heart's motion instantly suspended. I felt a swift flooding confusion in my mind accompanied by a sharp pang of piercing sorrow as though I had been sword-struck. For there before me was not a Queen in summer's joy-ance but in deepest grief, her gray face lined with tremendous sorrow and accumulated age, her features knife-sharp and her skin sallow as though with long illness. Tears welled in her eyes and left remorseless tracks upon her cheek. Her raiment was blackest mourning, royal widow's weeds, and near her stood not a party of pleasure but black-clad ladies-in-waiting crowding around her, their pale faces betokening great care and deep bereavement. I felt as though I were pinioned in an ice-bound darkness of heart and mind, helpless to move or cry out.

In another instant the vision passed and the present washed over me as a wave engulfs a careless wanderer upon the shore. Instinctively I took a faltering half-step to keep from sinking to my knees and as the Queen turned her head to look at me I took several more steps to conceal my confusion. My heart within me raced and I could still feel the fading grip of tightness in my chest. Raising a hand to my brow as though to shield my eyes from the sun I pretended to study the dogs as they splashed in the shallow stream at the meadow's far edge.

The Queen laughed brightly. "You see them, Jester, as I do? Their spirit? Oh, such spirit to behold! Delight and pleasure free from all the trammeling cares of the world." She paused but I dared not turn back to look at her for fear some confusion remained upon my features. What had I seen? Was it some passing fit of imagination or a shadow cast by some coming event ineluctable? I thought of the mad friar and in my heart knew 'twas the latter.

I continued to watch the dogs, willing myself to focus upon them. All four were now bounding exuberantly about in the brook, their splashing frolics sending sprays of water into the air, arcing jewels of silvered sunlight that for the ephemeral moment of their existence were haloed about with all the colors of heaven's rainbow.

"Such *joie de vivre*! It captivates me so," the Queen said, her voice softer now as thought o'ertook her. One of her ladies murmured something in agreement.

"I share in it as I watch them," she continued, almost abstracted now. "They seem to draw life from the very ground upon which they tread." She fell silent and the stillness was broken only by the splashes and occasional barking of the dogs – and the fading throb of my heart still in my ears. Her Gift of empathetic engagement extends to her dogs, I realized as I considered her words.

"Their freedom to be so fully, so comprehensively what they are," she continued as though musing half to herself. "Dog and dog only, and dog fully. No guile, no remorse, no melancholy, no meaning beyond the moment's fullness, which is the world to them. Never aught but what they are and always entirely so." Her voice was almost a whisper now and I, nearest her, was the only one who could hear her words. "It is a freedom and a purity of being that entrances, holds me so. . . ." Her voice trailed off into silence.

Abruptly the dogs stopped their play and after an instant's quick glance in the direction of the woods flew toward the trees as one, as though bidden by some silent command. The sudden movement brought me back to myself and I looked closely at the dogs and the forest edge but could see nothing. Some small creature, perhaps a deer or mayhap some will o' the wisp, as is the way with dogs. For a moment I was held again by their beauty in motion, the elegance of their forms and the rapid graceful flow of muscle under skin and coat, fluid and smooth. Dogs well-structured for speed, I thought approvingly. Briefly I was lost in delighted appreciation but upon the foremost dog's entering the fringe of the wood, the others close behind, I knew something must be done or the dogs could be lost to us for hours in the dank scent-rich world of the shadowed forest. But I had trained the dogs for this contingency, and for that thought I smiled to myself for I knew I now would please the Queen.

My whistled command was sharp and clear in the day's bright air and in an instant all four dogs had wheeled about and flew across the meadow toward us, tongues lolling and eyes as bright as the unclouded midnight's stars. I smiled as I watched them race toward us, stealing a glance at the Queen to see her smiling even more broadly now. I had realized my wish.

"How marvelous, Jester," she said happily as she bent to cup the dogs' muzzles and accept their exuberant affection. "I owe you great thanks for the care you have devoted to my favorites." She knelt, allowing the dogs to nuzzle and lick her face. I stood in quiet amazement, never having seen even a noblewoman do such before, to say nought of any queen. With her dogs she, though queen, sets aside all pride of station. What a rare woman indeed.

"Oh," she said, turning away from the dogs to speak to me, "they are so like young children before the world acquaints them with sorrow." She rose, her eyes again upon the dogs, her whole being directed to them and enveloping them in a love almost palpable. Her Gift. She draws them to herself as she does man and woman, high or low, so full and instinctively generous is she in her love of life, and there came with that thought some undercurrent of a grey sadness from which I instantly turned my mind. "They are as the children I shall someday have," the Queen was saying, "the children who shall bring to me and my husband even greater joy still." Her words brought to my mind the King's secret converse with me some months ago, his plan to adopt his nephews as his heirs should the Queen prove barren, and my heart misgave me.

I reflected often upon my vision of the Queen in mourning in the days which followed. It was of a piece with my earlier visions, for all such experiences had produced the same effect upon me, had arrested my being and rapt me out of the present into a dreamlike perception of what was not though which felt in my mind even more real than present sensation of being. This vision of the Queen had like the others been accompanied by the now-familiar sense of palpable thought brushing against my mind which attended all manifestations of my Gift.

What did this latest vision mean? I asked myself a hundred times in the weeks that followed. I struggled with the answer.

Or, perhaps, struggled against it.

The Queen in mourning. What of it? That the King would some day die – that all of us will some day die – is in the natural order of the Created World, for we are fallen creatures and death alone brings us to the grace and presence of God if we be not mortal sinners unforgiven. That a woman outlive her husband is not absolute but certainly is the common run of worldly matters. The Queen appeared to me in that vision as one old and recently unwell, but rare is the man or woman who finds advanced age unaccompanied by the travails of bodily woes.

Yet for all this reasoning I could not dismiss the vision. Was it, I wondered, because such visions were so rare? Or because of the three I had experienced thus far only one, the Baron in entreaty before the King, had been proven true to my knowing when that Baron was executed for treason, his family banished and his lands confiscated by the Crown and given in reward to another? If one could be true, would not the others also in their time prove true? But what even of that? Suspecting a nobleman of duplicity and treachery, one should not be surprised if his guilt is soon established and due punishment meted out. I so reasoned with myself, first on one hand then on the other, but for all my efforts I remained troubled.

Did my vision of the Queen indicate some special tenderness of heart toward her? Of course. She was my Queen, consort of a King who had elevated me to the highest rank a jester could know and for whom I already felt great love and deepest respect. She was possessed of great beauty, she was kind far beyond the routine courtesies of nobility, she shared with me a profound love of the dog and trusted me with the favorites of her heart, she had a grace of mind and heart, an embracing warmth of presence which felt almost transformative of the world . . . .

Was my vision of her but manifestation of a deep sympathetic compassion for a chance acquaintance of noble rank and nobler spirit?

I tried to convince myself this was so, for many weeks and months, just as I tried to convince myself the Queen loomed large in my daily thought simply because of her nobility of spirit and graceful possession of royal bearing and her kind and compassionate heart. I labored to convince myself of these things. Often and hard I labored.

In the end, all my effort came to nought for the simple fact these things were not true.

Or say, rather, they were true, but they were not the complete truth. But I was not yet ready to admit that complete truth to myself.

"Come, Jester, let us leave off our musicians and have one of your particular songs for the evening." The King gestured to me as he spoke, a wave of his arm accompanied by a gesture that appeared casual but was in fact one of our pre-arranged signals, one indicating there was no ulterior purpose, no need for provocation or scrutiny or aught but simple entertainment. The evening's feast was a small one by the standards of the court, a final entertainment for envoys from a foreign king with whom agreement had been reached regarding an arranged marriage that would strengthen an already firm alliance. With all business well concluded simple diversion would suffice.

I bowed with theatrical flourish and fetched a lute from the musicians stationed at the rear of the hall. My skill upon the instrument was rather limited, but for the simple ballads I wrote was adequate enough for accompaniment. I had quite recently composed a song I believed would suit the evening's purpose well. (As continual novelty is a jester's great ally, I had long made the regular composition of songs, tales, and jests a habitual practice.)

I stepped to a spot where I might command all attention and began.

A rose did grow in the forest fastness,
A honey'd rose of the palest gold;
A single rose in a silent clearing
And of this fair rose is a story told.

O there betimes did live a fair maiden
More beauteous maid than was ever seen.
Skin as soft as the touch of an angel
Honey-gold hair, her eyes emerald green.

Red were her lips as the deep-delved rubies,
Her smile shone like the radiant sun.
In her pure heart was a boundless joyance,
So many sought what was given to one:

She loved a prince who did love her truly,
And in their great love they went forth to wed.
To the wedding feast did come a harper,
And to the harper the fair maiden said:

'Play on your harp as you were an angel
So that for your music two hearts may join.
Sing magic for me and for my true love,
And rewarded you'll be with jewel and coin.'

'My harp shall ring as if played by angels,
I'll play you a music for hearts to join.
'Twill be a magic for you and your true love
But from you I'll take neither jewel nor coin.'

'Pray then, O harper, how shall I pay you?'
'Pay me, O maiden, with your last free kiss.'
Forth she did step and kissed him full blithely.
'Now mistress,' he said, 'we shall take our bliss.'

He struck on his harp and held her closely,
He struck again and in a swoon she fell.
'You, my fair maiden, are my own true love
For me and no other, so this I tell:

One bold touch more on my harp shall turn you
Into a blossom of rare beauty.
Of this I alone shall possession keep,
And thus never parted we twain shall be.'

He struck his harp with an angel's passion,
And found himself in the clearing alone.
A honey-gold rose did bloom before him
Which he forever did keep as his own.
Which he forever did keep as his own.

Light applause greeted the fading of the song but I could heed nothing about me for I was staring in dumbstruck amazement at the Queen as though I had never set eyes upon her before. Not for any look or action of hers, for she was but clapping softly and, speaking to the woman next to her, not even looking in my direction. No, I was stunned by my own foolishness, my own blindness. I had written the song but a few days before, somewhat hastily (as you may tell) and not without the assistance of Goodman Ale. There had been some vague and distant sense of inspiration or perhaps compulsion to write those words, for ale is a potent Muse, but I had not troubled myself to examine those feelings.

Or rather, as it now struck me almost with the force of a blow as I bowed before the assembled company, I had feared to examine my motives and inspiration. Feared it because now as the Queen turned from her companion and glanced at me, her honey-gold hair neatly bound and netted and her emerald eyes bright in the glow of torch and candle, I, standing frozen with lute in nerveless hand, suddenly understood what I had done.

I had written, to her and for her, a song of love and possession.

Upon the instant I understood what I had for months been laboring to deny.

I was in love with the Queen.

Not an idealized love of subject for royal, commoner for noble, servant for benevolent mistress. Neither agape nor storge nor philia, though containing elements of those, but eros.

How could this be?

In that moment there in the hall, before an assemblage of nobles some of whom were glancing at me curiously while I remained motionless, I felt a sudden rush of almost o'erpowering confusion. Had any understood the fair maid in my song was the Queen? That I, standing alone before the gathered guests with lute in hand, was the harper? Would the Queen be disturbed and insulted, the King leap to his feet and order me whipped before being driven from the castle in ignomy? I could feel my face grow flushed. How could I not have seen this? Why did I not perceive such hidden hubristic folly before now, burn the page the instant I had finished scribbling those hopeless words upon it? I struggled to fight down a rising surge of panic.

But none seemed to take any note. Some were raising food or drink to their lips, others spoke to those near them, the ordinary business of a minor feast continued. The King caught my eye and the slight arch of an eyebrow caught my attention. I suddenly realized I was standing, silent and unmoving, before an assembled party of pleasure as though I were a doltish servant struck dumb and senseless by his first sight of royalty. I had only presence of mind enough to make the signal requesting permission to excuse myself. When the King tipped his head I made as hasty a bow as ever I made and hurried to the privacy of my quarters, speaking to none I passed, my eyes intent only on the flagstones before me.

Had such folly ever been seen in the world before? I thought with a grinding self-anger as I reached my chambers and threw myself upon the bed in embarrassment and despair. How could I not have understood the implications of that song, as obvious now as the unclouded moon at night? I clearly am not the clever Jester, the subtle trickster of wit and uncanny insight I imagined myself in my vainglory to be, but a fool, a true and utter fool who has compounded one great folly with another.

No. A strange disturbance of my humours overtook me and I was suddenly clammy with sweat despite the coolness of the evening and my heart beat in my chest as though it would hammer itself into insensibility within me. I have not compounded one folly with another I thought as my mind whirled in a terrible confusion. Rather, I have committed one folly which has no equal and thus so fills the realm of Folly it is beyond the possibility of being compounded. Revealed, perhaps, yes, as I had almost unwittingly done, but in no way could my folly be made worse in itself for it was already the *ne plus ultra* of Folly. It cannot be it should not be and it must not be.

And yet it was.

This was impossible, I railed at myself in my thought.

But it was true nonetheless.

I was in love with the Queen.

I felt in that dark moment, in my torturous clammy bed, a wave of such despair wash over me as though a relentless torrent of black water, an ocean's worth of water, sought to bear me down, annihilate me upon sharp rocks of agony and grief before bearing my shattered remains away to some shadowy depth unimaginable. I struggled to breathe and feared almost for my sanity and my life.

In my grim despair I understood I longed for her in a manner I had not known before, my longing an enduring pang and irresistible compelling desire sweeping away all thought and reason and volition. I had had several dalliances while in the Earl's service and had even been much taken with a maid at the Baronet's who cared nothing for me and left my longing unrequited. So I was not unacquainted entirely with strong amorous feeling. But nothing I had known or even dreamt could begin to compare to such agony as I felt now, this soaring transcendent longing and consuming thought inextricably tangled with the dark despair of its utter hopelessness. How could I long so, long until I thought both heart and mind would fail me, long until my very being felt harrowed with pointless pain, long for that which is and always will be impossible for me to possess? It was worse than folly, worse than madness, and it could not be borne.

Nor could it be denied or evaded.

I loved the Queen. I loved her as a youth loves a maid of his own station, as a man loves one to whom he would join himself and his life so he might for all his days and nights bask contentedly in the quiet sustaining joy of reciprocal love and desire, the soft bliss of enduring supportive companionship and warm affection, the sharing of life so life may be doubly enriched. I longed for her as intently and as passionately as man may long and his heart not break within him and he swoon to death.

It could not be. By all laws, customs, dictates, mores, and practices of God and man this could not be. None may unclasp and reforge the links of the Great Chain of Being. None may slip from one station to climb to another. None may affect the turning of the Wheel, none may transgress the immutable and eternal laws by which the Created World is framed and ordered. All of this I knew. Yet would transgress were it in my power.

Commoners do not fall in love with royalty. In the ordinary course of earthly life they have no opportunity, no occasion, not even the proximity. But I had become an uncommon commoner, inhabiting a space disparate from the space and course of ordinary life. I had become Jester and held license to invade and subvert established order, to mock whom I chose and walk familiarly among royalty and nobility. What I did not understand until this dark moment was that such license and such familiarity created a risk no ordinary commoner could know. To such risk had I been exposed, and to such risk had I succumbed.

I had fallen victim to my own success, to the achievement of my dream. I rode the Great Wheel to its apex and now lived in close proximity to royalty and spoke familiarly to a queen who shared my devotion to a worthy monarch and my love of dogs and in consequence I now found myself prostrate and helpless before the impossible. I could no longer continue the self-deception which allowed me to call my feelings for the Queen by such names as "admiration" and "affection" and "honor." I had now no choice but to acknowledge the impossible true name of those feelings, and that name was "love."

My father's words again came back to me with terrible force as I writhed upon my bed of personal agony. "Educated out of your station but into none other." Has that indeed been my undoing? Through my education and my wit I have come into royal company, and being in royal company even for so short a span I have lost my heart to a woman as far beyond my reach as the quiet shining moon is beyond the yearning moth. Fortunate chance and years of learning and labor have brought me to the achievement of my ambition and to my heart's undoing.

"This cannot be!" I shouted aloud into the echoing darkness and immediately regretted my action. Sound travels too well in a castle of stone, in servant quarters especially where no tapestries or carpets muffle sound. Above all I knew, even then in the onset of my agonized love, I would never be able to speak of this to any. Somehow I must forever keep the love I would shout from every turret secret in my breast. I could never speak of this longing and the rending anguish which accompanies it, never in speech find any measure of heart's ease. I would love the Queen and suffer for my love in bitter and solitary silence. It came upon me that as my love would never know requiting, my heart would never know solace, and for that I wept.

Long hours I struggled with myself that night, tossing fitfully upon my bed or pacing the floor as does a caged beast in uncomprehending confusion, at times throwing myself into a chair to hold my head in my hands as I wept yet again or else to shake my head in alternating disbelief and despair. I told myself I was mistaken, a hundred times I told myself this was some illusion of the mind, a passing fancy, anything but what I in my deepest heart knew it to be. Shortly before sunrise I at last found sleep for a brief space, slumped in a chair, and when I awoke it was to bodily stiffness and the instant flooding knowledge I loved the Queen and thereby faced a life of hopelessness. And from that moment forward I struggled with little success to keep thought of her from my mind.

For some days after this I assiduously avoided both King and Queen, hoping to find beyond my confusion and uncertainty sufficient peace and calmness of mind so I might examine my thoughts and feelings with some measure of equanimity. But peace eluded me. With thought of the Queen dominating almost every waking minute I found myself by slow degrees seeking ever-greater distraction. In this, ale and dogs became my staunchest and most effective allies.

Until this time I had been in the main a man of moderation in drink, fond enough of ale and wine (and mead when I could get it) but well aware even from a young age of the manifold ways in which excess may cost a man a very great deal, for I had seen enough in the households of the Baronet and the Earl and the towns and taverns I visited to learn such a lesson. Even the boredom of the Earl's service led me only on rare occasion to excess.

But my feelings for the Queen, overwhelming and seeming utterly beyond my strength to constrain, brought with them a deep acute pain such as had never touched me yet in my life, indeed never had come within the scope of my imagining. I suffered an agony of heart and mind which seemed at times almost to impede the very intake of my breath.

To blunt the edge of this sharp despair I began to drink almost to regular excess. For drink did not make me melancholy or choleric, as it often does those whose characters are shaped by humours different from mine. With drink I became more sanguine, comic, even more fool and jester and always to the delight of those assembled in company. As long as I sought and found sleep while still filled with the distraction of ale or wine I could pass a night without pang or longing. Though should the elevating effect of drink pass while sleep still remained aloof from me, as it often did on account of the frantic working of my mind, and the night creep bitterly upon me in my growing sobriety, I would burn with anger or longing or, most commonly, both, and would rail against God. With a vehemence I heretofore did not know I possessed I would curse the ways of a Creation that gave me a heart with such capacity for love and brought me to the very feet of the one woman who could fill that heart, one whose being appeared to me as the only goal and purpose of my heart's longings, and then deny her to me. By God's Heaven and Satan's Hell I knew such seething anger and black despair in those suffocating nights and in the desiccated days that succeeded them, and I had no anodyne but drink. I began to keep wine always in my chambers so I might escape such pangs and hold such nights at bay.

"We have seen too little of you, Jester, these many a several days. I should have thought sooner to send to the kennel in search of you."

I started in surprise and confusion, the Queen having come upon me unawares, occupied as I was in instructing a kennel page in cleaning and binding a wound upon the foreleg of a greyhound. I leapt up in confusion, my materials falling to the ground as both page and I made a hasty flustered reverence to the Queen, my confusion surely greater than his both for the ale I had drunk already that day and for the unbidden surging of my heart as I looked upon her. Having haunted the kennel much in recent days precisely to avoid her presence I was all but shocked at her sudden appearance there, as though I had never thought to expect her in such a place. Why I should have thought thus was a mystery and a folly, of course, but such was my state of mind it did not occur to me she might sometime wish to visit the two of her favorite dogs not currently with her in the castle. I should have been all but anticipating her arrival, not thinking I had found distraction and calm refuge from her distracting presence and my torment.

As I raised my head I opened my mouth to speak – and words failed me. I, with a nobleman's education and a wit almost preternatural in its ready verbosity and invention, could summon no words. My mouth opened, my jaw worked but my mind could on that instant form no thought and know no sensation but blank surprise. To cover my confusion I turned my head to cough and pretended to clear my throat as though from an excess of phlegm.

"I do trust you are well, Jester, and that it is not infirmity which has kept you recently absent," the Queen said, her lids narrowing slightly in a searching look, though whether she saw through my pretense or was searching my face for tokens of true illness I could not for my confusion determine.

"But a slight indisposition, Majesty," I said, thinking to myself this was not entirely untrue though the indisposition was of heart and mind, not body. "My humours have all but regained their wonted balance and I shall be invisible no longer." A theatrical bow accompanied my poor jest.

"I am pleased of this, Jester, for we have been somewhat dull at table these past days without your wit and your songs to distract us." My songs? I thought. She has never mentioned them before. What might this mean? "My poor husband," she continued before I could pursue my thought further, "laments your absence, for now he has only the Lord Chamberlain and his ministers with whom he may speak his beloved Latin, and he assures me their wits are even duller in that language than they are in our own."

"I have been terribly remiss, my Queen, and for this I offer a thousand apologies," I said with mock distress. "Please assure my beloved master I shall soon Vergil him till the Aeneid leaks out at his ears and will Tacitus him till he cries out for mercy. In Latin." I found it hard to keep my eyes upon her as I struggled for wit.

"Punishment he will immensely enjoy, I am sure," she said. "But come, I would ask your advice on a matter quite dear to my heart."

As you are to mine, Majesty. The thought came to my mind unbidden and unwelcome. Instantly I grew both embarrassed and angry with myself. This is a child's foolishness, such feelings and their clumsy expression, nought but fevered nonsense from some idle dreaming troubadour's old *romaunt* or a marketplace ballad of chivalry's impossible love. Such thoughts should have no purchase in my mind or in this world.

"Ask as you will, madam, and I be not fool I shall nod and be scant of speech, or, being fool, shall speak you volumes." I struggled for wit to distract myself, to keep my mind from dwelling on her nearness, to keep my eyes from lingering on her face and to loosen the pressing bands that seemed again to be fastened about my chest, impeding breath.

The Queen glanced at her ladies-in-waiting. "Pray, good friends, translate for me if you understand jester-speech, for I fear it is a tongue unknown to me." Smiles and tittered laughter were their only replies.

"Oh, mistress," I cried dramatically, my jester-habit now beginning to come upon me, albeit weakly. "I would be no more common than I must be perforce, so would speak no more commonly than I cannot avoid." Some portion of my thought noted the fact I alluded to my commoner status as a regrettable condition, though there was no need to wonder why. I hurried on. "You ask for my advice. I say — " I stopped abruptly, holding up a finger as I turned to the kennel page still standing beside me, all but trembling and pale of face for his nervousness. "You, good sir, would you ask of a fool for wisdom?"

He stood silent for a long moment, eyes wide as though fighting back fear and I feared he might not be able to answer for his awe of royal presence. But he managed to force a mumbled "No, sir" from his lips.

I could not pursue the jest I intended with one so nervous so I turned back to the Queen – and registered my own nervousness, never before felt in her presence. My stomach seemed tight and sour within me as I looked upon her and I felt a quickening of my heart. I glanced quickly back at the page.

"On the counsel of this wise gentleman, Majesty, ask me only of that which I know, and that is but little, I regret." I bowed my head and wondered at the labor of my poor jest, such work for so little. My thought was scattered in her presence and this will not do. I cannot always be such, else for such ineptitude I lose my place. And thus her.

The Queen was studying me curiously, her head tilted slightly. Even she senses my confusion, I thought.

"What is it, Jester, you know best?" She waved a hand dismissively. "Aside from your jester-tricks and all your jester-work – for that is a given – what in this world do you know best? Books? 'Tis said you have a scholar's knowledge. Latin? You speak it like a studious bishop, my husband says." She smiled slightly and nodded encouragement. "Come, Jester, I would know this of you."

Do you have such interest in me? No. Foolish to linger on such errant thought.

I composed myself as best I might. "The answer is not in my head, Majesty," I said, tapping the side of my head with a single finger, which I then pointed to the ground, "but at my feet." The greyhound I had been tending was still sitting quietly just to my side. "These noble creatures, the greatest friend to man in all the Created World, are my love and my study." My love. . . . The word I had no business using in her presence lest it betray me lingered in my mind and for distraction I promptly knelt and quickly finished binding the dog's wound, struggling to control my suddenly unsteady fingers.

"As I thought, good Jester, for in this we are kindred spirits, no?" My heart seemed to stumble at her words. That such could be. . . .

A sudden movement surprised me. Gathering the folds of her dress about her the Queen knelt upon the straw-littered ground beside me. I felt a strange fullness of heart, a tightening of my throat. She was but inches from me, her soft eyes intent upon the face of the dog whose long muzzle she held gently in her hands, fingers stroking under the chin. I was all but overwhelmed by the urge to put my hand upon her arm, to touch her shoulder.

She murmured sweet words to the creature as I gave the binding a final inspection. I nodded to the page, not quite trusting my voice, and he led the dog away as the Queen and I both rose, I jealous of the lady-in-waiting who held the Queen's arm as she stood. Oh for such a touch. . . .

"It is concerning dogs I seek your advice," the Queen said, "so you see I ask a wise man for his wisdom." A brief smile, kind. "Attend me." She walked on and I accompanied her through the kennel, grateful for the rich cacophony of barking which made conversation all but impossible. We walked in silence until we arrived at that part of the kennel reserved for the personal dogs of the King and Queen, a special chamber, spacious and airy. It boasted comforts I had never imagined to find in a kennel. Most notable were the individual enclosures, each large enough to accommodate several of the largest boarhounds. Each enclosure here had fresh bedding of straw changed every three days, and a page was assigned to attend only to these dogs at all times. These were the quarters of the Queen's pampered favorites alone, for the King kept no personal dogs.

There were twelve kennel spaces in the room but only two were occupied and it was to those the Queen led me. These were the two bitches, confined now as one was finishing her season and the other had her season full upon her. They were released so the Queen might enjoy them and they leave off their barking, though being both in their season they had not quite their wonted sweetness of temper toward each other and we moved them some distance apart, I with one bitch and the Queen with the other.

"I would have more of these dogs, Jester. I would. Their love fills my heart but as it fills, my heart expands and I find room for more." She paused and I took the opportunity to show her I knew her mind, show her we were kindred spirits indeed.

"Your Majesty would breed her own, then. Create her own royal line rather than purchase more."

She nodded at me, gratification in her eye and a pleasing smile upon her lips. She understands our closeness of spirit, I thought wildly.

"I would indeed. When next these two come into their season I will have them bred, and I would have you select their mates from among some others belonging to the worthy gentlemen cultivating these dogs." I remembered all four of her dogs shared parents and so were too consanguineous themselves for proper breeding.

There were other concerns as well, and I could all but hear my father's voice in my mind as I quickly reviewed them.

"Both bitches are sound of form and structure," I said, "and both have proven well tractable. Temperament is sound in each, though

Onyx here," and I rubbed the ears of the dog before me, "shows more aptitude in the field." I nodded at the dog which the Queen was caressing. "Jet is too hard of mouth, still doing much damage to the small game she brings to us in training. I cannot yet say if that may be fully trained out of her, though we continue our efforts. She I would not yet breed for that reason, for her pups may be the same as she and those you do not keep might prove a discredit to the line should they behave as she does when in the field."

"And if I keep all the pups? Your concern becomes of no consequence then, correct?" She looked at me somewhat archly and I could see she was merely testing me.

"Indeed, mistress," I answered. "As long as you keep them all." I paused, looked at her. "And all of their get and produce, and all of theirs, and so forth." I smiled. "Her Majesty shall soon find herself awash in dogs. And mangled bloody carcasses of rabbit and otter."

A brief half-smile lit her face, its effect upon again me almost as lightning, its impact almost palpable and disruptive of thought. "Oh, what a pragmatical jester has my husband retained." Why did I not care to hear "my husband" from her lips? Jealousy of his possessing her love? One impossibility compounding another in the mind of a fool. Ludicrous to be jealous of that which cannot be. And I love the King as both man and master. What a bitter jumbled confusion of mind and heart.

". . . with your training." I had been so lost in thought I had not heard the Queen's words. "For I would have her bred if at all I might."

"As you wish, Majesty." As you wish indeed. Ask me aught and I would do it. I am driven by a strange relentless fire in my heart and there is nothing you could ask of me I would refuse. My heart began to race again and to rise in my throat so it was with great relief I heard one of her ladies remark to the Queen on their timely need to return to the castle.

From the kennel doorway I watched as the Queen and her attendants crossed the lawn, watched as the westering sun again brought the castle's stone to rich glowing life almost as though it was her approach kindling its latent glory. Her cloak, a rich burgundy, seemed almost incandescent in the golden light of the evening, a color as warm as love. Tears I did not understand came to my eyes.

Impossible, impossible, impossible. Yet as surely as this could not be, it was. I watched the Queen and her party until they were lost to my tear-blurred vision before turning back to the dogs, now being fed by their kennel page. Her love for these creatures will be the only love I will ever share with her, I knew, the only love I will ever speak of with her. My love for her – for love it was though I knew not how this could be – was forever to be the unutterable secret of my wracked and yearning heart. A love whelped by improbability and suckled by the impossible, I thought with every possible sadness as I watched her dogs devour their meat. After a few minutes I turned my own steps toward the castle and walked slowly there in full dejection.

My love for her could not be, yet was. Irrefutable as life itself, implacable as the day's progression. It was. From my liminal space in the Created World I had made the impossible possible, brought the unimaginable into being. And for such profane jester's trickery I am suitably punished, for in the very moment of knowing my love I know its loss. As I watched the sun set I thought how it would rise on the morrow and in so doing would for me be the harbinger of another day, the first of many thousands, of entwined longing and loss. I could foresee no end to this short of my own death.

There was indeed no end, as you shall see. There were periods of greater or lesser distraction and even respite, certainly, an ebb and flow of my heart's unhallowed yearning, for reasons I cannot fathom. There were the distractions of my duties, travels, dogs, ale, dalliances. There was the best and richest of all distractions, my family, of whom I shall soon tell, though even that could not completely divert my attention from the Queen, and that family lasted for so short a span I was soon left much as I had been before.

Why did I remain? Yes, that is the question.

Given the pain attending my longing for her, my occasionally flickering but always unfading love for a woman I could never have, why did I stay? I was free to leave at the time of my choosing, bound by no compact of law or custom. Why did I not walk away from a life which brought me such suffering and anguish of heart?

For a time the question vexed me considerably and I did fear at intervals I had become that other sort of common fool, crippled somehow in mind or will, lacking all strength of resolution or determination. I wondered even if it were the suasion of some agent of evil, some small revenge of the Devil's to make me suffer for the good I was doing in the service of a God-fearing and righteous monarch. Or perhaps I was more enduringly and profoundly the commoner than I thought myself to be, helpless and fawning before royal beauty despite the education I had received and what meagre store of wisdom I had so far accumulated, lacking the native wit and strength of character to save myself. Perhaps this and perhaps that – I surmised a thousand "perhaps's" and struggled with them all.

The result of my struggle, over the course of years and through the agonized darkness of empty nights and in the quiet reflectiveness of hollow afternoons, is that I came to know I stayed for what is both the simplest and most complex of reasons: love.

Not only the single and specific love I felt for the Queen, though I cannot deny the binding power of a love which often seemed an iron shackle fettering me to sorrow. I remained, I told myself, for Love as an idea, an ideal of what I came to believe was an emanation of the Divine within us that lest we actively seize it in its myriad forms slips our grasp, our lives, like mist through our hands and we are left only with the animal emptiness of our mortal earthly selves. We are ennobled by more than love, certainly – by faith, wisdom, goodness, charity – but might not love in all its multivalent grace be the greatest and the first of these, the Ur-force impelling our spirits to redemption and beauty and transcendence, to all other forms of nobleness and virtue? I do believe it is so.

I have, in my times of weakness and self-pity (and of such times there have been too many), felt I was too easily pained by all the many forms of love in this world, that God had somehow wronged me in this regard. Yes, a thought approaching to blasphemy I grant but a true and honest sign of the great reach of my anger in those moments. God had wronged me by making my heart too vulnerable, too easily and too greatly moved, too ready in surrendering to love: love of color, of knowledge, of beauty, of beast, of Queen. I have no answer or explanation, no sense of any meaning to this. In misery and anger I have demanded answers from God and in response was met with only black and indifferent silence. As it should be, many would say, and now in my later life I find I have no heart to disagree. I am a commoner, after all, no common jester perhaps but still a man of low degree who lived his life in-between the established stations of the world, one who still lives in those the only places he has ever known, the voids between the links of the Great Chain ordering our world and binding us to God. And to such a one as I no answers need be given, no response from Heaven due or expected. I do not know why I was made as I was; I know only it was my life. And perhaps that too was part of why I remained in royal service. In a sort of limbo, a halfway life of the heart which mirrored the halfway, interstitial existence I lived as Jester. Here yet not here, simultaneously at center and at periphery. Why then should the uncertain state and aching incompleteness of my heart, the epic misdirection of my longings, be of any great issue in whether I lived here or there? Would my love for the Queen have been lessened had I left? No interrogation of my heart and mind ever led me to believe that would have been true, though I confess I could not find the resolve to conduct the experiment. I eventually came to understand that "Why not leave?" seemed no more weighty than "Why not stay?" Put those questions in the balance and observe the scale draw level, the one side match the other dram for dram.

Perhaps that is why I did not leave.

I would say also I remained for reasons beyond my love for the Queen, compelling reasons of no inconsiderable value. I have already told of the castle's beauty, its multiplicity of enfolding spaces and pulsing vitality making it almost a living thing itself worthy of being loved, and after the boredom of the Earl's hunting lodge I had no wish to surrender such vibrant richness, Queen or no. A jester belongs nowhere and everywhere and if I must spend my life in the gaps of the world's hierarchy where could I find more opportunity to brush against those on either side of all those varied gaps than in a royal household? From lowest to highest all ranges of the human pageant came within my ken while I lived in the King's service, so though I could fully belong to none I could observe all. I could persuade myself, even if only with ale and self-trickery, that all the multiplicity of worlds swirling around me, the worlds of commoner, gentry, noble, royal – all those were if never fully available to me never completely closed to me either. So the royal household's rich tapestry of variety and what consolations I derived from my partial belonging in all of it were also no small part of why I remained.

The castle was also my home, the place where I lay my head at night more often than any other. For most of a quarter century it was my principle place of residence, small quarters in the servant's wing but among the best rooms in the castle ever given over to servant's use. I lacked for no physical comforts there, for the King and Queen were compassionate and generous masters. And for this too I remained.

I long ago accepted my Gift to be an essential and irreducible element of my very self and being, likely my *raison d'etre* and also a great joy to me, a making manifest in the Created World some compelling and ennobling aspect of my divinely-granted spirit. I could not, despite the near-constant aching grief of my unsanctionable feelings for the Queen, find it in me to surrender the greatest stage and most consequential opportunity any jester such as I could ever have. I stayed, in essence, love of my King, for to exercise my Gift in proper service to a monarch of such quality and probity I felt to be the fulfillment of ordained purpose. This was another anchor holding me fast to royal service.

There is as well the fame and fear which accrued to me. I enjoyed – nay, almost gloried in – my reputation and renown as the King's Jester, and this too was powerful inducement to remain. I know these words reveal a vanity and pride for which flames of purgation await me, but here in this reckoning of my life I would be as I said at the beginning full honest. For who does not love, even if only in the secret places of his heart, to find the skills he most values in himself and in which he takes his greatest pride are highly valued by others, regarded as a treasured rarity? Who would not be flattered to learn his talents are made the stuff of ballads and tales and his name has reached the shores of distant kingdoms? That his gifts inspire the envy and the fear of noble and commoner alike? Add to this as well the fact my skills were the cause of no small gain of worldly wealth. For these reasons too I stayed.

I knew some measure of joy in that castle as well. The joy of marriage and the joy of fatherhood both came to me there, and for a brief time those joys held the stage of my castle life, softening the ache of my unrequitable love for the Queen into something akin to mild melancholy. But those joys had far too short a lease upon that stage, as you soon shall learn.

That royal residence, the magnificent castle which was home to me, was then as you see a vexed and haunted place for me yet one I had not the strength nor will to leave. It held within its glorious golden walls the tangled skein of all my life's weavings and the tumultuous desires of the confused and anguished heart I bear within. All I longed for was there; all I would leave, had I sufficient strength and courage, was there.

And so I remained.

160

family

"If you would have my love be not Jester with me. Be only a man, one of truth and forthright honesty."

Those are the words I remember, words etched by guilt upon my heart for by those words a woman I believe I loved declared the condition of her love. A fair and simple condition, one to which I assented, and which I failed to honor.

In the two short years of our marriage I never spoke untruth to her and never violated our holy vow, never gave her cause for doubt or mistrust or aught but love. For I did love her in some manner. But in some deep-shadowed region of my heart my love for the Queen remained, potent still if somewhat quiescent for the distraction of my marriage, and of that love I never spoke. To keep such strength of feeling, one so strange and unnatural and all the more disruptive for its unnaturalness, from my wife was a fall from the concordant grace of the forthright honesty for which she asked, a betrayal of vow and promise. My silence, compelled by inflexible and absolute necessity, was a sin against love, a sin of willful omission for which I fear no penance will suffice.

"I shall play you no jester," I told her with a fervent earnestness hollow at its core. Yet my feelings for her, the strongest I had known for any woman other than the Queen, were as real as the thorn-studded rose, as real as the castle walls surrounding us and bringing into being the world through which we both moved and in which we found each other's love. Those feelings simply were neither the only nor the strongest feelings of love in my heart.

"I offer you no dissemblance, no trickery. Only what is true in my heart," I said to her. Oh, fair enough but not far enough, Jester. "In court and council I am Jester to serve my king and kingdom and there do take it upon myself to be whatever I needs be. I distract and disrupt, am fool and trickster and discoverer of secrets. I am too as puppet-master, for at times I can make some men dance in word and thought as though I hold the strings to their minds. I peer beneath the masks they offer to the world and I see them in their true guise and nature. I read them at times as I do books." I shook my head slowly as I held her gaze, looking softly into those large dark brown eyes, dark brown almost to black, that had been what first drew me to her, captivated me. They held me as in warm embrace and my heart stirred within me with a feeling I chose to call love. "I give you this token of my love and honesty," I said, my voice softened by my feelings and the confiding intimacy of the moment. "I give you my name." And I told her, in a whisper, the name I by which I had been christened.

It was a name I had revealed to none since leaving the Baronet's service. The Earl and his household ever knew me only as "Jester." The women with whom I had had dalliances knew me only as "Jester," though several had asked my true name but always fruitlessly. Even in royal service none knew my name. Not even my revered master the King, not even the Queen whom I loved above all else in the world. I kept my true name to myself, a cypher of absence marking my new identity, my new self, and thus a token of the surrender of my ordained and natural place in the order of the Created World. As commoner I had a common enough name, but when I became jester, became as my father said educated out of my station but into no other, I slipped into the gaps and leftover spaces in the hierarchy of worldly being and so my common name, my birth name, would no longer serve. In those unmapped uncertain spaces I was to spend my life as a man of tricks and deceptions, maskings and uncoverings, bringing low what had been high, making sport of the solemn and baffled fools of the powerful. I had become someone new, someone out of the common order and in no worldly station but the one I created for myself, created anew each day, each moment, and for myself alone. Who I had been born I was no longer. A new being needs a new identity, and thus I became Jester, and Jester only.

That I told my wife my birth name (with pressing injunction to reveal it to none, which she never did, not even in the fevered agony of her death-bed) was itself another failure of forthright honesty, I confess. It was, yes, a revelation of a truth known to few still alive but in my heart I knew I was offering it as a *show* of honesty, a pretense of revelation to hide a greater more troubling truth, a deeper secret I would keep locked away even from my wife. My revelation of the truth of my name was a lie, a deception, the hollow trickery of a hapless love-haunted fool.

"So you are to be married, my husband tells me. And to a body servant of one of my own ladies yet I learn of this neither from her nor from you. Are we not friends, Jester, that I must learn such important news indirectly?" The Queen smiled slightly as she spoke these words to me but the slight arch of her eyebrows and the directness of her look denoted a seriousness behind the question. Had she indeed felt somehow slighted? In some measure pained by the news itself rather than the means by which it came to her? Surely not, but my ever-foolish heart still would lead my mind to frame such idle hopeless damnéd thoughts.

"Oh mistress!" I cried in mock distress, "that the news of my foolishness has reached your ears by some path circuitous is most lamentable indeed, for who but a Fool should tell of a Fool's folly?"

"Why say you a foolishness, Jester? Surely you do not consider marriage to be folly?"

"Oh indeed I do madam," I said nodding earnestly. Let us play this game, I thought, for I must hide now the truth of my heart behind jester-wit. "'Tis the greatest folly enacted in the course of mortal life. Other than being born."

"Born? Jester, you speak conundrums today." The smile remained on her face though her eyes had grown yet more serious. "How is it being born is folly?"

"Why look you, madam, 'tis thus." I nodded sagely as I held up a finger, warming now to the distraction. "To be born is to become, to become is to be, and being we must perforce do. What we do, matters not," I said, waving a hand dismissively, "but being poor forked creatures we must forever busy ourselves. 'Tis the antic nature of our spirits drives us so. And being thus driven we blindly weave a web of such confusions we become hopelessly ensnared by the effects and consequences of our actions." I shook my head in exaggerated sadness. "As confusions lead to sorrows and as sorrows are best borne in company, we marry, and as from marriage is born more birth and thus more becoming and thus more sorrows, you see in the end we are born but to marry and marry but to breed more marrying. So to be born can be nought but folly. 'Tis inarguable. We put Sisyphus to shame, madam, to very shame." I paused, mock dejection upon my face and my arms spread wide in helplessness.

"You are quite misanthropic today, Jester, and I do protest," the Queen said lightly. "Your argument does not stand – "

"Stand, mistress? Oh, there is no standing. Could we but stand in place and be satisfied, we needs not marry. 'Tis the mad dance of life which drives us to wed."

She shook her head, the smile still upon her face. "Your words whirl about me, Jester, so that I cannot catch all their meaning."

"Fret not, good lady, for truly they are but airy things formed of nought but breath and of less substance than that which the glistening bubble encloses."

"Folly, you said, Jester. Surely you do not go to wed believing marriage to be folly."

"Why, if a Fool should turn from folly, mistress, how then will he eat? If folly be not fit for a Fool then belike 'tis fit for no man, and thus the poor Fool shall starve for lack of employ."

She held up an open hand, laughing. "Cease, Jester. This is but distraction, which I believe you pursue only to mask your true thoughts on marriage." Distraction, yes, my lady, but from a deeper and more painful truth than you guess. "You have been in my husband's service near two years' time now. We have come to know one another somewhat well, and while we have talked much of dogs and of the goings-on of household and kingdom I have not yet heard your thoughts on love. Nor have you spoken to me of this woman you soon will marry. It is a most grievous omission to keep from a friend the news of your love and betrothal. No more such silence, Jester." Her smile flashed broadly and again I felt the visceral pulse of my longing for her. "Come, Jester. Speak to me of love."

At those words my heart for a moment became a stone and unbidden to my mind came the thought 'Oh, that would I do, my lady. I would speak of my love for you until all word and thought were exhausted, until my tongue failed. Until I had won your heart.' In that instant all the sharp desperate longing I had ever felt for her came back upon me. I had found in the wooing of my bride-to-be some fair measure of distraction from my feelings for the Queen but in this instant my nuptials were forgotten and the ache of impossible love was full in my heart again and I feared for a moment it would burst.

To hide my confusion I bowed.

"Love, Majesty, is new to me," I lied, "and I fear I would speak of it as does the ten years' child who, rowing his little boat across the paddock pond, declaims boldly of the surging deep whereupon his armada sails to war."

The Queen laughed. "Is it not fit, sir, that love should forever be new to us? Even at the end of long life should not our love still feel vital, fresh each day as we awake to look upon the face of the one who fills our heart? My husband and I wedded five years gone now yet still to me my love for him each day feels new-born. Your love being new to you should be no impediment to your eloquence but rather encouragement, for who is more effusive and zealous of speech than the lover new to love?" She looked at me expectantly.

I felt as though I had been commanded to commit self-torture. To speak of love for another, if indeed it were love at all and not some pale shadow thereof, to the one woman whom I loved with a consuming completeness and intensity that kept me from myself — oh, it was an exquisite torture indeed, a harrowing of my heart throughout which I must smile.

I had misdoubted what I called my love for my betrothed since first she captured my attention. She was smitten with me, awed by my status and privilege in the royal court and taken with my wit and drollery and learning (she herself could not read), and I wondered from the start if in her feelings for me and mine for her I found not love but merely refuge. Is it not in our nature to be drawn to those drawn to us? Did I, I often asked myself, but exploit this common human love of emotional reciprocation, eventually convince myself our mutual attraction was "love" so in it I might find some surcease of sorrow, some measure of comfort for a heart, mind and body anguished by love for the Queen? Was I in truth pursuing not love but distraction from those feelings haunting my life, feelings simultaneously untenable and ineluctable and in that terrible paradox the great burden of my heart? If so, was I not the falsest of lovers, a very traitor to love? Yet now my Queen commanded me to speak of it.

I sighed deeply. The Queen's quick smile showed she thought it marked a lover's affectation rather than the resigned despair I felt in my heart. But let her think thus, I thought. There is no help for it.

"I confess I have thought much upon love of late, mistress," I said slowly as I thought with bitterness of the irony in those words. "Yet for all my thought and all my learning I know not that I approach closer to the truth of that great mystery than I did as a child."

"A great mystery now, Jester? So you find marriage a folly but the love which drives us to marry a great mystery? Explain yourself, sir. I fear I am lost in your conundrums still." The smile had not yet left her face. I would talk with you until Judgement if you would but always smile thus at me, my love.

I forced a half-smile of my own but all inclination to jester-wit had ebbed away, leaving me hollow, leaving me to feel a slow chill sadness creeping into the corners of my heart as a gathering fog slow encroaches upon the stubble field in autumn.

"It is for the very mysteriousness of love that marriage is folly, madam." There was no trace of levity in my voice and I knew I needed to choose my words now with care. "For if we do not understand that which goads us to marry, are we not acting upon that which we do not understand for reasons we do not comprehend? Is to act in the absence of all surety not great folly?"

The Queen looked at me a long moment in silence, her eyes narrowing slightly. She senses some seriousness behind my words, I knew.

"You speak of understanding and comprehension, good Fool. Is this how we are meant to experience love? Is it not to be felt in the heart rather than comprehended in the mind? You are too much the scholar in this matter, I think."

"A scholar by inclination, though a Fool by heavenly compulsion." I bowed my head, smiled briefly. "I do confess I live too much in my mind of late, mistress, 'tis the curse of a wise foolishness. At times I do envy the simpleton, free of weighty thought yet full of heart."

"From scholar to simpleton, Jester? Is there no middle ground?"

"Of course, madam, for those who may find it. You yourself do stand thereon, as does your husband and many thousand others I do envy." Oh, a statement most true, my Queen, for I do so envy your husband his possession of your love. "It is of myself alone I speak. But I am new to love as I have said and in my love do hope betimes to find balance. In matters of love I would be only a man in love, neither more nor less."

"Well spoken, sir. You shall find that balance as love grows upon you, for we all do grow in love as we love."

I smiled. "You have been too much in jester-company, Majesty, that you speak thus." I paused, for though I wished to escape this discourse and the pain it brought my heart I wished also to continue speaking of love with the Queen, of what I knew and feared in my heart as regarded her.

"Yet for all our growth in love," I continued, "does its nature ever reveal itself fully to us? Are we so constituted we may indeed someday come to comprehend it? Or is it to be forever a mystery, a force irresistible driving us to desires and decisions and actions we never fully understand? It is that which gives me pause."

She shook her head slowly. "Still, Jester, you speak of mysteries and understanding. Must all be reducible by thought, made particulate by reason so it may be fully scrutinized and duly recorded in the dull catalogue of common things?" She sighed lightly, her look upon me the look of one registering a regrettable, unreachable sadness in the one upon which she looks. You have found me out, Majesty, though your plummet does not fully sound the depth. "May it not be true," she continued, "that love, a gift from our Creator to ease the sorrows of the world by giving us in recompense the greatest joy we will ever know here, is a force irreducible, elemental and complete in itself? We accept matters of faith as distinct from reason. May we not do the same with love? Let it be apart from thought, Jester, sufficient in itself, a gift to which we must give ourselves without reserve if we are to receive it and all its joys and benisons. And they are many, Jester. You will see. Love's blessings are many."

I forced a mild look upon my features but was close to tears within. What love is for you, my beloved Queen, it may never be for me. The urge to leave, to be alone in my anguish, was almost irresistible. Our conversation had begun in wit and ended, for me, in a most grave and bitter melancholy.

The Queen smiled at me. "Come, Jester, we should rejoice at your coming nuptials, not surrender to melancholy." I glanced up sharply at the word. "It is to love you must surrender. You shall see, Jester, you shall see. I await the occasion with anticipation and great hope for the joy it will bring you, and do extend my congratulations to you and your bride. Felicitations, my friend, upon the joyful day."

I bowed deeply in gratitude and relief. "Majesty." I all but fled her presence.

So I married. Within two years of entering royal service, all but consumed by an impossible love for an unattainable woman, I married. In that marriage was some measure of distraction from thought of the Queen for I did find in my heart strong feeling for my wife, true affection of heart and spirit, for she was a good woman and a good wife, kind and attentive with a nimble native wit and admirable in all her qualities. She brought much delight to my life and I to hers, satisfaction to mind and spirit and body. Even, in some measure, to my heart. Yet I cannot say I ever completely untangled my love for her from that greater love I held for the Queen, and for that transgression I pray to be forgiven by her, by God, and by Love.

Or could it be, I have asked myself many times in the years since, I in fact knew a true love without then knowing I did so? Or say, perhaps, a love more honest because closer to the truth of human feeling and human experience. Perhaps the feelings binding me to my wife and my wife to me were in fact the richer for their completeness and their earthly realization than my exalted and idealized conception of my longing for the Queen allowed me to know.

How could this not have occurred to me at the time, nearly twenty-five years ago? Oh, the answer I know full well: despite marriage I remained, to varying degrees over those too-few years, caught up and enthralled by the potency of the Queen's presence and the dislocations, sometimes mild sometimes severe, of mind and heart which followed in the wake of that potency, the enduring distraction which despite its occasional ebb and flow was my endless longing for her.

Yet now, across two and a half decades of time's invisible distance, I wonder if my impossible love for an inaccessible woman was but my mind's construction of an ideal equally impossible to be realized, an ideal which then became the distorting optic through which I viewed all other women and experienced all other longings of the heart. My love for the Queen may have been an expression of some unrecognized, unexplained desire to explore the greatest reach and power of love by constructing in heart and mind a fantastical model of its abstract perfection, a model whose blazing glory so caught me up I could not recognize love's human manifestation when it came before my eyes in the form of my wife.

Or was my love for the Queen itself a compensatory phantasm, an idealized chivalric *romaunt*-love that was but an attempt to fill some unrecognized void within my heart, some deep unseen wellspring of loss and need? Be its source unknown, how is it one may not be helpless before it? What else might I have done, how otherwise have conducted the matters of my heart? Was my love for my wife an attempt to fill the emptiness of my love for the Queen which was itself an attempt to fill an even greater and subtler emptiness? How may a man escape this? Mask upon mask, distraction upon distraction, each attempt at fulfillment creating the need for another. Was my heart-life just such an impossible paradox? I do wonder of these matters still, these twenty-two years since the death of my wife and three or more years now removed from the Queen's company and by that temporal and geographic distance set free from the distractions of her physical presence, though even now what she represented to me remains in heart and mind undimmed, if more uncertain.

As what she represented to me lingers with me still I cannot know if I believe even now what I think and what I write. Did I overlook honest human love because of an abstraction, for if I truly believe so why do I find in my heart a passion for the Queen smoldering still? I should recognize it as abstraction and be done. Or perhaps my model of love's perfection became a trap from which I have never escaped; perhaps I became forever ensnared in a web of my own weaving. Or perhaps this too is rationalization, my mind's self-protective evasion of my heart's reality that the Queen was indeed the fitting object of a deep and compelling human love which only cruelly and by mischance of birth and station was impossible to be realized. Perhaps my longing for her was no mere model, no plaything of the mind or heart but the great and most exalted expression of a love-haunted mortal heart alive to the most intense reaches of passion and communion capable of existing between two mortals.

If so, all other love is a pale shadow of that one and I return to where I began. The futile Wheel of my life.

And perhaps, finally, this does not matter. What if the love I felt for my wife – for I did use that word to her and she to me – was not identical to the love I felt for the Queen, was different in quality as well as quantity? Was it not love nonetheless? Love knows many forms and facets, qualities and gradations beyond count. The love I held for my wife did not, could not, fully turn me from thought of the Queen but it existed and was named and caught my heart and mind sufficiently to hold me to my wife and her to me for the few years we shared. It led to children and no small measure of peace and to great heartache as well. So when all is considered, is that not love?

Yet if it is love, why have I for years now not been able to remember clearly my wife's face? Her death was near a quarter-century ago as I write these words yet still I see with painful ringing clarity the room in which she died – the luxurious dark green coverlet with edges traced in gold thread, a wedding gift from the Queen; the white ceramic pitcher on the dark oak table next to our bed; the sparse grey hairs on the back of the physician's hands as he sat helplessly by my dying wife – all this I see as though I have just stepped into that room again yet only by the greatest effort of mind and will can I summon even the most general image of my wife's face into my memory. I do not know what manner of failure this is, why my mind and heart should misgive me in such a matter, but there it is, the inescapable haunting absence of the face of the woman who bore my children. And again I ask myself what manner of love, then, was this?

Is my forgetting and the sorrow and guilt which accompany it a punishment from God? If so it is deserved and I make no complaint. Why should I not suffer the absence of her face, I who cared for her, even loved her though perhaps not enough because of the fact I also knew a greater love to which I never confessed and from which I was never fully free. May it be said I deceived my wife by telling her nothing of my feelings for the Queen? If you say so I will not argue. How my wife did not surmise those feelings I will never know. We were rarely in the

Queen's presence together, perhaps half a dozen times in the three years of our courtship and marriage, but I know the eyes of women are quick to perception in such matters.

Perhaps then my wife did know in some vague way the fact my heart was not entirely hers, some part of it always locked away as though held in reserve for unguessed purpose. She may well have seen it in my eyes or heard it in my voice when I spoke of the Queen, which I know I must have done much more even than I suspect. She may well have surmised it from my often-abstracted state of mind, my restless dreams, from the vague unacknowledged disquiet of my heart. Yet she said nothing, perhaps accepting the perfidy and vagaries of a man's heart as the given way of the fallen world. If this be true I should have loved her more than I did, for I deserved such a one as she less than I did. Although the affection I felt for my wife was true it was not all of which my heart was capable, and in that I did fail her. And perhaps myself. What I gave her may be called love, yes, but it was a love ever accompanied by the shadow of its own deception.

Yet from this marriage and the love, however attenuated and incomplete, that led to it came a great joy which my wife and I shared completely with all the passion and the fullest meed of love of which the human heart is capable. That joy was our daughter. Unlike my wife our daughter had no competition for my love, so in the common way of parents I gave to my child my full heart and was rewarded with an even fuller one. My joy in her was complete, unabated, and profound.

That any world not Heaven could have such a creature in it! She was in my eyes beauty in its purest expression, an exquisite rendering in elfin mortal form of all the human glories captured by any sculptor of Greece or Rome. Every aspect of her was perfect. She was a diminutive goddess somehow given us to grace our castle quarters and our lives with brilliant searching blue eyes and soft pale skin. I could not leave off looking at her, and with thanks to the Baronet for an education which gave me Latin I bestowed upon our daughter my obsession for her name: Miranda.

For more than a year she was our only child and in that time was blessed with all the love two devoted parents and a royal household's staff could give her. She was the most incredible of creatures in our eyes, as is the belief of all parents, but her beauty and her charming easy ways made her the pet also of every female servant in the castle and even of those male servants not too proud or gruff to spare a smile or a moment's amusement with an infant.

Perhaps my greatest joy at this time beyond the simple fact of Miranda herself was the delight the Queen took in my child. Though King and Queen remained childless after six years of marriage there was still anticipation and much hope, for all could see the Queen was a great lover of children. All infants born in the household received some gift from her, a gift she would bring herself with her own hands, and when she visited with the castle's children or encountered them at their play her pleasure in their ways, regardless of their station, would suffuse her face with quiet joy and swell with pride and satisfaction the hearts of onlooking parents.

Miranda seemed to be a particular favorite, owing something no doubt to my special place in the royal household though I love to believe it was due also to the child's own qualities. The Queen visited Miranda many times in her infancy and, as Miranda grew, would often keep the child with her for several hours together, playing with the Queen's vast wardrobe or being petted by her ladies-in-waiting or rolling with the Queen's beloved black dogs. My heart would fill with love and painful longing at the thought of the two people I loved most in the world, daughter and Queen, finding such pleasure in each other's company. Would, I often thought to myself with a secret desperate audacity, that we three were a true family, far from this castle so we might lose ourselves in full and undistracted love for each other. In such impossible thoughts I knew some small, passing touch of bliss.

Yet bliss was not to be the lot of my parental heart. Within three years of Miranda's birth my wife was again with child and we were in joy at the prospect of another such as Miranda, whose beauty and sprightly ways still kept her the castle favorite. Her birth had given my wife no particular trouble. The excellent midwives provided by the Queen said themselves my wife was born to birth babies, so well formed were her parts for the delivering of children and so free of difficulty was that first birth itself. Miranda's health was sound and with each passing month we found our worries for her fading as she grew in strength and vigor. We were fortunate in all this and offered thanks for a gift of such tremendous joy.

But no good fortune attended the birth of our second child, our son. As my wife's time neared a virulent contagion appeared in the city, spreading rapidly and killing many. Some called it plague, though the royal physicians disputed the claim with learned arguments which did nothing to stop many from dying of the fierce fever, wracking pains of the bowels, and bloody diarrhœic discharge that were the chief symptoms of this visitation. Efforts were of course made to prevent the disease from entering the castle but to no avail. Servants were the first to become ill but soon various councilors and ministers joined the ranks of the bedridden, their plaintive moans and pitiful pleas for mercy or release echoing in the hallways of the castle before they either recovered or perished. The King and Queen had gone to one of their southern estates near the sea to escape the pestilential air of the city but I remained by my wife's side, keeping to our quarters as much as I might out of fear for my family's health and my misery at seeing friends and fellow servants in torment. I should have done more to help, I know, for I loved many of those who suffered and some who died, but fear for my family's safety, for our unborn child, kept me from providing what comfort I could have given.

In the end my caution and my guilt saved nothing.

Some weeks before our child's birth was expected my wife took ill with the fever and within a day was suffering from gripping pains, sweating profusely and voiding more fluids than I would have thought the human form could contain. Her mind was at times swept away by delirium. The onset of the illness was terrifying in its swiftness, which the midwives attributed to her being with child. I say "midwives" but in fact only one remained, the two others refusing to stay for fear of the disease.

I of course remained though to do so was a wretched misery. My affection for my wife was genuine and to see her suffer so was a torment to me, a hell made worse by concern for our child in her womb. Her confusion and pain grew for several days despite the efforts of midwife and physician and in her agony came an early birth that caused her a suffering I could not believe did not kill her and which I could not bear. Yet bear it I did, offering my hapless assistance to the midwife through tears of pain and a bitter anger at God which consumed me, leaving no room in my mind for thought or Gift.

Our son was born alive but perilously weak in limb and breath and already exhibiting signs of the illness. My wife lay senseless on the bed, seeming close to death except for the shallow stuttering rise and fall of the coverlet, now stained with sweat and blood. I wished our son to be christened but the chaplain was himself gravely ill, unable to rise from his bed, and I would have carried the child myself to the nearest town church for baptism but the midwife forbade it with a sternness I could not refute. "The child is too weak and will not survive the chill air," she said, her voice as commanding as that of any man who has ruled a kingdom or led troops into battle.

"But he must be christened!" I cried, my mind clouded by dread and approaching panic. I took the child from her, desperate to undertake action of some sort, any sort, though I could think not what to do, could think only of how strangely warm the child felt even through the blankets which swaddled him.

"No!" Her command seized my attention and I looked full upon her, a fierce and overwhelming force evident in her eyes and I felt my own frantic energy drain away upon the instant. "Give me the child."

Thoughtless now, moving as though in a dream, I held my son out to her, some troubling shadow at the margins of my mind but I was empty, enervated beyond any power now of decision or thought.

"We may save him yet but he must remain within," she said, her voice as full of firmness as my heart was empty of hope. She unwrapped the child and laid him in a basin. "Bathe him constantly, as gently as you may," she said, handing me a cloth before stepping quickly to the room's small hearth and returning with a pot which had earlier been brought by the physician's assistant. She dipped a hand into its contents. "Fair warm enough. Keep him damp with it but none in eye or mouth." She turned her attention to my wife, still asleep upon the bed.

I did as she ordered, daubing my son's flushed tender skin as carefully as I might, my heart anxious and my hand at times trembling. Too warm he was, and despite his fever too pale, while his few movements were weak and lethargic. Never had I felt such helplessness combined with such despair. My son began to cry, a pitiful weak squall that nonetheless tore at heart and mind together.

"Is it hunger do you think?" I asked the midwife, knowing not what else I might do or say. "Where is the wet nurse? She was summoned." I could hear the approaching edge of panic in my own voice. "She should have arrived ere now."

The midwife shook her head as she turned from the bed where my wife lay as still as death. "I shall bathe the child," she said, taking the cloth from my almost senseless hand. "Seek you the wet nurse. The child must feed if he is to have strength."

I dashed from the room and rudely seized upon the first servant I saw, ordering her to find the wet nurse with a demand for all possible haste. I returned and waited in frustrated agony, my son's piteous cries now little more than a whimper but relentless despite the midwife's prayers and charms or the sugar-cloth she had given him to suckle upon. When at length the wet nurse did arrive, pale and with the hallmarks of incipient illness in her own features and manner, my son suckled but poorly and intermittently. He was soon asleep, surely more from exhaustion than satiety.

He awoke but a few moments later to a spew of vomit and his body even hotter to the touch. When soon after he weakly voided his bowels the discharge was bloody and noxious. His crying began again, weaker yet somehow still more piteous than before and tears sprang to my eyes. The midwife bathed him assiduously but his misery only increased and I was beside myself, distraught almost to madness with anger and helplessness.

"My child."

I barely heard the words my wife spoke, little more than a whisper on account of her own weakness. Our son's cries had awoken her from her deep sleep of illness though she could not rise from the bed, only gesture weakly with her hand.

"Bring him." Again her hand waved, the tremulous wing-flutter of a dying bird, pale grey against the green coverlet.

I looked to the midwife, helpless. She held my gaze for a moment then looked down at my son, her eyes studying him, lingering upon his damp feverish form. When at length she raised her eyes to me I felt as a blade of ice had pierced my heart for I read in her face my son's death. She believed now we could not save him and the tears which had been welling in my eyes now rolled, hot and excoriating, down my cheeks.

"Pray you now, Jester. He can hold no food so this must run its course as God ordains." She lifted my son from the basin, dabbed him dry before wrapping him in blankets. With an angel's delicacy she handed his swaddled form to me. "Take him to your wife. Let her hold him now. And pray you, Jester. Pray you." I could hear in her voice the tears that were in her own eyes but I would not lift my gaze from my son's face. His eyelids fluttered but did not open and his mouth moved weakly though no sound escaped.

"My son. . . ." Again my wife's whisper, fear and urgent need mingling in the reed-thin sound, a ghost's distant fading cry. With full gentleness I laid our son upon her breast, lifted her arms into place around him. She was as pliable as a rag puppet, so weak I feared she would not be able to hold him to her so I lay down upon the bed alongside my wife and son, my arm across them both so I might hold the child to her in safety. So I might embrace them both in love.

And in that embrace I felt life begin to leave my son's body, felt something vague and unformed brush against my mind with the now well-known intimation of palpable thought but I could sense only shadow, black and all-consuming. Without moving I called with desperate fear to the midwife to carry my son to the king's chaplain, bed-ridden and fever-struck as he was, so our child might be christened. I heard her approach the bed but my wife made a feeble effort to hold the child to her and I felt my own will weaken, overwhelmed by a sea of sadness even as the midwife spoke.

"Leave the child, Jester," she said softly as she put a gentle hand upon my shoulder. "Leave him with his mother now in her need. God's mercy is bountiful and we must trust to it." She leaned over me, placed a thumb upon my son's forehead, pale and beaded with sweat, and gently traced the sign of the cross. "Though I be but midwife I do beseech the Lord our God to show His greatest love and mercy to this innocent child – " She stopped abruptly. "His name, Jester. What is the child's name?"

He had none. As with Miranda, we would wait until the child was born, until we had laid our eyes upon him in joy and love before giving him the name he would carry with him through his life. I looked at my wife but her eyes were closed now, her face as pale as snow but for the hectic red upon her cheeks. Beneath my arm her chest rose and fell with such a shallow slowness as I must needs concentrate upon to feel. I kept my eyes upon my wife's face as I spoke to the midwife.

"I will not name him alone. As his father lives without a name let our child go to God only as Jester's son."

"He is not shriven, Jester, he – "

"No more, goodwife." I squeezed my eyes shut against the tears, against the thought of my son dying with the stain of original sin still upon his soul. I would not think on it. I shook my head. "With sorrow and anger my heart is overfull. I can no more."

Behind me the midwife spoke some combination of charm and prayer but I could no longer listen. My tears flowed freely as I labored to stifle the trembling sobs that sought their release of grief. In a moment, in an hour – I could not tell which – my son's breath stopped and I lay still, my mind overborne by shadow and my heart riven with an anguish such as I had never known before, would never have thought possible. It was long before my tears ceased to flow.

From that selfsame moment my wife released her own hold on life though she lingered for two days in an intermittent agony of mind and body I will not here describe, an agony which found its counterpart in my heart and spirit, in my own black and bitter emptiness and the dull consuming sorrow which alternated with a trembling anger at the God who would let such terrible suffering exist among the creatures He had created in His own likeness.

Let it stand as fit epitaph that even in her pain and delirium my wife called repeatedly for our son, her beleaguered body wracked with wrenching sobs it could scarce sustain, pleading through tears and wretched confusion for the child of her womb whose death she could not understand or accept. This was as tragic an expression of love as I have ever witnessed, and God help me that I wish never to witness again.

Miranda and I were somehow spared the fever-illness but the death of her mother – and, surely, my own transformation in the wake of that death – left Miranda changed in subtle ways I could not fully comprehend even though I myself lost my mother at a young age and thought this tragic similarity would have forged for us a stronger and still more intimate bond. But it did not. For months she puzzled and cried over the absence of her mother as any child so bereaved would do – as I must have done in my own childhood though I have no recollection – but even when the tears grew less frequent her manner remained altered, touched with a somberness never present before. I sought to ameliorate her sorrow as best I could, to fill the gap left by her mother's death and to return Miranda to what she had been before, but there is that particular love which a child can receive only from a mother and which I could not provide. My love for Miranda grew even stronger, demandingly so, in the wake of our shared loss but for Miranda a void seemed always to remain, a heart-space quietly and without effort resisting all attempts to fill it.

The Queen joined my effort to assuage Miranda's grief. She or one of her ladies or servants would attend Miranda or call for her almost daily, though she never seemed to enjoy these amusements with the bright abandon which had been her manner before. A nursemaid was hired by the Queen at her own expense to watch over Miranda and that was a great boon to me, but she seemed to find little pleasure in the nurse's company though the nurse was an excellent young woman of great patience and pleasant demeanor and well-skilled in the management of children. Even the company of other castle children could only on rare occasion draw Miranda fully from what appeared to be a premature and abstracting melancholy.

Contrary to nature this melancholy only deepened as the months passed. It was most strange to see a child of three and four years' age as silent as she, as . . . opaque. My Gift could show me nothing of her beyond what any parent could read in the face of a beloved child. And what I read there with troubling regularity was blankness. Opacity. A disconcerting stillness coming not from any profound inner calm, a saint's stillness, but from a deep distraction beyond reckoning. Her placid features had become a mask, one which I though a master of masks myself found impenetrable. I, with my Gift for the reading of men, of counsellors and envoys and princes, found myself confounded by the face of my own child.

I came to understand at length this change in Miranda was no simple consequence of bereavement but of something much greater and more permanent, something which caused my heart and mind increased misgivings. A bubbling laughing child become preternaturally placid, neither happy nor unhappy because she seemed beyond the reach of either happiness or its opposite, outside of a world that contained these because she had been taken by some other world. She played less and less with other children, began to refuse invitations from the Queen or her ladies and resisted, albeit quietly, if forced. She evermore preferred her own company, amusing herself with common child's toys in curiously tranquil and distracted fashion, or sitting quietly by herself, turning a leaf over and over in her hands or absently petting one of the castle dogs for great stretches of time together.

I began to fear for her mind. I thought of the mad friar and feared my daughter might end like him, wondered why if coming events cast their shadows before them I had caught no glimpse of the darkness which had taken my wife and son or now, it seemed, threatened to take my daughter. But I also well knew my Gift was of greatest utility with strangers, that the closer I approached my own heart the more clouded my vision became. So I worried for my daughter and worried too that despite my great love for her I could already feel the first intimations of a growing distance between us no effort of mine would ever prove able to bridge.

And then there came to me a very dark day of days, the only day when my Gift did come to me in regards to Miranda and showed me a glimpse of what I least wanted to see.

She was well past her fourth birthday, regarded now by the household staff as a precocious but odd child and increasingly left alone by those who once doted upon her. On this day, having spent much time with the King in council with a foreign delegation, I returned to my quarters late in the evening to find Miranda still awake. I dismissed the nurse and

sat quietly with my daughter as she played before the low fire, the highlights on her dark brown hair seeming threads of flowing gold as the
flames in the hearth danced their restless dance. She held in her hands
a rough wooden block carved on its various faces with fantastical figures,
the gift of a carpenter working in a nearby part of the castle who had
taken a special fancy to Miranda, saying she reminded him much of his
own lost child. Miranda turned the block slowly in her hands but
seemed to be paying it little heed. We sat in silence for a long while.

"Do you feel the river?" she asked suddenly, her eyes still on the
block but the question directed to me.

Her words surprised me. "The river? What river, child? The stream
in the meadow, do you mean? That's three furlongs from the castle
walls. How could I feel it here?"

She shook her head, her eyes still fixed on the now motionless block
in her hands. "Not that one." She placed the block on the floor in front
of her with great care, as though it were made of some delicate material
which would shatter with the slightest impact, then slowly raised her
arms so her outspread hands were just above her head.

"This one," she said, and slowly turned her head to look at me with
an implacable gaze I had never seen before and which chilled me despite
the fire's warmth. I looked at her for a moment in silence, my brows
arched in uncertainty even as I struggled to keep my features neutral.

"I don't understand, Miranda. What river could there be in the air of
this room?"

She shook her head again, a gesture of impatience reminding me so
acutely of her mother I felt a sharp pang. "*This* one," she repeated, again
holding her hands above her head and wiggling them slightly. "Not a
water river, a time river."

I was stunned, my mind stumbling to a halt and my spirit instantly
alarmed by a dark dread which seemed to have closed upon me like the
jaws of a hunter's hidden trap. I knew in some strange fashion everything was now about to change: my life, my hold on my child, all that
made up my existence and hers. Sweat broke out upon my neck and
brow as my heart faltered but I forced my voice to calmness. "A what
river?"

"A time river," she repeated, her voice perfectly imitating adult exasperation. "Time," she said emphatically as she lowered her hands and
gave me a wide-eyed stare as though daring me to not understand. I
would have laughed had I not had a clear sense of something terribly
wrong, some impending revelation about to change everything between

us and everything in her world and mine. And suddenly I understood what that was and my bowels turned to gripping ice for I knew now her words meant she saw the future. She too had the Gift, some insistent enveloping variant of it more potent than mine and one which I might or might not understand. I suddenly felt more alone than I could ever remember.

"A time river, child?" I said with feigned calmness, and as I spoke the look in her eyes told me I was not fooling her. "Tell me," I continued helplessly, "what is that? I've never heard of such."

"You know," she said with a hint of petulance. "Time." She drew the word out as though it were fully explanatory in and of itself. "Yesterday, today, tomorrow. Lots of tomorrows."

"Yes, but a time river? I don't understand." Though in truth I believe by this point I did.

She sighed. "A time river! It's time that flows faster than today."

"Faster than today?"

Miranda leapt to her feet, her fists clenched. "Stop copying me! Listen. Faster than today. Today is here, and I see it. Yesterday is gone but I can still see it." She paused to stare at me expectantly, a teacher wanting to make sure the slow learner comprehends before moving on to the more difficult lesson.

"Yes," I said nodding, "of course. We all in our minds see today and remember yesterday. But what of tomorrow? The time river?"

"The river is faster than today. So I can see tomorrow. Before it gets here. Sometimes lots of tomorrows." Here she paused, her eyes narrowing as though in effort to penetrate some obscurity. "Though it's hard to always see them just right. But I can sometimes because the river's faster than today." She paused again, her vivid blue eyes open now and looking directly at me but I did not recognize the child behind those eyes and I felt disoriented, as though the room around me had somehow changed and I did not know where I was. "Or at least I can see them," she continued. "I think lots can't. That's why I asked. Can you feel the time river too, father?"

I have been in numberless councils with many men – commoner, gentry, noble, royal – but never have I been so stunned to speechlessness as I was before my own child this night. I could hear the low crisp sounds of the fire and somewhere nearby in the castle a voice called out briefly yet I still felt as though all the vast Created World had suddenly gone silent, that the frost-bound winter's night had swallowed all sound and was waiting now for my answer to fill the terrible expectant void.

I spoke slowly, weighing my words. "To see tomorrow is a very rare gift, child. Very few have ever felt the flow of time's river as you say." I paused, uncertain. I did not want her to feel alone but she was too young to tell her of my Gift. How could I explain such matters to a child? Impossible. Yet, I reminded myself, she had just asked, had herself already sensed there was something of great if indeterminate consequence setting her apart from others. This was why, I suddenly realized, she had been so much by herself in recent months, avoiding those who she already knew instinctively would no longer quite understand her.

I was full of doubt yet needed to say something. "Yes, Miranda, it is said some few may be given small glimpses of tomorrow. A special gift from Heaven to help us find our way." I paused, very uncertain now of everything. "So you see tomorrows, then?" My voice was half-choked and barely above a whisper.

She looked into the fire before returning her gaze to me. "Not *all* tomorrows. Just some."

"Can you tell me one? Tell me one you have seen?" I spoke before I realized what I was asking, hoped I had not just made some blind foolish mistake.

She nodded. "I saw one yesterday. When you kissed me in the morning. I saw one day you will tell a story," she said emphatically. "A long one."

I laughed, an inchoate sense of relief upwelling in me. "I tell many stories, Miranda. I am a jester, after all. I entertain with tricks and rhymes and stories."

"No, no," she said with a shake of her head. "A long story. In a book. Like the monks and scholars make."

I smiled at her. "I have no such story to tell, child. I think your time river may be just a river of imagination." My sense of relief grew.

"No!" she shouted with a stamp of her foot, startling me out of my complacency. And before she spoke further I recalled again the mad friar and his coming events. "Tomorrow!" She closed her eyes again, suddenly silent and motionless for another long moment, arms rigid at her sides with tiny fists tightly balled. Then her eyes flew open in terror and she ran to me, nearly knocking me over with the force of her embrace. "They try to kill you, the bad men!" She began to sob. "Don't leave me! Don't let them kill you! Don't!" Tears and wracking sobs made further words impossible. I petted her and strove to soothe her, to tell it was just a dream and reassure her no bad men sought to kill me. She had no knowledge of the attempt on my life years before while in the Baronet's service, and though I knew many regarded me with suspicion and misgiving I had no reason to fear assassination. I feared only for Miranda.

As I held her to me, her small body shuddering with sobs which seemed each to press directly upon my own heart as though they would still its beating, I suddenly saw and felt in my mind the only Gift-given glimpse of her life I would ever have. She was in middle age, taller than I and dressed in a rough garment of a blue so deep it approached to black. She was standing quite still, one hand resting on a low gate of unpainted wood before an overgrown cottage garden with towering firs and witch elms beyond. Though motionless she had a sense of latent gracefulness about her, an elegance of neck and limb fully evident as she seemed to be looking at something, or for something, her chin slightly lifted and brows arched above slightly widened eyes. Her hair was the same dark brown as her mother's, loosely bound and quite long, and her face in maturity bore such a resemblance to that of my dead wife my heart ached anew for her. But it was Miranda's eyes that held me, sharp and uncannily blue as they always were. In those eyes was profound sorrow, an expansive ocean of the heart's deepest pains whose surface I could only glimpse but whose depths of crowding darkness registered heavily on my own faltering heart. The vision vanished in an instant but in its hollow wake left fear and emptiness and my own deep grief, and as I pressed my child closer I could feel the emptiness and fear coalesce as a swirling wind in winter gathers the dead leaves and dust of autumn into a simulacrum of animated existence. Though I could neither name nor clearly grasp the feeling its presence was irrefutable and brought me to dread. A deep touch of cold, as though of the embracing of a marble effigy in midwinter, unyielding and melancholy, crept into my heart and what I thought could never happen suddenly became real: an intimation of distance, the merest shadow but hauntingly and deniably present, slipped deftly and irrefutably between myself and the child I embraced so passionately, a feeling never to depart but only in the months ahead to grow inexorably. I understand not fully how or why but I know this moment as my life's greatest failure. Even the death of wife and son was not a darker time to me than this, for I knew she would soon be lost to me though I could not imagine how.

Miranda herself seemed further abstracted after this night, lost increasingly in the Gift she had been given and afterward saying very little of it to me again. I did not challenge this reticence despite a great longing to learn the nature of her Gift and give what guidance I could, if any. But I feared intuitively the distance between us would only grow if I sought to bridge that gap, a goal I would find receding precisely because I struggled toward it. The few half-hearted attempts I did make to tease out more knowledge of her Gift proved me correct and I soon ceased all such effort.

A mere three days after I learned of Miranda's possession of the Gift I had my proof her Gift was true, for on that third day another attempt was made on my life.

There had been for some weeks gossip among the servants, acquired from visiting tradesmen and merchants, of another pestilence in the kingdom. Though there had been no sign of such in the city rumor began to grow, as rumor does, for it had been not yet two years since the outbreak which killed many thousands, including my wife and son, and the pain of that suffering remained fresh in the hearts of many.

Three days after my vision of Miranda's future I ventured into the city to learn what I might, to gauge the level of fear among those whom I still and always regarded as my own people, those of the common ranks who shared my birthright. For some reason I chose not to trouble with disguise as I customarily did, relying, on this chill and sunless winter's day, only on a hooded cloak for some small measure of concealment.

I had wandered for several hours, stopping in various common shops and stalls to purchase small favors for Miranda (and for a laundry maid to whom I had taken a fancy, having had no intimacy with woman since my wife's death) and holding discourse with shopkeepers and those who gave them custom. I learned little beyond the fact many were afraid and every common ailment was now being taken as evidence of plague.

Having walked further into the city than I intended it was growing toward dusk when I finally approached the gate of the royal park where my horse awaited me at the gatekeeper's lodge. I was hungry and weary and the prospect of a cold gallop across the park in such a state lowered my spirits. Some small refreshment to fortify body and spirit was called for so I stepped into the last public house before the gate, the Hart and Lurcher.

This was my error. I had never set foot in the establishment before precisely because of its proximity to the castle. It was rumored to be a favorite of those who came to poach rabbit in the royal park but was most frequented, I knew, by the many tradesmen and merchants whose business brought them to the castle, and I feared I might be recognized. But this evening my hunger and unsettled state of mind – for I remained haunted by the recent discovery of Miranda's Gift – led to a foolish mistake.

And nearly my death.

I opened the door to the Hart and Lurcher to be enveloped in a warmth immediately comforting. I had become more chilled than I realized and the blazing fire and press of bodies in the low-ceilinged room created a heat that was a palpable embrace. Carelessly, I immediately removed my cloak but before I could take a single step a booming "What ho!" cut through the general din and I saw a tall sturdy tradesman rise with a slight unsteadiness to his feet, tankard in hand.

"Gentlemen," he cried, holding up his free hand for silence as he surveyed the room. "Aye, and the rest of you!" He paused to allow the laughter to subside. "It is our honor, friends, to have in our company a most excellent and honored fellow. A man possessed of more wit," and he paused to survey the room again before continuing after a rumbling belch, "than all of you put together." More laughter. "By God's wounds," he continued, his voice growing louder, "it is the King's own jester!" He raised his tankard in salute before draining it.

I had recognized the tradesman by this time, the journeyman carpenter who had been much at the castle lately and who had befriended Miranda as his special pet, carving her several simple toys. Although I regretted being recognized I acknowledged the greeting and the sounds of approbation which followed. But I also saw suspicion in some faces and fear in several more and watched a handful of men rise and with dark looks in my direction leave the tavern. Someone pressed a tankard into my hand as I watched yet another man, his eyes hard with menace, rise and cross himself before his hasty exit.

Such divergence of response to my presence was familiar to me, as I have written, for I met it constantly among the staff of the royal households: those who believed my Gift (wildly exaggerated in the rumors and tales) was from the Devil and with which I had bewitched the King, and those who knew me as an honest God-fearing man in loyal service to a proper monarch. I regretted always that many feared or reviled me out of base superstition but I had come in large measure to accept this because there was no remedy. If all the good I had done thus far – much of which, I grant, was not evident to those beyond the King's inner circle – could not convince those who doubted, their minds would not be persuaded otherwise now. I once also feared suspicions surrounding me might redound to the discredit of the King and that such sentiment could be used against him by some potential usurper, but the King was generally beloved and the kingdom of sufficient stability now that this fear of mine seemed increasingly ungrounded, and so it had long ceased to trouble me.

I was brought back from my reverie by a hand slapping my back and calls for some manner of amusement. I wished only to leave but did not care to be rude, especially to the carpenter who had been so kind to Miranda. So I nodded my assent and took a long draught of ale so I might have time to gather my wits.

Stepping onto a nearby bench I held up a hand and waited for the crowd to quiet. Most of the faces were friendly though several still showed some measure of distrust and I knew it would not do to provoke or linger. A rhyme, I thought. A moment, and one came to me.

"Bold friends of the Hart and Lurcher," I cried, "for bold you must be to drink the ale of an inn named for the poacher's dog here at the very gate of a royal domain." Cheers and laughter greeted my remark. "A song, then, for this establishment of renown and for its noble host!"

I began to stomp and clap a rhythm and soon several of the men joined in.

Sing ho! for the Hart and Lurcher,
Standing proud at the high street's end;
The fat old lord will have his greyhound.
I will take the poacher's friend!

I will live in a simple manner,
I will love my lurcher true;
If the fat old lord miss his rabbits,
He may find them in my stew!

Sing ho! for the Hart and Lurcher,
The finest ale at the high street's end;
Fat old lords may choke on mutton,
I will take the poacher's friend!

A simple rhyme sung in a passable voice but more than sufficient for the purpose, for applause and rough cheers greeted my bow and I quickly stepped from the bench to make my exit. All thought of food was forgotten in my desire to return to the castle before full darkness – or trouble.

I donned my cloak but before I could escape a hand on my arm detained me and I turned to confront the carpenter who had greeted me, his conviviality now dimmed behind a mask of worry.

"What do they say at the castle, Jester, of this new plague? What is known? I lost two children in the last – ." He could not go on.

I put a reassuring hand on his shoulder. "Rumor runs far ahead of truth always, friend, and even more so now. I lost wife and child – " here I too had to pause " – and would lose no more, yet here I remain as do King and Queen. The royal physicians say 'tis no plague so let fear do no more." With that I stepped into the street and huddled my cloak about me as the chill wind and deepening gloom rapidly dispelled the warmth of the Hart and Lurcher, sweeping it away like a fire's last embers fading to extinction in the frosty air of a mid-winter's night.

The park gate was only a furlong away and I had just rung the bell to summon the gatekeeper when I heard hurrying steps on the road behind me. I felt the danger even before I turned to see the man rush upon me in the gloom. On the instant I recognized him as the last who had left the pub upon my entrance. I sought to jump aside but his right arm blocked my movement as his left jabbed toward me. I felt a sudden searing pain in my side that made me gasp.

"Back to the Devil and his Hell," he hissed. "You shall bring no more plague upon us to kill those whom we love." He drew back his arm for another knifestroke but before he could deliver it his body gave a quick jerk and an odd sharp sigh escaped from him as his eyes suddenly grew wide. For a moment he was motionless except for a clenching of his jaw and mouth then sank silently and slowly to his knees before toppling over. I suddenly realized running footsteps were approaching: several men from the pub, including the carpenter. I glanced down at my attacker and could see even in the fading light the handle of a knife protruding from his back, its stark blocky rigidity at striking odds with his hunched and rounded form. As I stared, my hand pressed to my bleeding side, the carpenter took me by the shoulders as another man, small and dark, knelt beside my attacker and jerked out the knife, wiping the blade clean on the dead man's tunic. Rising, the small man sheathed his knife and gave me a wink. "Poachers love a good song, Jester," he said with a savage grin. Despite the burning pain in my side I felt a terrible chill.

The gatekeeper arrived in time to help the men from the tavern transport me to the nearest apothecary, who treated my wound enough to allow me to ride to the castle. With the further ministrations of the

King's physicians I recovered without incident, all the while thanking God the injury had not been more severe.

Miranda was joyed at my safe return yet seemed unperturbed to have predicted this event. She is accustomed to the Gift already, I thought. Several days passed before I worked up the courage to say to her that her "time river" had been correct, in consequence of which she merely looked at me as though I were a poor learner belatedly grasping the simplest of lessons. At that moment I knew she would spend her life much further in the Gift than I could ever understand. Though I do not know why, I felt a great sorrow surround that realization as clouds might gather around a lonely peak and tears came to my eyes again for the daughter I loved so deeply and whom I knew was already growing distant in a way none, not even myself, could properly understand. We were father and child together; both had known the early loss of mothers, the loss of a shared love, and we also shared a Gift which separated us, as best we knew, from all others. Yet by the very thing that should have bound us in fiercest love and inextricable closeness we were separated from each other. Her Gift would be my greatest loss while my insistent love for the Queen would be my greatest failure, and Miranda its foremost victim.

I had never before been much given to troubling dreams but soon after my learning of Miranda's Gift I found my sleep increasingly haunted by recurring nightmares of helplessness. In one frequent visitation I found myself waist-deep in a rushing river, struggling against the current to reach Miranda, whom I could not see but knew to be in some terrible danger. The press of the water made movement impossible and as I struggled even to lift a foot the unknown danger to my daughter grew greater and more ominous. I tried to shout, to call a warning to her but no words could I force from my mouth. In another dream I clung fiercely to Miranda with a father's urgent embrace of love but suddenly she was no longer in my arms but standing free some distance from me and was no longer Miranda but my wife and the Queen at the same time and I would wake from this dream with a pounding heart to lie awake in misery and confusion for hours. There were others too, diverse others, and all were a torment to me. I began to dread sleep and would force myself to remain awake long into the empty night so that, exhausted, I might find sleep without dreaming, a relief I was sometimes granted. I wandered the castle at the latest hours, never my habit before, and found the silent hallways and empty chambers in their hollow blackness to be fit emblems for the state of my heart. Even in the bitterness of winter I would pace the ramparts, avoiding the few guards as best I could for I knew from servants' gossip they were troubled by my late wanderings, for many were superstitious men inclined to harken to the most exaggerated rumors of my Gift. On those nights I would find in the cold sharp stars hanging above a dark and silent earth an apt metaphor for the incomplete loves of my life, remote and unreachable across a void blankly indifferent to my longing. And in my weakness I was ashamed.

I sought from my master permission to enter the Astrologer's Tower but was denied, for it was the special province of the King, who as I have mentioned oft found sleep elusive and would retire there in midnight contemplation.

I was in manifold ways bereft and found myself miserable and in as dark a humour as ever I had known. My wife I had in some way loved, my child I held deeply in my heart, and to my Queen I was devoted with a passion which equaled my love's hopelessness. All were lost to me now.

Efforts on my part to stem the growing tide of distance between Miranda and myself continued to prove fruitless. She was as mildly pleasant a child as ever when she could be engaged but those moments grew ever rarer. Her play was almost always solitary and her lessons – she was well ahead of other children in her mastery of letters – continued but while she learned swiftly she took no apparent joy in the process. She grew more passive in her relations to others, adult and child, speaking well enough when spoken to but otherwise so remote and solitary some began, I knew, to suspect her mind was touched.

I soon found I could barely reach her. Lost in her Gift, she would study intently the faces of everyone who passed within her ken, or would sit silently yet fully absorbed when conversation flowed around her, or would stare blankly at some object in her hands or into the vague distance with unnerving preternatural calm. My efforts to find beneath her stillness the child full of life and vivacity my wife and I had once loved were now futile, painfully so, and I began to lose all hope I would ever greet that child of love and joy again.

As Miranda drifted slowly but inexorably from me, I powerless to stop that drift and she seemingly unaware of it, the full force of my hopeless love returned and brought with it its full freight of misery renewed. The Queen began to occupy my thoughts almost incessantly and the sight of Miranda and the wan half-smile that was now her customary greeting became a haunting reminder of my incapacity. Could I have taken the Gift from her and thus won back my child and some measure of my heart's ease I would have done so, but such could never be, and the only solace I could find was in drink.

Miranda was victim in this as well, for there was little time when I was calm enough in my mind to be comfortable in her presence. I was often distraught, the growing distance between us intertwining itself in ways incomprehensible to me with my feelings for the Queen and leaving my mind and heart to feel as though caught in a dark descending whirlpool of despond. When not drinking I slept, and when not sleeping I drank. For weeks, for months. For many months. Miranda seemed barely to notice my distance, a fact which only increased that distance and my despair, a foul black creature of my heart which grew the more readily the more I fought to subdue it, unceasingly. I began to grow alien to myself as well as to my child.

I also grew, for the first and only time in my life, almost constantly angry, an emotion in me which, as I have told, was usually dispelled by drink. But now anger and agitation became my constant companions. I began not to recognize myself. I had railed against God many times before for having so formed me that I would hopelessly love one whom I could never possess, but anger had grown to become a seething rage for now Queen, wife, son, and daughter were all lost to me. All four losses I did not feel I could bear, especially the cruel loss of Miranda to a Gift I too possessed, a loss I felt most acutely when in her very presence. The injustice and unfairness of this pain struck me as the deliberate spite of God, a terrible haunting punishment for no sin of mine.

Or *was* I guilty of sin? I loved the Queen, thus I coveted another man's wife. Yes, I was guilty of that. But to have *all* I loved taken from me? No, it could not be borne, could not be justice either here on Earth or in Heaven. I have known those who committed adultery and lived their worldly lives in happiness; why should I be punished so grievously for a sin transpiring only in my heart? I took my anger and my grief to the King's chaplain though of course I could say nothing to him of the Queen, and in his kindness and friendship for me he sought to ease my burden. But his recounting of the story of Job and his assurance that suffering precedes mercy were no balm to my tortured spirit. I began to avoid him, and have since had nothing to do with churches or their ministers. In my misery God had become my antagonist and I suffered too deeply and too acutely to forgive him.

I found sleep ever more elusive and my nocturnal wanderings in the castle became regular. I would often walk without intention or purpose but many times found myself passing the door to the Astrologer's

Tower, its iron-barred oak a somber cypher of mystery for it was by now the only door in the castle I had not either passed through or peered beyond. I was perhaps for that very reason drawn to the spot, and I wondered as well if some trace of magian wisdom lingered there atop the tower where the carved stone parapets gave way to the cold empyrean of stars. But the tower door was opened only by the King, possessor of the only key which he was known to keep always on his person, and only he passed through.

Long past midnight on a night when I was only slightly the worse for drink I passed that door to find it flanked by two of His Majesty's guards, the usual practice when the King was in the Tower. They greeted me quietly and I was about to pass on when the door swung slowly inward and the King emerged.

"Ah, Jester, you too find no rest tonight," he said softly in Latin. He locked the door carefully, pocketing the large iron key with deliberation before turning to me with a tired smile. "We two find ourselves awake in the cold and dark, wandering spirits of the midnight world, eh? Come, walk with me a moment." He motioned the guards ahead to light our way.

We walked for a time before he spoke. "Your spirits give you great trouble of late, Jester. Even old eyes like mine can see as much." I gave him a quick glance, for he and the Queen were but a scant few years older than myself; he deprecates himself in jest to ease the pain of what he would say, I thought. "Others too: the Queen, the Chamberlain, the Exchequer, my Equerry, even the Lord High Constable have mentioned to me your evident sorrow and loss of spirits. We know of your wife and son, of course, and now there is some word that your daughter – "

In his pause I spoke quickly for I would not hear it from his lips. "Is touched, yes, lost in her mind in some unaccountable fashion." I could not bring myself to speak of her possession of a Gift akin to mine and how like an ocean breaching a dike it was flowing to separate her from me, from the world. Let them think her touched. It is a simple explanation and close enough to the truth.

The King nodded. "It is a great trouble, Jester, I am sure, and your sorrow is shared. Do know that many miss their jester and I – " here he paused and placed a hand on my shoulder – "I miss a counsellor and a friend, for you have not been yourself of late days. Perhaps a respite, or a pilgrimage, would restore your humours to balance."

I winced inwardly at the word "pilgrimage" but held silence as we paced slowly along the silent stone hallway, our footsteps echoing briefly in the soft stillness of the dark.

"A respite might be good, yes," I said at length. "A short journey, perhaps. I don't know."

"Choose any of our residences if you wish, Jester, and visit there until your spirits are restored. Perhaps by the sea. . . ."

"Thanks to your Majesty for his generosity, but I feel a journey simply for the sake of journeying might be best." In truth the idea of a sojourn in one of the royal residences offered little promise of relief. To move, to be in motion, to leave behind, if such were possible, the demons which seemed to follow always at my very heels seemed the only chance of escape from my present persistent misery.

"Yes," I said, warming to the thought, "I think to travel would suit me best, some wandering to clear my mind and refresh my spirit." Though in my heart I doubted such could ever be accomplished.

The King nodded. "As you deem best, Jester. Know you have full freedom and our best love. And rest your mind as regards your daughter – she will be well loved and well cared for by us."

At that moment and for the first time the thought struck me and to this day I do not know why: Miranda should be sent to my dead wife's parents for a time. Perhaps to be among new and welcoming faces, yet still in the care of those who loved her, would draw her back to the world somewhat, and I could wander for a brief time with freedom of heart and perhaps recover something of myself.

I thanked the King as we went our separate ways and the next day set about to implement my plan. A messenger was sent to Miranda's grandparents, many leagues distant in the eastern part of the kingdom, and he at length returned with word they had agreed to take Miranda, no doubt my generous offer of funds to offset the trouble of her care encouraging their agreeableness. The King had offered transport for Miranda so on the appointed day I walked her to the courtyard and the waiting wagon. She had said little of her departure though I had spoken of it to her often for several weeks now, she seeming to accept it in the same spirit of equanimity and quiet indifference with which she accepted everything in recent months. Tears and remonstrance I had expected, but her quiet compliance disturbed me much more than I let on.

By the side of the wagon I held her fiercely to me. "You have all of my love, Miranda," I whispered as I kissed her. "Be a good child and we shall be together again soon, I promise."

She leaned back to look me in the face and the expression in her eyes haunts me to this very day. Always a brilliant blue of jewel-like clarity, her eyes then were as though carved of ice with a hard glittering quality

I first mistook for the onset of tears. But the only tears were mine. Her eyes seemed to me as the eyes of one who has responded to some great pain by sealing it away so deeply its presence is no longer felt, as a corpse in a forgotten tomb. You are too young to have such a look in your eyes, I thought, and too young to know that such a burial as you think you have effected is impossible. But I could find no words for Miranda and embraced her again in silence and helpless despair.

She clung to me lightly for a moment then spoke softly, little more than a whisper, her lips pressed almost to my ear.

"You won't be able to send for me, you know. You won't see me again."

I started in surprise and guilt-driven anger, grasping her shoulders and holding her at arm's length so I could study her face. "Why do you say so, Miranda? That's foolishness. Of course I will send for you, as soon as I return from my journey. We will see each other again soon, in just a few months. Oh, don't think such thoughts, child!" I pulled her to me again and stroked her hair. "Parting is a sorrow, yes, but it is only for a time. You shall see. You shall be back at the castle before you know."

I could feel her shake her head but she said nothing.

"All is loaded, Jester," I heard the wagon driver say from behind me. "Ready."

I rose and lifted Miranda to her seat in the back of the covered wain. With a dutiful air she leaned out and presented her face to me to be kissed and I did so with as heavy a heart as I have ever known. What did she mean by saying I would never see her again? Is that her Gift or her child's uncertain heart speaking? I told myself it was only the latter, a peevish melancholy of the moment, but my own heart misgave me and I felt a dry hollowness within, a chill evacuation of spirits leaving me to wonder why it seemed I could be shown no mercy, never find solace for a grieving heart that of late years seemed always to be struggling vainly against an implacable force bent on draining it dry.

Miranda was to be proven correct, as she had been in her vision of my attempted murder, as I think in my deepest heart I even then knew. But I had not the strength to visit that place within me and confront what I found there, to stare into the grim inevitability of yet more sorrow. So I looked away, convincing myself it was only her child's anxious heart which spoke on our parting day.

Thereafter I undertook my wandering, thinking I was healing myself though I was, unwittingly, only increasing my own sorrow. Declining the King's offer of a horse I set out on foot, a commoner among commoners, as I was born and should have remained, I thought, dressed in commoner's weeds. For two months I travelled, hostels and stables my inns, sometimes in company with merchants or pilgrims but often alone. I wandered in the southern reaches of the kingdom, in weather often pleasant for it was a mild spring but just as I began to think of a return I fell ill. For more than a fortnight I lay in a monastery bed with a recurring fever, dosed with herbals and prayers in equal measure and finding neither to be helpful. Even after the fever passed and I was sent from the monastery, where beds were needed for others ill with the same sickness, it was nigh on three weeks before I had sufficient strength to resume my travels, and even then they were at a slower pace for I had to travel entirely on foot, having been robbed of my remaining coin by whomever had helped me to the monastery. The monks had given me enough for the purchase of food but I could not engage a horse or even send a message to the royal household.

By the time I finally returned almost six months had passed, and while the time away had at first seemed salutary (until I became ill), my weak health and the absence of Miranda now left me vulnerable in heart and upon my first sight of the Queen my feelings for her came upon me in full strength, an almost physical tide of emotion which unsettled me for many days. I felt nearly as helpless again as I had before I set out, as though all my time away had been squandered. I cursed God yet again and wished for a dead heart and oblivion but could find neither but for their faint and fleeting shadows in inebriation.

I could not yet find in myself the strength of heart and will to send for Miranda, a weakness and a failing for which suitable punishments surely await me in Purgatory, where for my life's many sins I will keep the devils long busy I know. But I simply was too frail in spirit, hollow and joyless and adrift. I sent more money to Miranda's grandparents for her care and education. I had sent enough with her upon her departure that this additional sum was unnecessary but it helped to assuage my guilt. I wrote several letters to Miranda, simple enough for her to read as her grandparents were illiterate, assuring her of my love and offering my lingering illness as an excuse for her delayed return. I ended all my letters with a request for her to send some message back but only once did she comply, telling the messenger to thank me for the small gifts I sent and wishing me good health. No word of love, and my heart was yet more deeply riven.

The last messenger reported also that my father-in-law seemed in very poor health, his skin a bilious yellow and complaining of pain in the bowels. This increased my anxiety for he and his wife were indeed quite aged – my wife had been the youngest of their children by many years – and I began now to regret both my initial decision to send Miranda to them and my delay in returning her to the castle. I could hesitate no longer. I sought to reduce my drinking and bethought myself again of leaving the King's service. I had considered this many times before, of course, in my vain attempts to wrestle with my feelings for the Queen, but had never truly believed I had the strength to deny myself her presence despite the pain of heart it caused me. But on this occasion I allowed myself to believe Miranda might prove sufficient to pull me at last from the Queen, that my love and care for my own child, however distant her Gift kept her, would overcome my hopeless and idealized love for a woman forever denied me.

"This I will do," I thought, but I could not leave the castle at present. An important delegation of foreign nobles was arriving in several days and the King had commanded my presence. I told myself it would serve well for Miranda to be back in the castle for a while, among old playmates and acquaintances, so she and I might reacquaint as it were in familiar surroundings, adjust again to each other's company after so many months apart before leaving for a new life of our own. So I arranged for her return, thinking it clever and appropriate for it to mirror her departure. The same wagon, the same waggoner, even the selfsame horses were dispatched to fetch her home. My daughter would return as she left, and in a few months' time we would leave the castle together, father and daughter, bound in love and uncertainty, longing and distance, but together.

But Miranda never returned.

The wagon came back empty three weeks later, detained by poor weather and worse roads, and the waggoner's news could not have been grimmer.

"Gone, Jester. Cottage was empty." The waggoner was a great hand at managing horses and oxen but was otherwise notable for few words and less wit. "Old man died, they said, and the woman took the child to kin in another village."

"Did you not follow?" I was frantic and growing impatient with his slow speech, as plodding as the beasts he spent his life behind.

"Aye. But kin had moved on too. Crops be very poor this year again and work and food hard to get. Half the village empty. The old woman and kin set out but none could tell where." He stopped, his stolid features seeming an embodiment of the placid calm of one of his oxen. Oh, to feel as little as you, I thought. What a boon that would be!

"There was no word left, no message telling where she might have gone?" Impossible to believe, I thought.

"None that any knew of. Apologies, Jester. I tried as best I knew." His blank face and simple shrug told me there would be no further help here.

As soon as I could I went myself in search of Miranda, a search which proved as fruitless as the waggoner's. I learned only, to my bitter anger and tearful sorrow, that Miranda's grandmother had sent word to me at the castle, but for reasons undetermined her message never reached my ears. One villager told me the old woman may have left some word with a neighbor, her closest friend of many years' standing, but the neighbor had been away when the waggoner had come for my daughter and by the time I reached the village she had herself moved on. Many had been displaced by the near-famine conditions of the year and those who remained knew too little to be of any material assistance. I knew not what else to do but with the King's blessing sent several men out to scour the region in search of any news of my daughter or her grandmother, but all came back with nothing.

Miranda was lost to me.

exile

With this realization I slipped into the darkest days of melancholy I ever knew. I could find little solace in sleep or even drink, and none of my customary amusements or diversions provided any comfort. Even the dogs, always a source of pleasure to me, could not lighten my spirits or much distract my mind. I avoided company as best I could, for many still expected wit or japes or tricks but my heart was far too heavy and my mind too dark for aught but despair. Words seemed utterly empty while nonetheless too burdensome to be spoken. Even my Gift failed me. When I looked into the faces of those about me I saw only my own misery mirrored back to me, so I kept my eyes from those faces until I became almost a hermit, seeking solitude during the day and wandering the castle halls at night, a forlorn ghost of myself.

Impetuously I undertook another journey, wandering for weeks, the thought of finding Miranda uppermost in my mind but beneath that thought was a shapeless dark fear I might find her only to learn she did not want me, or that what I found in her I would not have the strength or courage to face. I thought of her with love but those thoughts came always attended by shadow and by the pained recollection of the strange distance, the disquieting gulf, between us and between Miranda and the world which was the consequence of her greater Gift.

During my wandering I had come to change my mind regarding the King's suggestion I make use of one of the royal residences so I might recover some measure of equanimity. Still preferring solitude and quiet I chose the most remote of the royal residences, a small manor house in the northeast reaches of the kingdom, one not visited by King or Queen in years and maintained by only a very small staff. I knew I should be returning to the castle and my service to the King but the thought of again being in the Queen's presence and in the domestic spaces which would remind me even more acutely of Miranda's absence made me postpone day after day any thought of travel. I wandered the barren fields and naked woods – it was the very end of winter now but at that northern estate the season still felt to be in its depth – and I could find no release from the black and melancholy sorrow seemingly rooted in my spirit and bearing it down like a suffocating weight of misery. The manor had a small but well-chosen library yet what little reading I could manage gave me no comfort, the words lying flat and lifeless on the page before me and my mind wandering restlessly from the Queen to Miranda and back a thousand times. I loved what I could not have and I sought what I feared to find. How, I wondered, could my despair be any more acute?

I had taken to wandering through the several nearby hamlets, small and miserable collections of poor cottages along muddy lanes, their sagging roofs and grey stone walls seeming to reflect back to me the emptiness of my own spirits amplified by the quiet despair of those who lived within. Yet to walk was to me something of a liberation, the sense of movement giving me the illusion of progress, a pretense of journeying toward an unknown something which perhaps would provide solace or resolution. I knew that sense was illusory, a chimerical self-deception, but at times I was able to allow myself to believe it to be true.

On one such walk – I would never permit myself to use the word "ramble," for it was the Queen's term – I passed an old woman combing through the seasons' remnants jumbled beneath a hedgerow. She was one I had seen before in the neighboring hamlet, for her considerable height and long thick thatch of gray hair spreading as wide as her shoulders made her most distinctive. We had never spoken but on this cold day of brilliant sun in a cloudless sky she rose when she saw me and stepped into the ice-muddy roadway. Her garments were of the coarsest common cloth and seemed to me inadequate for the weather yet she appeared indifferent to the cold.

She peered at me closely as I approached, her long heavily veined hands clutching an ancient woven basket filled with what seemed forest detritus and the wild meadow's leavings. I could form no idea of her purpose in gathering such at this time of year and thought to inquire when she spoke first, her voice an abrasive rasp but it was her surprising words which stopped me short.

"You will not lose your melancholy here, Jester. The soil will not accept it, the air will refuse it, the streams run dry before they could wash it away."

I recovered myself by the time she paused: servant gossip, of course. There were only a handful at the manor but that would be more than enough. So I was known. As was my sorrow.

"A melancholy jester," she said with a slow shake of her head and a harsh cough of a laugh. "God sends us such for a jest of his own, I suppose."

"I find no jest," I said sharply, "in my private concerns being the fodder of common gossip."

She looked at me intently and I was struck by the fierce unfaded blue of her eyes. I immediately thought of Miranda.

"Some say you have trucked with the Devil, Jester. But I think not. You do not look such a fool as would strike a deal that cost him his daughter. Yes, servants talk and talk spreads, especially in a small backward place as this. And the wind blows from all quarters at one time or another, so little remains private for long." She paused, looking at me slyly. "Besides, what is done can't be undone but solace may yet be found for those who seek it."

"Solace? You know nought of me or my melancholy, grandmother, and it is beyond all reach of your twigs and leaves. Godspeed." I turned from her abruptly and began to walk.

Behind me I heard her cackling laugh again. "We are a dangerous pair, Jester, for some say I am a witch and you league with Satan. In honor of such foolishness may we not walk together? Perhaps you will find me not so ignorant as you suppose."

I turned to give her a dismissive glance, not wishing for the company of a meddlesome gossip but as I turned I also realized I was desperately tired of my solitude and glad almost even for some small diversion. I nodded curtly and waited for her to shuffle along the road beside me, her movements halting and stiff as of who suffers some ailment of the joints.

We walked in slow silence for several minutes, the old woman occasionally muttering to herself soft words to which I paid no attention.

"They say your daughter is lost to you, Jester," she said at length, her voice without emotion, "gone with kin in the famine migrations. And before that wife and newborn to plague. Heavy losses indeed."

"Aye."

"Many others have lost those they love to the same causes."

I gave her a sharp look and she held up her hand abruptly.

"I mean not to diminish your loss, Jester. I know the pain too well for, like all, I know such loss too." She paused, lifting her head slightly and her eyes narrowed as though she peered into some remote distance. "Yes, even I. A husband who went to fight a king's war some forty years ago and never returned, and a child lost three years later to a cause known only to God." She turned her face to me and I could see the recollected sorrow in her features and her eyes. "All know loss. That is why the land here," and she swept her thin arm before her, taking in the quiet winter landscape before us, "has no room for your melancholy. We who live here have filled it well enough and beyond. As is true in all places."

I studied her again and pursed my lips but in truth knew not what to say. Her words were true, certainly, but my loss and my continuing pain seemed somehow beyond the common sorrows to which she referred, far beyond the common run of heartache and loss.

"All sorrows are unique to those who feel them," she said as though reading my thoughts, and she cackled softly again at my look of surprise. "You are not the first to feel such things, Jester, nor will you be the last. It is the way of God's world and those who suffer in it. They say you have uncommon gifts but I think still you are a man, and as a man you feel as others do. We all know love and we all know its loss, the great and common heart-pain of life."

I shook my head. "My situation is different, grandmother. Few live in the court and none of those are such as I."

Again her brittle crackling laugh. "Yes, yes, each is special, all are unique. None has suffered such as each of us suffers." She paused to wipe a thin thread of spittle from her lips with the back of her hand. "Oh, Jester, none is such as any. That is the way of the world, court or hamlet, castle or hovel." She abruptly stopped in the roadway and turned to face me, a strange earnestness suddenly in her eyes.

"Would you have full surcease of your sorrow, Jester? To be done with it all, forever?"

I studied her face, its seriousness. "Aye, grandmother, I would. But self-murder is the greatest sin, and though God seems to – "

"Keep your God-fears, Jester," she said, waving a bony hand, "I mean not self-murder. I mean what I say: your pain and sorrow gone, all loss and grief blown to airy nothingness like fine dust in the wind."

My look narrowed. "Short of death this cannot be, good-dame, unless you are indeed a witch."

"A witch," she said with a sad shake of her head. "It is told you are an uncommonly educated common man, a scholar-jester, so if the tale is true I think you may hold scant belief in witches as the superstitious and the simple do. Even if you grant the existence of such, know I am none. I am only healer and herbalist, providing what small solace I can to those too poor for apothecary or physician."

"How then can you speak of erasing a sorrow deeper than you can know? What you offer cannot be achieved in this world." I began to suspect her mind's soundness and thought of the mad friar in the cathedral years ago.

Her look was suddenly stern. "There are powers in the world unknown even to scholar-jesters," she said with dark earnestness. "I speak not of any witchcraft but of plants, of pale roots reaching into the yielding dark earth, of green herbs drinking of sun and air and rain, of tawny mushrooms drawing life from death in the deep-shaded woods. They say you have the skill to read men's thoughts – "

"Tales grow in the telling."

She smiled. "A clever answer, yes. Well, my skill is not to see into men's minds but with my knowing of the vegetable kingdom I can render those minds empty of all their memory, all their pain."

I looked at her closely but could see neither deception nor mockery in her wrinkled face. Her look was earnest again and utterly calm.

"You speak a riddle, grandmother."

She shook her head, her thick mane of hair brushing audibly against her coarse tunic in the silent stillness of the day.

"The mastery of plants is what I speak of, Jester. Gaining that mastery has been my life's work and with my mastery I offer you now a new life, free of all past sorrows and grief. But the price is high, oh, very high."

That was her game then, to cozen me for gain. "You are a mountebank, good-dame, and would beguile with foolish promises for the mere sake of filthy lucre. Begone!" And I began to stride away in anger.

"You mistake me, Jester," she called. "I ask for no money but offer you relief as a gift and a courtesy." I stopped but did not look back at her. "You and I are not so different, Jester. We both know the edges of the world, no? The small leftover places for those who are not as others, for those whose gifts and graces make them almost as strangers among their own kind. We both wander a narrow and lonely way and in sympathy and fellowship I freely offer you what you seek."

I turned to look at her across the few yards separating us.

"The price I mention is not coin or treasure. The price is yourself. My medicines will take your pain and grief, yes, but they are blunt and the mind is oh so delicate. They will take all your memory but also some, perhaps much more than some, of the rest of your mind. You would awake to blankness, to no recollection of wife or daughter, court or even Jester. You would be in mind as a newborn babe fresh in the world, but not even I can know how much you would be able to relearn, how much regain of that which we all needs know to live in the world and to live among others. A great risk and a high price, yes, but it is all I have to offer."

"Why think you any would consent to such a fool's bargain?"

She looked at me slyly, her eyes suddenly dark. "You have lost much already, Jester. Wife, son, daughter. Solace and peace of mind seem forever gone from you." She nodded. "You have already well begun to lose yourself. Indeed I think you stand upon the edge of the precipice, unable to keep your eyes from the abyss, wondering what sweet release that darkness offers you. All you need is a nudge, Jester. I offer it to you."

I shook my head in disbelief. "You would take me from myself? Madness!"

"Is that not what madness is, a taking of us from ourselves? Some find peace in madness."

"And many do not! What you offer is madness of the worst sort. I would not surrender all I am and have been and even may yet be for the sake of forgetting my burden of pain, as troubling and perpetual as it may be. You ask far too much."

She shrugged and turned away, began to walk slowly on. Without conscious thought of what I was doing I began to follow.

"Your heart and your mind are known fully only to you, Jester, as is their pain," she said when I had caught up to her. "Tally your griefs and sorrows – and I know they are greater than is told; I see it in your eyes and hear it in your voice – and put them in the scale with oblivion on the other side. See which weight is the greater and which the less, then choose as your heart tells you."

"My heart and mind are decided, grandmother. They will remain mine as I know them now."

She nodded, falling silent as we walked at her pace for several minutes. Her offer held no appeal for me but I confess as we walked I attempted to imagine a life without the pain of separation from Miranda or without the ache of hopeless longing for the Queen. So much of my life since entering royal service has been defined by negation, by not having that which I desired, that the prospect of having no experience of such defining absence, of having heart and mind not drawn to impossibilities, seemed indeed to be an offer of such freedom and such peace my spirit for a moment seemed near to acquiescence. But not at such a price.

I looked at the old woman shuffling along beside me, her head bowed and thick hair falling forward to cover her face. What did she know? I wondered. What salvation could she really work?

She paused by a narrow path leading from the rutted lane in which we'd been walking, a path barely more than a trace of sodden earth in the tangled brown undergrowth of late winter.

"Here, Jester," she said as she nodded toward the path. "My cot lies this way."

I looked at her long in silence. She steadily held my gaze and I could see in her eyes her knowing I had a question for her yet.

"Come, Jester," she said softly, "what would you ask?"

"I have made my choice, grandmother," I said again, "but would know: do you really possess the skill to take a man from himself as you said? To empty a troubled mind, gift it with oblivion?"

She waited, still holding my gaze and I longed for my Gift to show me something of her thought but her mind was inscrutable to me. A slight breeze moved a wisp of hair across her wrinkled cheek.

"There are many plants dangerous to mind as well as body, Jester, even to the point of madness for some. But no, I have nothing to take the mind and leave the body quite as I said."

The fleeting look of surprise on my face caused her to smile.

"Think on it as a riddle, Jester, a conundrum you have already solved."

"I do not take your meaning. You told me a falsehood, not a riddle."

She shook her head. "No, Jester. I acquitted myself much better, for I have given you yourself."

"Now you do speak riddles."

"You believed my offer to be true when you turned it down in the name of who you are and who you may yet become. In the name of yourself, do you see? You reject my offer of oblivion because you embrace the man you would still become. And where will you find that new self, Jester? Not here, hiding in some remote manor far from the world. You suffer great griefs, Jester, but you have been fleeing them, drinking too much ale – yes, they talk about that too – and wallowing in a slough of your own pity instead of wading forward." She paused. "Leave, Jester. That is the wise course of action and you are a wise fool. Return to your world, to the court. Men say you provide loyal and valuable service to our King but you do him no good here. Go to your world, Jester. That also is why I say this place cannot accept your melancholy. You cannot master your grief if you do not grapple with it, but you come here in flight from it. You cannot master pain but by walking through it, not away. Return. This you know is right, for you rejected my offer of oblivion." She smiled, her face a mask of fine wrinkles but her eyes glittering. "Like the wise fool you are, Jester. Go back. Get you gone." And with those words she turned from me and moved with her hobbling gait along the narrow track of dirt. I watched her for a long moment before I turned away and began my walk back to the manor.

And to my life at court.

chamberlain

If the King is the axis upon which the world of the court turns it is the Lord Chamberlain who keeps that world in constant steady motion. In his office he is the King's most trusted advisor in all matters of state-craft and polity, and it is he who oversees and orchestrates the deliberations and dispositions of all matters which come before the King. There is no man in the kingdom more powerful than the Chamberlain save the King himself.

For the first decade of my royal service the Lord Chamberlain was, for all purposes and intents, a nemesis to me. He was an old man though not long in office, clean-shaven but with thick white hair worn long so as to be nearly a mane about his face, strangely smooth for one advanced in years. For some reason his appearance sat ill with me, and his haughty, almost regal bearing did nothing to endear him to me. He was scion and patriarch of one of the oldest families in the kingdom – the very family which, several generations gone, had lead the war of succession against the family of our present king, which at the time had held the throne but a few years. The Chamberlain's ancestors and their allies were decisively vanquished, many executed or banished.

Thus it was a considerable shock to the world of the court that the present King my master, upon his ascension to the throne only three years before my arrival, offered the descendant of that same insurrectionist family the office of Lord Chamberlain. Almost as many were then surprised the offer was accepted. I came quickly enough, once in service, to see this not as the naïve miscalculation many gossips held it to be but as a gesture thoroughly consonant with the King's character and vision of that kingdom which was his royal charge and his passionate love. To secure the enduring peace of his realm by binding it irrevocably into a more secure and cohesive whole was his driving purpose, one he sought to effect in every manner possible: the granting (and revocation) of titles and lands, the arranging of marriages, even embracing as it were his family's former foes. A strategy not without considerable risk, of course, but one that for many years did seem successful.

The old Lord Chamberlain was a fiercely proud yet resolutely venal man, so the honor and wealth accruing to him in consequence of his position at court did much to mollify him as regards his family's honor though it did nought to improve his temperament. To all but King and Queen he was acerbic and arrogant, condescending often to the point of cruelty. Courtiers feared him in their hearts, mocked him in private, and groveled obsequiously before him in public. Servants feared him too, but hated him more and avoided him as best they could. In my privileged position as jester I took it upon myself to be an annoyance and a trouble to him as oft as I might. I had so quickly gained the King's trust and confidence the Lord Chamberlain could do me no harm, a fact which I knew frustrated and infuriated him in his heart. Had he been king my head would long ago have been separated from my shoulders. Indeed, in retrospect I find myself somewhat surprised he made no attempt to have me murdered. As it was, he suffered my jibes and mockery and couched derision in silence and no doubt dreamed, however impotently, of revenge. He well recognized my value to the King and could not gainsay the value of my insights and advice which were, by virtue of my Gift, rarely in error. He could not have me dismissed nor even ordered from the room if the King were present. So he was left with treating me with as much contempt as he might, particularly in the King's absence. I was to him a walking affront to his pride and sense of station, a common Fool whose Latin and learning were superior to his and whose insights into men and their purposes were surpassed by none. I took great delight in tormenting him, in proper jester-fashion, at every opportunity. The King often sought to soften me toward the Chamberlain but met with little success, so strong was my loathing for the man.

In the spring of my tenth year of service, after my mind and heart had at length begun to regain some of their wonted tenor following the loss of Miranda, I found my prayers concerning the Lord Chamberlain answered. I had wished, simply and devoutly and for years, that the Lord Chamberlain be gone from the court and my life, and finally the event came to pass.

I received the good news of my delivery – every servant's delivery – from the Lord Chamberlain's reviled presence directly from the King himself and as fresh as a turnip just plucked from the yielding earth. I was making haste through the castle in answer to a summons from the Queen, who wished me to attend her as her current favorite dog, a beautiful bitch elegant in form and tireless in the field, whelped her first litter. Rounding a corner I came abruptly upon the King and Lord Chamberlain emerging from a room of state, their look and manner clearly that of men emerging from close and weighty discussion.

I would not long delay lest I miss the whelp but I could pass no opportunity to jest with my master if by so doing I might be to the Chamberlain as a noxious stinging gadfly.

"Do you now seek Leviathan or Kraken, you former fishers of men?" I asked brightly as I stopped directly before them, my eyes wide in mock wonder as I glanced from face to face. The King was surprised for only a fleeting instant, more I think by my abrupt appearance for he was well accustomed to my jester-fashion of speech. He suppressed the beginning of a smile as he glanced at his Chamberlain, whose annoyance was already evident in his curled lip and condescending glare. I smiled inwardly.

"Leviathan or Kraken, good sirs? Which? Come, I would know."

The Chamberlain's mouth was set in the sour look of contempt I knew so well and it was clear to me he would not speak.

"Why bethink you of the ocean's monsters now, Jester?" the King said after a moment. "We are no fishermen and are far from the sea." His tone was kindly. 'Thank you, Majesty,' I thought. 'You and I shall play this game if the Chamberlain do not.'

"Oh, but sirs, I do seem to see a great woven net strung between you twain, binding you one to the other in your labors," I said, spreading my arms dramatically. "A prodigious great net such as would sieve the ocean's watery reaches and ensnare only the greatest of creatures, the fearsome monsters of the darkest deeps." The Chamberlain's eyes were icy and hard, which gratified me much.

"I take no meaning from this, sirrah," the King said calmly. "There is no net."

I struck myself on the forehead in mock dismay. "Pardon me, my masters. My wit's diseased today. I see something where there is nothing and nothing where there is something. Yet all honest fools know nothing can come from nothing so wherefore do I see something where there is nothing? I cannot say, 'tis a puzzle beyond my weak head." I looked at the Chamberlain directly, met his sour gaze and smiled. "Why, this very gentleman here will vouchsafe the truth of my maxim. For if I do not see nothing before me I see one who knows the truth of a foolish wisdom, having proven it so oft himself. Is this not so, sir?" The Chamberlain's face darkened as his choler began to rise. "Faith, la," I said lightly, "here's one will not speak for fear of the old proverb that –"

"Jester," the King interrupted mildly as he held up an open hand. "It may be our Lord Chamberlain is not in spirits for your jibes at present. We are just come from treating of a matter of great moment, news of which we would even now have spread to the general court." He smiled. "And if you would spread this news, good sirrah, look you your speech is of such fashion it be not misunderstood."

I bowed with mock gravity, then straightened abruptly and snapped my fingers in the Chamberlain's face. "Your news, sir, pray, quickly, before the pains of a lady bring forth beasts."

"Jester," the King said, a measure of firmness in his voice now, "take with you on your way the news my Lord Chamberlain, wishing to spend his remaining days in peace and quiet reflection, surrenders, to our great regret, his position at our court. To which I upon the time and with fullest confidence do appoint his son."

My broad instant smile was genuine. I took a step back from the Chamberlain and made him a great sweeping courtier's bow, cap in hand. "Then fare thee well, my good Lord Chamberpot, and take with you all these thanks I do here give you." I held out an empty palm. "I shall lament your absence, my lord, quite gladsomely."

"Jester," the King said slowly, "the Lord Chamberlain has served us loyally and well these many years. Pray leave off your japes."

"I do protest, my lord, most protestingly. You understand me not. I shall truly and indeed miss this worthy good scowling sir, grim eyes and furrowed brow and all, for he has been to me as is the meat upon which a starving man, finding another's meal ready to hand and its owner absent, may feed himself with no effort and much satisfaction. I shall miss this good Lord Chambermaid as a cow would miss the grain it finds left in a fallow field, as a dog those scraps which fall from the table, as a fly . . . his pile of reeking shit. Good day good sirs I must haste!" And with that I scampered off to kennel and Queen.

With due ceremony the old Lord Chamberlain's tenancy of office was ended – 'good riddance old crow' was my chief thought amidst the pageantry and ceremony but I held my tongue and wit in check out of deference to my master – and his son was thereupon granted title and duties of Lord Chamberlain. Although I never in my heart felt much at ease with the King's decision to continue his embrace of the progeny of those now-mouldering insurrectionists, I never made mention of my doubts either in earnest or in jest. Reflecting upon this now as in my old age I pen this accounting of my days I cannot say why I did not speak. Perhaps because my master's mind seemed on this matter so thoroughly set I knew I could neither reason nor rail him out of his determination. What I can say with certainty now is how deeply I regret not making the attempt, given all that followed.

The new Lord Chancellor, only a handful of years older than the King, was much unlike his father in both manner and form. Indeed, so different did they seem it was a common servant's jest to conjecture the old Lord Chancellor had been well-cuckolded. The father was tall, lean, and acerbic, while the son was some deal choleric and in body as much like a bear as a man may be. The father was sly and subtle, spare of word and always cloaking thought and intention behind calculated reticence and reserve. The son was direct to bluntness in his manner and fearlessly forthright. If the father had sought to kill a man it would be with stealth, a stabbing from behind in the black-shadowed night. The son would charge a man in the bright golden daylight, bellowing and with mace in hand.

Yet I soon realized his outward manner concealed great subtleness and cunning. He was a man of relentless energy whose love of statecraft and its intrigues was well matched by his grasp of their intricacies. I came to see him, in the execution of his office, as the leader of a troupe of skilled players, one who understands not only the role each man plays but grasps as well the shape and essence of the play they perform and precisely how each must contribute to make the work a pleasing whole. His management of a chamberlain's duties was from the start masterful, as though he were born to the work, and I was struck at how a man of such gruff physicality could be possessed also of a mind so capable of sharp insight and nuanced cunning.

He even used his physicality effectively in office. He was rather fierce in form and countenance, with a large head atop a stout solid body, his full black beard a monstrous affair helping give him a bear-like mien he used to great advantage. I have sometimes seen him, in dispute with some envoy or another, approach his adversary with a slow lumbering gait, bearing down upon his antagonist like a beast closing for the kill, his eyes hard and glinting like polished swordsteel, shoulders hunched slightly forward, coming to a stop only inches from his opponent's face while roaring his displeasure with a vehemence that unsettled all but the most heartstrong men. This blustering, I soon came to see, served for him the same purpose my japes and witticisms and provocations served for me, drawing forth from men reactions which unwittingly revealed something of those men's true nature, something of what they would conceal in their hearts and minds. And later, in privy council with the King, the Chamberlain would laugh boisterously about his intimidations, deriving great pleasure and amusement from his power to cow others and win his way.

I had not known the new Chamberlain well prior to his assumption of office, though I soon had ample opportunity to study him, as we were regularly together in the King's company, the two of us his most trusted advisors. The Chamberlain's greatest skill was somewhat akin to the first aspect of my Gift, though in lesser degree, for we both were astute readers of men. Our insights into the men who appeared before the King were rarely at odds and we were impossible to entirely deceive.

Yet neither of us could refrain from turning his skill upon the other. The Chamberlain, knowing the stories and rumors concerning me, always comported himself with great wariness, as though he were unsure how much I might know of him and his heart and how my insights might be used. This wariness indeed became for me a caution regarding the Chamberlain, for if he knew anything certain about me it was that our mutual master had my full love and loyalty. Did his wariness then grow out of his desire to keep from me matters he feared I would reveal to the King? I came to believe this was true, to believe all the Chamberlain did and said was shaped by considerations never fully disclosed. The hint of careful calculated secrecy about the man became a lingering shadow in the corner of my mind, a shadow never quite in focus and the more troubling for that.

On account of these doubts and calculations the Chamberlain and I found ourselves wary and reluctant allies, serving the same monarch but from very different stations and for very different motives. For all of our mutual suspicion, however, we nonetheless proved quite effective in our working together.

Although our skills were similar, in matters of practice they also proved quite complementary. His blustering and my japes and mockery combined to unnerve many a man in audience or parlay with the King, much to the benefit of our mutual master and the business and state of the kingdom. I do confess I even came to enjoy the Chamberlain's "performances," as I soon thought of them. He had a theatrical bent he exploited to considerable advantage and with which I came to work in sympathy, for in his behaviors he abetted and furthered both my reputation and our joint usefulness to our sovereign. I could neither love nor trust him yet together we served the King more fully than either man could have done alone.

Of particular delight to us both were those instances when the second aspect of my Gift manifested itself and I caught a word from the mind of minister or envoy or supplicant before the King and quickly whispered it to him before he spoke the word himself. If a man's reaction betrayed the slightest hint of confusion the Chamberlain would be upon him in an instant, pressing the attack, bearing down upon him physically like a bear upon a wounded fawn and, moving in close, issue in sharp whisper a warning disguised as platitude: "God's ways are a mystery to men, are they not? Passing strange it is some men's thoughts are as plain to read as a verse on parchment" or some such phrase that would invariably unsettle these men further, at times making them even more susceptible to my Gift. Those whose composure was not visibly ruffled by my uttering the word they were about to speak would receive a subtler treatment: upon seeing me speak to them, the Chamberlain would take a single step closer to the man who had been speaking, his dark eyes under their bushy brows levelled directly at the eyes of the speaker. And the Chamberlain would wait. If I caught another word from the man's mind and spoke again the Chamberlain would take several steps closer, and yet a few more should I speak a third time (though indeed that was quite rare). His closing presence was a palpable thing, unsettling and even ominous. The tack of negotiation or discussion would always shift once this happened and the King and his kingdom were the better for it.

It was not many months after the new Lord Chamberlain took office that the King himself gave me to understand my vague reservations about the Lord Chamberlain had their counterpart in his own and that our shared doubts had compelling basis. From that day forward I began to grow anxious for the peace of the world I had so quickly come to love.

It was often the King's practice, after certain important councils or events of state, to meet with me in private, knowing that even with jester's license I as commoner would necessarily at times have been somewhat guarded in remarks made within the hearing of men of rank, or else so elliptical in speech my meaning would be couched in ambiguities. Though he came to understand my jester-manner quite well, it yet remained that the King preferred to hear my frank and undisguised opinion so he might understand with all certainty the full scope and reach of what I had gleaned.

At one such private meeting the King directed the conversation to the character not of the envoys with whom he had just met but of the Lord Chamberlain. We were in his private chambers and had been speaking the vernacular but the King abruptly switched to Latin when he mentioned the chamberlain, marking this as a matter of great delicacy. We had never spoken directly of the Chamberlain to each other as yet but I knew I must now speak full freely. Reticence in a matter of this importance would be as a barrier between us, a hindrance to our mutual trust and this I would not abide. I would find no better master in this world and I would keep from him for my own purposes nothing but the secret of my impossible unsanctioned love for his Queen.

"He is a clever good reader of men and their purposes, Majesty," I said frankly, "and his grasp of matters of state is second only to your own. He does you great service with his counsel and management so I am glad you keep him close."

The King looked at me with a half-smile upon his lips and grave seriousness in his eyes. "Who should we keep closest, Jester — our friends or our enemies?"

This surprised me, for I had not yet thought the Lord Chamberlain, however limited or conditional his friendship might be rendered by his deeper purposes, could be considered as enemy. At the same time I realized the King was testing me, seeking to know not only what I believed but what I was willing to reveal. I did not hesitate.

"Some enemies, Majesty, will be forever such and forever beyond conversion. Others may as circumstances change become our friends. And there may be some who forever resist final classification."

He laughed lightly. "A courtier's answer, Jester, for it purports to be an answer yet is no answer at all. I see you have learned much at court, and I applaud you. Yet your seeming non-answer hides no thought for it tells me you think of the Chamberlain much as I do — as a man of indeterminate loyalties."

"He serves you well at present."

"Yes," the King said with deliberate slowness, "he does. There can be no denying the acumen of his insights and the value of his advice and management of the state's business which comes before us. But it is as much for what he does not say that I prefer to keep him close."

I simply raised my eyebrows, inviting the King to continue. I knew now his trust of the man was closely circumscribed but hoped to hear precisely why.

"He is a man of both considerable ambition and long memory, Jester, and loves the power which I believe he feels he is owed. A hundred and twenty years may be two lifetimes for a man but for a proud noble family may be but as yesterday. The Lord Chamberlain, like his prideful father before him and so many of his kin, has not forgotten the war of succession which put my great-grandfather on the throne but cost several of the Chamberlain's ancestors and their partisans both their lands and their heads. I begrudge no man his memories or his family honor but my commitment must always be to my family and to the peace of the kingdom it rightfully holds. No man in this realm can claim more power or wealth than what the Lord Chamberlain possesses except myself. I give him this gift to satisfy him and those of his line, just as I had done with his father. A generational obligation, one might consider it, and an obligation I am content to maintain in the interest of my larger purpose. But I am not such a fool as to fail to recognize my largesse may have other consequences." He paused, studying me. Testing me.

I gave a short nod. "Too oft generosity proves but kindling for the fire of ambition."

The King smiled. "Is that then your thought? Have I appeased the Chamberlain's sense of family honor or merely whetted his appetite?"

"A blunt question, Majesty, and I recognize the honor you do me in asking it." I lowered my head, then spoke in the vernacular for the sake of the pun: "Most of those who lay in chambers prefer to lay close to others, so the closeness of a chamber-laying must surely be good."

The King smiled briefly.

"We understand each other, I see." He slipped a ring from one of his fingers and tossed it to me. "For your candor, Jester, and as a token of more to come for your vigilance as this matter unfolds."

I understood that from this moment King and Chamberlain were bound in a subtle dance of mutual benefit and suspicion, and for the remainder of my years in royal service the Chamberlain was to me a subtle and crafty opponent never to be given full trust, a man to be watched as closely as one could watch.

Yet in the end all my vigilance came to nought.

My signal error came some eight or more years after that conversation with the King, an interval during which I could detect no evident change in the Chamberlain's manner or mind, though I grant I was oft distracted during those years by my love for the Queen. It may also well be that in consequence I grew somewhat complacent regarding the danger posed by the Chamberlain's dubious loyalties and family history. My signal mistake, however, was underestimation of the role played by the Viscount, and the Viscount's death, in all of this. What at the time I took to be an unfortunate but necessary turn of events was in fact the beginning of the end of the court and the life I loved.

The Chamberlain had two daughters and but a single son, the last of his children. The latter, having reached the age of majority, became in his own right a high-ranking noble, a Viscount. He had also become, well before this point in his life, an utter brute.

Even the best of us is a fallen creature, our souls stained by sin bequeathed from Adam and darkened almost daily by our own thoughts and deeds, redeemed only by the mercy of God and the sacrifice of his beloved Son. While none of us may be angels, we should look to them and to all the heavenly cohort to strengthen our frail will and more frail flesh as we seek to follow the difficult path of righteousness even though we often stumble.

The Viscount, however, looked only to the devils and it was certain he would one day be pulled down among them. He pursued not righteousness nor common decency but power, corruption, and hedonistic pleasure, and the devils surely urged him on with glee for he was entirely of their party even before he joined them in hell. All men commit sin, and some men actively pursue the commission of sin for the perverse pleasure it gives them, but men such as the Viscount, with their wealth and privilege and freedom from the constraints under which most of us live, magnify the inherited failings of man to grotesque proportion. To the extent they know not shame nor guilt they celebrate moral grotesquerie and urge it ever further, finding in the tortuous arabesques of their sinning ways a soulless path to Hell. Men such as he are devils among us, devils clothed in human flesh and devoid of all possibility of redemption.

A full rehearsal of the stories told about him would be a burden to my spirit, but let it be said what was pleasure to him was often misery or even death to others. I know well the ways of men and how tales grow in the telling, and no doubt many tales of the Viscount's turpitude have grown beyond truth. Yet the maleficent cast of his spirit is beyond doubt.

Though rarely at court the Viscount was a common subject of servant gossip, fresh rumors of his depredations and sins finding their way to the King's household almost monthly. Poaching, robbery, rapine, theft, violence, murder, rape, hints of a clandestine assembling of what was said to be a small army – as the years passed the tales grew steadily more grim. Thus it was I felt no surprise when the King summoned me to private council one day and with his first words asked me, in Latin, for my sense of the Viscount.

"He is as oft among us as a falcon among the swans, good sir," I said lightly, not yet sure of the King's purpose. "I have not seen him since the day you gave him a Viscount's title despite the fact his father had not bestowed upon him a Viscount's character, and that is near two years a-gone. Afore that, he was as seldom in my company as a priest among harlots, which is to say but now and again and gone as quickly."

The King's smile was brief and grim. "What know you concerning his character?"

"Nought but hearsay, gossip, tales having such stench as a good man may nose from a league's distance. And if he go there, search as he may he will find no flowers growing from that offal."

"The gossip is of poaching, robbery, violent acts unwarranted, no?"

"Mere preamble to the main text, my lord."

"And that main text, Jester?"

"It is said he killed a coiner as the man climbed the scaffold to be hanged. Some hold it was for revenge at being cheated by said coiner, others say 'twas but to test the blade of a rare foreign sword. Either way he is a robber indeed, for he kept from your hangman his fee that day." I shook my head. "Yet even this is but prologue still. The main text is written in darker ink and tells a tale not of one man but of many, led by one possessed of a noble's title but a beast's heart." I paused, looked searchingly at the King. "As I read this text I, a mere Fool, find myself confounded by a question which I would put to your Majesty."

"Speak."

"How comes such a man-beast to have such freedom? Surely he should have been caged ere now, put on display for gawkers to marvel at and children to mock and throw stones."

The King nodded slowly. "Theft is a matter for constable and sheriff, not King, and the Viscount's wealth may buy many a man's silence in sundry matters. But when a man usurps the King's law as in the killing of the coiner he comes to my attention, and the attention of my agents, men of stealth and cunning from whom I learn much. I learn of his growing band of companions and their depredations in the far provinces, of their crossing of borders for rapine and murder and, perhaps, purposes darker still – purposes disguised and served by the treasonous falsehood that those borders are breached with my covert blessing. I hear rumors also these incursions are yet themselves deceptions intended to distract from what may be overtures to certain noble families and ranking gentry, both here and abroad, whose allegiances have not always been with my family. At this, Jester, I come to a matter which cannot and will not be brooked."

"How, your Majesty," I said softly, "does a man of little wit and less subtlety initiate and manage intrigues domestic and foreign without guidance from one subtler and more informed? It is difficult of belief the Viscount fully orchestrates his own actions."

"That is the rub, Jester. That is the question. There is evidence enough to hang the Viscount but no evidence yet unequivocally identifying whomsoever spurs him to such action and directs him aright. Yet I can brook no more delay. This must and shall cease anon."

I was surprised. "You would not draw him out? Dally with him longer so you might learn whose hand guides him and to what purpose?"

He shook his head. "The Viscount is summoned to me in three days' time, and with him and his father I shall hold council. If the meeting not effect the immediate change I must have, then change shall be effected by other means."

I thought for a space then removed my jester's cap from my belt and held it toward the King.

"Be this cap or bird, sire?"

He gave me a brief narrow look, his customary expression of exasperation, but his features quickly settled for he knew that with him my jester-ways were never mere folly.

"Of course cap, sirrah."

"How know you this?" I asked lightly. "Both may be seen in the air – " I tossed my cap upward and caught it again " – and both may perch on the hand." With a flourish I dropped my cap upon the floor. "Both may be seen upon the ground. How then may a poor fool tell one from the other?"

"By life and song, sirrah, as cap has neither."

"Indeed, Majesty! Oh, sire, you are as wise as any fool. To know the truth of a bird we look and listen and thereby discover life and joyance. Thus it is with our friends. Though with them we look and listen not with eye and ear alone but with our hearts, and if thereby we descry life and joyance we have found true friendship indeed. If we discover not those then we discover no true friend."

"The Viscount – "

"Oh, I speak of no viscount, master," I said briskly, holding up my hand. "A fool may query a puppet to learn how it is he jigs and ambles but a wise man asks of him whose hand is upon the strings. Your Viscount has been weighed and measured and found wanting, though I see now your too-generous purpose in summoning him is to give him a last chance to save himself from himself. But I with jester's license will speak the fuller truth, that in your heart you suspect his father the Lord Chamberlain to be the puppeteer, albeit an imperfect one for his puppet at times escapes his control, dancing recklessly and turning the performance to farce." I stopped, pointed abruptly at the King. "But you see no strings to link the loutish marionette to its master, so you must perforce speak to the puppet after all. But this is too hasty a business, I say."

He shook his head firmly. "No. I will speak to the puppet now but in the hearing of his master and thereby end the show ere the stage is o'ertaken by preventable tragedy. When there is no secrecy for the puppet the master will withdraw, for though his puppet be a fool the master is not. He will draw the curtain while he may yet save himself and his puppet, for he has no other."

"And would you save yourself?"

The King looked at me askance. "Your meaning?"

"If a farmer spy the fox creeping upon the henhouse and sets no trap, he must shed no tears when he finds next day his favorite hen to be taken. You know the fox is near but you will not set him a trap nor follow him to his den where perchance you may find others of his ilk who would also do you harm."

"The fox will know he has been seen, Jester, and having learned of our vigilance will henceforth do us no harm. I will act now because I will have peace in this realm and I will have quiet borders. I shall allow no foolish upstart puppet nor his master to threaten the many years' labor I have given to the ordering of this kingdom." He paused, stepped closer to me and spoke in milder tones. "Some years ago when we treated of the Lord Chamberlain in our talk you spoke of the fires of ambition. I grant they seem to have been well kindled, but I shall extinguish them now before they grow to conflagration. Once extinguished they shall never be relit. Of this I am confident, for the Lord Chamberlain will have learned my reach is greater than his. He knows he will be discovered should he venture again beyond the limits I now impose. Trouble yourself no longer on that head, Jester. Be with us in three days' time to attend the Viscount's audience, for I would have your thoughts upon him."

I nodded and bowed my leave, my concern greater now for I could not share the King's confidence in the success of his plan. The Lord Chamberlain was a formidable man, and I could not think that, finding his schemes currently thwarted, he would retreat forever from the field of contest.

On the appointed day of audience I arrived at the King's private presence chamber ahead of the decreed hour. Finding it, as I expected, empty but already guarded I paused to entertain the guards with some trivial sleight of hand. I had good reputation among the royal guard and castle wardens as one who despite my place and all the rumors swirling about me did always have pleasant jest or diverting trick for them, and who for the shared bond of commoner's heritage was one who treated them with a kindness they too seldom saw from those whose very lives they protected.

I knew I would be privy only to some small part of the audience soon to occur, for while of considerable political moment this was no formal matter of state. At issue was an intrigue which inextricably entwined questions of family and honor and as such no commoner, not even a favored jester, was likely to be given full freedom of presence.

This was of no concern to me for I believed I would need little time to take the Viscount's measure. No rumor concerning him indicated anything but that he was a man of simple albeit violent temperament and little wit, and as such would be as easy to read as any mere beast. I suspected as well that the true purpose of my presence had less to do with the son than with his father. The King had already reached decision concerning the Viscount and at most I could but confirm his suspicions and the reports of his agents. The Chamberlain, however, was another matter altogether, one delicate, complex, and potentially quite dangerous. He would remain, though suspected of intrigues suggesting treasonous purpose, as Chamberlain so the King might keep yet closer watch upon him even while believing the Chamberlain would be sufficiently chastened that he plot no further. I harbored grave doubt. He would call off his son, surely, but then bide his time. Neither reform nor capitulation were in his nature. Of this I was certain. The Chamberlain would be now as a snake in the darkness, an adder dangerous to approach yet even more dangerous to ignore.

I took myself to a corner of the room and sat upon the floor crosslegged, waiting. In short while the King arrived, surprise in his face when he saw me seated as I was. But I held a finger to my lips and, nodding once at me, he said nothing before seating himself. Heavy footsteps soon after announced the approach of Viscount and Chamberlain. I began to mime the reading of a book.

The Viscount and his father entered the presence chamber together. My head was lowered so I did not see their surprise and, I am certain, displeasure at my presence. They spoke greetings only to the King. I glanced up as they approached him, tension and unease mingled with defiance traced upon their features and their forms.

215

The King occupied the only chair in the room. It was a simple one but stood upon a raised dais small enough to leave no room for any other person to stand upon it, so the King while either seated or standing would always be above the level gaze of even a tall man. A simple but effective trick, of course, one which would serve to remind all who approached the King even in this private chamber of their subject and inferior status.

While it was not necessary to kneel before a royal in the less-formal confines of the presence chamber, even there protocol demanded a bow upon first approach and upon leave-taking. The Lord Chamberlain's bow was exemplary – for his son's instruction, surely – but the Viscount ignored the lesson, offering only the shallowest dip of his head, the merest hint of deference constituting an expression of haughtiness verging on insolence. At that moment I felt certain the young Viscount was unlikely to see old age, though whether it would be his recklessness or his stupidity that would get him killed I could not guess.

With only the slightest narrowing of his eyes the King ignored the improper bow and instead glanced at me. I rose slowly and walked toward the Viscount, still pretending to read the imaginary book in my hands. I stopped just inches from the Viscount and looked up abruptly as though I had just noticed him.

"What slanders are written here, sir!" I cried, holding out my hands as though presenting a volume for his perusal. "Look you, it is written here a man may oft be as a mouse, but a mouse may never be as a man. For while a man may creep about stealthily in the night to avoid discovery, a mouse is unable to lie." I shook my head vigorously. "Oh, I would have him whipped who writes such falsehoods! For your mouse is a great dissembler. He runs squeaking from the cat but only to draw him into a purlieu so he may be set upon by fleas. That is no fearful honest mouse but a prince among villains! I would give all my gold for such a clever henchman. I will not have such calumnies before me. No, I will not have it!" I acted as though slapping closed the covers of a book. "But you may have it, good master. Here, I give it you." I held my imaginary book out to the Viscount. He glared at me in silence, unmoving, and I took the opportunity to examine him well.

He certainly looked every inch the Viscount, his raiment costly and his bearing haughty, but his choleric nature was readily evident in the lines of his face, the set of neck and shoulders, the hooded eyes and a hand that even as I still held my invisible book toward him twitched as though moving toward the sword hilt that was not there. (For no man may appear in the presence of the King bearing arms except his guards.)

In his person he was much like his father, a very large man though little more than twenty years of age, broad of shoulder and strong of limb as well befits one whose great passions were the hunt and the sports of the military field. I could see that like his father he reveled in his physicality, used it readily and expertly. A hasty glance at his face suggested a pleasing-enough countenance, but close scrutiny dispelled the deception of surfaces and hinted the darkness which was his true nature. His eyes, a flat and lifeless green, were cold and oddly blank, harder even than the eyes of his father and fully suggestive of an absence of spirit within and I could read in the set of his cheeks and jaw and the tautness of his brow the traces of hard cruelty. He quickly struck me, in short, as a very dangerous and unintelligent man.

"I believe you have little acquaintance with my jester," the King said blithely, gesturing toward me with an open hand. "A most entertaining and informative fellow, you will find him, if at times somewhat obscure."

The Viscount turned his slow gaze to the King. "I have never found use for fools," he said curtly, his voice a thick bass rumble that would suit an actor playing the role of a demon in some mystery play.

"Oh, but this is a wise Fool, Viscount, the wisest I have ever seen. His Latin is excellent, though his Greek, I am sad to say, is somewhat poor. But he has read as much as any scholar, and I think is wiser than most."

"I have the same use for scholars as I do for fools. A sharp blade and a sound horse serve me better than all the books ever written."

The King gave the Viscount a long silent look, then glanced at me.

"Well, Jester," the King said brightly, though the hint of uncertainty in his voice was distinctly apparent to me – and to the Lord Chamberlain, whose eyes flitted not to my face but to the King's – "what think you of our Chamberlain's son? Neither your learning, your Latin, nor your wit impress him, I am afraid, but he is an imposing specimen of a man, no?"

I stepped back from the Viscount, whose glance at me was all but an open sneer, and gave him a deep, exaggerated bow and flowing flourish of my arms, a hyperbolic gesture meant to mock his insulting bow and to let him know his slight had not gone unmarked, though whether he understood as much I could not say. I then comically half-danced my way around him with theatrical excess as I continued to scrutinize him.

I stopped in front of him, crouching so as to exaggerate his already impressive height, and peered up at him with mock awe writ large upon my features.

His annoyance with me was growing, for his brow furrowed further and his features grew darker still, a touch of crimson along cheek and neck marking the beginning of genuine anger. Precisely what I expected and intended so that in his stronger emotions he would reveal himself more fully.

Not that the Viscount understood my presence or my purpose, I think, for while he would have heard the stories told of me what he made of them I could not say. He was clearly a man of little wit and understanding. All reports I had heard of him testified to such, and looking now into his empty eyes put to rest any lingering doubt. No, the Viscount had no sense of my purpose here, for even men as perceptive and astute as his father the Chamberlain cannot read me well. For I am after all Jester, master of wit, misdirection and evasion, and like all true jesters I wear many masks, one on top of another in so many layers even I have lost count, yet I manage those masks with consummate dexterity and skill. (This, Heaven knows, is not vainglory. I speak but what is true.) Indeed, I wear so many masks it may well be, as I have come to think now in my later years, that I have at length lost the knowledge of where the final mask ends and my true self begins. I may, I think in my darker moments – and who can be jester without those? – have no identity other than those masks.

But these doubts were to come later. None of it mattered there in the presence chamber with the Viscount, for he needed no masterly handling. To him I was but a buzzing fly of the moment, an irritation among other irritations. But I had already taken his simple measure.

"*Fronti nulla fides*, your Majesty," I said with a knowing glance at the King – and then at the Lord Chamberlain, whose command of Latin would let him know I had said appearance could be deceiving. I could see in the Chamberlain's eyes the turning of many wheels, the calculation and the uncertainty. He understood the weightiness of this moment, perhaps even in ways I did not. The Viscount's face was blank. No Latin. Had the man been taught nothing? No wonder then he behaved as he did and had managed so poorly whatever scheme to which his father had set him. 'Oh Chamberlain,' I thought, 'crafty you may be but infallible you are not. You should have been wiser in your choice of son, sirrah. You would keep your machinations secret but had only a foolish brute to make your puppet.'

218

"Indeed, my King," I continued, "a rare specimen among men, a most imposing and impressive young Viscount," I said cheerily. "Were I skilled in the sculptor's art I would model him for a statue of a god, or perhaps of Hercules." As I spoke I slowly circled the Viscount again, my exaggerated gestures seeming now to trace the contours of his form. His lips pursed and his jaw tightened as his anger grew further though he remained still. "He could model for a great man cast in bronze, yes. Or sculpted of marble, the finest marble." I paused. "No, no," I cried, "adamant, surely. Only the veriest adamant that ever yet was quarried will do." I came to a halt in front of him, my hand at my chin as I pretended to examine his form while studying closely the set of muscles in his face and shoulders, the glint of steel in his eyes as he sought vainly to stare me down with only beast-simple intimidation in his look. "Yes," I said after a long pause, "I think only purest adamant could best represent such a specimen as this."

As I spoke those last few words I tapped him lightly on his thick chest directly over the heart, more than half thinking he would slap my hand away or perhaps even strike me down though my person had long ago been declared inviolable by the King. But the Viscount remained rigid though the effort of self-control was evident. "A man of solid and most adamantine stone," I said as I quickly stepped behind the Viscount and tapped him on his back, directly behind his heart. This time he did move as though to swat me away, turning abruptly with his left arm half-raised and his fist like a mace of flesh and bone clenched for the blow but he arrested his movement before striking me. Saved, I thought to myself, by the presence of the King. I had no wish to be battered about like some *jongleur's* ragged monkey. "Adamant through and through," I declared with a flourish as though nothing had happened. I glanced at the King, who was watching me intently. "Such as this world has seldom seen, my lord." I bowed dramatically to the King again and stepped away from the Viscount, glancing at the Chamberlain only to meet a gaze as full of dark suspicion as I have ever known.

The skin at the corner of the King's eyes crinkled slightly as he spoke to me. "We shall make an artist of you yet, Jester," he said with a slight smile although his tone carried no amusement. Then a gesture so slight as to be imperceptible to all but those such as I (and the Lord Chamberlain) who were accustomed to the close scrutiny of men and well attuned to the smallest nuance of the King's features: a fractional inclining of the head, a gesture of both gratitude and dismissal. I bowed myself from the room with a sense of considerable relief.

Which was, alas, very short-lived.

No sooner had the guard closed the chamber door than I heard an unaccustomed sound, quite wrong for the time of day. The routines of a royal household are firmly established, so unless variations from that routine are known in advance one must always regard the unexpected noise or the out-of-place servant with due measure of concern.

What I heard was boisterousness, some raw amusement – not yet recognizable as trouble so the King's guards seemed unconcerned. But my encounter with the Viscount had left me disquieted and in that state I did not think it prudent to leave such irregularity unexamined.

Following the sounds from below I soon encountered two kitchen maids, breathless and in a passage where they had no business being. Oh, trouble indeed, I now thought. I stopped as they ran to me, and even before they reached me both began speaking urgently, fragments and phrases tumbling over each other like dice spilling from a shaken cup. A few minutes passed before I could assemble a narrative of any sense from their voluble distraught outpouring.

The Viscount had flouted decorum even before setting foot in the castle. Any man of rank, knowing he had been summoned before the King for some form of censure or admonition, would, if he were truly penitent or at least wished to appear so, have arrived with some show of humility, perhaps entering the castle grounds with only a few companions, his customary retinue and equipage having been discreetly left in the city. Even a bolder and less repentant spirit would have had the wit to arrive with some show of restraint. The Viscount however lacked both wit and shame (and a good many other of those qualities elevating us above the beasts) and being endowed with an abundance of arrogance arrived with an entourage of some dozen companions, half of whom were in their cups before they'd dismounted while those who were still somewhat sober upon arrival soon busied themselves in a dining hall making up their deficiency. The house steward, having no preparation for dealing with this unexpected and uncooperative company, sought to keep order as best he could by complying with their boorish demands, so while the Viscount went before the King his boon companions feasted and drank and in short order began depredations upon the female staff. Liberties were being taken, it seemed, and some of the women had fled into the castle's further reaches for safety.

Calming those two servants as best I could I sent them to the marshal, for if the Viscount's companions were much like the man they followed it could well be some soldiery would be needed should matters go awry. I hurried to the dining hall, not entirely certain what I would do when I arrived but while I have never quite been a man of action I have also never been a man of fear, and my profound dislike of the Viscount, I realized as I hurried onward, instinctively extended to his companions.

The steward, I later learned, had in his initial confusion first tried to seat the men in the servant's hall and had been threatened with violence for that effort, though fortunately the Viscount's men proved content with the smaller dining hall to which the steward then led them. I burst into that hall with deliberately dramatic flourish, knowing my motion and jester's costume would draw all attention. I would have taken a small flambeau from its wall sconce on the way and entered with it in hand – nothing makes a flourish more arresting than a flaming torch in one hand unless it is a flaming torch in both hands – but at this time of day no torches were lit and I did not wish delay while I sought a flame.

But I was not without means of distraction. I had learned long ago the value of simple tricks in winning the favor of those in service, so almost always I went about with some small accoutrements of entertainment upon my person, secreted in the several various pouches and pockets I had caused to be sewn into my jester-garb.

As heads were still turning in my direction I produced three balls and began to juggle, standing first upon one leg then the other, alternating more rapidly until I was dancing a slow jig, the balls managed perfectly all the while. Every man in the room was intent upon me, some with cup or morsel still half-raised to their mouths, and I took a moment to survey them, take their measure as best I could in the instant. A few of the faces were familiar to me, second or third sons of lower nobility and gentry in fealty to the King, though any man in this company and following the Viscount must be suspected of being in some degree a villain and a danger. Nine men were seated at table with food or drink before them while two others stood against a wall in close conversation. I could hear another in the passageway at the far end of the hall, laughing and speaking boisterously to some woman who was responding with half-muffled protestations.

"Welcome, masters all, to the royal residence!" I boomed out, dancing my way slowly around the table so I might study them more closely. I doubted my reminder they were in the King's home would serve to curb their crudities, but try I must. "And all such proper felicitations as are due to your worships," I added. Of course no courtesty was due to blackguards such as these, but their sodden wits heard this only as compliment and several cheered and pounded tankards on the table, calling for song or jest.

"A song, gentlemen? Oh, let me see …." I pretended to think as I continued my scrutiny of the men. Most of those at table seemed relaxed enough but the men standing against the wall were somewhat taut in their bearing, as though anticipating action or some decisive event.

"Certainly, my good friends, but first I must solicit some kind assistance." I stopped dancing but began juggling the balls more rapidly. "I well know how to begin juggling, and I am quite able to keep juggling, but I have I fear quite forgotten how to *stop* juggling." I looked about in mock helplessness. "I would not drop these balls for fear they will break, being of a rare and delicate wood from a far-off realm." I nodded at the man by whom I had deliberately stopped, having seen little villainy and less wit in his face. Just the sort of man I wanted. "Kind sir, I beg your assistance. Stand, please." Taking a last draft of ale he set down his tankard and stood, remaining between chair and table.

"Good sir, that helps me not. You must be able to move your feet should needs arise. If you would step toward me." I took several steps backward as the man clumsily pushed his chair aside and took a half step in my direction. "Oh master, closer please, and face me full." Dull-witted indeed. He moved toward me, a sheepish grin on his face and uncertainty in his eyes as his companions looked on, several already preparing to laugh at his expense.

"Now sir," I continued, the balls still moving, "I shall attempt to throw one of these to you so you might catch it as delicately as you may. Are you ready?"

He nodded and half-raised his arms.

"Good. And remember, friend: delicately, for my balls are most tender." Rough guffaws greeted my remark. "Are you ready?" I asked again, more urgently.

"Aye."

"Then here!" I made as though I were throwing a ball to him but he grabbed at empty air as I had instead bounced the ball off my arm and continued juggling.

"Did you catch it, master?" I cried, pretending to watch the balls closely.

"You did not throw it," he said slowly, uncertainty in his voice.

"Say you so, master? I thought surely I did."

"You made as if to throw but no ball came to me."

"Count you these balls in the air before me, good sir, to vouchsafe the truth of your words."

His head bobbed comically as he followed the balls.

"Three."

"Ah! It did not leave me, then." I glanced quickly around the table to take the men into my joke. "I find, gentlemen, my balls are as fond of me as I am of them! For in faith I would not care to lose a one of them!"

"Nor I one of mine!" one of the men shouted as several guffawed again. Bawdy humor never fails with such sordid company as this, I knew.

"A good wise fellow you are, sir, to keep your balls close," I said, nodding vigorously. "But let me try again, for I cannot juggle all the day." I looked at the man standing before me. "Are you prepared, sir? I shall try again."

"I am."

Again I motioned as though tossing one of the balls to him but again it was a feint.

"Did you catch it, master?" I cried.

"There was no ball again," he said, a hint of annoyance at the edges of his voice. Time to strike, I thought.

I abruptly stopped juggling, adroitly catching all three balls in my cupped hands.

"Do you mean to tell me, sir, that after all this you still have no balls?"

The man's face grew flushed as his comrades laughed and made remark. He looked about uncertainly as I quickly returned the balls to their hidden pouch. Even such a playful jest as this may have dangerous consequence in such company so I could not let the moment linger. Immediately I began clapping a simple rhythm, nodding at some of the more drunken men in an attempt to get them to join me. Several did, banging their fists or the butt ends of their knives upon the table.

"A song, gentlemen," I said quickly, "was requested, a song was promised, and by God's balls a song shall be delivered!"

Give me a maid who loves to worship,
Give me a maid oft on her knees;
Hark to her words of supplication:
'Sir, remove your codpiece please.'

Give me a maid who looks to heaven,
One who truly loves her saint;
On her back she may always see him
And I will always find her queynt.

As I sang I circled the table, peering at the men with my eyes agog and brows comically raised. I could see the weight of the ale in their eyes and the dust of travel upon their clothes. Which gave me further inspiration as I ended my song to scattered applause and drunken approbation.

I bowed. "You have ridden far today, my masters," I said with mock awe in my voice, then paused as I glanced theatrically in the direction of the far passageway, where the woman's voice I'd heard before was still making ineffectual protest. I cupped a hand to my ear and leaned toward the sound as though intent upon hearing what was being said there. "Yet there is at least one among you," and here I waved an arm in the direction of the passage, "who fain would ride yet another filly!" Boisterous laughter and bawdy remark followed. I espied a dagger used by one of the men to cut his food lying on the table very near me. A good jester finds ready props everywhere and sight of the knife gave me an idea. I reached slowly for the dagger with a look of inquiry in my widened eyes as I carefully watched the face of the man to whom the dagger belonged, for even a jester with all his privilege must exercise caution when reaching for a drunken man's weapon. "May I, friend?" I asked in confidential tone. The man smiled and dipped his head, his reddened eyes good indication he was well gone in drink. I picked up the dagger and stepped up on an empty chair then onto the table itself.

"To ride all day is hard work, and so to ride all day a man must be hard," I said in my booming theatrical voice. "To ride yet further," and here I paused, holding the dagger in front of my crotch then slowly tilting the point of the blade upward in imitation of an erect phallus, "a man must be harder still." More bawdy remark. Drunken dolts such as these were child's play to entertain, and though this would likely keep them from further trouble for the moment, my true wish was to draw off the man in the passageway. "Your amorous companion," I continued, and here I turned slowly about so I was facing the passage, then slowly lowered the dagger's point and dangled the blade loosely in my hand, a look of exaggerated surprise upon my face. "Alas," I said, my voice now a low growl meant to suggest the man in the passage, "it seems I have ridden too far after all!"

More laughter and now several men began calling to their companion in the passage; one of those at table rose unsteadily to his feet. "Let us see," he began, speaking with the strained care of a man seeking to appear more sober than he is and spilling some ale from the tankard in his hand, "what —"

He did not finish for at this instant the Viscount appeared in the doorway. Though he was mostly in silhouette from where I stood atop the table the set of his shoulders and head made clear the barely contained anger within. I was surprised he had appeared so soon. That he did so surely indicated his audience with the King had gone poorly.

The man who had begun to speak turned toward the Viscount but before his eyes could focus the Viscount strode into the room and with a brusque sweep of his arm knocked the tankard from his follower's hand, causing the man to yelp in pain. (The tankard, as I saw later, hit the wall with such force part of its pewter rim had been flattened.)

"To horse!" the Viscount growled. "Now!" He spun abruptly on his heel and strode back down the passage he had come. His men, several of them unsteady on their feet and many taking last quaffs of ale or mouthfuls of food, made the best haste they could to follow him. The man in the further passage was the last to leave and among the most sober, judging from his gait and the glare of unabated animosity he gave me as he passed. I was relieved to see his garments were still fastened. When the last of the men left the hall I jumped from the table to attend to the servant in the passage but she had already fled, and I found later had come to no physical harm or violation, which was to me some relief.

The Viscount's meeting with the King, though brief, had at first appeared to effect some change in his behavior, for the rumors of raids and violence waned. But within little more than a twelvemonth the disturbing reports began to be heard again. I could never learn if the political intrigues hinted at by the King had also begun again, for no word of these matters ever reached my ears nor were they ever again alluded to by King or Chamberlain in my presence. I am certain however those intrigues did in fact resume, the Viscount again acting as the agent of his father in sounding out possible alliances among those who might be susceptible to other loyalties. So I was not surprised when, less than a year after the Viscount resumed his lawless behavior, came word he had met his death in a hunting accident. A hunting accident which was no accident, of course, but warning to all who would think to challenge my master's sovereignty. Not least among those, I also knew, would be the Lord Chamberlain himself. It was certain that now he would have to be watched with utmost vigilance, so it was as well the King had chosen to keep him very close.

Yet for all that proximity, and all my careful observation, the Chamberlain eluded me, outfoxed us all, in the end. For this I can never forgive myself, and for this I will grieve the rest of my days upon this earth.

tragedy

Perhaps it was for my jester's life of trickery that Providence demanded I make requital by being tricked myself, all of my thousand small deceptions, jests, and unmaskings paid for with a single grand subversion of my own intention. All of my insights into the characters and minds of so many men paid for with a misperception and culminating in an ironic inversion worthy of Oedipus. For as the Wheel carries us up it must perforce carry us down, and my miscalculation became the means and mechanism of my descent. The scales of Creation must find their balance, so all the good I sought to do in service had set as counterweight against it a foolish, selfish desire to keep what I did not possess in the first place. Were God a jester he could have performed no subtler trick, prosecuted no grander or more ironic jest. My foolish love of the Queen and my selfish desire to remain in her presence was paid for by the loss of all I loved.

A loss which was the consequence of my weakness.

The Queen never produced an heir. By the sixth year of her marriage the whispers which had begun years earlier became open talk, and very soon that talk became counsel. More and more of the King's advisers urged divorce and remarriage so a second queen could produce the heirs who would establish direct unequivocal succession. But the King flatly refused to consider it. His love of the Queen was too rich, too deep, the bedrock of his life, he declared, and all the accomplishments of his reign were built upon the foundation of that love. He was fully confident in his long-established plan of succession, and truly none could deny Arther was a young man of great promise and in direct line of succession even prior to his being adopted, along with his brother Edwin, by the King and Queen.

I confess I marveled admiringly at the King's adamantine refusal to consider divorce. Surely because I understood all too well how a man could be devoted to the Queen, bound to her with bonds ineradicable on account of her generosity of spirit, her profound empathetic compassion, her warmth of heart, her grace of character, her beauty – by the full totality of her being drawing and holding me as if she were a beneficent and hallowed Siren and I the sailor powerless to resist. Did I not feel precisely what the King felt? None could understand his love better than I, of this I was and remain convinced.

Yet I still must own to a certain confusion in this matter. The King had another great love, a sterner one: his kingdom. To secure its stability and durance was his life's great labor, his constant concern and the engine of all his polity. He had arranged near a dozen marriages since I had entered his service, subordinating the feelings and desires of all parties involved to the greater need, as he understood matters, of the state. Love mattered less than kingdom. Until it came to his own love.

Hypocrisy? It was true that many, perhaps most, thought so. I heard the gossip, the innuendo, the whispered slanders. I often thought so myself, yet I understood better than any man the power of the love binding him to the Queen and on that account I forgave him his Janus dealings in the matter of marriages. Perhaps, I thought, this was for the King his own in-between existence, his own dilemma of indeterminacy. Like a man to double business bound he was drawn in antipodal directions, on the one side love and on the other calculated decisions made for the sake of his realm, his duty, his greatest responsibility. For himself and his Queen, if for no others, love outweighed all other consideration. So it was I forgave him.

Of the very few voices urging the King to reject divorce mine was loudest and most insistent. Though I had no more power than any man to determine the King's mind on any matter, neither was my counsel valued less than any man's, not even less than the Lord Chamberlain's, and all my persuasion was for the King to remain married to the Queen, much to the Chamberlain's dismay and even anger. We disagreed on nothing so much as this matter, the Chamberlain and I, and I confess had I been a disinterested counsellor my voice may well have been added to his and the others in arguing for divorce. But in my love and my weakness I could no more do that than I could leave the Queen. I argued in favor of the marriage and I argued in favor of Arther and his brother but in my secret heart I argued so I might remain in the presence of the woman whose being was the inaccessible lodestone of my life. And for my selfish pains I must always know that my arguments, born of hopeless love and feckless will, helped shape the destiny of a kingdom by leading to the death not only of Arther, but also of my King.

Yes, I contributed directly though without intention or design to the death of the monarch I loved and served for a century's quarter, and a day does not go by but I implore God's forgiveness for my actions and their consequences. But I could argue no other course, pursue no other persuasion. To remain with the Queen consumed me even after all those years of unanswered longing. Or perhaps because of them. I know yet more flames of Purgatory await me for this weakness and my heart misgives me in fear of those flames, but I implore God's mercy because God Himself knows it was my love, and only my love – the love He planted in the heart He gave me – which drove all my words and all my actions in those days and years in the court.

None can be fully certain divorce and remarriage would have prevented the calamity that ensued, but I do believe it to be so. Had the King and his new Queen produced male offspring Arther and Edwin would not have been adopted, would have been much less at court, further from the throne, and less exposed to the corrupting influence of power which overtook Edwin's mind and spirit. The turning of the Great Wheel would have brought us all to a very different fate.

But such was not to be.

When Arther fell ill shortly before his thirtieth birthday there was at first little concern. His malady seemed not serious and the physicians were fully confident of recovery, for his health had always been good and his vigor considerable. He was fond enough of the chase and an excellent horseman, and was particularly skilled in fencing which he practiced regularly and with passion. He even sought to educate me once in the rudiments of the sport despite my low origins, but my lack of stature being exacerbated by a lack of confidence born of acute awareness of my station, my efforts proved to be of comic value only.

It was the King's confidence which prompted my own deep misgivings regarding Arther's illness.

For more than a fortnight Arther had been bed-ridden by his illness, all his customary activities suspended and his appetite in rapid decline. I had not seen nor spoken to the King for some days when we met by chance in a hallway. He gestured me aside.

I could see in the altered lines and contours of his face and hear in the forced determination of his voice his evident struggle against the press of bad news, and even as he greeted me with hollow optimism I felt a darkness encroach upon my spirit, a vague but irrefutable misgiving for which there was no cause but the King's denial of cause. It was, I felt with a cold and most unwelcome clarity, the shadow cast by some coming event grim in both its consequences and its iron implacability.

"No cause for worry still, we are assured," the King was saying, his eyes glancing restlessly about the stateroom into which we had stepped. Portraits on the walls looked down upon us in what seemed forlorn sympathy and unbidden to my mind came the memory of those pictures in the Baronet's house so long ago, frightening me with their stern somberness. I all but shook my head to clear the melancholy which seemed gathering about me like a fast-thickening fog.

"He remains weak but will recover quickly once health returns," the King said, nodding in self-reassurance as though the hoped-for event had already begun. "His sleep was sounder last night, a good sign. Good sign indeed."

"Yes, Majesty. Good indeed, and let us pray for its steady continuance for I would this court regain its wonted order soon."

"We shall, Jester, we shall. Of this I have no doubt." The King walked slowly to one of the tall windows in the room. I followed. We stood in silence for a moment, the rampart of the east castle wall below us many yards distant, beyond that the meadow where the Queen and I together first watched her beloved black dogs, the creatures of her heart, splash in a long-ago summer's stream. That same meadow where I in my Gift-vision saw her in mourning, transfigured by sorrow. My own heart now faltered and I suddenly felt certain some strange doom was making its slow and ominous approach.

"No, Jester." I started at the King's words, seeming as they did to indicate he had divined my thought. "No one in this world" – and I realized he was merely teasing out his own thought – "has brought more peace to our mind than Arther. Except my wife, and I am fortunate in the grace of Heaven to know such love and such security for the future of this kingdom."

"Let us always thus move *ad meloria*, Majesty," I said quietly, hoping the Latin would pleasantly distract, hoping also that what I spoke could somehow prove true.

The King's brief smile was wistful. "Yes, Jester, always toward better things." He turned from the window and looked at me in silence a moment. "We have spoken too little Latin of late, Jester." I waited for more but the King slowly turned away and began walking toward the door. Halfway across the room he stopped. "*Ad meloria.* Such has been the purpose of my reign," he said without turning to face me. "Good even, Jester. We do not require your presence tonight." As you have not required it for many days now, I thought. You struggle against a melancholy you wish to deny and I pray for a victory I do not foresee.

I waited until I was certain the King was well away before I left that silent stateroom, the portraits beginning to grow obscure in the gathering dusk though I seemed still to feel the weight of their gazes upon me as I left, as though even those figures from the past were compelled to look upon whatever dark fate was approaching.

Despite the King's willed optimism and the continual ministrations of his doctors Arther grew steadily worse. Other physicians were consulted to no avail and as Arther's decline began to accelerate, their efforts grew increasingly desperate but still met with no success. He was bled, he was cupped, physics and potions were administered, his diet was altered this way and that a dozen times, prayers and Masses were offered by the score, all to no avail. His doctors were unable even to agree on the cause of his sickness and its source in the body and I heard them argue amongst themselves so often I began to avoid them entirely, relying on servant reports for my news, for it had become evident to me no human intervention could save Arther now. If he lived it would be through the grace of Heaven only. Week after week passed and as Arther's health grew ever more precarious doubt grew among all who would confess the truth of their feelings, and doubt soon darkened into despair.

Edwin, uncharacteristically, had been continually in residence at the castle during the entire period of Arther's decline, making a great show of love and concern for his brother and spending much time tending to him personally. This touched members of the court and many of the castle staff as profoundly moving, a compelling instance of fraternal love given that Edwin had never before showed inclination to remain at the castle for more than the briefest of periods even upon high occasions of state.

I however remained troubled. As he had always done since his earliest manhood Edwin avoided me assiduously, the few times we did meet, and those but fleeting moments, leading only to the increase of my general distrust of him. He had a firm composure of temperament that in some way did not ring true, his face and eyes always a player's mask, as it were, one which even I could not readily penetrate. His customary manner seemed almost a cautious dramatic performance rather than genuine expression of his heart and mind and so he was to me in a way I could sense but not truly fathom a fundamentally false man, a creature of pretense whose truth of being was deeply and carefully hidden. On those rare occasions when we spoke even the simplest of greetings it were as though the shadows in the room's corners crept closer. There was a darkness to his spirit, some willfully obscured region of mind that left me uneasy.

Arther's illness had been of near three months' duration when the Queen began to display similar symptoms. The heightened consternation throughout the castle, much of it centered on the possibility of plague, was nothing compared to the panicked dismay I felt when I first heard the news. Arther's seemingly irreversible decline confirmed the helplessness of the physicians in the face of this malady and I feared the Queen would meet the same fate. Among the servants talk also began of witchcraft and a curse upon the royal house, and I knew some were whispering of me as well.

Even Edwin himself suggested as much to me in one of our rare conversations. Although it would not have been proper for me to see the Queen in her illness I often lingered in the passages leading to her rooms so I might catch what news I could of her condition. One evening as I loitered at a late hour in that part of the castle I was startled to see Edwin himself emerge from a servant's passageway which led to the Queen's suite. He seemed as surprised to see me and for the briefest fleeting instant his discomfiture showed in his features. But he quickly collected himself. He was an adept at deception and dissimulation, I had long known. Few men can recover from surprise with such speed and equanimity and those who can are rarely to be trusted completely.

"Ah, my uncle-father's diabolical and all-licensed Fool, wandering the halls at the very witching time of night." His smile was a cynical mockery of good humor. "I have heard of your nocturnal rambling habit, Jester, and have wondered what troubling ghosts keep your old bones so oft from your warm bed on so many cold nights." He tilted his head slightly, brows raised, inviting a response.

No. The slight tightening of skin around his eyes and the barely hinted pursing of his lips made it evident he was not so much inviting a response as challenging me to deliver one. I could sense also that Edwin's manner of dealing with me had changed abruptly. In this accidental encounter in a hallway he had no business being in, Edwin instantly decided to set aside his customary evasion of me – he could simply have brushed by me without a word, as he had done so oft before – but had instead decided on what could only be regarded as a confrontation. Our battle, as it were, was suddenly joined and his swift and masterful self-command caught me for an instant off-guard. But for the briefest of instants only. I have grown old in jester-service but my skills and my Gift have not. Yet I knew with a chilling certainty I was facing one of the most dangerous men I would ever meet. Not dangerous in the way of the Lord Chamberlain's son, dead these several years, whose danger was in his anger and brute strength. Edwin was a subtle fox to the Viscount's charging boar. As the fox is among beasts the king of cunning and guile, for his cunning and his position at court Edwin would be far the greater threat.

"We in the royal household do now live in a moment of much wondering, Prince," I said, "so what wonder some of us" – and here I nodded at him to note his own nocturnal foray – "deal with our wondering by wandering in search of that which would end our wondering."

Edwin's mouth widened in a smirk which was itself an evasion. I focused all my thought upon him in the hope my Gift would serve me here, help me to catch a word from his mind or glimpse of his future.

"I too wonder, Jester," he said slowly. "So much to wonder about now. These tragic and mysterious ailments which strike my family so . . .'

'Selectively' – the word came to me with the familiar brush of thought, freighted with uncertain meaning but I could not speak the word for Edwin's pause was too brief.

". . . selectively that one cannot but be struck." His eyes bored into mine but I held his gaze unflinchingly. "And of course one prays no one else is struck." He flashed a quick and hollow smile.

"You see, Jester, I too enjoy a bit of wordplay. Perhaps I should have been jester myself." His lips spread in an empty grin and he stroked his dark beard in mock contemplation. "Yes, perhaps. And you, Jester, with all your many wearying years in my uncle-father's court, would you now be a Prince? A King? What say you, Jester, on this wondering night? Would you so far turn the world upside down as that?"

There was no humor in my voice or mien when I answered him. "A prince might indeed become a jester to learn humility and honesty, but what would a jester learn should he become a prince?" I spoke softly but held Edwin's gaze with an intensity that would have disconcerted most men. "I know already of prevarication and flattery and dissembling, so courtiers could teach me nothing. I know of machinations and deceptions and subterfuge already, so ministers of state could teach me nothing. I have seen in my years enough of grandeur and ritual and ceremony to know I prefer a simple stool and an honest handshake so I believe, your Princeliness, I stand to lose much by such a bargain." I flashed a wicked grin. "A jester's head under his cap is safer than a prince's head under his crown, and as my shoulders have grown quite fond of my head, as poor and empty a thing as it is, I say thank you, sire, and sire thank you but keep your crown upon your crown, Prince. I shall remain Jester, you shall remain . . . who you are." I stepped close to him and lowered my voice almost to a whisper. "Yet still we meet in a midnight hallway bound together in wandering wonder and worry for the health of our Queen." I bowed my head as I stepped back, hoping he would linger a moment longer for still I would learn, if I might, something of this late visit to the Queen's chambers and the reason for his use of a servant's passage.

"Yes, worry for my aunt-mother and for my brother-cousin keeps me from my rest. This unaccountable malady puts in jeopardy the stability of our kingdom. . . ." He paused and in that instant I caught a second word from his mind – "perilous" – and before Edwin could resume I spoke quickly.

"Perilous times indeed, sir," and I was pleased to see the slight contraction of his brow, "and let us hope our prayers may please God to restore the health of our Queen and Crown Prince" – and again Edwin's brow twitched; oh, you resent he has precedence for the throne, yes – "in rapid course. And to thereby deliver our King from his troubles and return him to his wonted peace of mind."

His eyes narrowed slightly at my mention of the King. Why does that touch you so? I wondered. "Yes," he said, "I am troubled much in my mind by my uncle-father's . . . despondency, for he much neglects the affairs of state and I do now at times fear for his health and for him."

Here I was startled yet again, betraying my surprise by a slight lifting of my own brows, for again came the familiar sensation of palpable thought brushing my mind as I caught words from Edwin's mind. Those words were "his death." Edwin must have registered my reaction for he nodded once, slowly, his eyes on mine as he repeated his last words.

But I am never betrayed by myself for long. I bought a moment by giving him a slight bow. "Your concern for the health of our King is a reassurance to all," I lied, knowing he understood my words for the mockery they were. "Our beloved Majesty does find himself beset by great worry, to be certain, with his wife and heir both desperately and mysteriously ill. Yet as one who knows the King, I presume to say, as well as any other excepting his Queen I believe his current despond shall soon yield to his customary strength of character and will. Had your worship been able to spend as many years in the royal household as I have, you would rest easy on this matter." I dipped my head yet again, more mockery meant to gall him for his studious avoidance of the King's household for almost the full span of his life, but not before noticing the quick and barely perceptible twitch of the skin around his eyes which told me my arrow had struck home. Edwin collected himself instantly and his manner grew cold and aloof, making clear he was about to leave.

"Be that as it may, Fool, I bear great love for my uncle-father and as long as my aunt-mother and beloved brother-cousin suffer from their malady I shall remain consumed with worry for them all. And I shall pray too this strange malady strikes none other." He stepped brusquely past me then suddenly halted.

"Take care, Jester," he said over his shoulder, "that you linger not overlong near the Queen's chambers, lest you be stricken yourself." And with that he strode quickly off into the gloom of the ill-lit passage. He had no love for me – indeed, I could find no evidence he had love for any but himself – so I dismissed his words as hollow.

It was only some time later I realized those words were a threat.

Within two days Arther was dead and the kingdom was plunged into mourning. All affairs of state and governance came to a standstill and the King seemed lost to himself in his melancholy.

Arther's funeral was as dark a day as I have ever known beyond the deaths of my wife and son and my loss of Miranda. The Queen was too ill to attend and her absence rendered the ceremony all the more oppressive for those of us haunted with worry for her own fate. The King was as grim and morose as I had ever seen him, wooden and mechanical in speech and gesture. The funeral ceremony's elaborate grandeur was befitting the untimely death of a Crown Prince but it all passed for me as a dream glimpsed through a veil, distraught as I was over the Queen's imperiled health, the King's black melancholy, and the loss of a prince I genuinely loved.

Everything was out of joint. The castle was all a blackness: black drapery, black flags, blacker thoughts. The King's Privy Council met to keep affairs of state on course as best they could but their meetings were rancorous for in the King's absence there emerged long-nursed grudges and disputed prerogatives which made the council sessions of little value to the kingdom. The King spent much time alone in the Astrologer's Tower when he was not sitting with the Queen or meeting with Edwin, who would soon be formally declared Crown Prince. Yet I also knew there was still hope among some that the Queen might die or, somehow surviving, be divorced so the King could remarry and produce an heir, although strange to say the Lord Chamberlain seemed to have lost his taste for this argument. His counsel was now that the matter be left in God's hands and for the sake of stability in this difficult moment the King should proceed with Edwin's elevation to Crown Prince. This puzzled me much and no thought I could bring to bear and no whispered rumors I pursued could shed light on the Chamberlain's change of heart.

Arther's death also gave wings to the rumors of plague already circulating, and rumors of witchery likewise were fanned by the unflagging winds of gossip. Many eyes were on me, I knew, for every untoward event in the kingdom always lead to renewal of the popular suspicion my dealings with the Devil were the root of all our troubles. But I had become accustomed to such talk and aside from taking great care with my disguises when I went about in public I paid this superstitious chatter little heed.

Of course this was no plague, for none other than Arther and the Queen ever took ill, but the severity and sudden onset of a fatal malady which did not spread continued to puzzle me greatly, troubling my thought like a problem the answer to which was lost in some secret part of my mind while yet it felt nearly to hand.

The King suffered most of all, becoming a changed man both in temperament and appearance. He grew ever more morose and silent, particularly in private, and while a man normally meticulous in his raiment and grooming he was now all but careless of appearance. It was painful to see him lose himself, not only because of the love I bore him but because of the evident increase in influence which Edwin gained upon him. They two were often in company while the King's requests for me to attend him nearly ceased. My mind could not rest easy with the idea this was entirely accounted for by Edwin's preparation for the monarchy. I suspected something dark but could find no shape to my suspicion, no name for the unease I felt. I would bring my Gift to bear upon Edwin if I could but he had resumed his long habit of avoiding me as completely as he might.

It soon was rumored Edwin also accompanied the King to the Astrologer's Tower, the first man I had seen in all my years of service given leave to enter that secret place. My heart misgave me when first I heard this – I recalled the denial of my own long-ago request to visit the Tower – and had I been capable of yet more suspicion of Edwin I would have given my mind over to it. But my distrust of him was already utter and absolute, and my heart was made bitter by the inescapable sense this latest development was, in a way I could not fully grasp, a lurching forward of that grim coming event bringing great doom upon us all.

That event, the tragic denouement of my life's tale, came all too soon, altering forever and darkly the course of my life and the lives of those I loved more than any others left to me in the Created World.

"All too soon," I write, though for two and a half decades I had been in service to my King and in hopeless love with my Queen. Nearly half my life, yet still it felt all too soon, so consuming had been my devotion and my love and so eternal did I wish them both to be. King and Queen and I had as it were grown slowly from youth to age in each other's company, yet the end felt as though it had come rushing upon us like some fell beast from a child's fable, an unseen and unsuspected destroyer laying waste an entire world.

Several weeks after Arther's funeral, with the royal household still in deep mourning, the Queen appeared at the point of death. Her physicians had declared the case hopeless, final rites had been administered, and it appeared we had but little time to wait. The King seemed almost undone by the burden of this impending loss. His face was lined with such care and set in such a grim mask of grief he appeared even to me almost as a stranger. It was pain to look upon him, and for the first time I was glad he had ceased requesting my attendance, for my own grief was the equal of his own and I was fit for nought but misery and ale. The business of the kingdom held no interest for him now and Edwin had become Regent in all but name, conducting state business and wielding the King's personal seal as though it were his already. I was utterly excluded from his affairs. A sense of great impending change filled my mind though my Gift brought no clear presentiment or vision. There was yet more tragedy in the air, in the very stones of the castle it seemed, but no sense of the direction from which it would come or the shape it would take.

The final tragedy came, as it befell, from above – or, at least, from the highest point of the castle, the Astrologer's Tower, before sunrise on a warm spring morning two months removed from Arther's funeral.

I had been awake well past midnight, haunting the passages near the Queen's quarters in grim expectation of hearing of her passing, but still she lingered and finally, overcome by a weariness which seemed now my constant companion, I retired to my bed.

Only a moment later – in truth several hours but it seemed to me only an instant – I was startled awake by violent pounding on my door. I leapt from the bed with my mind still clouded by sleep and the effects of ale. With my heart pounding alarmingly and my swimming brain in an aching fog I rushed to the door. The pounding was repeated ere I reached it and I could hear as well the sounds of hurried footsteps and general turmoil.

"Jester!" a man's voice called from the other side of my door just as I reached it. I flung it open to find the second under-butler, still in his nightclothes and with a look of distress and panic on his face such as I hope never to see on any man's again. Tears welled in his eyes as I stared at him, too startled to speak as an icy cold filled me like a swiftly rising tide of fear. My knees began to quiver.

"The King, Jester, the King!" he finally managed, trembling, tears now coursing down his cheeks and not knowing what else to do I reached both hands and took him firmly by the shoulders.

"What? What's the matter? Is the King now ill too?" For this had been much on the minds of all in the castle. "Speak, man. What?"

His trembling increased and what little color had been in his face faded as he opened his mouth, his jaw seeming to twitch as he struggled to form words. I could feel my bowels tighten.

"Not ill, Jester. Dead!" And he sagged against me, his body racked with sobs.

I pushed him roughly back — he was not much larger than I, fortunately, else he might have carried me to the ground with his weight — so I could look him in the eye. What I saw and felt remains with me vividly to this day: the under-butler's naked fear and gaping confusion, his recognition that a world had fallen away and what was to take its place unknown.

"What do you say? No foolishness, man. This cannot be." I barely knew what I was saying but as I came more awake and gathered my wits I could see he was speaking only plain and terrible truth.

"Dead, Jester. The truth of God. In the Tower," he said, pointing weakly down the passage.

With that I ran dressed only in my nightshirt in the direction of the Astrologer's Tower, passing others standing helplessly in doorways and passages, joining others hurrying toward the dreadful news, finding as we neared the Tower all passageways blocked by members of the Royal Guard. A swirling and confused maelstrom of rumor was all that met our panicked questions and distraught concern.

For several hours, through the course of a slow and cheerless sunrise and into the long reaches of the morning we waited for answers. Order was slowly restored as servants were dispatched to their work and some rough approximation of castle routine was haltingly restored, but distraction and uncertainty dominated all that was said and done as we awaited news.

I had returned to my chambers only long enough to dress, donning no mourning as many already were doing but my customary jester's costume, close enough already to mourning-dress. Perhaps, I thought to myself, I did so for the last time, but I hoped it might gain me access to information to which others would not be privy.

I sought first the Lord Chamberlain but was denied. The Marshall, the Steward, the Head Butler, a half-dozen others – they either would not see me or knew nothing definitive. I returned to the Astrologer's Tower and found the passages now clear but the door guarded.

Or what was left of the door.

I made no attempt to speak to the guards posted at the Tower's only entrance. The grim set of their faces and the evident tension in their arms and shoulders told me plainly enough what the answer would be should I request passage, even though the King's body had long since been removed. But the door. It stood open and awry and bore evidence of considerable violence, its thick oaken planks hewn and shattered, particularly in the vicinity of the lock, with some of its iron bands bent and gouged, the fresh sharp edges glinting like silver scars.

It was the sound of the door being breached which first alerted the general household to tragedy. My quarters are far from the Tower and the sounds of the axe-blows did not wake me but other servants and castle officers had rushed toward the noise only to be turned back by the already-present Royal Guard. As I spoke to more of the servants I was able to piece together a rough account of those terrible and unparalleled events, an account later collaborated and supplemented by official pronouncements from the Lord Chamberlain and Edwin.

The King had gone alone into the Tower somewhat earlier than was his custom, taking with him as he often did a flagon of wine. He refused to allow servants to enter the Tower even to keep it stocked with food or drink, so always took his own. He was in the habit of leaving a particular goblet in the Tower, an heirloom from his grandfather too worn for formal use but beloved by the King, so that he on his visits need not carry both wine and cup.

Several hours had passed uneventfully until Edwin came to the Tower door, clearly excited, declaring he had great good news for his Majesty: the Queen had begun showing small but unequivocal signs of improvement. Knowing such news would prove an immense boon to the King's laden spirits Edwin pounded on the door, shouting for his uncle, but to no avail. This was of no immediate concern; the Tower's flat roof is far above the level of its only door and were the King out on that roof, as was likely on a pleasant spring night, no noise made at the door would reach him. As there was a parapet walk, reached from elsewhere in the castle, which passed near the Tower only some half-dozen yards below its roof Edwin hurried hence, thinking he could shout to his uncle from there.

He returned a short while, showing evident concern at having been unable to gain the King's attention. It was unlike the King to have fallen asleep in the Tower, Edwin claimed, which had long been rumored to hold little furniture beyond a chair or two along with bookshelves and cabinets filled with various instruments and mouldering curiosities.

Edwin tried again at the door then again at the parapet walk to get his uncle's attention, his shouts and increasing agitation now causing servants to begin gathering in the surrounding passageways and cham bers. Edwin sent for the Lord Chamberlain, who arrived in state of deep vexation.

Taking a sword from one of the guards the Chamberlain pounded with its pommel upon one of the iron bands of the Tower door, the force of his blows causing the door to shudder and the very stones of the floor to tremble. Though advanced in age now the Chamberlain remained a hale and robust man, still formidable in his bluff ursine physicality.

"Our King is no sound sleeper to snore his way through such noise," the Chamberlain declared as he paused. But there was no response from within, only an increase in the number of servants peering around corners. The Chamberlain ordered the passages sealed off as he again pounded the sword against the Tower door, each blow leaving a visible mark upon the dark iron. Again no response. He sent for the Yeoman Herald, a stout young fellow of magnificent stentorian voice, ordering him to the parapet walk to call for the King.

No response.

At this the Lord Chamberlain seemed to grow furious – unreasonably and dramatically so, the Herald told me when we spoke later.

"He seemed to me almost like a player in a mystery play seeking to out-Herod Herod, such were his gesticulations and shouts. I truly feared the Lord Chamberlain would strike me where I stood," the Herald said, "on account of my failure to rouse the King. 'Let his Majesty sleep,' was my thought at the time; 'the King has more than earned the right to his rest.' But the Chamberlain was adamant and ordered the door broken down. Axes were sent for as were several particular members of the Royal Guard, large men such as might have been termed giants in the ancient days and who even now would be fearsome to look upon in battle. Yet even they spent exceeding great labor upon the door and broke three axe handles before the door finally yielded. The noise was as thunder in my ears for near an hour. I stand astonished it did not wake your worship."

I nodded, eager for him to get to the salient moment. "And then?" I prodded.

"The guards began to rush up the Tower stairs but the Lord Chamberlain ordered them back. He and the Prince went into the Tower with orders for none to follow. They shortly emerged but a few moments later with the terrible news the King was dead, his cup of wine nearby and his face and limbs discolored and distorted in agony. Poison, the Prince said, by his own hand on account of his great melancholy. 'Just as I had come to give him the good news that would have saved him from suicide,' he said. 'A terrible and untimely tragedy,' he said."

"This he said before guards and all?" I asked incredulously. A rush to judgement, surely, and a breach of all protocol and common decency. But I said nothing. This matter would require further thought, but later.

"Aye, Jester, as soon as they emerged from the Tower. The Prince was shaken, I think, to speak so rashly, though he appeared composed enough in his features."

Of course. Few men are colder and more calculating.

"The King's body was soon brought down," the Herald continued, "and though the Chamberlain had just ordered me away I caught a glimpse as they carried the King out of the Tower, his face empurpled and much contorted. Such an agony must have been his death, Jester, it pains me to think upon."

"Yes, a great pain of heart for all who loved him. But was anything else said by Chamberlain or Prince?"

"The Chamberlain," he said slowly, "looked at the Prince in most distraught fashion but said nothing. But then the Prince took such action as I never would have dreamed on." The Herald paused, inhaling sharply and gathering his wits. "I avow he did a deed as rash, or as brave, as any I would have thought to have looked on in my life. When he and the Chamberlain emerged from the ruined door the Prince carried the King's flagon. When he uttered the word 'suicide' there was disbelief, of course, some murmurs of outrage and denial from those of us still gathered. But the Prince merely nodded and held up the flagon. 'We do believe it was self-murder,' he said, 'for this flagon carries no taint of poison, only the cup from which the King drank and which had been in the Tower many days, touched only by my uncle alone, as I have witnessed myself. I stake my life upon it.' And with that he took several great quaffs of wine directly. Many of us expected him to fall dead before our eyes but of course there was no ill effect. The poison must truly have been in the cup only, must have been the King's sinful and damning choice, Jester, for he was alone in the Tower, unquestionably."

"And now Edwin shall be king," I said softly, as though musing to myself. "Who would have thought it?" I thanked the Herald and left him. Keeping my confusion and my troubling thoughts to myself, I wandered the castle for several hours seeking to learn what more I could. Of wild gossip and flying rumor there was plenty but of clear and reliable fact nothing beyond what I already knew.

Until I sought to return to my quarters.

The castle, I have remarked, was an accretion of parts built over time, expanded and altered by generations of monarchs to match their purposes and the needs of an expanding kingdom. This slow process created its share of architectural quirks and curiosities, particularly where new and old portions of the structures met. There was one such place I knew well, using it regularly when desirous of passing quickly from the part of the castle which housed servants' quarters, including my own, to the stately rooms used for grand entertainments. What was now a flanking tower of the castle had once been a corner tower when the castle was originally constructed, and when the castle was extended in that area and walls removed or reconstructed the masons had, perhaps for reasons of illumination, left several loopholes of the tower unfilled, creating the odd circumstance of loopholes which now gave view into interior spaces of the castle. One, on a higher level of the old tower, overlooked a tall and rather narrow chamber originally used as a trophy room by a long-dead monarch in love with the instruments of martial combat, though all that remained there now were several incomplete suits of armor and a few weapon racks, empty and grayed with a layer of fine dust. I was passing through this spot to my quarters, my mind scattered and lost in the events of the day, when I heard as I passed that armory loophole the sharp closing of a door below. I stopped instantly. For more than two decades I had passed this very spot regularly and could count on one hand the number of times I had seen anyone in that room, the last of those times many years ago when the room had been briefly used for linen storage. For someone to be in such a forsaken spot on this day of all portentous and unsettling days struck me as quite odd. I moved carefully to the loophole, peering cautiously I know not why to see who had what business in such a neglected place.

My surprise was as sudden and sharp as a physical blow and to this day I know not how I refrained from crying out. There in the dim light of the dusty, disused armory stood Edwin and the Lord Chamberlain, their faces set in tight masks and every aspect of feature and limb bespeaking such tension as one witnesses when wary men come together in reluctant alliance. Here, I thought, was a matter of deep connivance and machination though I could not imagine what might bring these two together here and now.

To my dismay they remained standing just inside the door which they had closed firmly behind them, as far from my position as they might be and Edwin with his back to me. I strained to hear their speech but could catch only some of the words spoken by the Lord Chamberlain, for Edwin's voice was habitually soft. He was as thoroughly as anyone I ever met a man of whispers and shadows, of secrecy and guile.

"Events approach fruition, Majesty," the Chamberlain said, his beard now gray with age but as thick as ever and seeming almost to bristle with some barely contained energy. "With your ascension and your marriage to my daughter we will have placed ourselves precisely where we wished. Where we were meant to be."

Edwin nodded, speaking for some moments as I burned with frustration at my inability to hear his words. He paused, then clapped the Lord Chamberlain on the shoulder as he spoke again.

"Indeed," the Chamberlain said with a brief bitter smile. "Long overdue, but yes, it does. All scores reckoned and settled. And with the month's coming parleys all will be secured. We meet . . ." and I could catch no more. The Chamberlain turned to the door, caught himself, and spoke more words I could not hear as he fumbled beneath his tunic, withdrawing a large iron key which he handed to Edwin. And then a curious incident: Edwin pulled from his own tunic another such key, identical I knew for he held them in his two hands next to each other. He made some brief remark which caused the Lord Chamberlain to chuckle grimly. And then with another dark smile the Chamberlain muttered something unintelligible and slipped from the room. Edwin pocketed the two keys, waited briefly, then slipped out himself.

I could make nothing of this at the time, my mind in swirling confusion with the events of a day so monstrous and irrevocable I knew I would be unable to think clearly of these matters for some time yet. But with a deep misgiving I understood I had just witnessed part of some sinister enterprise the implications of which reached far beyond my current knowledge.

The afternoon was well advanced when, still unable to find any respite from restlessness of mind and body, I donned full disguise and set out to wander, in a state close to despair, the streets of the city, now filled with people and the frantic uncertain energy of the moment. The King's death had already been formally declared and I heard among the people no whisper of suicide, for the official proclamation mentioned only the King's sudden and lamentable passing. The proclamation already included praise for Edwin as the monarch who would lead us through this time of sudden disruption, and my heart grew heavier and more bitter with each mention of his name.

I kept revolving in my mind the troubling curious fact Edwin had called the King's death a suicide when he first descended from the Tower. It was impolitic beyond comprehension, yet that alone did not account for my unease. The circumstances of the death itself were mysterious and baffling and surely not fully revealed. Both heart and mind refused to accept suicide as the explanation. I knew the King too well to believe he would take his own life. Yet even if the King had committed self-murder why would Edwin speak it publicly, even if only within the hearing of a few dozen servants and soldiers? It was most unmeet. Had he spoken carelessly and out of shock or overwhelming feeling, as most people would? No. I could believe that no more than I could believe the King took his own life. Edwin was a dark paragon of self-control and dissembling, a calculating man who plotted, planned, and manipulated with scrupulous care and as naturally as the cock crows at sunrise. He had a reason, a coldly crafted and considered motive, for everything he did and said and this would most certainly be no exception. But for what reason? I had only uncertain conjecture. He spoke of suicide – why? To discredit the King's memory? Perhaps so, for several months later at his coronation he spoke, as I later heard, of a "new moral and spiritual tone" of rule in the kingdom. The Lord Chamberlain used similar language (if clumsier for he was no rhetorician) on several public occasions. Though no formal accusation of suicide was ever made – thus allowing my King the Christian burial he most assuredly deserved – the mere hint, the whispered rumor, was I believe sufficient for Edwin's purpose. It would serve as a compelling if publicly unspoken assertion of moral reclamation and legitimacy regarding his reign, allowing Rumor to do the work of constructing his ascension as redemptive, cleansing the kingdom of the spiritual stain of a king's moral and spiritual failure.

Edwin as redeemer. The thought was a vile bitterness rising in my gorge, for I knew the truth.

I discovered that truth on my surreptitious visit to the city the very afternoon of the King's death, and that truth is a most terrible judgement against Edwin and the Chamberlain. Nothing less than regicide, though the only proof I had was the truth of my own feelings. But those feelings were and remain more than proof enough for me. On this gravest of all matters I harbor no doubt.

As I wandered the streets, stopping at various shops and taverns to eavesdrop upon the talk of those who are the unconsulted majority of this and every other kingdom, I chanced upon a small lane, a twisting rutted path lined with small shops of trade, and I paused, recognizing the place but uncertain at the moment as to why I should. And then it came to me: here in this very spot some months ago I had come upon a commotion in the street, an agitated gathering which captured my attention. There had been, I now remembered, a murder: a locksmith of some repute found in his small shop with his throat slashed, his garments soaked in blood. And no explanation: coin was found in his safebox, he was remarked as an aged man of fair reputation and placid temperament, so all at the time wondered why such a thing might have occurred. I gave it then little mind, thinking it merely one of those inexplicable tragic occurrences that befall in a large city almost daily, consequence of the vagaries of human folly and the manifold weaknesses of poor fallen creatures.

Until now.

Standing at the head of the lane my mind filled with the recollection of it that previous time, the clutch of peasants and commoners before the locksmith's shop crowded together in a mass of muddy color and confused noise, and succeeding that image in my mind was the sight of the Lord Chamberlain handing a large iron key to Edwin, a key only now I realized was the one which opened the door to the Astrologer's Tower – that ancient tower with its ancient door and its ancient clumsy lock. I had seen the very key in the King's hand many times, and having seen but a short while ago Edwin produce its twin now I knew, I knew as certainly as if coming events cast no shadows but their own very images, that there had been a copy made of that single and singular key, purloined somehow from the King, and thereby Edwin or the Lord Chamberlain had acquired secret access to the Tower, slipping in unseen while the King was distracted elsewhere. And I knew in that selfsame moment of recognition that they, yes, they two had contrived to murder the King. Their monarch, their benefactor, uncle, adoptive father.

A foul and most unnatural murder.

244

I recalled at that moment, standing motionless in the street like a man bereft of his wit, a long-ago remark of the King's, something touching on the long memory of the Lord Chamberlain and his family's honor. Then the death, surely ordered by the King, of the treacherous Viscount, the Chamberlain's wayward puppet-son. For several years the Chamberlain nursed his grievance and awaited the moment and the means. And those means presented themselves in the form of Edwin with his secret fire of ambition and his masterful guile and the utter blackness of his corrupt and damnéd soul.

The King's physicians declared the cause of death to be traumatic failure of the heart brought on by the great melancholy oppressing his spirits in the wake of Arther's death and the Queen's grave illness. I however held in my mind the Herald's description of the King's body on that fateful morning and the sight of Edwin and the Lord Chamberlain in the abandoned trophy room and I knew the truth. I had no tangible proof of course, and to speak my thoughts to any would have been as much as my life was worth, so until this very moment as I consign these words to the page before me I have kept this secret truth hidden within. But now the truth will out and may it bring about the great and everlasting dishonor and damnation of the Lord Chamberlain and Edwin. I know too that Edwin was responsible for Arther's death and the Queen's illness – why he did not kill her I do not know but am as grateful to God as mortal may be that he spared her life. I recall too the stories told of Edwin in his youth, his travels in foreign kingdoms and the curious company he was known to keep and I am convinced he learned enough of poisons in those years, for poisons would naturally be the subtle treacherous tool preferred by one as fundamentally devious and secret as he. My heart burned with hatred for the man, and burns with that hatred still.

When the nuptials of Edwin and the Lord Chamberlain's youngest daughter, widowed recently (here I thought of poison again for the cause of her husband's sudden death was mysterious), were announced I knew the Chamberlain's revenge was both personal and familial. 'All scores reckoned and settled,' he had said. Indeed. The death of the Chamberlain's monstrous son was settled in the death of the King's beloved heir and nephew and adopted son, the long-ago calumny of the Chamberlain's family avenged in the public-secret besmirching of the King's moral and spiritual character, that family's failed usurpation decades ago requited by the Chamberlain's daughter becoming queen of the land his ancestors once fought to rule, a land which henceforth will be ruled by men in whose veins course the blood of his family.

But I will have my revenge too, such as I may effect. My revenge will be these words, this story of my life which shall serve also as the revelation of regicide and treasonous duplicity. I know full well no monk in his scriptorium would copy these words, no masters of the new presses of which I have heard set its pages now, for Edwin and his agents would ensure that any who sought to assist the spreading of this story would not live to complete the task. Yet words will live, do live beyond the time of their makers. They enter into history and in that record they shall prove a satisfactory revenge and a fulfillment of the justice I seek for my master. And may history's record drag Edwin and the Chamberlain through the foulest slough of disrepute and thence to the gates of Hell where the devils might await them with sharpened hooks and gleeful anticipation.

I shall yet copy this book myself, copy it many times here in my empty days, and dispatch those copies to certain noble families both here and abroad who I know will, for various and several reasons, take keen interest in Edwin's ascension and its consequences, and who also have the will and means to act should they so choose. If I do I shall pay a price, I know, for then the remainder of my days must be spent in caution and anonymity but I would have that anyway. Anonymity and a reclusive life far from city or town is my only wish now, for it is just such an existence which best suits my melancholy and troubled spirit. In such a life I shall bide my time and work my stratagems as I may. Of friends and acquaintances I have accumulated a bountiful store in my many years in court and I shall advantage myself of them in coming days. In the fullness of time my King's name shall be cleared and I shall have my vengeance. The truth of this matter shall be made known and its shrouded secrets revealed. Of this I am certain.

For coming events cast their shadows before them.

reckoning

And the Queen? She survived being brought to the very threshold of death by Edwin, who wanted only to create a pretext for the King's apparent suicide. With the murder of the king accomplished Edwin ignored her, let her live, dismissing her from his mind and his life as readily as he might dismiss a scullery maid after a night's wanton pleasure. The Queen slowly, very slowly, returned to a shadowed semblance of her former health though she never fully regained her wonted vigor or previous beauty of face and form. She was too weak to attend the King's funeral, though with much assistance did pay one brief visit as his body lay in state, mastering her weakness long enough to bid him a final farewell. She had ordered the chapel vacated during her visit but I was compelled by an irresistible urge to be in her presence again even in the smallest of ways, so when I learned her visit was imminent I stationed myself secretly in the chapel where the King's body lay, hiding behind a tomb in a far corner. When at length she and her ladies did arrive, the Queen having been carried on a litter, she remained only a few minutes but more than enough time for me, peering over the carved effigy upon the tomb behind which I hid, to see what I both feared and expected.

With much help she was assisted to the bier holding the King's coffin and there spoke a word upon which her ladies and the royal guard attending her stepped back several paces. She swayed slightly as she stood and her ladies reached their arms out to her but she did not fall. In silence she stood a brief space, an audible sob escaping her, and in that moment my vision many years before of the Queen in mourning now seemed to manifest before me again, every detail just as I had seen it in that summer meadow long ago. But this was now no vision. The rarest aspect of my Gift was again proved true. I could see her no more as tears filled my eyes and I crouched down to await the Queen's departure from the chapel.

The funeral followed the next day. I more than half-expected the Queen to make some effort to attend but the castle gossip proved correct: she had taxed herself the day before and was too weak to endure the lengthy ceremony.

Several days later, however, she summoned me so I might speak to her of the ceremony, to describe as best I might the solemn grandeur of that grim and most oppressive of all lamentable sad events.

I was admitted to the Queen's sitting room by one of her ladies-in-waiting, a long-time particular favorite of the Queen who touched me lightly on the shoulder as I greeted her. In her face, drawn and pale, I could see the agonies she had endured as her mistress suffered so.

"She is quite weak yet, Jester," she said quietly, "but much gladdened to see you." I nodded acknowledgement and she retreated to a corner of the room.

I approached the couch upon which the Queen was half reclined, propped up by a mass of white silken pillows, a luxurious nest for a woman of highest station. But sight of her stunned me almost to immobility, my breath stopped in my chest by an audible gasp as tears sprang to my eyes before I could even think to control them.

Other than my brief and distant glimpse of her a few days before I had not seen the Queen for some months, though she had loomed large in my thought even through the most difficult days following the King's death. While I knew her illness must have taken great toll upon her I was unprepared for what I saw before me when I approached her closely. Her face, customarily so expressive of the vitality and warmth of her compassionate spirit, was pinched and drawn, the rose-tinted honey-gold of her skin replaced now by a greyish pallor that seemed somehow less than fully human, a hue more of the churchyard than of any living place let alone a royal household. Her hair, knotted tightly, was now much streaked with grey, and the hand and wrist emerging from the sleeve of her gown were skeletal in their thinness, every joint and sinew stretching taut the skin that seemed barely sufficient to contain them.

I approached her as though in some terrible numbing dream, unable to see clearly for the tears in my eyes and for the moment thoroughly incapable of speech. I knelt before her and could do nought but allow my tears to flow and half-stifled sobs to be torn from my breast like bereft children ripped from the arms of a grieving parent.

She reached to me but I had knelt too far from the couch and her hand fell back to the cushions as a wounded bird flutters to the ground in its exhaustion. Just as well, I thought through the disruption of my agony, for her touch would have only magnified my pain.

"Oh, Jester, I too grieve deeply for the loss of our king my husband, and your tears mingle with mine to do justice to a great lord's memory."

Even at that instant I understood she misread my grief, for the tears falling from my cheeks to the grey flagstone floor on which I knelt in such sorrow were tears for her alone. I said nothing, could say nothing for the deep anguish constricting my throat and heart. I knelt in long silence as I struggled for control of both tears and voice.

"There are no words, Majesty, to do justice to our loss," I finally managed, my voice thick as with straining effort I all but forced the words from my lips. "I cannot believe —" and I stopped abruptly for I was about to say "the cursed lies that attend his passing" but I realized on the instant I did not know what the Queen had been told of the circumstances of her husband's death and the rumors swirling around it.

"Nor can I yet fully believe he is gone," she said softly. "To lose to natural cause one who had always enjoyed robust health, whose life they say ebbed for grief of my own when yet I survive. . . ." Tears came to her eyes as her voice trailed off. She had so far been protected from the whispered rumor of suicide, I realized with great relief.

I found my hand had strayed, seemingly of its own volition, to the head of the dog lying quietly against the Queen's couch. It was her current favorite of the sleek black dogs she still loved so deeply, and it gladdened my heart to see she had at least that comfort.

She dabbed weakly at her tears and to fill the painful silence I spoke briefly of the funeral ceremony, of its fitting pageantry and solemnity, of the wise gravity of the archbishop's elegy and of the gathered nobility in the chapel and the common throngs lining the streets and crowding the castle gates. In truth I remembered little of these events and much of what I told her was fabrication, but every word was spoken out of consideration and love for her and I hope when I am judged I shall be forgiven those compassionate lies.

I concluded my brief dissembling account and she nodded, her eyes half closed.

"Thank you, Jester, for your kind words and the ease they have given my heart. I fain would rest now but there is one matter yet I must address with you." Half raising a trembling hand she gestured me closer and I inched toward her couch still on my knees.

"I am Queen Dowager now," she said, her voice little more than a whisper, "and as a supernumerary royal will be sent from this castle as soon as health permits. Neither Edwin nor his bride will wish me here as a reminder of those whom they replace."

I opened my mouth to say something in protest but she shook her head and with some effort held up a finger to silence me.

"Thus it must be, Jester. It is the will of God and the way of kings. When I leave my retinue will be a small one —"

"Allow me to petition the new King to add one to that number, Highness," I blurted out. "I would remain in the service of one who shares my love for your late husband." I scarcely knew what I was saying.

"With your permission of course. The new royal household, even the very stones of this castle will be to me painful reminders of the loss we share and I will under no circumstances remain."

"But the new King has already informed me he much wishes you to remain in service, Jester."

That made no sense. Edwin and I shared only a deep and mutual, if still not openly declared, mistrust. Some other game is afoot here, I thought.

"This I cannot do, Majesty," was all I said, my head lowered.

"I leave you to your own sound judgement and know you will choose wisely, for as my husband was wont to say you are the greatest of Fools who never yet was Fool. But I fear you cannot join my household, of which I will not be full mistress."

Of course. Edwin will control the purse-strings and will surely have spies, for he would always be master of all contingencies.

"Yet I would do you a kindness, Jester, for all the many years of loyal service you have shown to me, to my late husband, and" – here she glanced at the dog in front of her – "to my beloved dogs. I have always cherished and never forgotten your great labors in their management and breeding, and for those efforts you will always have my deepest gratitude. Ask me what is within my limited power to grant and it shall be done for you."

I lowered my head and held the bow for a long moment, in no small part to conceal the tears again brimming in my eyes but also to buy time for myself and gather my disarrayed thoughts. I had understood already I could not safely remain in the new royal household, so a plan which had been half-formed in my mind since the King's passing now sprang fully shaped into consciousness, bringing with it both a sense of relief and the realization of a coming finality I would have given all to avoid but which by no imaginable effort could now be evaded. I would leave, yes – I had no choice – but if I must leave I would take great care to leave as wisely as I might.

"There is indeed a boon I would ask, Majesty, and I do humbly thank your Highness for her offer though I deeply regret its necessity." Oh, how true was that! "If I may not be a retainer in your household I would remove myself from all service and the busy world of court, seeking out in my old age a place of simple retirement where I might live the remainder of my days at my quiet leisure. Such a remove from this household will, after so long and so joyful a residence here, require some effort on my part, so I would ask your Majesty this humble favor: to take, along

with her retinue and possessions, some small particular boxes of my be-
longings that I might later claim at my convenience."

She gave me a long wondering look, the slight suggestion of a smile
at the corner of her mouth a clear sign she understood the unspoken
implications of my request.

"Such a simple boon to ask. Of course it shall be granted." Her eyes
flitted for an instant to her lady-in-waiting in a far corner of the room.
"And yet sometimes the simplest gifts are the wisest, are they not?" As
she returned her gaze to me, holding my eyes firmly, my heart was
cheered for in her face was some hint of the spirited expression of years
gone by. I returned her look but feared to speak lest my tears overflow
and my heart cleave again. I knew the direction of my remaining days
was determined now and what lay before me appeared an empty desert,
waste and desolate and lacking all which had given my life meaning and
fullness since that day in the Baronet's household when my lightly mock-
ing rhyme inaugurated my life as jester. A bitter emptiness swept
through me, filled me with an ache I could neither name nor assuage.

"We will speak once more, Jester, ere we part. For now, I must rest,
so I thank you again for your kind words of my husband's ceremony."

With my vision blurred again by tears I bowed and all but stumbled
from the room in my misery and haste.

edwin

"Come, Jester, I would parlay with you."

Edwin's hard smile belied any suggestion of companionability his words may have been intended to convey. The subtle modulations of his voice, the slight straining of muscles around his eyes and in his cheeks, the tension in his shoulders – all made clear this conversation would be as all conversations with Edwin were, full of subterfuge and cloaked purpose. Was this ever not true of you? I wondered as he motioned me into a private chamber. With a gesture of invitation he directed me to the far corner of the room as though in confidential talk though the chamber was empty. You are so habituated to secrecy and deception you employ them without need, without thought.

"These are difficult times, Jester" he continued in a firm quiet voice, "and when a kingdom knows duress it is every good man's duty to serve that kingdom as best he may and with fullest fidelity. Do you not agree, my friend?"

Friend. The word, from Edmund, is both insult and warning. He will have no cooperation from me, for I know his heart and his intention, yet I would not confront him openly. I have been Jester far too long and too well to now be fool.

"I posit you this," I responded in jester-manner, sweeping my arms wide with a flourish. "A man and I might agree, or a man and I might disagree. I would fain be friends with he who agrees with me, for wise he must be to agree with me and I would be friends with all wise men. But he who does not agree with me, well, at him I laugh for he is a fool if he agree not with me and I care not for fools. On this we may agree, no?" Edwin's face was impassive, rigid in its intensity as he willed himself to resist my goading words. I shook my head theatrically. "Oh, to sort this out good master puts one's head in a muddle," I continued, "so I can but say what I have been told by many a friend: that fidelity's fiddle oft plays loudest where its music is least desired."

Edwin's eyes narrowed slightly as I finished but he otherwise appeared unperturbed. Too canny and devious, too much master of himself to betray his heart or thought to others, he was one who could seethe with anger yet appear outwardly as calm as the well-guarded lamb in May, a man who could plot your murder as he warmly clasped your hand.

"What continuity we can muster," he said, continuing as though I had not spoken, "is in the interest of the kingdom and its people, Jester, and well I know my uncle-father the late King valued your counsel most highly. You and I have had little chance to learn much of each other, I grant, but in this time of the kingdom's need I ask you with all my heart to remain here in royal service, at least for a time, and provide your new king with the same wise counsel you provided your old. You will have my full trust and confidence, all my love and gratitude. And of course my generosity." Again the false smile and with a movement as smooth as practiced hypocrisy he reached into his tunic and tossed something to me. A ruby.

The set of his features, to all appearance expressive of warm appeal, was to me but the face of long-cultivated insincerity, for Edwin had lost all my trust long ago. I believe he knew I suspected the King's death was no suicide, and whether or not he suspected I knew of his hand in the matter he was no man to take chances. I was convinced he wished me to remain close only so he could ensure I died as surely as did the King and Arther.

I studied the ruby in my palm for a long moment as though engaged in true deliberation. Then I spoke again in jester-fashion, the irreverence and insult giving me considerable satisfaction despite the risk of Edmund's displeasure:

A gem is a jewel and a jewel is a tool
To be wielded by the rich.
But though a Jester's a Fool nary a Fool
Does willingly drink from a ditch.

I tossed the gem into the air and let it fall on the stone floor between us, its sharp brittle clatter making a hollow echo in the empty room. "I humbly thank your Prince Majesty but must decline his generous offer. The loss of my master has quite undone my wit and I beg leave to retire from all service." I bowed deeply with mock sincerity.

Edwin cocked his head at me and smiled as coldly as ever man smiled. "Oh, Jester, there is much more than a simple stone which awaits you. Besides, my late uncle-father would surely have implored you to advise his successor, no? And to his ghostly supplication I add my own voice, and my increased generosity." With that he tossed another stone to me, an emerald the size of a quail's egg, which I made no attempt to catch. It glanced off my chest and tumbled to the floor near the ruby.

"Again I thank your Princely Majesty," I said, wondering how much longer I could get away with the insult, for Edwin was now king, "but a

Fool's mind once determined is as difficult to sway as a wayward donkey's. I seek repose now for mind and spirit and would leave your new Majesty to conduct his kingdom's affairs in his own manner. I am, I fear, too much imbued with the spirit of your late father-uncle the good King to provide you with properly disinterested counsel." That, I thought, and I have no wish to hand you my head.

Edwin stepped toward me, placing a hand on my shoulder in a manner utterly foreign to him and thoroughly insincere. He knew himself poorly, I thought, or believed me a much greater fool than I was.

"I believe, Jester," he said quietly after a moment, "we understand each other better than either would care, or find safe, to admit. Consider then, carefully, my offer. I have heard often of the late King's generosity to you but I am ready to double that generosity, triple it, if you will serve me for even a little space as this my beloved kingdom moves from one monarch to the next. Besides, there are many dangers on the roads these days, even to revered old heads such as yours. Here you would be safe. Remain with us." He paused, his eyes on mine and his hand remaining firmly on my shoulder. "Tell me you will consider my offer." His look was intended to be imploring but I found it laughable in its cold insincerity, coming as it did companioned by a threat.

"Your generosity is most affecting, Majesty, and conjoined to your appeal does now begin to tempt my heart," I lied. To abet my deception (and further fill my purse) I stooped to retrieve the fallen jewels, considering them a moment before hiding them away. "But I must ask you grant me leave while I consider this matter a few days."

Edwin nodded, the slight smile on his lips a certain indication he thought he'd begun to sway me. "Of course, Jester. As you wish. And remember: triple."

I bowed my way out of the room.

Within four days I fled the castle in disguise, leaving behind the life of a quarter century and the place, the home, whose walls had once contained so much of what had shaped that life but now gave shape only to that loss which, of necessity, attends the implacable mutability of all things.

exodus

I fled the castle, yes, though not as a thief who, finding himself startled by a sound at the door, slips hastily away without the treasure he had come to purloin. Long recognizing that age crept steadily upon all of us in the court, I had for some years given careful thought to my future. Though it was my decided wish to die in royal service of either my King or of Arther as I had anticipated, their sudden deaths caused me to accelerate the measures I had already begun to take to secure my well-being.

Over my many years of service to a generous king I had been able to save a goodly part of the material bounty with which I had been favored. Often rewarded with jewels or coin, most from the King and other members of the court but some of it bribes by anxious envoys seeking to curry favor with a fabled Jester (though all they ever gained was the loss of their lucre), I had conserved these valuables as best I might. When, as often transpired, I was rewarded with valuable cloth or exotic curiosities, I would sell or barter such for coin in the city, for though coin is weighty it is more readily hidden and transported than bolts of fabric or strange exotic creatures. Some of my wealth I had already sequestered with a few trusted friends in various reaches of the kingdom. Rupert, long since elevated to Baron and still ensconced in his scholar's paradise, was by far my greatest ally in this scheme, though by the time I left the castle a good part of my wealth was still to be taken by the Queen when she began her exile in the remote manorial estate Edwin had given her, far in the southeast of the kingdom where she would forever be removed from his thought with no discredit to him. I am pleased to say in the end I recovered much the greater part of my wealth, somewhat less than a quarter of it lost to highwaymen or other cause.

The days following my encounter with Edwin were consumed by my surreptitious preparations for departure, for it was paramount that no suspicion or gossiped speculation reach Edwin's ears. I trusted no one. I myself carried several small stout trunks to the Queen's quarters so she might have them conveyed with her own goods to her place of exile. I slipped into the city in careful disguise to convert some last few gifts into coin, careful to spread my commerce among several various merchants so as to raise no suspicion.

By late afternoon on the fourth day it came upon me, almost as a sudden revelation, that my efforts had reached their culmination. Suddenly, it seemed, nought remained but to leave. Yet there was no satisfaction in the thought, only a sense of vacuity in my heart and in my life.

I stood silently in my quarters, my eyes running over all the material goods which had surrounded me for years, created the texture and tangibility of my daily life: a few books upon a shelf, an aged wooden chest stored with linens, the bed where my wife and son had died so many years ago. There had been no change in these quotidian things, all appearing to the eye as they always had, yet now these familiar items of the day spoke only of the emptiness that follows upon utter change of life. I stood in my rooms and felt all the life I had lived till now slipping from me, receding as a fast-withdrawing tide, leaving only a forlorn emptiness within me which I did not think could ever be filled.

My need for secrecy meant I could take no farewells, a necessity which was further burden to my heart. I had stored some few personal goods with a trusted merchant in town but would have to leave the castle itself with nothing but what I could carry inconspicuously on my person, to all appearances simply going to the city for another of my customary visits.

Only one exception would I make, for I would take my leave of the woman I had silently and hopelessly loved for a quarter of a century. Though I had already vowed to myself a hundred times it would not be the last we would look upon each other in this world, I still found my mind filled with a vague dread, my heart somehow overflowing and empty at the same moment, devoid of any prospect but anguish yet compelled by the hopelessness of my situation and hers. Take my leave I must, yet in doing so I would be grievously torn. To remain in service would mean the loss of my life. To be separated forever from the Queen I loved was another sort of death. Despite the urgency of my situation and even after all the long years of my foolish unrequitable love, of what I had always felt as an incompleteness of being and life, I could but struggle confusedly to grasp the simple enormity of the fact I would no longer be in the Queen's presence. Often in those four days I recalled my father once speaking of how his heart took the shape of the woman he loved and how thereafter none other could fit the space of her absence. What then of me, I wondered, whose heart and very life seemed to take the shape of the Queen's potent presence? What dread looming absence awaited such a fool as I? What among all the glories and transports of the Created World could fill such a void as will be in my life henceforth? I could see no hope, feel no promise of aught but loss and blank, cheerless vacancy. Yet I could not remain. Time the vanquisher, Time the implacable juggernaut, waits for no man nor woman and my time was at hand and could be denied no longer.

On the fourth day I attended the Queen in her chamber, again only a single lady-in-waiting in the room with us, her look this time one of sadness and understanding mingled and I felt with my first glance at her how utterly our worlds had changed, how complete the dismantling of all prior joys and contentments. Even the old acute anguish of my earliest love for the Queen I would now embrace if I could, hold to myself like a treasured friend if by so doing I could avert the greater loss to come, could keep from myself and my Queen the terrible fate which had befallen us and prevent my coming separation from her. Before I even approached the Queen my eyes brimmed again with tears and my heart was as a drum within me.

She smiled at me as I knelt before her, the effect upon me as striking and visceral as it always had been though she looked no longer the woman she once was, her skin still of the churchyard's grayish pallor and her features taut and strained by the sorrows she had known. I bowed my head deeply, for the moment not wanting to look upon her.

"You end as you began, Jester, with a formality which touches my heart and does you great credit still. Do you remember, Jester?"

Indeed I still well recalled our first meeting two and half decades ago, but at the time was most struck by the knowledge that she still held fresh in her mind the memory of our first meeting. I would always so touch your heart and live thus in your memory, Majesty.

With great effort of will I raised my eyes to meet her gaze and as I feared my tears began to flow. I knew in that glance, that look into a self rarely guarded and now in consequence of its recent sorrows fully vulnerable, that it was her spirit more than any bodily vigor which carried her through days which, I could sense, were heavy and grey and empty to her heart. I could see her loss and sustained anguish, feel it as I and countless others once felt the warm embrace of her profound enfolding empathy. For the wrenching pain in my heart I all but cried out in grief. I struggled to find voice, knowing I must speak but floundering helplessly in the confused torrent of thought and feeling coursing through me almost with violence.

"I learned no Latin nor Greek, Jester," she said with a weak half-smile, "but I did learn of Alpha and Omega. And with your endearing formal gesture I know it is to Omega we have come."

I shook my head in silence, not wanting to accept her words, not wanting this moment to be what in my mind I knew it could not but be. Still the heart will wish against the mind, wish against all the senses, against all the memory of all experience, wish against the fierce cutting pain it would o'erleap but cannot. The heart doggedly confronts what it will never accept, is perhaps unable even to recognize, the limits of loving and desiring, and in that confrontation the heart is filled by and knows only itself in its complete and abject failure. Such was my heart. There was nought I could do, there in the room that will forever be in my mind the room of my heart's greatest anguish, but cry. I let my tears come without restraint. I had no will with which to resist them, no strength of heart in that moment of absolute despair to summon any measure of resolve or courage. I sat helplessly back on my haunches and with my head in my hands I wept. Like a frightened child in the face of a fearsome sorrow it cannot comprehend, I wept. For long minutes I wept.

When the tears at length ceased and the choking grief within me subsided I rose to my feet, unsteadily and with the bodily pains which had become, in my age, as familiar as my lined face in the mirror. I sought to speak but composure yet eluded me and for some minutes longer I could not even look at the Queen, not bring myself to show her, as I would if our eyes met, the wretched churning disarray of my heart and mind. I turned away, took several steps, turned back and turned again, almost knowing not what I did as though I were some confused and stricken victim of a sudden and overwhelming tragedy. Never had I felt less master of myself.

"Life gives way to life, Jester, until it gives way to Heaven." In her kind instinctive way she spoke to cover my confusion, to fill the silence I suddenly realized must have been as awkward and unsettling as the sound of the sobbing which it had succeeded. "None pass their full meed of days without sorrows great and small, but always beyond those sorrows is more life if we but welcome it. My heart and mind and spirit like yours know great loss, Jester, loss of husband and king, loss of a life we had known for so many years it seemed it would go on ceaselessly, unchanging except for our growing old in joy and contentment. But we know this cannot be, not in this world. Only Heaven is immutable, Jester. Let us remind ourselves of this. In this world we must know change, for better and worse. Yet even when change takes from us that which we think we cannot bear to lose, we must know that more change will follow and it may bring us benison. Of this we must think, even in the darkness of our grief. This sorrow will pass and though our hearts and spirits may never be as blithe as once they were, we will know peace again. Of this I am certain."

"I thank my Majesty for the hope she would share with me," I said, my voice thick and uneven with grief. "But I can find none at present."

I was still unable to meet her eyes. My grief and my loss are so much more than you know, Majesty, so much more than can be spoken. I felt almost torn asunder, filled with the desire to rage but finding no object or agent upon which I could vent my anger and despair, for I would not rail against God in presence of my Queen.

"Allow your heart its span of grief, Jester. It will not heal unless its sorrows are fully acknowledged."

I shook my head grimly, felt tears return to my eyes but could find no words to express the confused welter of thought and feeling that roiled mind and heart. The greatest sorrow I know is the one I cannot speak, I thought with bitter agony of heart, and so it remains lodged within me like a large stone swallowed by a foolish dog.

From the corner of my eye, even through tear-blurred vision, I saw the Queen make some small motion and an instant later I heard the door behind me open and close. She had dismissed her lady-in-waiting and in a rush of suddenly clearing thought I realized that for the first time in all my quarter-century of service the Queen and I were truly and entirely alone together. The first time. As I have come to take my leave. What gall and bitterness in that irony, what a twist of the dagger whose blade had so long been lodged in my heart.

"Are you ready, Jester? Are your preparations for departure complete?"

I nodded.

"I have done as I vowed," she continued. "Your chests are secured with my own possessions and they shall be kept safe until you send for them. You have hinted at concern for your safety. Have you taken all due precaution? I would have you be safe, Jester, for all the service and love you have given to my husband and to his kingdom. And to myself. You have been a true friend and wise counselor to my husband in matters of state and to me in matters of the dogs I have so long loved."

I bowed, again not trusting myself to speak, and with eyes now free of tears looked at the Queen's face for a last sight of her still-emerald eyes, the one feature of her being left untainted by Edwin's poison. I saw her eyes, yes, brighter than I expected and I saw as well the sudden enigmatic smile which surprised me.

"I have one final gift for you, Jester, the truest token of gratitude my mind could light upon. I present it now to you, but if you wish will keep it for you until such time as you deem proper to retrieve it."

I could not imagine what she meant. Why she had a gift for me at all, having already granted me a boon? Some bulky treasure? A book? I shook my head, my open hands spread in a gesture of helplessness.

"Decide as you wish," she said, her smile growing. With that she clapped her hands twice, a side door opened, and into the room stepped a kennel page, the very one I had most recently been instructing in the management of the Queen's dogs. He was accompanied by one of those very dogs, a sound elegant male from the latest litter several months ago. He had become my favorite from that whelping, though in truth I had spent rather little time at the kennel on account of the tragedies of recent months. The page approached directly, the scrabbling puppy straining at his rope.

"He is yours if you wish him, Jester. A living token of my thanks for all your years of service, of jest and counsel and wise insight into men and dogs."

"Majesty." I again found myself speechless as I sank to my knees to caress the dog, his exuberant wriggling and fiercely wagging tail near to bringing a smile to my face. My heart, for all its wounds, went out to him and I felt a stirring within that only after the passing of a long moment did I recognize as delight.

The Queen gestured a dismissal to the page, who left the room as he came. "We shall keep him for you as I said, or you may take him now if that will serve," she said after he was gone. "Though with your need for haste. . . ."

"This is a greater treasure than I deserve, mistress, greater than any I could have imagined. Your kindness and generosity humble me even as they do me great honor. Thank you. A thousand times I thank you, and that is not enough." I stood, a sense of resolution forming within me despite my grief. Driving my grief away, I realized with some relief. My heart may be undone for all my remaining days but I will not surrender to grief.

I knew I should go, now, while this feeling was upon me.

"I shall take him, Majesty, for he shall well serve as part of my humble disguise. Yet I ask this further favor. Summon back the page so he might convey this dog outside the east castle gate and wait for me in the woods just beyond, for I would not be seen with him by anyone within the castle. If it is known I leave here with a dog for my companion I may the more readily be spied out upon the road. And this page you must swear to secrecy."

"This I have anticipated, Jester, and have done. He departs with some of my retinue in three days' time, for Edwin does allow me all my dogs." She clapped again and the page returned, standing silently by me as I handed him the dog's lead.

The Queen smiled again, the broadest I had seen since the King's death and once again I felt a trace of that familiar pulse in my heart as though I had been touched by some benign o'erpowering force. Oh, I would take that with me as my last experience of her. With a final bow and farewell I turned to leave, the puppy half-pulling the page behind him as the dog sought to regain my side.

With my hand on the door I suddenly stopped and turned back to the Queen. "As you give me one of your beloved dogs, Majesty, I would that you have the honor of giving him his name. Pray, what shall it be?"

She looked at me in silence, her head high and tilted slightly to the side in thought. Her eyes suddenly grew brighter and she smiled again.

"Why, surely, there is but one name this dog could have, and have it he will. He shall henceforth be . . . Jester."

Instantly tears sprang to my eyes again and I gave a quick acknowledging nod of my head. I clenched my jaw, swallowing hard as I looked at the Queen and sought to speak through the grief and joy that contended within. I could see her only as a blur of color now, the long-beloved woman of my heart.

"My farewell gift to you, Majesty," I said with halting voice, speaking as though the words had to be forced past my swelling heart before they could be uttered, "as poor a thing as it is, is this trick by which I double myself. Though but a single Jester entered this room, two shall now make their humble exit." I made a final bow and stepped swiftly from the room lest grief overtake me utterly. The page and puppy went one way and I another, hastening to my rooms to collect my last few goods. I hurried through echoing hallways, the sound of my own footsteps haunting me, then swiftly out the main door, across the entrance court-yard now quiet in the afternoon stillness and then out of the castle, my home for a quarter of a century, forever.

Having a young dog as companion was little impediment to my plan of escape – for that is how I thought of my departure, given what I suspected of Edwin – for all along I had intended very little travel on foot. No longer young and evermore feeling the aches and travails of an aging body I knew that even were I traveling alone I could not make the progress I wanted at first, for I needed quickly to be as far from the castle and Edwin's reach as I could. As I had dressed in lowly garb for the purpose of disguise I could not travel by horse or coach, so while it did not allow me the rapidity of movement my mind constantly longed for I often travelled by paying carters and waggoners to allow me and my dog, my living reminder of the Queen's long presence in my life, to ride upon the seat beside them or among the sacks and barrels they ploddingly transported along the rutted roads of commerce. We fled, my Jester-dog and I, often at oxen's pace while I wished for wings so I might race at arrow's speed to the refuge I knew I would find in the far northern reach of the kingdom, farther even than the domain of the Earl in whose service I once found a great boredom which led to the rest of my life, to the apex of the Wheel and now its nadir. My former master was dead these twelve years or more, passing to God's mercy while drunk asleep in his bed, I had heard. I would have wished him a better end, the one I know he would have preferred: to die on horseback or on foot, in the heat of the chase. My intended place of refuge was some twenty leagues from the furthest corner of his domain, and given the passage of time since I had been in his service and my intention to live a life of considerable solitude I harbored no fear of discovery.

As the days of our slow travel accumulated to weeks my mind grew easier. I had been recognized by none, suspected by none, for I was now almost exclusively among those of my own station and far enough from the castle and other royal residences that none had experience of or direct commerce with the royal household. I was among strangers, among none who had ever seen my face before. Some of the new printed ballads about me which circulated in the market fairs featured crude woodcut illustrations of a jester-like figure but as all were products of some artist's imagination, not taken from the life, they posed no danger. Only a single painting had ever been made of me in all my time in royal service – for I had no personal vanity, being a man of little physical beauty – and that was many years ago, a small work which hung in a little-used salon in the castle. I had no fear of detection by casual recognition, though I still suspected Edwin would send agents in search of me. He was as profoundly suspicious as he was careful and would have no compunction about ordering my assassination based on mere suspicion. The stakes were too high for him to abide any measure of risk.

As we gained distance from the hub of courtly life I would occasionally delay our travel briefly. At times Jester and I would spend several days in a single inn or hostel, though in general I preferred not to linger o'erlong in any one place so as to leave little impression of my presence or passing. On occasion I would change direction almost at random, hoping to frustrate any effort of tracking or pursuit.

As the weeks grew to months and my dog grew in size and strength we would travel more by foot, though after a long day or two of walking my age would make itself felt and we would again hire a passing cart or wagon. Jester now being too full of life's red vigor to remain long seated with me among the sacks of cabbages or casks of salted beef, he would race about the fields and forests through which we slowly passed, always returning to my whistled call and excellent at leaving oxen or horses un-molested, a never-failing concern of the carters when first they saw us by the wayside. I pursued Jester's management with as much pleasure and fervor as ever, in no small part because to do so kept alive within me memories of working with the Queen's own dogs and the joyful sat-isfaction I always found in bringing pleasure to her. At times my heart would grow so full at the recollection I would have to cease my efforts, sitting upon the ground while Jester sought my attention or distracted himself. I would have to wait, at times for long empty minutes, until some measure of composure returned to me and we could continue our work or our travels, all the while my mind wondering if ever I would find the memory of my time with the Queen not unsettling to my spirits, if ever I would find equanimity of heart. And I wondered if perhaps I did not wish to, did not wish to surrender the power of those memories despite the pain that followed in their wake, for was that pain not the evidence of a living heart, a heart still alive to love?

We were still by my rough reckoning a fortnight away from the area where I intended to settle when I stopped at a small inn at the edge of a remote hamlet whose name I never learned. My stops were growing more frequent now, and I often found myself eager to rest at the first place of accommodation which presented itself rather than push on until twilight and risk another night in barn or field. My decades in service had accustomed me to comfort more than I had allowed myself to real-ize, and as well I was already beginning to wish for some sense of be-longing, of rootedness. Of something akin to home. Poor country inns and hostels served only to remind me I was now in-between in yet an-other manner, wandering somewhere between a source to which I could never return and a destination I did not yet know. In the guise of a poor commoner I was not what I appeared, and while I was no longer what I had been I was not yet what I would become, did indeed not know what that was to be. Could I, I often thought to myself on this journey, this flight from Edwin and my past, be any more in-between or indetermi-nate than this?

The inn at which I stopped was nondescript, small and ordinary in every manner of such drooping-eaved dirt-encrusted places, but when I glanced – for my eyes are instantly drawn to horses and dogs – at the small stableyard behind, a poor plot of weeds with but a single tying-off post, I stopped abruptly for tethered there were two fine horses, large bay geldings both of them, almost a matched pair, well beyond the common quality of horse one would ever expect to find in such a place in such a part of the countryside. Horses of squire or gentry, perhaps. Immediately I grew alert, my several months of incognito travel having done nothing to dim my fear Edwin would seek me out. I thought to pass by but it had already been long since my last meal, and I thought too I might be over-concerned, here in this place far from anywhere. The horses of passing successful tradesmen, perhaps. I could not set my caution entirely to rest but I determined to enter.

They were seated at one of the inn's two small tables, simple dark oaken planks stained and scarred with years of rough use. Though the light was dim I could see the remnants of a meal before them, their hands on battered pewter mugs and their eyes upon me even as I was yet opening the door. One of the men nodded a brief acknowledgement as he studied me and I returned the gesture with an obsequious smile as I moved past them to the other table, at which sat a man and a boy, obviously father and son from their similarity of feature. We exchanged a simple greeting as I sat. Their clothing was common and of poor quality, the man's rough hands and brown weathered features speaking of a life outdoors, a life of hard work. To spend coin at even an inn such as this must have been some small extravagance for him so it was clear to whom the horses belonged.

Surreptitiously I studied the two men at the other table. They spoke softly in low tones between themselves so I could distinguish few of their words. Both were large men of solid substance and vigor, dressed in the garb of ordinary yeomen but I could see that was pretense for their clothes were too new and sat ill upon their frames. Their features were rough and their movements slow and heavy with the suggestion of physical strength. In a moment I knew: soldiers. I immediately thought of Edwin.

I did not concern myself that I might be recognized. I was dressed in common peasant's clothes, worn and patched, and since departing the castle had abandoned my lifelong habit of keeping myself clean-shaven, sporting now for the first time in my life a beard, heavily streaked with grey. Besides, these men were unfamiliar to me, ordinary soldiery who had not been part of any royal guard.

One of the men abruptly gestured in my direction with his tankard, causing his companion to turn in his chair. Jester, who had been laying quietly at my feet, had risen and was stalking slowly toward the men, head and neck straining forward in quest of food.

I opened my mouth to call him back but even as I began to form the first syllable of his name realized the error I had made in accepting the Queen's suggestion for it was a word I dare not utter in a situation such as this. I caught myself and instead whistled him back, caressing his head when he returned to sit beside me.

"Fine dog," the man who sat facing me said, his voice gruff and sharp in the manner of a man accustomed to blunt speech and giving orders. "I have not seen his like."

I nodded, smiling obsequiously. "I thank your worship. He promises fair indeed, for already he catches squirrel and rabbit with regular success, and in all things is a dog of good manner and noble heart."

He nodded abstractly, eyes still on the dog, and I was beset by a new fear. What if this man knew the Queen's dogs, knew of their relative rarity?

No, I told myself. If he were often enough at the castle – the only residence where the Queen's beloved dogs were kenneled – to be able to recognize her dogs then I would recognize him. I was safe in that regard, though my heart still misgave me and I regretted the hunger which had driven me inside despite the presence of those horses.

"Live you hereabouts, grandfather?"

"Some dozen leagues to the west," I said with a vague gesture, doing my best to feign the accent of this district.

"Far from home."

You probe with the subtlety of a battering-ram and the wit of a chamber pot, I thought.

"Indeed, good sir, far indeed. But I will take what chance I must to see my latest grandchild, the first boy, for one of my years should tempt not fate with delay. His mother, you see, the youngest of the six vouchsafed by the grace of Heaven to my poor dear wife and I, has the quinsy and would not travel with an infant, so I took it upon myself to journey hence. A fair long way, aye, but a journey worth all the trouble and more. For my reward was a double one, masters. I had the joy to look upon my grandchild – my fifth, sirs, my fifth! yet the first male. Oh, I hope you both live to know such benison yourselves, gentlemen. And for my troubles and from his love my daughter's husband, a good man, true in heart and righteous in spirit, did give to me for companionship's sake in my old age this dog from a recent whelping. For my wife is dead, sirs, dead these seven years next month, and nights alone are nights too long. Those of my children which yet live, you see, have moved far from their home, moved for cause of famine or work or love and I may not see them near as oft as my old heart desires." I smiled within to see the rapidly growing boredom on the man's face. "So my nights are long, sirs, yes, and alone but now I have this dog, this wonderful fine joy of a dog, and I do feel my burden lightened already, and thus I – "

"Thank you for your tale, grandfather," the man said rising abruptly, "but my companion and I have much road yet to travel today. We seek one from whom the new king would have particular council only this fellow can give, but his whereabouts have become unknown."

"He must be a singular fellow," I said jauntily, "that in a kingdom full of wise men his council is so valued our new King, God save his grace, would send such good masters as yourselves upon the road to seek him." I shook my head in feigned pity. "But a tremendous task for two men even though they be as bold and stout as you, to search an entire kingdom for one wise councilor. Better to look for a single grain in a field of stubble, no?"

The second soldier snorted a laugh and shook his head. The first spoke again. "More than two are upon this task, grandfather, though make it a thousand and I think we still would have little hope. But we do as we are bid. Besides, this is no common man, though he be commoner."

"You puzzle my aged wit, sir."

"He is a commoner but they say a man of great wit and learning, skilled in tongues and a good horseman besides."

"And in dark league with the Devil himself," the second man said bitterly. "If he be not in hell already I wager he's made himself invisible. We are sent to hunt a wisp of fog in the desert, I say."

The first man shook his head, weary I could see of his companion's superstition and doubt. "More likely taken ship to some foreign land before watches were set upon the ports. But search we must." He looked pointedly from me to the silent man seated across from me. His hand had gone to the boy's shoulder at the mention of the devil and the child was uncertain, nervous, glancing from his father to the soldiers and back again.

"There is reward," the first soldier said. "Keep watch for a man who looks common but speaks noble, of middle height, slender, growing to old age. His speech is that of the west. He will stand out from all others, they say, will fit in nowhere. Keep watch, report any suspicion to constable or sheriff and if correct you shall have the King's reward and his thanks." He nodded once brusquely and the two men left the inn.

"Godspeed sirs," I called out after them, then turned to my table companions. "Fear not, lad," I said cheerily to the boy. "Their talk of hell is but a gossip's tale cloaked in a soldier's roughness." I patted his shoulder as I stood, for the inn's host had at length reappeared and I bespoke some food I might take with me. As he prepared a small bundle for me I stepped outside into the road for a glimpse of the soldiers. They were riding south, cresting a low hill now brown against the purpling sky just as I looked after them. Northward still I go then, to what future I may cobble together from the uncertainty and loss that seemed now to constitute the primary raw materials of my life.

place

Two Jesters.

One, a dog. The other, a ghost.

The first lives joyously. Has some of what I once was passed to this four-legged Jester now sleeping at my feet as I write these words? For he has been and to this day remains the most playful and child-like dog I have ever known, even among all those others of the Queen's special breed. A full four years of age now he is yet still more pup than adult, living proof of that *joie de vivre* upon which the Queen remarked so many years ago. He is a great joy to me, companion and distraction and un-fillable receptacle for all the love my weary heart bestows upon him. His very being, his mere physical presence in the world, is a celebration of life which daily renews my spirit and resolution even here in my remote solitude and somber quiet. A trickster of a dog, forever at his playful thievery or upon gymnastic gambols. Perpetually expectant of adven-ture, food, chase, ramble, love — forever open to the infinite possibilities of life. Is he a type of the youth I once was, an avatar of the eager ambitious would-be Jester I as a young man was? I cannot say. But he is eternal delight to me, and for that gift I do know that to him, and through him to the Queen, I owe much more than I can ever requite.

The second Jester, living now only within me, is the ghost of my for-mer self, the lingering trace of the role I assumed for so long. Jester is what I had been, what I once was. But I am Jester no longer, either in life or mind. I think of myself no longer by that name, would not answer to it even instinctively if it were called out to me unexpected. The name I go by here in my new home is the name I hid most of my life, the name known to perhaps two or three now living. My true name.

All masks forever stripped away and discarded.

As Jester I inhabited gaps and voids, the empty spaces between the established stations of the world, between the Divinely forged immuta-ble links of the Great Chain. As no-longer-Jester I find in myself the desire to recover what I may of my original self, knowing full well the experiences of my Jester-life shaped me as the man I am but knowing also the commoner I was born as remains alive somewhere and some-how within me still. I cultivated that originary self in all my disguised wanderings over many years, and would now reclaim as much of that self as I may even while recognizing that Jester shall never fade entirely from heart and memory. So be it. He will be a quiet ghost, I know, never to be summoned again even if never to be forgotten. For now I will be what I may be, traced from my origins to this late present moment, all tricks and japes and costumes of Jester foregone forever. Only thus will I find peace.

I would put by my Gift as well. I have no use or need for it here in this quiet place. The cottagers and villagers about me are, in the main, honest simple folk, their intentions and travails plain enough on their faces that no special skill is needed to discern them. In the three-some years I have been here I have experienced no premonitory visions, caught no word from any man's mind, and I would have it so. For I am Jester no longer.

And in the retrospect of my life that has been the work of my days in this new home, I confess I have come to wonder if I ever truly was the Jester I thought myself to be.

To consider the course of one's life has scant merit if it be not conducted with unstinting honesty, for no deception blinds more completely and renders the meaning of our life more elusive than self-deception. I have written forthrightly of my origins and aspirations, my ambition and my failures so profound I do at times fear there are no flames in Purgatory hot enough to drive the dross of my transgressions against love from my soul. Yet even the magnitude of those transgressions has not turned me from the need to hold to honest truth and honest truth alone.

In this spirit of truth I come now to the Gordian knot of my life, and having learned from the story of Alexander I approach that knot as with new-sharpened blade in hand and sinews well-braced. For there can be no dissembling at this moment, no hesitation or weakness. No jest nor sleight of hand nor distraction will avail. Only a swift revealing cut to the very core will serve now.

And that cut is this: I have come to doubt my Gift.

I mean not doubt its potency now but doubt its existence ever and always in my life, for the full duration of my life from the first intimations of its presence to the very moment I sit here scratching these words at my simple table. I wonder now if I ever possessed any Gift.

Yes, perhaps I had some skill in the close observation of men, of gleaning from the shifting of their eyes or the set of their lineaments or the manner of their speaking what their character or intention might be, but this is no more than a skill other men also possess, if perhaps it has been more acute and potent in me than in others.

To catch words from other men's minds? Perhaps a mere instinctual parlor trick, the clever anticipation of the direction of a man's thoughts and words after I had already taken his measure or, so often, met many others like him before.

And the rarest aspect of my Gift, to see brief glimpses of the future? Nothing more than imagination perhaps. I believed I saw that cathedral in the full glory that was to come with its completion and consecration, but it is unfinished still and my vision may have been only an active imagination working at heightened pitch in the presence of a grandeur new to me, my mind weaving the tales and images I had known in books into a fanciful dream. My vision of the Queen in mourning? Oh, how common a thing it is for a wife to outlive her husband. My sight of Miranda as a grown woman? Perhaps also mere imagination, fueled by my fear her difference would lead her to a life of estrangement and loneliness. Having lost her at four years of age how can I know if this vision, like that of the cathedral, indeed was a glimpse ahead in time's swiftly flowing river?

As for Miranda's "time river" and her presentiment I would one day tell a story and there would be an attempt on my life – both of these you know now to be true. I confess I do not understand how this may be. She may well have a Gift, the true Gift I spent so much of my life believing I possessed. I do not know. If as it seems her Gift is a true one I can only hope it has served her well here in the fallen world where such a Gift seems a terrible burden, an estrangement from all that should provide solace and comfort and which will instead I fear render hers a life of sorrows, as mine has been. I can only hope such is not her story.

I find myself wondering now if it was my own experience of loss which led me to such unfounded faith in my Gift. Perhaps my continued belief in it for all the years of my life until now was a compensation for my life's disappointment, a consequence of my need to understand the great reach of love only in terms of the capacious negative space defined by its incompleteness in my life. Perhaps it was only an illusion of empowerment for one who from his earliest adulthood found himself displaced, hollowed out by his own dislocation, a dislocation accompanied by such great unfulfilled need of the heart. I may have turned, it seems now to me, a few parlor tricks into a rich tapestry of compensatory fancy and self-deception.

How fitting it would be, then, that a jester find his life's greatest trick to have been one played upon himself.

But it matters little now. Let Jester be gone and take his Gift with him.

To be Jester, then not to be Jester. From nadir to apex to nadir, kennel to castle to cottage, threshold of manhood to fullness of life to declining age, the Wheel of my fortunes has steadily turned. I accept this with equanimity, accept the sorrows and joys, losses and gains, for if I have found any wisdom in the course of my days it is the ineluctable necessity of acceptance. We are not the empty puppets of Fate, our strings pulled by an unseen unknown hand so that we dance a dance of another's contrivance. I long knew great anger at God and blamed Him for shaping my heart in a manner which brought me great sorrow, but I understand now, at long last, I was not God's victim but my own Fool. Only in the embracing of our freedom to act and choose, our will to persevere in the face of all consequence and acknowledge and accept all consequence as our own creation, may we find the self-redemption which is the final meed of an honest life. Only through such acknowledgement and acceptance do the troubled waters of our days come at length to reflective stillness. And in that stillness we will see ourselves not as we were or as we wish to be, but as we truly are.

The Wheel turns ceaselessly and brings what it shall bring. This has been and forever will be the enduring truth of the Created World, yet I know many strive to evade this truth, to deny the mutability of all the facets of our lives. They would cling to that which they would keep unchanged, to delight and revel endlessly in the joys they find at the Wheel's apex while refusing to see that the Wheel pauses for none, must always and relentlessly turn for all. Nought endures but Mutability, so these come in the end to find themselves surprised, bereft, disarrayed in body, mind, life, heart, spirit. They become their own Fools, they who seek to misdirect or restrain the inevitable. For always will come a final hour in which no preparation, no will to deny or confront or withstand, will avail a jot. Bring what rage and denial, grief and confusion, sorrow and dismay you would bring, in the end the Wheel will turn, endlessly and implacably. Some who cannot embrace this truth live in fear, some die in great distress of heart, some even in darkest despair their own quietus make. Such as these never understand that only through the full embrace of Being and all its requisite vicissitudes have we of the Created World any path to the spirit's peace and the heart's ease.

No longer Jester, I now follow that path.

For me, now, no longer enthralled by the distractions of Queen and court though bound always and inextricably to them by the unfaded memory which keeps them as close as thought, as close as the words upon these pages, I consider what I have been, what I have sought, what I found and lost and what I may yet be.

Though I feel the accumulated sorrows of my life acutely, I find now as I stand upon the threshold of my final years the ache of those sorrows begins to subside. Perhaps it is through the catharsis of writing this my story, of gathering in memory those events which gave shape and substance to my life and coming to see them not as a series of serendipitous or calamitous occurrences following one upon the other almost as by accident, but as a continuous unfolding path. A path not laid in advance by Fate or Providence but carved out of the raw materials of worldly experience by one who never knew where his next step would take him. Through will and accident and mischance my journey was realized upon and within each moment, a continuous present ever and always creating itself anew while yet always being shaped by what had been. Swept up in the worldly rush of that journey I, like most others, could see no pattern or sequence, determine no direction giving meaning to all that was. Whirled forward by ambition and pride and love, my sight obscured by the veil of an ever-present impossible longing and its attendant sorrow, I knew only the moments and my own dislocation within them, too often consumed and distracted by the pain of my foolish love for an unattainable woman and the loss of my family.

But having paused now in my journey, having found place and measure of peace enough in this quiet hamlet to look back upon the track of my life, I discern there has indeed been more than whirling, frenzied motion and persistent sorrow. I have found, I believe, some measure of wisdom, for I have found, contrary to what I so long feared, that Melancholy will not write my epitaph.

In this remote place I have gathered in mind the weighty moments of my life, those moments of which I have told as honestly and as ably as I might, and I have put them all in the balance. What I find – a surprise near to revelation – is that it is not a matter of which outweighs the other: joy against sorrow, love balanced with loss, victories weighed against defeats. What matters now, to this *quondam* Jester and this living, present man, is the balance itself, the very desire and will to weigh, the act of loading the scales and the mind's mechanism of assay. I have found this to be my truth: in the gesture of careful self-scrutiny, in the work of thought and memory and heart turned back upon themselves, there inheres the full sum of self-redemption we may know here on earth.

For we may end our days with little. We may end without love, without home, without friends, without means. But if we have honestly and scrupulously weighed, if we have been assiduous in the gathering and the assay of all the matter, large and small, of our lived experience, we end with the great gift, the final gift of highest value: the knowing of our true selves.

I have lost "kennel-master's son." I have lost "husband" and "father." I have lost the presence of the woman whose love I could never know but to whom I gave the richest of mine. I have lost "Jester." But in losing so much I have found – and I am late, yes, distressingly late to the discovery, for only in the writing of this book have I achieved understanding – I have found myself. Not a ghost, not a mask or a fiction behind a pretense, but what underlies and is prior to all of those and which in the founding essences and the final reaches of life cannot be transmuted or altered or denied. Myself.

That self is well acquainted with melancholy, and there is undeniably within me a lingering vacancy though whether it was created by a misbegotten love or was that which the misbegotten love sought to obscure I cannot say. But I see now even emptiness has a shape, even the echoing voids of the heart have their form, and those forms are created by the ineradicable traces of what was loved and lost throughout our lives. And by the very fact traces remain we know all has not been lost to us even if what remains is memory or echo only. A traveler leaves a footprint in the damp clay and that print although giving shape only to present emptiness nonetheless also testifies to presence, sings in celebration of presence for those who would hear. The heart, as long ago my father first told me, takes the shape of our love and though our love be lost the heart in some degree remains as it was, the trace of love remains, and by that enduring reminder we may be brought to mind of all the fullness our hearts once knew and thus may yet know again. Memory must be understood as ally, not antagonist. In the emptiness we know within, the restless persisting absence which unsettles the heart and disrupts the equanimity we seek for our days, there is much pain, yes, but a pain we must recognize as our own, sorrow and loss we needs accept as some of the material of which we are now constructed. Show me one who has known no pain and I will show you a statue. But if sorrow is the price of our presence in the Created World, our dark birthright, love is our reward and our redemption. Even in its loss, its absence. If we study the track of our lives and the arc of our enduring longings, this we will know.

On account of this knowing I find a spark of hope alive in my heart still. I have learned, so belatedly, that to love before we know ourselves is to build upon quicksand and that no idealization from the world of romance can resolve to satisfaction such a fundamental instability. But when the world of romance is recognized as chimera, as seductive illusion but nothing more, then hope returns. Even to me, even here in this remote place. I am but a few years shy of threescore and do not know if the chance of love remains to me yet but I will not close my heart to that hope. And should I again know a woman's love, she will know me not as a mask, not as Jester, for she will meet me and know me only as a man who goes now by his true name.

She will know me only as myself.

Socrates was right, all those long echoing centuries ago. The unexamined life is not worth living. But he neglected to add that only in examination is redemption. From the study of ourselves we achieve ourselves. And if sorrow is the price we pay for wisdom and self-knowledge and love, so be it. The scales do prove the gain far outweighs the cost.

incipit

I will go to see her yet once more before our lives here are complete and we are called to whatever lies beyond. I know full well the stories and homilies of the churchmen, their words of enrapturing grace and transcendent glory in the presence of an Everlasting God and all His Host, but my thoughts upon such matters take no final form, remain a grey, slowly shifting veil of fog through which nought may be discerned distinctly. With my death that fog will lift, I suppose, and I will learn what I shall learn, but for now this present life is sufficient reward. I have in this world come to know myself as best this flawed and fallen spirit may and I am content with the sum of what I have learned, sorrows and doubt and hope and all.

I have been kennel-master's son and confidante of a King. I have known comfort and danger, love and its agonizing loss. I watched a wife and son die, sent a daughter into the world and thereby lost her, loved more than any other woman in this world a woman I could never have.

But breath remains to me, if perhaps less vigor than once animated this corporeal frame, and breath remains to her, and though the distance between our stations remains as has been ordained by the strictures of God and men I will go to see her yet. I will undertake one last journey, a final pilgrimage of the heart.

She will greet me kindly and will speak fondly to me, though as across a distance through gathering shadow, and when I leave she will bid me tender farewell though glad to see me depart in the hope I will take with me those sorrows which shall revive within her when again we meet.

And I will take my final farewell of her so I may forever dispel the illusion with which I was self-deceived for so long, thereby opening myself to life and love again with a heart untrammeled by a past which though unalterable must no longer be allowed to bind me irrevocably to sorrow.

This I know, for coming events cast their shadows before them.

When again we meet the wound that is my love for her, the wound that has never quite healed, will bleed afresh. And by that blood I will know my heart lives, will know from my heart's great loss its still greater embrace of love and the hope of love, than which there is no more glorious and redemptive consolation here on Earth.

So through the welling tears and the lancing pain I will be glad.